Rhona Ma[...]
history of [...]
Academy [...]
as a thea[...]
novel, *Gallows Wedding*, won the
Georgette Heyer Historical Novel Prize
in 1978, she gave up work to
concentrate full-time on writing. Her
second novel was *Mango Walk*, a
modern love story with a background of
racial tension, published in 1981. She
lives in Pembury in Kent, is a
committee member of The Romantic
Novelists' Association and her
miniature paintings have been exhibited
by The Royal Society of Miniaturists.

Also by Rhona Martin

GALLOWS WEDDING
MANGO WALK

and published by Corgi Books

Rhona Martin

The Unicorn Summer

CORGI BOOKS

For Diane and Jill
who changed my life

THE UNICORN SUMMER

A CORGI BOOK 0 552 12508 3

Originally published in Great Britain
by The Bodley Head Ltd.

PRINTING HISTORY
The Bodley Head edition published 1984
Corgi edition published 1985

Copyright © Rhona Martin 1984

Conditions of sale:
1. This book is sold subject to the condition
that it shall not, by way of trade *or otherwise*,
be lent, re-sold, hired out or otherwise *circulated*
without the publisher's prior consent
in any form of binding or cover
other than that in which it is published
and without a similar condition including this condition
being imposed on the subsequent purchaser.
2. This book is sold subject to the Standard Conditions
of Sale of Net Books and may not be re-sold in the U.K.
below the net price fixed by the publishers for the book.

Corgi Books are published by Transworld Publishers Ltd.,
Century House, 61-63 Uxbridge Road, Ealing, London W5 5SA,
in Australia by Transworld Publishers (Aust.) Pty. Ltd.,
26 Harley Crescent, Condell Park, NSW 2200, and in New
Zealand by Transworld Publishers (N.Z.) Ltd., Cnr. Moselle
and Waipareira Avenues, Henderson, Auckland.

Made and printed in Great Britain by
Hunt Barnard Printing Ltd., Aylesbury, Bucks.

CONTENTS

PART 1

1550 Winter, 7

PART 2

1561 Spring, 31

PART 3

Summer, 147

PART 4

The Horseman's Word, 245

ACKNOWLEDGEMENTS

For the detail of Elizabethan London and its low life I am indebted to the works of Christopher Hibbert and Gamini Salgado.

PART ONE
1500 Winter

1

All day it had rained. Not the soft benison of summer rain lisping gently from leaf to leaf, but bitter needles of sleet that drove relentlessly down between naked branches to beat on the forest floor, stitching black leaves of winter to the iron ground. The natural sounds of the greenwood were stilled. Fox and badger stayed snug in their earths, deer stood silent and dispirited. Even the birds found little to say, their occasional voices drowned by the incessant drumming of the rain.

Through it, chilled to the bone, scuffling their chilblained feet through a sodden mat of leaves too cold to rot trudged the tinkers: Tim Kettle, his two sons and the girl Joanna.

'Best stick to the greenwood,' Tim had said. 'Put your hand on a tree it do always feel warm. Like us, they be, living — or thereabouts,' he added with a weak chuckle that brought on another bout of coughing. He went on coughing while they held him up, until he had voided his mouth of bloody phlegm; after that they plodded on in silence, heads down against the misery of the weather, mouths tightly clenched to guard their teeth from the vicious probing cold.

They were not in the habit of conversation. They had little enough to talk about and in winter needed all their resources merely to stay alive. Comments on the

9

weather or on their own state of wretchedness would have seemed to them pointless, both being inevitable and unalterable and no more than they were used to. Except to Joanna. Even now, after four years, she knew she would never be used to it.

Her moods swung between apathy and rebellion. Rebellion brought wild fantasies of reinstatement in her rightful home...but today was not one of those days. Today the mere thought of hot food, blazing fires and mulled wine made her ache with misery. At times like this, when her stomach gnawed and water seeped through the sacking that failed to protect her head, she knew there was no hope for her; this life was all there was, all there would ever be, and the memory of her home was the sharp edge of a sword from which she could only turn her face away.

Tim and the younger boy had fallen behind, Tim because of his breathing, Potter because of the great swollen belly that prevented his ever moving with agility. She quickened her pace as she saw the bigger boy closing on her. She hated the boys, especially this one who gave her no peace. If they had Christian names she had never heard them, their father gaining their attention with 'You!' or the simple expedient of the back of his hand. She had dubbed them Pot and Pan — being tinkers' brats — in a wan attempt to make sport of something that menaced her. Not that Pot had proved any threat. He was too young and too sick, his ailment, whatever it was, had effectively stunted his maturity; time and a degree of compassion had modified his nickname to Potter. His brother was another matter: not for nothing had she named him Pan. Not only had he an affinity with animals that left malodorous traces on his clothing but he was downy-faced with a breaking voice and a precocious eagerness to test his new equipment. Lately she spent her life avoiding him, listening apprehensively for the thin tuneless whistling he produced from the pipes he cut from reeds and attempted to play upon.

Now, as he reached for her, Tim's voice rasped out,

10

'Let 'n bide!' and she was able to evade his groping hands and dodge back to the others. Pan gave her a side-long look which said plainly, One day, just wait. And she thought, not for the first time, If Tim should die, what then?

Although she judged herself to be the elder, Pan was the taller by half a head and the stronger by far; and she had seen her first flux on her twelfth Saint's Day. Her sole gift, she reflected wryly; at home there would have been a feast, with dancing to celebrate her womanhood. And gifts — she remembered them on past Saint's Days, a lute, a jewel, a Book of Hours — once a trained jack-anapes suited like a jester. Now the only jewel she possessed was a pectoral she had snatched up in her flight, stitched into her ragged gown between two folds of cloth where thieving hands could not find it. Her hand moved towards it unconsciously. Her talisman, her last bulwark against death by starvation — her one link with her identity, her proof of birthright should she ever realise her dream...

She sighed. She had fled with good enough reason: even in her darkest, most desperate moments she knew that return was a folly for which her life would pay.

She reminded herself that any sort of life was better than none, even this among the tinkers with their evil smells, their resentment of her, the grinding deprivation of their existence. What galled her was their accep-tance of poverty as their natural lot, as if there were nothing more in life worth struggling for. But there was, there was! Her ragged nails drove into her palms as depression smouldered into anger. Even at her lowest ebb she clutched stubbornly at the conviction that some-where between what she had lost and the depth to which she had sunk, there was something better than this...

Tim was coughing again, bent over the cart on which they carried their stock-in-trade, racked and fighting for breath while Potter stared blankly.

'We stop here.' She heard her own voice sharpened by

11

anxiety. 'Let him rest. Try and get a fire going while I make him comfortable.'

It was a sign of the times that she ordered the boys about in his presence as though he were not there, as though he were already dead. He had gone downhill so rapidly that it was hard to reconcile the bowed, grizzled figure with the sturdy little tow-headed tinker she had known. Less than a year ago he had seemed tough as a hawthorn root, stunted in growth but tanned and wizened like a walnut, wily and pugnacious and in unquestioned dominance of his coarse-grained sons. In the past her own unbending spirit had flared often enough into conflict with that dominance. Now she could only pity him, and dread his final loss. Not that she held him in affection — she would not have cared to admit it if she had. But she sensed that, for some oblique reason she did not know, she was under his protection.

Pan was muttering sullenly, "Taint time to stop.'

'Don't argue!' she snapped. 'We're stopping.' She glanced uneasily at Tim where he wilted over the handles of the cart.

'I want to stop,' whimpered Potter. 'I'm bad. And he's bad an' all, just look at him, see if he anna.' He pawed ineffectually at his brother's sleeve.

Pan glowered. 'We dunna stop afore dark. Not never.'

'Do you want him to die!' spat Joanna furiously. 'Light a fire, can't you, is it too much to ask?' She felt powerless in the face of Pan's defiance, trapped by the thought of impending death, the fear of not knowing what to do — suppose Tim died in the night? She felt tears of panic building inside her and tried to stifle them. No one must see her cracking. 'We're stopping! This instant! And you're going to light a fire.'

'Am I now?' For a moment their eyes wrestled, burning with mutual venom. 'Oh-ah. And what are you going to do for me, then?'

His meaning was unmistakable. Joanna's cheeks flamed. 'It's not for me, it's for your father! Don't you care at all?'

12

'He'll not be needing it, not above an hour. And I anna doing nothing for you, not afore you do something for me.' He looked her up and down, went on jeeringly, 'Just like all your kind, you are. Take all, give nought — well, I've had enough taking orders from him, I'll not take none from you. My turn to give 'em now, and I says we're going on.' He turned away. 'Anyways, wood's wet!' He tossed the words back over his shoulder and went slouching on ahead of them.

'He's going!' wailed Potter in disbelief. He started to cry. 'We got to go on or we'm left behind —'

'We'll manage.' Joanna choked down the sob that rose in her throat. 'We don't need him, we'll manage without. Take your father in out of the rain while I make a fire. We're staying here.' She bundled them both under the cart and forced herself to move with a show of reassuring briskness, stumbling about in the undergrowth, hampered by her sodden skirts in a futile search for dry wood. Only by physical effort could she keep command of herself, of her situation, her overwhelming need to give up, to lie down on the drenched ground and sob out her despair. She hated and despised Pan for deserting them; the only one among them with strength enough to be useful yet uncaring enough to abandon them, unconcerned even for the dying...but to her personally his departure was also a relief. 'We don't need him!' she repeated stoutly. She turned to the sniffling child. 'Stay there and keep the old man warm, we'll manage. And stop grizzling, God's life, I cannot endure your noise!'

The boy glanced fearfully at his father. 'I dunna want to, not on my lone. I'm coming with you.' He started to scramble out.

'Do as you're told!' Ruthlessly she pushed him back. 'When I've made a fire, we'll eat. Now lean up against Tim, try and warm him.' At least, she thought, they were out of the rain and resting. Tim, unprecedentedly docile, put up no resistance. Limp and grey-faced, he crouched, dull eyes staring before him, scrawny knees drawn up to his chest, his only sign of life the occasional

13

sucking in of his rib cage, as though it hurt him to breathe. 'Keep him warm,' she snapped at the cowering child. 'I'll search for firing.'

Pan had been right about the wood. It was too wet for firing even with tinkers' expertise. After futile efforts that almost exhausted their store of dry tinder in the box she gave up and joined the others in the dubious shelter of the cart. Potter's whimpering increased at her approach, as if he hoped it might bring some response from her, some answer to his misery. She had no answers, to his or to her own. 'Stop it!' she ordered sharply, making him flinch. Her own fear and misery were all she could manage, she had no reserves to deal with his as well. Seeing him drive his knuckles against his teeth in an effort not to cry she knew a moment's remorse. 'Here, eat this.' She thrust at him a crust of black bread she had been hoarding in her pouch.

'What is it?' He sounded querulous.

'Bread. Be thankful, it's all there is.'

He peered at it in the failing light. ''Tis mouldy.'

'It's all there is,' she said again. 'Eat it. There'll be less than that tomorrow.' Tim had always done the foraging, had provided rabbits, pigeons, squirrels, hares — even occasional eggs, whence no one asked. Tim — and sometimes Pan. Curse him, curse him for going off and leaving them to flounder!

Potter sat obediently mumbling his bread, sniffing loudly from time to time and swallowing tears with the tasteless crumbs, until the pressure built so high inside him that he could go on no longer. The dread of his father's death, the cold, the weariness, the never-ending pain that nagged his belly suddenly burst forth and he bawled loudly and unashamedly, his eyes screwed shut and his mouth wide open, spilling half-chewed bread and tears and saliva all together in a helpless cascade.

Joanna could take no more. She turned away, her own face distorting uncontrollably, her head buried in her arms to shut out the sound. 'Stop it, stop it, stop it!' But he could not. He howled unrestrainedly. Reluctantly she

14

took her hands from her ears to stare at him, useless in the face of his distress. At last some instinct came to her aid: she reached across the insensible body of Tim to pat the child's bony neck where his tousled hair lay in filthy matted strings. 'Come, be of cheer.'

He nodded mutely, unable to speak. She pulled the damp sacking from her own head and arranged it inexpertly about the thin shoulders of the others. 'It will be all right, you'll see. Things are always better in the morning. The rain will cease and we'll go on to the fair, sell the pots and be able to eat again.'

'He's about to die,' sobbed Potter.

'No, he's not!' She could not countenance the possibility, would not even consider it. 'There are herb women at fairs with cures for all manner of ills. You must not talk like that, you make him worse. No battle is ever won by giving in.' She gave him a little shake. 'Come now, brace up! We're not beaten yet.'

With a mighty gasp he regained control, scrubbing the backs of his hands across his nose. 'You reckon?'

'I'll warrant!' She spoke with a confidence entirely false. 'We have to look after things until he's well again. You're the man now.'

He gulped. 'Pan said —'

'Who cares for Pan! We are well enough without him. What does he care for any of us, going off to the fair on his own? Best forget him.'

'I want him back.'

'He'll be back.' She knew a twist of uneasiness. Back he would certainly be, if only for the cart and its contents. If he should find her here while Tim was helpless...She pressed a hand against the old man's ribs. He was still breathing. She pushed her misgivings to the back of her mind. 'Forget him. It's Tim we must think about. Keep close, and we'll warm him between us till morning.'

After a time Potter was quiet. They huddled in silence, clasping each other's cold hands, watching the curtain of water dribbling past them from the edge of the cart. Cramped and cold though they were, they slept at last from sheer exhaustion.

At dawn, when they roused themselves to ease their constricted limbs, only two of them moved. Rigidly set in the attitude in which he had fallen asleep, Tim was dead.

2

They stood looking down at the shallow scrape with its inadequate cover of earth and leaf mould which was all they had been able to manage.

'It's not very deep,' said Joanna. 'What about the foxes?'

Potter stood beside her in a hunched attitude of pain, his thin arms folded across his swollen body, strangely white and dry-eyed now that the worst had happened. 'Canna dig no more.' Even his voice seemed diminished. ''Tis what we did for Ma.'

Joanna glanced at him sharply. 'What, like this, out in the forest?' She had not realised that people were interred in this fashion, without benefit of Mass or hallowed ground.

Potter nodded. 'Only then he were there for the digging. Him — and Pan.' He caught his breath as at a sudden spasm of colic, then straightened up again. 'He anna come back — '

'Not yet. He will, though. When he knows what's happened.'

'Who's to tell him?'

'I will.' She drew the sacking tighter about her shoulders. 'I'm going on ahead to find him.'

Alarm flickered in the child's eyes and she had to look away. Did he guess that she was lying, that she too was

17

running away, abandoning him to a fate too awful to be shared...?

'What if he dunna come back?' The unnatural quiet that had descended on him since this morning threatened to give way again to whimpering. She hardened her heart.

'Of course he'll come back. He's your brother, he won't leave you when he knows.' He won't leave the cart and its cargo, she thought cynically. She said aloud, 'If I see him I'll send him back.'

'If! You said you was going after him —'

The rising note of hysteria in his voice stroked the raw edge of Joanna's nerves. She said cruelly, 'You're going to walk with me then, are you? All the way to the Cold Fair — that's where he'll be by now, you can stake your life —'

'I canna, you know I canna —'

'Then you'd best stay here and guard your father's goods like a man, not run away snivelling like a half-grown cur. A fine way to serve him now he's dead!'

The child crumpled under the lash of her tongue. But she was driven by the spur of her fear of Pan, her dread of his return before she could make her escape; she went on remorselessly, 'See — see, I leave you his pouch — and his knife — it's day now, you can sit quiet and rest till Pan comes — he'll bring food — he'll not be pleased if you desert —' Hurriedly she snatched up her few belongings and fled, not looking back.

As soon as she was out of sight she was running blindly, aimlessly, anywhere away from the squalor she had left behind her, from the growing menace of Pan, from the memory of the morning's awakening, the misery of Potter and his pain, her own inability to relieve it. Pan would go back to him, she assured herself. Potter was his brother, his responsibility, not hers, she did not have to feel guilt at leaving him. It was not as if she could do anything for him — and if she saw Pan she would keep her word, tell him to go back. She could safely approach him at the fair, safeguarded by the presence of

18

so many people. That was where he would be, it had to be, that was where they had all been heading before he churlishly pushed on alone. She would seek him out, send him back...the brothers would be together by nightfall. Potter would be all right. He would. He *would*!

She slowed her steps, composing herself as the forest path was joined by others to form a well-beaten track. Folk were travelling to the fair; in ones and twos, in family groups and some on loaded wains, their goods and livestock carried in bundles or baskets or herded before them churning up the mud, the doomed geese honking ineffectually in protest. Tim in his heyday would have cut one out from the flock undetected, and they would have dined right royally for days. Tim had been an expert, with a lifetime's experience to hone his natural cunning; yet he had died like a starveling dog and been buried like one, naked in the frosty earth, his few mean garments stripped from his emaciated body, too precious to be wasted underground. If she, Joanna, were to stay, her end would be the same...involuntarily she quickened her pace.

Yesterday's downpour had dwindled to an intermittent drizzle, the wind backing to a sharp north-easterly. A lazy wind, the peasants called it: too lazy to go around you, it blew straight through. Small wonder this was known as the Cold Fair; held in icy November it dealt mainly in geese and pigs fattened for the Yuletide table, in plum puddings and minced meat pies and similar fare — by daytime. At nightfall the innocent merchandise disappeared and was replaced by stolen horses with dyed coats, broken-winded jades doctored up by dishonest curbers, fake jewellery, stolen property of all descriptions. Here, by the light of links and dark lanterns, robberies were planned, plots hatched, loot fenced and fortunes gambled away. So it was here, in the itinerant thieves' market where no questions would be asked, that she planned to sell the ring.

She had little idea of its worth although she knew it must be valuable, its weight of gold alone was enough to

ensure that. It held, moreover, a heavy purple stone —
an amethyst perhaps, or even a ruby — that had glowed
like a drop of blood in the light from the fire. "Tis yourn,'
Tim had whispered, in a rare moment of confidentiality
at the onset of his sickness. 'If I go, 'tis for you. It were
hers,' he added darkly. She had frowned, mystified.
'Hers,' he went on, impatiently. 'Her that you sheltered,
her as had my babby. I kep' it in memory, see. Dunna let
the boys know, they'll have it off you. 'Tis yourn,
remember.'

She shook her head, unable to think whom he meant.
'Why me?'

'You was good to her — oh yes, you was, you and your
ma. I saw her, well fed an' all, her and the babby. So
you'm to have it when my time comes. Not yet, mind!'
He rubbed it on his sleeve and stowed it out of sight,
reverting to his normal foxy common sense.

She had had to suppress a smile. She did not recall
anyone to whom she might have been good, but she'd
said, 'Very well' to humour him and thought little more
about it. This morning, turning out the pathetic contents of his pouch, she had found it and remembered.
Furtively, almost guiltily — for should she not after all
have given it to the equally destitute Potter? — she had
slipped it unseen into her pouch. And now she was going
to sell it, to set herself free.

3

She could hear the noise of the fair long before she saw it, a sprawl of tents and booths and milling stallholders shouting their wares. Their voices and those of their animals wafted towards her on the gusting of the wind, mingling with the scents of manure and warm spiced gingerbread, mulled cider and perry and the hot sizzle of roasting pig to torment her empty stomach. She set her teeth and swallowed the saliva that welled unbidden into her mouth. She judged that it must be about noon; she would have to endure the penniless afternoon before dusk brought out the receivers who would buy what she had to sell. Until then she must contain her hunger as best she might. Despite Tim's fanciful story — or perhaps because of it — she believed that the ring was stolen; to offer it for sale to an honest trader would be to arouse suspicion and invite disaster. She tightened the rope girdle about her waist and mingled with the crowd, half-heartedly scanning their faces for Pan in an effort to keep her mind from the subject of food.

Even allowing for the shortened days of winter she knew that hours must pass before the light failed. It was tantalising to move in the midst of plenty and be unable to partake of it. A child threw down a roast codling half eaten and she pounced on it, brushing away mud and straw to sink her eager teeth into the warm sweet pulp of the fruit. Like a beggar, she thought. But she was past caring. If only she could be warm! Her clothing, still heavily damped with rain, lay like a cold plaster against her skin, drawing away the little warmth she had gained by walking. She followed her nose to where a swarthy man was roasting codlings and chestnuts on a brazier of charcoal, and felt the blessed warmth of it on her hands and face. She drew nearer with his customers, revelling in the glow that embraced her and drew a cloud of steam from her clothing.

The vendor was doing a brisk trade with his piping hot wares. Although his clothes were almost as ragged as her own they were worn with a certain flamboyance, a scarlet neckerchief and a large gold ear-ring combining to give a rake-hell semblance of good looks. He said something to her in a language she did not understand, and when she shook her head to indicate that she was not buying tossed her a broken apple and a couple of chestnuts. She seized them gratefully, cupping her blue hands about their heat, attacking the chestnuts with her teeth because her fingers were too numb to deal with the husks. He laughed, and threw her another, and she saw his eyes kindle in the way that Pan's had done. As she edged away, a woman in a gaudy skirt appeared from nowhere and screamed at her; Joanna caught the flash of a blade and fled as another joined her, waving a broomstick.

Instantly she was surrounded by a romping troupe of tumblers. Whooping and laughing, they caught her up like a mad March wind, twisted her around with them, whirled her off her feet and just as suddenly left her to pick herself up, cursing and scrabbling after her scattered fruits. 'Scurvy drunken knaves!' she yelled after them. But her protests were lost in the good-natured ribaldries of the onlookers.

She devoured the last of her spoils behind a booth. In front of it, out of her sight, she could hear an old man beating on a tabor and pleading with passers-by to come and behold his five-legged calf for a farthing. Peering through a rent in the hangings she could see it, an aborted foetus in an advanced state of decay suspended by string from the roof pole of the booth. Wrestling with a nausea not entirely due to having bolted the chestnuts, she moved on.

Judging it best to avoid the gipsy vendor with his jealous womenfolk, she was drawn helplessly by the smell of food to where a whole suckling pig was roasting on a spit. It was surrounded by children with glowing faces and hands outstretched to the fire. Rich droplets of fat oozed from the blistered hide and fell with little explosions of flame on to the charcoal; each time the children jumped back with squeals of delight in feigned alarm. From time to time someone would stop, offer a coin to the woman wielding the knife, and she would slash off a succulent slice and hand it over. Joanna hung about the fringes of the group watching the diners, hoping for one of them to throw down a piece unfinished. But it must have been too good; without exception they ate to the last, crunched up the hide and went away licking their fingers. She sighed, and moved on to where a pedlar's ribboned cap bobbed among the throng. Sometimes at fairs they added toys and sweetmeats for children to their more prosaic wares, and a gilded gingerbread man would be welcome indeed.

Pulling the sacking up over her head she made her way towards him. She could not buy, but a judicious jostling could bring a trifle tumbling from the edge of his tray; she had witnessed it many times, and while she could not lower herself to beg, thieving was subtly different. Involving as it did a degree of skill, it did not lay her pride in the dust in quite the same way.

She edged up beside and a little behind him, feigning absorption in the antics of an acrobat some way away. When his attention was diverted by a couple of girls haggling over the price of a comb, she fell heavily against him, clutching at him as though swooning, and deftly spread her tattered skirts over whatever might

23

have been dislodged by the collision. 'Help me —' she murmured weakly.

'By the Solomon!' The pedlar, who was no fool, sprang back clutching at the contents of his tray.

The two girls, more naïve, stood peering down at her. Fools! she thought, exasperated. How was she to make off with her loot while they stood there gawping! She clutched at her stomach. 'The sickness,' she moaned. 'The plague — from the town — succour me from Our Lady's sake...'

Predictably, they shrank back. 'Don't go near her!' cautioned the pedlar, and moved off smartly leaving them exchanging fearful glances. Joanna groaned again. 'We'll get help,' promised the elder, and seizing her companion's hand dragged her away and ran.

Before they could look back Joanna was on her feet. Clasping several interesting shapes under her skirt, she scuttled away and dived behind a booth to examine her spoils. For all her effort she had gained very little of use to her: a scroll that might be a letter, one only of a pair of perfumed and embroidered gloves, a paper of pins. The last she could sell, though not here where the pedlar might catch her; but the gingerbread men she hungered for had eluded her, saved perhaps by their sticky texture and so not easily dislodged. She would have to survive until nightfall on the scraps she had already half forgotten.

She tucked the pins and glove into her bodice and looked again at the scroll. Tim had told them repeatedly: 'Never throw anything away, no matter what, you can always make use of it one way or another.' Perhaps it was a letter. If so she could deliver it, exact some payment for the service. She opened it out, frowning as she tried to decipher the ill-formed characters. It looked, she thought, as though someone had slavishly copied them who had no understanding of their meaning. Among the blots and scratchings she made out '...Justices of the Peace, Bayliffs, Mayors, Constables, and all other...Majestys officers, ministeres...Know that I,

Thomas Cooper, Knighte...that the bearer...' After
'bearer' came a long blank space. This was no letter, it
was a —

'Give me that!' The pedlar, his face hot and furious,
was bearing down on her. 'Just as I thought, recovered
already, you tinkers' bitch! What else have you filched
from me?'

Lighter and quicker on her feet than a man encum-
bered by a tray, she contrived to evade his grasp. 'Nothing — nothing!'

'Give it here!'

'Not so fast, how do I know it's yours?'

'You thieved it off me, that's how —'

'Not so! It was lying underfoot, I but picked it up —'

'D'you think I was born yesterday, you knocked it off
my tray.' A crafty look came into his eye as he tried
wheedling. 'Look you, girl — the thing's no use to you
and 'tis my passport for the road, I can't trade without
it —'

'No? Then why does it not bear your name in that
space so cunningly left blank?'

'That means nothing. Hand it over, or I'll —'

'That means it's a forgery.' She spoke firmly, with
such conviction that the man was clearly taken aback.
He looked furtive for an instant before making a blustering recovery.

'You're making it up, you lying brat — you couldn't tell
that without you'd learned to read. Give it here before I
get you put in the stocks!' He made a last desperate grab
but she was too quick for him.

'Not without you to keep me company. I can read as
fair as any and this is a forgery, you're hoping to sell it to
the first rogue to offer you coin — ah-ah! Touch me and
I'll proclaim you, there's plenty near enough to hear.'
She laughed. 'We'll make a pretty pair in the pigeonholes, billing and cooing —'

'You little —'

'Soft, or you'll get us taken up. Let us rather come to
agreement.'

25

'Agreement?' He eyed her suspiciously.

'Why not?' She smiled maliciously, savouring the situation now that she had turned it to advantage. 'No doubt you have a selling price in mind. We'll share it, half and half. How like you that?'

'Share it! With a half-grown, thieving trollop that did none of the work —'

'How else can you be safe? Share the snap and we're in league, I dare not go to the constables. Otherwise...' she shrugged.

He glowered, furious at being bested. 'Five pence,' he offered sullenly. 'Not a farthing more!'

'Done!' She was delighted, not having expected so handsome a sum.

'Hand over then.' But he showed no sign of producing the coins.

'Throw the money on the ground.'

Grudgingly he did so, foot poised ready to cover it if need be. She picked it up, producing the scroll only as she reached it, and stood watching the pedlar as he moved off swiftly to lose himself among the crowd. She was well pleased with the transaction. She had five whole pence, enough to feed her for a week, enough that she need not sell the ring tonight; she could keep it for another time, secreted like the pectoral against a worse day yet to come — and she still had the paper of pins. Strange, that he had not troubled her for that, nor for the expensive glove. The forged passport must be worth more to him than both of them put together...She stood still, pondering the value of a scratched and blotted parchment, a couple of seals, her satisfaction faintly dimmed by annoyance with herself. Tim would have seen that, would have haggled and extorted more...still thoughtful, she moved on. She too had once learned to write, and had a fairer hand than the pedlar's any day...

A freezing mist congealed about the revellers, suffused with rose from a sun that had not broken through all day. Soon it would be dusk. It occurred to her that she had not

26

seen Pan at the fair. Now she was nagged by doubts that he would go back to his sickly brother. Perhaps he had already pushed on to another town. What did he care — no, to be fair, he did not know that Tim was dead. Would he go back? If he did not...She was not going to think about it. Curse him, oh, curse him to Hell! He had known his father was dying, had said so, brutally. It was up to him to go back. The burden of Potter was his to take up, not hers — not hers. She could not. Could not. If she went back now...

A waft of roast pig brought an anguished response from her stomach. Wondering if any was left she retraced her steps. There was little now on the carcass and the pig woman was selling off cheaply what remained. She bought a sizable chunk, raggedly carved, for a farthing and stood near the fire to eat, enjoying the warmth now she had bought the right to it. Some day she was going to always have that right. Somehow she was going to wrest from life something better than shivering barefooted, sleeping rough, going hungry, something better than being — what had he called her? — a tinkers' bitch! Something nearer to the life she had known and almost forgotten, that of Joanna the pampered child, who had dined on roast meats and marchpanes and French wines...her eyes misted, remembering the gracious rooms, the fur covers piled on her testered bed, the music of lutes...

She started nervously as something tugged at her skirt. Two children lean as rats gazed up at her with hollowed eyes circled with want, and she realised that she had stopped eating. They were begging for what she might leave. She tore off a fragment of the meat and dropped it and, like rats, they fell upon it, scrambling and fighting over it, darting away between the legs of the adults.

For a long time she stood staring after them. At last, scowling and on the point of tears, she purchased another farthing's-worth of meat and started walking back towards the camp.

* * *

After a long cold lonely trudge she reached the place where they had slept last night. The mist had lifted. The night was clear, with a brisk wind polishing the stars. A scent of woodsmoke greeted her and, she thought thankfully, Potter must have got a fire going. She was hurrying forward with her gift of cold pork when she smelt, unmistakably, rabbit. Could he have pulled himself together enough to catch one, skin it, cook it? She halted. Perhaps she had mistaken the path, stumbled upon some other vagrants' camp where she would not be welcome. Or perhaps...cautiously she made her way forward under cover of the brushwood. Potter sat alone, huddled in his usual uneasy posture close to the red glow of the fire, watching with dull eyes the small carcass impaled on a hazel stake over the embers.

As she moved into the circle of light he looked up and saw her. In his face she saw relief, and a shortlived pleasure that was swiftly chased by doubt...apprehension...

A twig snapped. Potter twisted awkwardly around to look behind him, made a gesture to her that she could not interpret — her eyes following his widened in shock. At the far side of the clearing, weirdly lit from below by the flickering light of the fire, she was looking straight into the grinning face of Pan.

Too alarmed to utter, she dropped the meat and doubled back the way she had come. Then she was running, running blindly and in terror, stumbling — crashing into tree boles — tripping on long harsh trailers of bramble — hearing nothing but the thudding of her own heart, the heavy pounding tread of her pursuer...

And then he was on her. Laughing. Swearing. Ripping at her ragged garment while she writhed and struggled, slashed with her broken fingernails, tried to sink her teeth into his throat...His scream of agony tore through the forest, startling some wild creature from sleep to go clattering away through the darkness and dead leaves. Joanna froze. Without warning he released her, rearing backwards with a choking gasp. In her frenzy to free herself she heaved at his weight, shuddering violently, able to think of nothing but escape as she fought to get out from under him. Pan rolled on to his back, his cry cut short, his mouth still open in a silent scream of pain, of disbelief. Slowly, clawing at the ground, he dragged himself half on to his stomach, his face livid, his eyes staring at nothing. Joanna wrenched hers away and scrambled free. It was then that she saw Potter.

White and shivering he crouched, staring at the worn handle of Tim's knife protruding from his brother's back. His breath came in short painful jerks, as though he were trying to cry and had forgotten how, unable to sustain the enormity of what he had done. 'I didna mean to —' The words were barely audible. 'I wanted to help you, that's all — I didna mean...'

'It's all right.' She said it quickly to convince herself. 'He's only hurt.' She did not say, Not dead...not yet, she thought. She did not want Potter to know that, did not want him to think that he had killed his brother. 'Come.' She gathered the shivering child in her arm. 'We'll leave him to rest, it's better so. Come to the fire and leave him, he's all right. Come —' She herded him away, not allowing him to turn his head and see the feebly writhing figure on the ground, settling him at last by the fire, shielded from the scene by distance, by her sheltering arm, by the piece of sacking over both their heads. Presently he spoke, through chattering teeth. 'He'll be cold.'

Numbly she said, 'I'll take him a cover.' She took Tim's clothing from the cart. 'Stay where you are, don't move.'

She approached Pan with caution. She need not have troubled. He lay moveless, she thought unconscious, until as she laid the clothing over him, he moaned faintly. She knew she should feel compassion for him, dying there slowly in the biting cold. But she could not, it was wiped out by the memory of her fear, her revulsion. She made her way back to Potter.

'Is he dead?' he asked fearfully.

'Of course not.' She forced cheer into her voice. 'Resting. It's what he needs. You too.' She remembered her errand. 'Do you want to eat?'

29

He shook his head. Uneasily, their hunger evaporated, they dozed on and off until first light.

Before Potter was awake she crept away to look at his brother. Pan had not moved, and she knew that he was either dead or deeply unconscious. If she touched him she would know which, and she did not want to know. There was nothing she could do, she told herself. He would die or he would recover; she could not, dared not, wait to find out. And if he died, she did not want Potter to know; he had enough to bear without that dreadful burden of guilt. It was Pan's own fault, she reminded herself fiercely: he had brought it on himself.

When Potter awoke, she told him, 'He's gone. Recovered in the night, taken your father's clothes and gone off. We must go on without him now.'

'How will we live?'

It was a fair question, not one to be answered easily. 'We'll manage. We've got the cart. Maybe the Egyptians will take you, they like children with fair hair, Tim said.' Steal them, was what he had actually said...but they would feed him, she thought, in exchange for the cart.

'What about you?' She did not answer. She could feel his eyes searching her face. They walked on for a while. Potter said, 'Why are you crying?'

She had not known she was but he was right, the tears were streaming down her face. 'I'm not!' She fought it, but now Potter was crying too, not bawling as he had before but soundlessly, painfully, like a man. 'You're leaving me...'

She meant to deny it, tried to force the words. Suddenly she was weeping helplessly, unable even to go on walking, the tears making streaks down the grime on her face. 'I'm going home,' she sobbed. 'I am, I am! Some day, somehow...God help me, I'm going home!'

PART TWO
1561 Spring

1

Gold coins of light dropped from between the high branches, dappling and dazzling on the surface of the water, making a screen between the watcher and what he wanted to see. He lifted the rawhide eye patch and held it like a visor, squinting down with both eyes through the green depths, past the lances of weed laid flat by the current to the river bed.

It was still there, its blurring frog-shape just discernible among the pebbles. As he watched, a fish no longer than his thumbnail appeared from nowhere, funnelled its mouth towards it briefly, tail quivering, and then flickered away out of sight. He leant lower, peering hard in his effort to penetrate the gloom. Down there the water scarcely seemed to be moving. He was tempted to reach down and touch it, to help the dissolving flesh on its way — but if he did that, it would not work. It must be left undisturbed, at the mercy of the twisting glassy sinews of the stream until only the one bone was left: the special bone, the magical bone. The frogbone that gave dominion over horses.

It was Jody who had told him about the frogbone. Jody was the smith, and knew all there was to know about horses. Or reckoned he did. But there was one thing he did not know: how to talk to a horse with his mind, see response dawning in the large watchful eyes.

33

Only he, Angel, could do that, and in the light of what he had gleaned from Jody, he was determined to have that bone. That meant that he would have to come back tomorrow...and tomorrow, and tomorrow, until the last of the flesh had washed away and left the frogbone clean.

A sudden gust of wind shuddered the trees and he shivered. He did not much like this place, it was darker and colder than the greenwood had any reason to be and since childhood it had sent a prickle — albeit unadmitted — down his spine. Nobody liked it, no one ever came here, not even to fish — which was why he had chosen it. The gossips held that on the eve of May Day Black John and his woman could be seen hereabouts, galloping through the treetops on a ghostly black horse, their eyes burning fire and their faces livid. There was no way of knowing if it was true. Everyone he knew took care to be clear of the place before the sun went down.

Straightening up he felt the hairs on his nape march upright to the crown of his head. Two pairs of eyes were looking back at him from the water. And only one of them was his own.

'Who's there!' As he whipped around to defend himself, hand flying to the knife at his belt, he slipped on the mud of the bank and sprawled backwards into the water, his eyes raking the undergrowth and finding nothing. 'Who's there!' he challenged again. Floundering out, he staggered to his feet, armed and dripping with water weed. 'Show yourself!'

No answer. Only the trees stood over him, gaunt and menacing, their blackened trunks leaning towards each other like the bars of a cage. For a moment he waited, motionless...watchful...listening...until a sound half sigh, half moan, sent him walking briskly back the way he had come, telling himself it was the wind, only the soughing of wind among the brushwood. Using all his willpower not to break into a run.

*   *   *

34

Kate looked up from her butter-making to see him coming up the path, the sunlight glinting on his bright thatch. He was stripping off his sodden shirt as he walked and the burn scar on his chest made a pale smear on the tanned skin. How he had screamed, poor mite! But there, it had had to be done, there'd been no other way. And it was better so, with that and the eye patch he might yet go through life without bringing down disaster on all their heads. She had brought him up strict enough, God knew, kept him at a distance as far as she could. If the worse came to the worst she could disown him now he was grown: 'No son of mine,' she heard herself saying, 'I fed him out of pity along with the others...'But that time had not come so far, he had given no cause for real alarm. Uneasiness, yes — this nonsense of his over animals had set the idle tongues clacking about familiars more than once — but there, they could say all they liked, they had no proof. Only she knew what was wiped out by that scar. Well, she and one other...but that one had gone with his secret to the grave.

As she watched he crossed the yard through a gaggle of geese and goslings to where the stables backed on to the outer wall and disappeared into the gloom within. Horses! They could well be his undoing if he persisted in haunting the stables without leave. He knew well enough where his duty lay: in the brewery throughout the winter and spring. Only in the hottest months when the weather closed the brewery of necessity, then and at no other time was he allowed to help with the horses, and Lord Eustace was not one to tolerate disobedience. Her lips compressed in an angry line; God knew she had warned him often enough. But there, that crazed he was, there was little more she could do.

Angel sidled in alongside the towering hindquarters, whistling softly under his breath to warn the horses. They did not like to be surprised, even by him. A muted whickering, a soft gusting of grassy breath down their nostrils told him that they knew who was there and were pleased. For a moment he stood still in the shadows vibrant with their presence, savouring the warm air heavy with the odours of dung and hay and sweaty harness leather before moving on to where the bright chestnut mare was turning her head to greet him.

'Hallo then, my old beauties.' He ran firm hands over her flank and that of her neighbour. 'What cheer then, how's my Young Bess?'

The mare flicked her ears forward and blew a cloud of chaff from the stable floor, and her head came reaching to nuzzle him. He chuckled, fondling her. 'Ah, Bess, I do believe if I was to sit you'd be climbing on my lap.'

She nodded, tossing her mane, her bright eyes moist with love. He laughed again, happily, and reached across to greet the massive animal beside her. Although Young Bess was his favourite he was brother to them all, and the Warrior commanded his admiration and profound respect. Warrior was proud and strong, bred from destrier stock to carry his lord in battle if need be; it angered Angel to see him ill ridden about the home farm like any old jade. When, he asked himself, had their master the Lord Eustace shown any feeling for anything! He had tried talking to Warrior; but the aloof spirit that allowed him to rise above his owner's mistreatment had also put a distance between him and Angel.

With Bess it was different, he could commune with her without effort. He and Bess were somewhere of an age, he could not remember a time when she had not been here in the stables, gentle and uncritical for him to run to for comfort when the humans in his life had proved unkind. In theory, she was the property of the Lady Edith, a palfrey for a woman too sickly to ride who had always to be carried on a litter; she had been fortunate in escaping the callous hands of Lord Eustace by being too small to carry a man of his bulk and her sole duty now was as a spare mount for guests whose horses arrived lamed or exhausted by overlong journeying.

She had come to Buxford Place already named Young Bess after the copper-haired 'Tudor wench' of Hatfield, then only a young princess sharing the stigma of bastardy with her half-sister Mary. Angel had been in his infancy when the old king died and the shufflings and scufflings for the throne that followed were still a confusion in his mind, but he did recall that when Mary had at length ascended it her short reign had been so bloody, so unpopular that now young Elizabeth was queen at last the sighs of relief were audible even in Buxford. Not that he personally had been much affected; kings and queens were too remote to engage his interest unless he was directly threatened. Horses, now...that was another matter; he preferred their company to that of humans any day, finding them kinder, warmer, more loyal — and a lot less difficult to please. Young Bess, now — well, she was no longer young except in his memory; but he recalled with love the sight of her flying by at full gallop bearing some guest bent on chevying the deer, a sight that had fired his childish spirit with a longing to ride a horse of his own. It would never be, not while he stayed at Buxford; such glories did not fall to the lot of brewery hands. But once let him gain the Horseman's Word...he sighed. He could never abandon Bess. As a child, seeing the old horses slaughtered when their useful days were done, he had promised himself that when Bess's turn came he would steal her and run away with her to save her from that fate. Time had taught him the futility of such a dream, had shorn him of it along with many another; but stay with her he could and would, until her time was up. Then, with nothing to keep him here, he would shake the dust of Buxford from his feet. He closed his eyes, leant his head against the mare's warm neck, feeling rather than hearing her soft munching...

> We travel the night wind...drink the moonlight...follow the fall of the star...

He stirred. What was it that he heard? He was never

sure. It might be Bess — or perhaps some other horse, past, present or to come — what did it matter? Here it came again...drawing him...enclosing him...

> *You and I alone in the scent of the dew...the whisper of morning...listen...*

He listened — trying to lose himself in it, neither knowing nor caring what it was, only that it was beautiful — and it was fading...fading as the voice of Kate came jarring upon his consciousness. He tried to get back to it but he could not. Her strident voice dragged him back to reality against his will and he cursed mildly. Kate was always calling someone — usually him — and it was mostly fussing over nothing. He nuzzled Bess and did not move.

A shriek and a crash of fallen crockery were followed by a cry of alarm. 'Angel! Come quick, for the love of Heaven! Angel!'

He relinquished his dream and went out blinking into the sharp spring light, the sweetness of clover hay still in his nostrils.

Two of the children were racing towards him through the honking geese. 'Come quick! In the dairy —'

'A girt black cat, so big as a hound —'

'Its eyes was all afire —'

'And it vanished!'

'Oh-ah.' He took his time, accustomed to their excited exaggerations. 'Is that all?'

'There's something in the cream!' They shrilled in chorus.

Udderstones, most like. He'd noticed the young heifer flinching from being milked. In the dairy doorway he paused, peering one-eyed through cool dimness richly scented with cream. It was difficult to see clearly after the brightness of the yard, for the windows were small and set high up to keep out the mischief-making sun, but after a moment he made out, flattened against the far

38

wall, the butter paddle clutched like a cudgel and her face as pale as the whey pouring from her overturned pail, the sagging figure of Kate.

'What's all this about a cat —' he began as the children crowded in beside him to watch the excitement.

'Send 'em out — dunna let 'em see!' gasped Kate, her eyes dilating wildly. 'Oh 'tis horrible — look there!'

He followed her stricken gaze to the shards of the broken vat, the pool of cream slowly spreading over the stone flags of the floor. In the midst of it something was squatting. Something that moved. Something that blinked greasy fluid from protuberant eyes and with eerie deliberation lifted its obscene bulk on wart-encrusted legs and took a ponderous step towards Kate.

'Kill it, kill it!' she screamed, beside herself, swinging the paddle aloft.

Angel sprang forward. 'No, dunna! 'Tis harmless — just my old toad —'

As he grasped the slippery creature his own foot skidded on the greasy stones, the paddle descended with a crash on the side of his head, and Kate's cry of anguish faded into a darkness stabbed with dancing lights as he and his quarry went sprawling in different directions.

He did not remember walking across the yard but he knew that he must have done because when his head cleared he was lying on his back in the ingle of the cooking fire in the kitchen where he had spent his earliest years. He was staring up at the hams hung to cure in the vast smoke hole and Kate was shaking his shoulder, wailing and scolding by turns.

'Spit on your hands, wake up and spit on your hands! You got to do it afore you're a minute older —'

'What?' he said stupidly, his head swimming as he sat up. 'Spit on my hands, what for?'

'A charm against witchcraft, that's what, just do it and dunna mind why. What with the cows bewitched, giving toads with the milk — as if that weren't enough you have to go and touch it — now do as you'm told and spit!'

Angel rolled his eyes heavenwards. 'Giving toads with the milk! All right, all right — I'm spitting, look, see?' He felt his skull tenderly. 'That old toad's no more give with the milk than I am. Fell in — or was put there. One of them children most like, just to hear you yell.'

'No Christian child would touch such a thing!'

'Well, I've touched her often enough. Lives in a drain end she does, over by the stables. Here, you didna —'

'I couldna go near it, not if you offered me gold! What you got to do's kill it, then take its heart and stick it full of pins —'

'I'll do no such thing, nor you neither, poor old thing. 'Tis harmless, like I said —'

'No, 'tis evil, evil I tell you! All toads is evil, like black cats and hares, they'm all in league with witches and sent to do their errands. I don't know who I've upset but there'll be someone somewhere with a grudge — you saw it step towards me, 'tis come to carry her curse! You got to help me, Angel, your father's still in the fields.' She burst into tears. 'Get rid of it for me, Angel, I dunna want to be bewitched!' She collapsed on to a stool, bawling loudly.

Angel got slowly to his feet. 'That's old wives' talk, Ma, you know it is. I'll get her out of the dairy for you. You must be content with that.'

'No, kill it, kill it!' Kate's hysteria was mounting. ''Tis not enough getting rid of it, you got to kill it!'

'And I'm telling you, no!' He turned to her, appealing to her compassion. 'How can I take and kill her? She knows me, poor old thing. No, I'm sorry you're afrighted. But I dunna kill creatures as trust me; there's the long and the short of it.'

Kate's tears ceased abruptly. She levelled at him the same look of fear and mistrust that she had fixed on the toad.

'You do it!' Her tone was ominous. 'You do it now. You got to. If you dunna…I'll know what to think.' As Angel stared, she backed away from him. 'Are you going to do as you'm bid?'

Bewildered but still determined, he shook his head.

Kate crossed herself. 'So…'tis you! I know now what you are, there's no more blinking it. Oh, I should have done it when I had the chance, 'tis too late now!'

'What is?' He tried to peer into her face but she turned it away, refusing to look at him. 'Come, tell me…what's too late — what you talking about?'

Kate seemed to struggle within herself before she turned her reddened face to him and blurted, 'I should have put out that Eye of yours!' Involuntarily, his hand flew to protect it as she blundered on. 'Oh I should, I should! Only I couldna, you was so little and so lost — and her an' all — and I didna want to believe ill of neither of you, it seemed so hard — and that was my mistake, I see it now —'

'Wait, wait…' Angel pressed his hands to his throbbing head. 'Look, I canna understand what you're on about. Who's "her"? What mistake?'

'Why her, of course, your poor mother —' again she crossed herself — 'hanged for a witch and never a word proved against her! No trial nor nothing, and I thought… well, I reckoned theyda killed you too — and they would if so be I hadna kept you hid…' She turned away, wringing her hands. 'I had you baptised with the fancy name she give you and hoped it would be enough. But it wasna enough, I was fooled to think it would be. You canna cover up the Evil Eye, what's bred in the bone will out.'

Stunned, he stood still in the familiar kitchen that was the only home he knew, chilled by the revelation that he was an outcast in a hostile camp. Slowly it came to him that he had always known there was something. Buxford had fed him, sheltered him, employed him; it had never wanted him. And Kate? 'I thought…' He faltered, made himself go on. 'I always thought you was my mother.'

Insensitive as ever to what was in his heart, Kate turned on him in reproach. 'Aye, and if youda growed up Godfearing you'd never knowed no different! But you couldna, could you, you had to go messing with animals, setting the tongues a-wag, and now look what you done!' She burst into hoarse howling.

'I anna done nothing — oh, give me strength!' Angel felt his patience fraying, his manhood slipping away from him, the boy who had sheltered within it ready to weep. 'This is madness, all madness — just for me not killing a poor harmless thing —'

"Tis never harmless! And 'tis yours — *yours*, that's what you said! Your familiar, from the Devil, that's what they'll say, oh, how could you! How could you, after all I done for you...' And her words degenerated again into noisy sobs.

Angel could find no answer, no way to convince or reassure in the face of such prejudice. And his personal anguish prevented him from trying. Others were coming into the kitchen to make preparation for the meal in Great Hall, making private conversation impossible. He noted their curious glances at Kate who was still weeping. 'Come, there's nought to cry for.' He reached to pat her shoulder but she twitched away from his touch. 'Best we talk later,' he said unhappily. 'I'll go and do what has to be done.' He left her there, uneasily aware of the eyes that followed him.

When he had gone, Kate scrubbed at her tears with a corner of her apron and hurried out into the yard while the others stared after her. Running as fast as her bulk would allow, she went out through the postern gate and made towards where she could see a straggle of men returning from their work in the fields.

'Clem!' she called, panting. 'Clem, come quick — I got to talk to you!'

Angel walked slowly across the yard to the dairy, trying to come to terms with what Kate had told him in the kitchen. They had had many spats in the past but she had

42

never before disowned him, and the story had a sinister ring of truth. Looking back over the years to his infancy as one of the uncounted children of the manor servants, he knew that there had always been a distance, a coldness in Kate's care of him; the children of other mothers had been scooped up, tickled, made much of in rare moments of warmth and laughter...he had waited in vain for his turn to come. He had been sharply aware of the lack of affection, but he had at least believed he had a right to the little there was. Now even that little was snatched away, replaced by the sour face of pity, and the reason — that was ugly enough. Who could say what his real mother was like, what dreadful inheritance was his? He shivered. He felt confused, at one with the toad that had ambled into the dairy in search of shade and found every man's hand against her — the servant of Satan, no less. He remembered that Kate had spoken of putting out his eye; he wondered how close she had come to doing it. He still harboured the dim vision of a moment of terror, of red-hot iron and searing pain, the awful singed smell of his own flesh...and Kate's hands holding him prisoner, Kate's voice saying, 'There now, dunna cry, 'tis all done...' It had been a time of horror to be put out of sight and forgotten; he had been too shocked to ask her what it meant. Now he began to see that he must find out.

He found the toad huddled in a corner of the deserted dairy, under a fragment of the broken vat. No one had come to clear the mess, unless you counted the tabby cat and her kittens who were busily lapping the spilt cream. They hissed at his approach like a nestful of tiny vipers. He smiled wryly. 'Not you, too...'

He picked up his unlovely friend and carried her out to the well. Setting her down on the stones he poured a bucketful of water over the warty skin to rinse off the clogging cream, and another over his hands to remove the venom the frightened animal had released. He watched while the long sticky tongue flicked out and vanished again with one of the many flies that droned about the yard, saw the bulging eyes disappear downwards as

43

the creature swallowed and pop up again as if on springs.

'You'll be all right.' He nudged her gently with his toe, smiling as with ungainly gait she waddled away in the direction of her drain. No animal however grotesque was repulsive to him and he found the repugnance of others incomprehensible. Like having one eye the wrong colour, he thought: Canna help how you look, whatever you are.

He sat for a long time on the coping of the well, aching with the need to discuss his problems. But the reluctance bred of too many childhood rebuffs held him back from trying to talk again to Kate.

There was Jody. Old enough — almost — to have fathered him, yet young enough to understand, he had been the recipient of many a confidence, had consoled past grievances, laughed him out of occasional heart-aches and unfailingly lent a sympathetic ear. Jody more-over had been the Buxford blacksmith for as long as he remembered, doctoring the villagers, bandaging their wounds with cobwebs, remembering their family his-tories and knowing everybody's business. Jody, if any-one, would know the facts behind Kate's outburst this afternoon.

Still preoccupied, he set off down the hill towards the forge.

He did not notice Kate and Clem, their heads bent close in conspiracy as he passed them near the gate. In fact, they were quarrelling bitterly in undertones.

'You had no right to wed me, pretending he was yours!' Clem said furiously. 'If Lord Eustace finds out whose spawn he is we'll all end up on the gallows!'

2

'Well,' Jody folded massive arms across his chest and leant back against the chimney breast. 'So now you know.'

''Tis true, then?' Angel's spirits dropped a little further. What he had hoped for he scarcely knew — anything but confirmation. He said, 'I reckoned you'd know, if anyone. Only I somehow thought you'd have told me.'

'Why would I tell you what you was better off not knowing? As for me knowing, I guessed as much when she brought you here that day.' He flipped a finger towards Angel's chest. 'Don't tell me you've forgotten that so soon?'

Angel's knees felt suddenly weak and he sat down on the anvil. 'That was never you!'

'That it was not!' Jody's expression was one of lively rebuttal. ''Twas a cruel hard thing to do to a child, such as I'd not do to a dog. I was only a prentice then, no more'n a lad myself, I could but stand by and see it happen. The old smith did it, him as died a few year back and left the forge to me. Your Kate come in with you that day a-begging and pleading, swearing it was the only thing to save your life and I don't reckon the old man had a lot of choice. There, on that very anvil you sat, her holding you, and he took the hot iron from the fire and burned it away.'

45

'Burned it away...burned what away, Jody?'

The older man looked at him long, considering. 'Some things is better not known. Or being known, forgot. I've a mind not to tell you if Kate hasn't.' He turned his attention to picking a strand of meat from between his teeth with a broken thumbnail.

Angel felt strangely helpless, as if he were a child again and denied essential knowledge by a conspiracy of adults. He tried to keep his voice patient. 'I need to know, Jody. 'Tis my right. And I'd sooner hear it from you than some I could name. Besides, there's other things I got to be sure about. Like being born of — of someone else. You dunna reckon Kate maybe said that out of spite — because I crossed her?' It was a faint glimmer of hope, extinguished by Jody's next words.

'Never!' The big man shook his head ponderously. 'No natural dam would ever ask what she asked of me.'

Angel caught his breath. 'Did she — did she ever ask you to put out my eye?'

Jody did not answer at once. Instead he piled charcoal on the bed of his fire and applied himself to the bellows. 'Stand back,' he cautioned. 'Best not to breathe the fumes.'

'I'm standing back.' He waited. 'Are you going to answer me?'

'I'm thinking it over,' said Jody. 'Could be you're going to wish I hadn't. 'Twas all a bad business, Angel. You really sure you want to know?'

'I didna want to know none of it,' said Angel heavily. 'But since I started I best know all. Then at least I'll know where I stand.'

'Very well. Don't say I didn't warn you. What do you want to know?'

'Everything, good and bad. Start with the burning and go from there.'

'I'll have your word on it that you'll keep silent. It could be mortal danger to us both, folk and their suspicions being what they are.'

46

'My word on it,' promised Angel. 'Cut my throat if I break it.'

'I'll have better than that.' Jody took a short black-handled knife from his belt and drew its razor edge across the pad of his left thumb. 'Now yours.' Holding the two thumbs together he intoned:

> *'Blood of mine, blood of yourn*
> *Bind the oath that here be sworn.'*

'Well?' Angel sucked his bleeding thumb and spat upon the straw.

The brown eyes regarded him piercingly for a moment. 'You had an extra teat, like they reckon witches have. For suckling the Devil, so they say, though I can't say as to the rights of that. But Kate held that's what your dam had; like mother like son, she reckoned, and that's why she wanted it off. And burning's the only way she could be sure.'

After a long silence, Angel said, 'And she's dead, like Kate said?'

'Aye, lad. Hanged with her man, these many years. They reckoned the Devil had caught her young.'

'Young?' Angel was surprised. He had imagined her old. Ugly, and covered in warts. His mother...A new thought struck him. 'Did you ever see her?'

Jody sucked at his teeth. 'Reckon I might have, just the once. I was at the hanging, see. The old smith and his goodwife took me to it for a pleasance — or so they said. I reckon it was more to show me what comes to bad boys, them being a Godfearing lot. Still, that's as may be. But if you was about to ask me what she was like... well, she'd been "swum", see, and the Lord knows what else afore I clapped eyes on her; just a wet bundle of rags as could have been anything. No good to ask.' He smiled his regret.

No, he could see the truth of that. Just the same, he wished he knew what she had looked like; all he could picture was a faceless woman, weirdly endowed with an extra breast...He picked at a loose end in the tangled skein. 'You said she had a man. You reckon that's who sired me?'

'Seems likely. And you want to keep close about that too if you'd make old bones, I'm telling you.'

Dear God, thought Angel, it gets worse. 'Why?' He passed his tongue over dry lips. 'Was he a bad'n too?'

Jody lowered his big voice with some effort to a whisper. 'Ever hear of Black John, the outlaw?'

Angel slumped despondently on the anvil, his head reeling as it had from the blow with the paddle. In the space of an hour his quiet life had distorted into a nightmare. He stared with blank eyes at the bellows, the assortment of irons, willing himself to wake up to a normal world again. Finally it was borne in upon him that Jody was still speaking. '...safer to be the Devil's own than claim that one as your sire!'

Oh yes! And yet — and yet — in spite of himself he could not suppress a throb of illicit pride. Black John had been a villain indeed, but he had been a great one! A legend in the district, his bloody exploits chuckled over, his terrible death spoken of in whispers; a sire of whom no young man could truthfully claim to be ashamed. But he too was dead, disgraced, unmentionable...He sighed, straightened his shoulders. 'So, I'm on my own.'

Jody smiled. 'I don't know as I'd say that, exactly. That oath we swore, that binds you to me in a manner of speaking. So you got a friend if need be. That's if you want.'

At this moment he could think of few things he wanted more than Jody's friendship. He shook his head. 'I dunno, Jode — seems to me I'm the sort of friend to keep away from. Why saddle yourself with my misfortunes? 'Tis none of your doing.'

Jody eyed him thoughtfully. 'Well now, there's a question! Say — fellow feeling. I felt for you the day you was brought for the burning and I'm not one to forget; I had a sister once with your affliction, I was sold away from home in the hungry days but I always remembered her. I'd like to think someone'd do the same for her...' After a

48

moment's silence he cleared his throat, and added briskly, 'So there it is: any time you're in trouble or wanting advice, you come to Jody. Any time at all, just like you was my own. Just you remember.'

Angel felt his eyes prickle shamefully and turned away to hide his embarrassment. The big man's laugh came romping out to rally him. 'What lad, dunna fancy being kin to a blacksmith?' He lowered his voice again and teased, 'Not grand enough for the heir to Buxford, is that it?'

Angel forced a laugh. 'That's what they say, isn't it? That Black John were the true lord, home from the wars.'

Jody sobered. 'Aye, and them as says it pays for it. You keep your lip buttoned tight on that as on the rest. Try proving it and you're like to end as he did, food for the crows. Better to live a pauper than die a prince.'

'Aye...' He shivered. To be hacked to death at the crossroads!

Jody brightened unexpectedly and clapped a warm hand on Angel's shoulder. 'But that's all past and done, now. You're a fine young fellow with good years afore you and wishing on the past won't butter no parsnips, what you got to do now is think about what to do with your life. What about coming to work with me at the forge?'

Angel looked up, a sudden ray of light piercing his gloom. 'You mean it?'

'Why not? Good muscle you got, humping all them casks, and I can use a strong lad with the way you have with beasts. Go back and fetch your things.' He winked. 'Don't forget the frogbone.'

'Oh...that. Still in the river, waiting for the flesh to melt.'

Jody did not look at him. 'You did it then?'

Something in his tone made Angel wish that he could read his face; but he kept it turned away. 'I did it all right. You didn't make it up, Jode? I mean, it is true — about the Horseman's Word?' It had always seemed somewhat improbable, but worth a try. Now it seemed more doubtful than before.

"'Tis true enough — from what I've heard. Mind, I never took the Horseman's Word myself. 'Tis just I wondered at you killing the frog. Knowing you, I mean.'

'I found it dead. 'Tis all the same.'

'I don't know so much.' Jody pursed his lips. "'Tis not so powerful as if you'd done the killing. You'll have to go and watch over it, day and night till it be ready.'

In that unwelcoming place? 'Day and night,' he repeated without enthusiam, privately debating the necessity.

'Day and night,' insisted Jody firmly. 'Got strong nerves, have you, a stout heart? Because they do say —' he lowered his voice and leant closer — 'they do say that when the last bone floats upstream it screams like the mandrake root, fit to rob you of your wits.' He drew back, eyed Angel speculatively. 'You reckon you're man enough to take the Horseman's Word?'

Man enough? What did Jody take him for — him, the son of Black John! His cheekbones burned. It was the braggart left over from boyhood who answered for him. 'I'll take it from the Devil himself if need be.'

Jody's great laugh went booming through the forge. 'And there's many a true word spoke in jest — just watch he don't run off with your soul!'

The sun was drawing long webs of shadow from the trees as he walked reluctantly homewards up the hill. 'Go back for now,' Jody had said, 'and make your peace with Kate. There's more to be done than just waiting for the frogbone. When it's clean you'll have to take it to the stables, and wait there three nights for a man to come that can tell you the Horseman's Word.'

Angel frowned; this was something new. 'A Buxford man?'

'That he's not — though he may well look like one.' Again he lowered his voice. 'He could come in any guise so don't be deceived, for he'll be up to tricks to put you off. 'Tis a man as knows the Word, and having been hard put to gain it he's not about to give it up easy — he's only there by the power of the bone, too strong for him to resist. So no matter what form he comes in, who he may look like, if he's there on the third night he's the one. And the Devil himself to beat.'

'You're saying, I got to take it by force?'

'That you have! Beat it out of him, squeeze it from his throat — and look to it, Angel — ' the bearded face leant so close that he could see clearly the red network of broken veins across the cheekbones — 'be sure you win! They do say if you lose, he'll have your soul.'

Angel was silent. Jody drew back, and with a deep chuckle clapped him on the shoulder. 'What, wilting already? Takes a man to do my work, no greensick boy ever made a blacksmith. Away with you now, and prove yourself. Meantime I'll tell my Nan, talk her sweet so she gives you a welcome. Like the horses, Nan is, don't like things sprung on her, but she'll come round.' The heavy hand steered him out into the yard where he stood blinking in the light. 'Come back in about a sennight, that'll give you time. Come back a Whisperer.'

Come back a Whisperer, he thought now; it had been made to sound so easy. But if it was, why had Jody himself not achieved it? The whole project was beginning to have a bad smell, altogether too close to the witchcraft he only half believed in but which terrified Kate and her kind. Could it be so nasty, so dangerous that even Jody fought shy... He should not think such things of Jody. Jody was his friend, had proved it today beyond all doubt. Why dishearten himself with old wives' tales, casting about for excuses to back down! He was ashamed. What if Jody meant to come himself to the stable — what had he said? Whoever he may look like — what if he came to test his mettle and found him craven, failed! He would lose the respect of the man he so admired, the only one whose opinion mattered to him. And his own respect for himself might well go with it.

It seemed that he had made up his mind. But he did

not want to see Kate, not just yet. He still smarted, not only from her rejection but from the heartless manner in which she had told him such bitter news. Better to wait until his wrath had simmered down. He would go now to the greenwood, wait for his bone to be ready; he could make his peace with her when the time came. Perhaps by then she too would have softened a little...He changed direction and strode out purposefully towards the place that sensible folk avoided after nightfall.

The dark bulk of the greenwood crouched like a waiting animal; he pushed to the back of his mind the thoughts that it evoked. The shadows closed about him like a trap as he moved forward between the trees. A faint mist wreathed in wisps above the forest floor and he found himself treading stealthily, as if it were forbidden to disturb the unnatural silence. A twig underfoot cracked like a whiplash in his ears and he started like a nervous filly. He shivered, wishing he had brought his shirt, wet as it was. It was always cold here, colder than anywhere else he knew, as though the warm world of sunlight was fenced out by a dark-boled palisade of trees.

If he was to spend the night here he would need to gather bracken while it was still light enough — he caught himself up. Of course he was going to spend the night, there was no question of 'if'. Jody had been baiting him with tales to frighten children, no doubt to see if he had the gut as well as the muscle to make a smith. And he needed that bone with any skills it could give him if he was to make a life for himself beyond Buxford and its brewery; horses were his life, he had long known that, and whether or not his destiny lay with Jody at the forge he knew he was heading at last in the right direction, his own direction, setting his feet on a road of his own choosing. If he could stay awhile with Jody so much the better; he could linger within tidings of Bess while he learnt his trade. What he had to do now was collect the bone...and acquit himself at the stable with whoever Jody might send!

He smiled in the darkness and pushed on, plunging through the undergrowth now with as much noise as he could make, striding through brambles, crashing through brushwood, lashing out at low hanging branches that slashed at his face. He even thought of whistling; but his mouth was unaccountably dry and his memory refused to produce a tune. There would be moonlight later, he reminded himself. Light to bring back normality and dispel the dark fantasies his mind persisted in inventing, to reveal the shadows slipping furtively past the edges of his vision as those of owl or weasel…and then he heard it.

A sound neither animal nor human, it started low and anguished and rose in a crescendo that froze every hair on his body as upright as the green shoots on a field of young corn. It was coming from directly ahead of him.

He stood his ground. Gritted his teeth, sweated under his hair. But nothing he could do would force his legs to take another step forward.

3

'But he hasna been home all night,' wailed Kate, her hands tormenting her apron. 'He an't never been out all night before!'

'Then he's gone, and good riddance to 'un,' growled her husband, hauling up his breeches.

'Oh, I wish I'd a never told you, I never thought you'd be so hard.' She stared miserably out at the grey dawn sky.

'What did you suppose, then — I'd go out looking for 'un, shouting "Come in to your supper, lad", is that what you thought?'

Kate swallowed. 'I thought you'd give him a tongue lashing and kill the toad, that's what I thought. Not talk of turning him out of doors, not that! I wish I could unsay what I said, I didna mean the half of it.'

'Well, *I* do, Every word and more — and half a mind to send you packing with him, and all! A deceiving woman be a bane to a man as he's a sight better off without.'

'I dunno how you can say that, not to me! Not when I been a good wife to you these seven year and borne you three of your own — '

'Aye, and stillborn the lot of them — and now we know why, don't us? Witches breeds witches and a witch-child be like a cuckoo, dunna tolerate no other in the nest! You should have knowed, you poor dummy, you'd

54

never raise a child of your own with that one in the house. Well, he anna coming back here, I can tell you that! I'll tell Dan Brewer — and the steward — aye, and Lord Eustace hisself if need be —'

'Not Lord Eustace!' Kate paled, less at the thought of what Clem might say to him than at the daring of approaching him — Clem, a simple farmhand! Such a thing was unheard of. 'Oh, Clem...not him...'

'Well...mebbe not him, not this time.' He squared his shoulders, blustered a little. 'No reason we should be blamed and he's a hasty man, is that. Just dunna you let me see that certain face in here again. Understand me, woman —'

Kate cried out in pain as his hard hand bruised her arm. 'I understand you!' He released her, and she sank down sniffling on to the floor of the pallet room they shared with the other servants. She watched him go, thinking: 'Yes, you are a hard man. I did what I did in fear, said more than I should and now I'm sorry. I'd take it back if I could...but you never will. Poor Angel...' She dropped her face in her hands and began, quite quietly, to cry in earnest.

Angel peered down through the water in the growing light and sucked in his breath in disbelief. It could not be so. Nothing, but *nothing* could float upstream! It was like saying that rain could fall upwards. And yet there it was, a tiny perfect echo of the frog of a horse's hoof, lying a full hand's span upstream of the rest. He pulled off the eye patch, scrubbed at his eyes and looked again. It was still there. And it was clean.

He ran his tongue over dry lips. Then carefully, very gingerly, he reached down his arm through the reeds to the river bed. At the moment of contact he recoiled, expecting...what? He did not know. He pulled himself together, plunged his hand deeper and the prize was his. He drew it out and sat looking at it for a moment, gleaming pale in the wet palm of his hand, still with a dank green odour clinging faintly about it. It looked fragile and yet quite ordinary. He recalled the scream of last night that had kept him rooted where he was until first light, and was ashamed. Ridiculous to think...It was just a bone after all. Quite ordinary. And his heart sank a little with the loss of his belief.

He stood up, feeling foolishly disappointed. He supposed he might as well go through the rigmarole, even if only to satisfy Jody; but now he had best go home and see what could be done to pacify Kate.

Kate leant her weight against the iron handle of the well, her muscles protesting with every turn of the crank. It had been Angel's habit to wind up the buckets for her, and she realised that she was missing him already. He was gone, she thought; gone without a word. And that was maybe for the best, at least he had been spared the wrath of Clem. She only wished she could take back the hasty words that had provoked that wrath.

Halfway through the long grind she paused to wipe the sweat from her face with her apron, and in the lull from the noise of it children's voices reached her across the yard.

'Angel, Angel, fly away to Heaven!'

'Silly old Angel, canna catch me —' The rest was lost in a burst of excited giggling, the scuff of romping feet.

The handle slipped from her grasp to go whirling like a mad St Catherine's wheel as the rope unwound and the bucket plummeted to hit the water with a muffled splash. Kate barely heard it. Hoisting her skirts she fled back to the kitchen; she seized the end of a loaf from the board and, filling a tankard from the barrel, ran with them into the yard and down the path towards the postern gate. If the lad must take the road because of her, at least she could see that he did not go with an empty belly.

Before she had gone a dozen steps she was knocked off her feet by a blow that came crashing out of nowhere.

'Where d'you think you'm going — and who give you

56

leave?' It was Clem's voice, roaring with anger. 'No call to victual him, he don't live here no more!'

"'Tis only a crust of bread,' she whimpered, struggling to rise as Angel came into sight. 'Dunna grudge him that —'

"'Taint mine to grudge nor yourn to give. 'Tis Great House victuals as he's no more right to. Now get up and go back to your work!'

His rough hand jerked her to her feet where she stood wilting, hugging the ribs that had landed on the bruising tankard. It hurt her to breathe, but her anger was rising: she stood her ground as Angel came running towards them. "'Tis bread and small beer,' she said stubbornly. 'The Lady Edith dunna turn no one away empty.'

The high colour drained suddenly from her husband's face leaving an ugly greenish pallor about the mouth. With an inarticulate choke of fury he drew back his arm as if about to stun an ox. At its zenith it was seized as he was grappled from behind and he and Angel went down together in a snarling, thumping, grunting tangle in the well-manured straw of the yard. Over and over they rolled, fighting barehanded and using fists, knees, feet and even teeth in an orgiastic eruption of mutual anger. They were too evenly matched for a quick result and might have battled on until exhaustion overtook them had not Big Daniel overheard the commotion on his way to the brewery; with a massive hand on each he hauled them apart, slammed their heads together with an alarming crack and flung them down in opposite directions like a pair of slavering dogs.

'Had enough?' he boomed pleasantly. 'Or do you want a bucket of water each?' Seeing Angel already gaining his feet, 'Hold hard!' he warned. 'What's heating your blood so early in the morning, you've no business here at all from what I'm told.'

Angel checked, surprised. He looked at Kate, who could not meet his eyes; then at Clem, who regarded him slyly.

'Caught him thieving a tankard from the kitchen,' Clem volunteered, pointing to where it had rolled. 'He was trying to make off with it.'

'Was he now?' Angel felt a heavy hand on his shoulder.

'You take that back, 'tis a barefaced lie and you know it!' He turned to Kate. 'You know it, you tell Dan!'

Kate's eyes were fixed on Clem's like those of a rabbit in a snare. She stammered weakly, 'I — I never saw...oh, husband, no — not that! They'll lop his hands, dunna let them lop his hands!' She threw wild beseeching looks at Daniel, at the stony face of Clem, the blanching one of Angel. 'Oh, Holy Virgin —' She threw up her kirtle over her head and blundered sobbing back to the kitchen; they could hear her crying noisily, the other women clucking over her like hens.

Big Daniel looked gravely from one to the other. 'You certain about this, Clem? 'Tis a sorry thing to lose a hand. He ain't never stole before, not so much as a handful of malt. You better have a witness.'

'Course I'm sure.' He glanced sourly at Angel. 'You going to take my word or his?'

'Not for me to say, thank the Lord. But you best be sure if it come to a hearing — you know Lord Eustace, have your tongue soon as look if so be he holds you're lying. Think on it, man.'

'Who says I'm lying — pox on it!' Clem had started up but now he fell back, nursing his head. 'Reckon you cracked my pate,' he said fretfully. 'Don't know your strength, you don't.'

Big Dan bent over him, his face anxious. 'Dunna jest about such matters, 'tis unlucky. Come on, get on your feet.' He stretched a hand to the fallen man, releasing Angel who backed away. He felt cold in his stomach and a little sick. It was hunger, he told himself, not eating since yesterday; but he had no desire for food. What he wanted was to turn back the sun, to lose last night and yesterday and start the time afresh.

Clem made an effort. He grasped the proffered hand and lurched forward. But as he got his legs under him he swayed, his eyes rolled wildly and he vomited. He sank to his knees and remained there, rocking slowly and holding his head. 'Kate...' he moaned feebly.

'Kate!' echoed Daniel in his customary bellow. 'Where is the woman — Angel, go fetch your ma, say her man's took bad.'

There was no reply. When he looked about him, Angel was nowhere to be seen.

Tight-lipped, Kate wrung out a cloth in vinegar and held it to her husband's brow. 'Serves you right,' she was thinking. But she dared not say it aloud.

Clem seemed to be recovering. He looked up, growled abruptly, 'All right, where've you got him hidden?'

'Hidden?' Kate stood back, arms akimbo. 'Hidden who?'

'Dunna give I that!' He reached forward, snatched the cloth from her hand, and soused it in the vinegar. 'You know well enough — and you'll not win over me with playing the booby.'

'You mean Angel?'

'Course I mean Angel, who else?'

Kate stared, bewildered. 'But — he's took off to the lock-up, he went with Big Dan...'

'Oh no, he ain't!' bellowed Clem. And winced at the power of his own voice through his bruised skull.

'Dunna shout —'

'I'll shout all I have a mind to. And you'll tell what I want to know if you'd save a clout. Now, where is he?'

'I don't *know* where he is, I wish I did!' Kate burst into tears. 'Just leave me be, Clem, you've bullied me enough for one day.'

'Well...that's as maybe.' His tone was surly and his eyes flashed a warning. 'And mebbe you know and mebbe you dunna — but let me find you do and look to it, woman! Big Dan never saw the going of him, no more did I, that's all I know of it.'

Kate blew her nose on the end of her apron. 'Then he's had the good sense to run away from here, he dunna

59

want to lose a hand at his age.' Her tears welled up again. 'I don't know how you could say such a dreadful thing. I wouldn't have believed it of you, not of you.'

'Oh...Kate,' Clem leaned forward, his expression earnest. 'Look, love... 'Tis for us, for you and me, for our safety, see? We can't never have no sort of life with that varmint hanging about, and except he's flushed out proper he'll keep turning up like one rotten apple in a basket. We got to get rid of him, see? Afore he rots us all.' As Kate continued to cry he lost patience again. 'Oh, stop blubbering, can't you! See sense, it was your complaining started it all.'

Kate shook her head. 'It's that dreadful wicked lie as sticks in my craw. Why couldn't you just let him go without you have to say that?'

'Well, I had to say summat, didn't I? What else could I say, that he's a warlock? They'd have us all suspicioned, you know what 'tis like, no sooner accused than condemned. Is that what you want?'

Kate made an effort, mopped at her tears. 'No — no, course not.' Her mouth pulled away at the corners. 'But you got to allow my feelings, Clem. I raised him like my own, he was all I had.'

'And we know why that was, don't us?' He shoved a hand up her skirt in his notion of a comforting gesture. 'Come, be cheery. He's no loss — sooner spend his time with the horses than he would with you —' He broke off suddenly. Kate looked up to see him struggling to rise, an odd expression on his face.

'You've to rest!' She pushed him back against surprisingly little resistance. 'You set where you are till I come back with a simple; sovereign it is for broken heads. Dunna move, mind.'

'I got to get on my feet —' But he sank back, defeated.

She left him complaining in the pallet room and went in search of her herb, reminded of Angel's mother who had taught her what she knew. She sighed; why couldn't the Devil keep his meddling hands to himself! She prepared the comfrey and took the infusion back to Clem, who took it from her without his customary protest. He downed it at a gulp, merely pulling a face at its taste. 'Kill or cure,' he muttered.

'Dunna you want to know what's in it?'

He shook his head. 'You keep your secrets and I'll keep mine.' He laughed, not merrily but as if at a joke too unpleasant to be shared.

In a cramped corner of the loft above the stables, Angel lay huddled under the hay and waited for nightfall. His insides were uneasy, churning and aching with hunger, and the hay that concealed him was alive with rabbit fleas. The dusty residue of last year's crop invaded his nostrils and made his eyes stream but he dared not sneeze. Men and horses came and went in the stables below him; from time to time he heard his name mentioned in undertones, but only the horses knew that he was here.

They alone had seen him creep out between dusk and moonrise to drink at the well or stay his hunger with a handful of bran; from the beginning they had sensed his presence and greeted him with soft breathy sounds of welcome. He thought unhappily of Bess, and heard her answering whicker from below; she always knew when she was in his thoughts. Did she sense that he was leaving her? Be still, he told her silently, be still...

Tonight must be his last here, before dawn he must be on his way come what might, Horseman's Word or no. It was not for that he had sweated out two days and nights in constant peril of discovery, nor even for the sake of impressing Jody since any hope of working at the forge was now blown to the winds. It was, he told himself, his natural singlemindedness that had always kept him bound to a course once set. In fact, events had moved too fast for him, had left him clinging like one drowning to a pre-set plan, a crumb of stability. And deeper, pushed still further to the back of his mind where he need not look at it, lay the memory of his cowardice that night, the knowledge that only by carrying the project

61

through to the end would he ever live down his shame. It mattered not at all that nobody knew: *he* knew, and must vindicate his courage to himself. This was the third night. Whatever the outcome, whether anyone appeared or not, he would lie low and await his daemon.

The last of the animals was brought in for the night. The shouting of the children, the intermittent squeak of the pump handle, the to-ing and fro-ing in the busy yard died down. The geese were herded in protesting; as doors were barred and windows shuttered the distant voices faded into stillness, Kate's among them dull and dispirited now that her anger had cooled. He felt a moment of remorse. She had in her fashion been good to him who was no kin of hers; he had had no right to expect her to love him as well. He wished he could have let her know he was safe.

Far off he heard the postern gate slammed shut. A breeze sprang up, wafting in through the cracks the smell of the midden, the rank odour of the privy towers that drained into the moat and nourished the lilies. He thought not for the first time how much more wholesome was the smell of horses. For a time he lay listening to the soft sounds of mice in the hay, waiting until he could be sure that the house was asleep; at last, overcome by warmth and inactivity, he drifted off himself.

He was aroused by a sudden restless movement among the horses. He listened for a moment while they stamped and shuffled, alert to the ever present danger of fire. He sniffed. No smoke. No smell of burning. Cautiously he crawled to the edge and peered over. Both sections of the main stable door stood ajar. Dimly in the gloom, outlined by the moonlight nosing through the crevices, he made out the shape of a man.

He lay still as an icicle, while within his thoughts ran like a millrace. He had waited for this moment hardly believing it would come: now it was here, and he was unprepared. He had been so concerned with restoring his self esteem that he had all but discounted the possibility that someone would actually appear on the third night. It had dwindled to a matter of going through the motions in order for honour to be satisfied. Now he saw how he had deceived himself. Could this be Jody's devil, some unnatural being come to tell him the Horseman's Word? A creature summoned from Hell against its will by the power of the bone — was this why even he had quailed! He recalled with a shiver his warning of the consequences of failure.

One thing was clear, there was no going back. The figure, whatever it was, stood between him and the door. And if it was here in answer to his challenge he was bound to fight it, must get his attack in first, gain the advantage of surprise — but suppose it were not! It would be foolhardy indeed to betray his hiding place to anyone else...

In the silence that followed he could hear his own heart thudding in his throat. How was it that the man below him did not hear it? If he did he gave no sign. He was absolutely motionless. Silent...

The figure had now been so still for so long that he began to question the evidence of his eyes. Was there really anyone there at all? If there was it was no one with a right to be here on the ordinary business of a stable; such a one would have walked in boldly and set about his task. This man — if man it was — was moveless as masonry. Soundless...listening...waiting...for him? He scrubbed his sweating palms among the hay.

The faint rustle brought a response from the watcher. The head jerked around and a familiar voice growled, 'I know you're in here somewheres. You better come out.'

His stomach gave a sickening lurch. It was no faery horsemaster who awaited him down there but Clem, bent on his destruction for reasons he could all too easily guess. He eased himself back under the hay, hoping for the sound he made to pass for that of mice. He waited.

'Up in the loft, are you? Come down!' A pause. 'If you dunna come down I'll take a pitchfork to you!'

He pressed himself lower in the hay, trying to remember whether in the normal clutter of the stables a

63

pitchfork lay readily to hand. The next words banished all thoughts of personal peril from his mind.

'Come out I say, afore I smoke you out!'

Smoke — he could not mean it! Surely not even Clem would — as he reared up to look he heard the telltale chink of flint, saw the face briefly lit by the flying spark. Fire among the horses! Nothing Clem could do to him matched the enormity of setting fire to a stable. He launched himself to land with a thud on the man's stooped shoulders; the tinderbox flew out of his grasp and the flint with it, his cry of alarm set the horses stamping and whinnying as he went spreadeagling backwards on the straw with Angel on top of him slamming blow upon blow into his upturned face while he struggled in vain to defend himself.

Clem quickly realised that he was now the one in danger. He made frantic efforts to recover himself, defeated every time by the punishing fists driving into his face. Already his head was swimming again, as it did all too readily since he had quit his pallet while Kate was busy in the dairy. And the darkness that swamped him and receded only to wash over him again, was that entirely due to lack of light? With a strength born of panic he fought to free an arm and landed a blow on the side of Angel's head sufficient to knock him off balance. Seizing the moment he staggered out from under, heaving him off to go sprawling among a fall of buckets into a corner. Clem flung himself towards the crack of light that marked the doorway and was through it and out into the moonlight, reeling away from the stables in a dizzy search for the refuge of the house.

He made for the nearest open doorway and stumbled through it in a surge of relief.

Inside, he stared bemused. He was not in the kitchens as he had hoped but in a building unfamiliar to him. The reek of ale told him that he must be in the brewery. He stood blinking, trying to clear his vision. All he could make out were the shapes of three pale towers looming like ghosts in the gloom, their dark fire doors gaping open, and beyond them a tunnel of denser shadow yawning. There was no safe refuge here. He turned back and looked out to see Angel running across the yard in determined pursuit. As well he might, thought Clem, just let me get back to the house and there'll be a hue and cry out after him — Jesu, Maria, he's seen me! Barely checked at the pump, then looked this way and come charging straight for the brewery — dear Heaven, what's to be done! The tunnel, that's it, that's all there is — maybe there's another chamber beyond — if I can hide there, take him by surprise...

Angel felt the rope tighten across his throat from behind, his arm seized and jerked agonisingly upwards to a point somewhere between his shoulder-blades. He twisted and bucked, flailed wildly with his free hand in a futile attempt to strike his unseen assailant. Twice he lost his footing, twice regained it, slithered and kicked to no avail until his heels slamming back against stone told him that he was on the steps leading up the side of the great fermentation vat. It was still full of the last brew of the season. If he could get them both up there somehow — anyhow...one step...two...four more to go — only four, yet they felt like a mountain — if only he could draw breath! Dragging his attacker with him he forged on painfully, bracing his feet blindly against whatever they found...two more to go, or was it three? He was losing count...his hand met the warm brick of the chimney — he was there! His eyes were crackling with coloured lights...his lungs bursting...he heaved the combined weight of their two bodies towards the brimming vat that he knew must be just below them...if he could just force Clem's face under the ale...he would have to...let go...he felt himself arching backwards...Clem's body beneath his...felt it stiffen in alarm — heard him shout — felt the warm fluid lap the back of his own head...

The shout became a long gasping gurgle and he was free. As the choking rope slackened and released him he clambered back on to the steps to cough exhaustingly until he retched.

He sat for a long time limply recovering before he thought of Clem. He stood up cautiously and peered about him in the darkness. Where was he? He listened intently for the giveaway sound of breathing, half expecting to be ambushed again. He could hear nothing. An unnatural stillness had settled over the place. It came to him that he had heard no sound of the other man splashing his way out of the vat. Could he...could he be...still in there...

'Clem?' The effort of speech set him coughing again. 'Clem, where are you?'

There was no response. He groped over the side of the vat into the tepid seething brew...and felt cloth. He felt along it, slowly at first and then more quickly in growing alarm. He hauled out the inert body and dragged it laboriously down the steps, out through the outer chamber and on into the yard. In the greyish glimmer of moonlight the face gleamed wet, blank, unknowing. Clem was dead. He, Angel, had murdered him.

His sole emotion was horror. His knees began to shake at the thought of what he had done, of the inevitable consequences of being caught. Until now he had only stood in peril of losing a hand — and even that was arguable since he was falsely accused. But, now!

He was not sure of the penalty for killing a father, albeit a surrogate. Might it not be heresy, like killing a husband? If so it would be the stake. Death it must certainly be, and the form of it savage.

Stunned, he stood staring at the body until the thought formed in his mind that it must be hidden. The longer before it was discovered, the further away he could be by the time it was. He could heave it back into the vat...but it would float. There must be somewhere. He wrestled with his reeling brain, trying to force it to come up with an answer quickly, quickly before it was too late — suddenly he had it. The fireplaces under the heating vats! Surely one of those would take it, and there it could lie undiscovered until September when they started brewing again. He would have to force it in through the fire door; it was not an easy task single-handed but he could turn to no one for help, not even Jody...

Any time, he had said: like you was my own. But he could hardly have foreseen a catastrophe such as this...or had he? With the strength of desperation he wrestled the body back into the brew house, and closed the door behind him.

Weary and shaken as he was, the walk to the smithy seemed even longer than usual; but Jody was his only hope. He could not ask his friend to hide him and was firmly if reluctantly resolved to say No if he should offer: he had no right to expect so much, to put the whole family in danger. But Jody, if anyone could be trusted with the truth, could be relied upon to give sound advice from the wisdom of experience.

He reached the forge at last and stood looking at its shuttered windows: of course, they must be all a-bed and asleep. How to wake Jody without rousing the neighbourhood? He made his way around to the back in search of a way in. The shutters stood ajar at a tiny window under the eaves, about twice a man's height from the ground. By clambering on to the rain barrel he could just about reach it. He pulled open the shutter carefully and called softly, 'Jody?'

There was no reply. He was looking into the bed-chamber, the only one possible; a timber staging built up off the floor about the chimney breast, reached by a ladder and accommodating a large straw mattress with an assortment of coverings. But no bodies rounded out the covers, no muted sounds of sleeping came from within. The cottage was empty, the fire dead on the hearth. Of Jody, his sloe-eyed Nan and their family there was no trace.

Angel came down slowly on legs unwilling to hold him. He looked helplessly about him at the cottage, the herb garden, the forge sleeping under its thatch, unable to take in this final blow. On the stack of horseshoes behind the forge a large black cat crouched and stared. It widened its glowing eyes, swore softly and disappeared.

He wished he could vanish as easily. For vanish he must — out of the manor, out of the county, as far and as fast as he could travel. And one pair of legs was not going to be enough.

4

Lady Edith Pengerran mounted the stairs to her withdrawing room and sank down gratefully on to her straight-backed chair, gripping its arms to ease the settling of her body. The days when she was free of pain became fewer as time went by; the daily round of inspection of Buxford Place and its many outbuildings had long ago become a penance, but still she dragged herself from shambles to kitchens, from dairy to cellars, supervising the running of the vast estate down to the smallest detail. It was the daily pattern of her existence, her duty as chatelaine: she would not know how else to spend her life.

She thought of the dairymaid, Kate, blubbering noisily into the milk with a garbled tale of disappearing relatives. A son, was it, or a husband? She passed a weary hand over her face. It made her head ache to try to remember. But she pitied any woman who had lost a child. If only...ah, if only. She stirred restlessly in the hard three-cornered chair. There was nothing to be done against a husband — and such a husband. Eustace had been a tyrant all his life, a bluff and merry jester, yet a tyrant underneath; and Joanna had been of other blood than his, a true child of her father...Her lips compressed at the thought that came unbidden. She preferred not to remember her first lord. He had left her

69

with a bitter fate, a doomed and wayward child. Old age, they said, was prone to bring such memories flooding back: if that were so she would hope to die soon, before the pain and the memories became too much. She sighed. She had instructed the steward to institute a search for the dairymaid's man; no doubt he would be found bundling with some younger, fresher wench...

Her attention was caught by a commotion in the Great Hall below. She rose to her feet with difficulty and moved to the niche in the panelled wall from which she could see down into the hall.

Eustace, his face an unprepossessing purple that clashed with the fading ginger of his hair, was bellowing and thumping on the table while the deerhounds leaped up in alarm and retreated, tails under rumps. The man who stood humbly before him with bowed head was the head horseman.

'Gone!' thundered Eustace. 'How can she be gone? Was the stable not locked, not guarded — who's to blame, I'll have his ears for it!'

The unfortunate man cowered, but the cockatrice glare scorched past him and up to where Edith leant palely down. 'Your mare is stolen, madam! Kept for you and never ridden, there's a pretty waste of good horse-flesh.' He turned back on the wretch before him. 'Don't stand there with your knees playing knock-a-penny, go after her! I want that palfrey back — show your face here without her and you know what to expect!'

As the man made his escape Edith wilted against the tapestry. Her woman moved to support her but she waved her away, composing her face as the gallery reverberated to her husband's onslaught. The door of her room burst open.

'Lord Eustace, madam,' stammered the frightened maid, and retreated like a rabbit.

Lady Edith mustered her self command. 'My Lord, what means this intrusion?' she demanded.

It had its usual effect. The man who had entered the tiny room as though leading a cavalry charge checked, blustered a little and said gruffly, 'Send your woman away.'

'So early, my lord?' she enquired icily.

His eyes snapped. 'Let us not play games. I wish to speak privily on a matter of some import. Send her away.'

Edith dismissed her. 'If this concerns my mare,' she began wearily.

Eustace cut her short. 'It does not concern your mare. It concerns your daughter.'

Edith stared, caught momentarily off guard. Her *daughter?* He must mean — could only mean — Joanna, the only one to survive her infancy. And since she vanished in childhood fifteen years ago their disinclination to speak of her had been mutual. 'Has...has she been found?' she asked weakly. Perhaps she had been guilty of injustice; perhaps her brutish and ambitious husband had not murdered her only child...perhaps after all she had misinterpreted his chilling words: 'Have no fears for her safety, madam, I assure you I have none; rather light candles for her soul.' No, there was no mistaking his meaning! Their marriage, never one of liking, had withered to a sour exchange of duties; she had eschewed his company as far as she dared, addressed him with searing civility and only when she must. Joanna's name in particular had never passed between them; why then, did he drag into the light the agony of it now? She raised a limp hand to her brow. 'My daughter?' she echoed faintly.

'Your daughter, madam.' His voice had a biting edge. 'You had a child, I think, when I wed you? A girl, as I recall. Or does your memory fail you along with...other virtues?'

Edith suppressed her anger; it ran, a still cold trickle of depression, to join the great reservoir already inside her. 'My lord, you must know that the subject is painful to me. I pray you be brief.'

'Painful?' His pale eyes narrowed. 'Indeed, your sentiments do you credit. Who would have thought that such chill blood could run so warm — and to so little purpose.'

'To little purpose indeed, since she is dead!' It had burst out before she could stop it, the accusation she had kept locked within her over the years. Thank God she had managed to hold back the rest of it. She gripped the arms of her chair, avoiding his eyes. 'All the world says so, my lord,' she added in the hope of placating him.

'The world may say as it pleases.' He lowered his voice. 'You and I know differently, do we not?'

Edith turned to look at him. What was he saying...'My lord, I do not understand you. If this is some cruel jest I pray you stop, I am somewhat discomposed.'

Eustace bent over her, but not in solicitude. 'Madam, I have no time to waste in bandying words. I am well aware that you have your Cornish brat secreted somewhere, some nunnery nicely endowed to keep her safe, and of the goodness of my heart I have blinked the fact. But the time has come for the tidying of loose ends. The girl Joanna must be brought out of hiding. Produce her, madam. At once!'

'At once...' Why was he going through this elaborate pretence? A tidying of loose ends — it had a sinister ring. It was like, she thought, a deadly game of chess in which she had to be always on the defensive...and she was so weary. What was he plotting, did he hope — Heaven forfend! — to lay the murder at her door, to be rid of her and marry again like King Henry in his fruitless search for heirs! She drew a deep breath. The lists must be entered, the game however deadly played out: she must make her move. 'Why at once, my lord?' She contrived to keep her voice ambiguous. 'Why, of a sudden, is the matter become so urgent?' A flicker in his expression told her that her intuition was right, that whatever his scheme it relied on her compliance, and the knowledge gave her a weapon. She gazed at him calmly under lowered lids. 'Why, my lord?'

'My reasons are my own.'

'And I would know them.'

For a moment they deadlocked, as he tried to glare her

into submission. 'You will then produce her?'

Outwardly, Edith did not waver. 'Nothing will induce me otherwise.' Within she felt an unaccustomed throb of excitement, delicious, terrifying. She was deceiving and defying her lord and master...she must have taken leave of her senses!

Eustace's face worked and reddened before his voice filled the room like thunder. 'Oppose me at your peril, madam! I will have the girl in spite of you, I have been thwarted long enough. There is that to be done which cannot be accomplished in her absence *and I will have her!*'

Edith was scarcely listening. She sat bereft of words and blank of face, trying to grasp the fact that her husband truly believed that she could tell him where Joanna was to be found. Something fifteen years ago had removed her child from her sight — but it was not he! His long silence had been occasioned not by guilt as she had imagined, but by God alone knew what sullen child-ishness that prevented him from humbling his pride — until now. How they had deceived one another...and now he was hoist with his own petard. Eustace the bully, the tyrant, was to be baulked of some cherished dream. What it was hardly mattered in this moment of sweet revenge, only that he was to be for once the loser...

As she sat there her body began to shake at the bliss-ful thought of that, and in distant rejoicing for her daughter who had somewhere survived in spite of him. And something so unusual started to happen to her face that Eustace took alarm and shouted from the door for her serving woman, 'Come quickly, your mistress has need of you!'

He had it in mind that her womb had come loose and was running wild about her body, the result of all those miscarriages. Having never seen her laugh before, he thought she must be ill.

5

In the malt-scented gloom of his deserted brewery, Big Daniel looked unhappily at Lady Edith. He scratched his head and shuffled his large feet. 'I don't know as I can make no promises. 'Tis over late in the year for brewing, 'twill likely not cool of itself but keep on working and ruin the brew.'

Lady Edith said wearily, 'I do not ask for promises, merely for effort. Should Her Majesty decide to honour us on her coming progress there must be sufficient for her retinue. This means that we shall need at least one further brew. Look to it, Daniel; I rely on you.'

Daniel bowed his head in deference; when he looked up she and her waiting maid were gone. He sank down heavily on to an upturned barrel and gloomily contemplated the flagged floor. What was the use of trying to explain about brewing to a woman, they didn't understand nothing about nothing anyways. True, there had been a late frost — but that didn't signify the weather would stay cold day and night for another month! And they hadn't got the last brew clear of the vats and barrelled up yet, another couldn't even be started until they had. And he hadn't got Angel to help him now, and the new lad didn't know his arse from his elbow and couldn't even handle the big barrels without help — oh dear, oh Lord, oh dear — what was he going to do?

He heaved a sigh. He'd have to do something to impress her ladyship, show willing before she made her round again. He supposed he could rake the old ashes out, lay the furnace fires ready for lighting. He stood up, reached for the shovel. Yes, he'd better make a start on that...

As he opened the fire door, an evil odour met him. Sickened, he stepped back and almost at once moved forward again for a closer inspection, his curiosity engaged by what he saw. Slowly across the brewery floor was crawling a dark, sluggish fluid. Daniel peered, his first thought that someone had dumped a dead animal into the fire too late for the dying embers to destroy it. But this did not look like anything that might come from a sheep or a goat. He touched it, sniffed it, rubbed a little between his fingers: it felt greasy yet sticky, like partly burned fat, and as the ashes sighed and settled a waft of thick oily smuts came belching out. Daniel went down on his knees, thrust his hand into the opening and groped. For an instant he froze. Then he staggered to his feet and rushed out into the air to vomit in the rank straw by the wall.

Kate straightened her back with difficulty, leaning on the handle of the butter paddle. 'I swear it do take longer to come every time,' she complained. Seven-year-old Prue looked up from her task of scrubbing the cream vats and nodded sagely; she knew better than to disagree with her elders. Suddenly her eyes brightened with interest as something outside caught her attention.

'Look at Big Daniel, something must be ailing him!'

'Where?' Kate followed the pointing finger to where the big man lurched across the yard from the brewery. 'Stay there!' she ordered Prue, and hurried after him.

She caught him up at the door to the kitchens. 'Daniel, whatever ails? You do look like a ghost.'

'Where's the steward, get someone to fetch the steward, 'tis some fearsome thing has happened in the brewery — nobody's to go there, mind, not till he's seen it — oh Kate, my poor woman, poor good woman...' He sank on to a bench, his shaggy head on his hands. The naked spit-boy goggled at his post. Kate paled. She had had enough shocks and dreaded the thought of more. She steeled herself to say it. 'Why me...? What is it, Daniel?' as the kitchen maids came crowding round.

He shook his head. 'I don't know how to tell you and that's a fact.'

Kate's nerves snapped and so did she. 'Well, tell me and have done, dunna keep me dangling! Who is it, what's happened, Angel or Clem, or what?'

'I couldna tell, I only found but one foot —'

'What!'

'That's what I found, just a foot and the rest all...burned away.' He raised his head to stare incredulously into Kate's blanched face. 'That's the God's truth, Kate, that's all there was, I don't know if 'twas Clem or Angel but I reckon it had to be one or t'other — here, come back!' But Kate, her face breaking up into anguish, was already out of the door, running towards the brewery with the women close behind her. When they caught her up she was kneeling on the floor in front of the fire door, her apron over her head in a state of hysteria, rocking her body from side to side and screaming or laughing wildly, it was hard to be sure which. Trying hard not to look at what protruded from the fire door they closed ranks and hustled her outside, with some difficulty because she fought them all the way. 'Clem, oh, my Clem! My Clem's in there!'

Daniel came out to meet them and between them they brought her back into the kitchens and sat her down. The steward arrived with the scullion who had run to find him and now stood stern and a little aloof, as if he wished to register that this was not the part of the house where he belonged. 'Calm yourself, woman!' he commanded sharply. 'Someone give her ale to quench her noise, I have not all day to waste.'

Kate took a long gulp, belched, and began to howl in a

76

fashion that was normal to her. 'My Clem,' she sobbed, 'that witchboy, he's burned my Clem.'

A gasp ran round the assembled company. The steward merely looked mystified. 'Clem?' he queried of Daniel. 'Who is Clem?'

Daniel tugged his forelock. 'That'd be the ploughman as disappeared a while ago, sir.'

'I see.' He turned back to Kate. 'And what makes you think this...remnant is of him? Speak up, woman, and stop blubbering,' he added testily.

Kate blew her nose on the end of her apron. 'I know 'tis, sir, and couldn't be surer. Clem was my husband, see. And I'd know his foot anywhere.' Tears overcame her but a gesture of impatience from the steward rallied her to defiance. 'I do know it by the scar he had from treading on a scythe when he was young, and if you do but look you'll see it there, plain as day. And if it anna the work of that witchboy — oh!' She looked up with round eyes as if she had suddenly discovered something. 'No wonder he made off! And all this time I thought him dead or lost, the varmint! He killed my Clem and run off on his master's mare, you see if he didn't, that's where she'll be, find one and you'll find both —'

'What is she babbling about?' The steward enquired wearily. 'Who is this witchboy of whom she speaks?'

'I don't know, sir,' mumbled Daniel unhappily, his sympathy for Kate diminishing. 'Nobody from here, not that I know —'

'Oh yes, you do, you do!' Kate was up in arms. 'You know him, it was you had to separate them fighting —'

'And he hit Clem to save you from a thrashing, ungrateful jade as you are!' Daniel had lost his temper, and with it his discretion. 'How can you speak so of one of your own! Hold your tongue, woman, where's your loyalty?'

The steward answered for her. 'To her master, as is yours and mine, brewer. Now,' he turned to Kate. 'You, woman — speak! I've no time to waste with Lady Edith sick.'

*　　*　　*

77

Lady Edith lay back against her velvet pillows and took a soothing sup of her mulled wine. It was good, she decided, but not perfect: the cinnamon had been left in a fraction too long, and she made a mental note to have a word with the backslider.

Until her visit to the brewery this morning, she had not left her chamber since the day her husband came rampaging into her withdrawing room to demand the return of Joanna. Not that she was ill; such an admission of weakness would have been foreign to her nature and she had been surprised to find herself savouring the rest. But since Eustace had imagined her to be collapsing she had been quick to seize her advantage, hiding behind a feint of sickness while she tried to get to grips with the situation. She still found it difficult to grasp that Joanna might be alive, when she had for so long been resigned to the fact of her death. Now she saw that it was not fact at all but a myth that had grown in a web of deceit and silence. She had long been certain that Eustace had done away with her daughter. It had seemed incontrovertible in the light of events and her knowledge of his nature. Since his ruthless ambition had encompassed the father's death it had seemed naïve to hope that it would cavil at the child's. Now she must ask herself another question: If Joanna had not died at his hand, where was she?

She must if she lived be a woman grown, sole heiress to the great estates of Buxford and Pengerran. 'A tidying of loose ends...' The phrase clanged in her brain like a death knell. Why else should Eustace the usurper want her back! Edith shivered. Was there nothing she could do...she must think, think...but here was a knot which would take time to unravel. The pain that dogged her body had eased during her unwonted spell of inactivity. Now it was her head that ached; every tread on the gallery outside, every echo of her husband's voice made her flinch, in dread of a savage bid to drag from her knowledge she did not possess. If she could but stave it off for a while, something might come to her...she

78

reached for the goblet, took a long steadying draught; it was clear that she must be ill for a little longer.

Kate continued to cry after the steward had left, huddled by the kitchen fire with a tankard of mulled ale; despite the warmth of the day she still felt chilled. Big Daniel, returning half an hour later, eyed her sourly. 'Best you get back to your work, take your mind off your woes. There's a bucket of butter half made in the dairy and young Prue asking can she come out yet. Finished her scrubbing, she has, says you told her to stay where she was. You best get over there, I reckon. That's if your face don't sour the milk.'

Kate looked up to make a retort but thought better of it. Still clutching the tankard she made her way back to the dairy, averting her eyes as she passed the brewery door where a knot of men had gathered. Prue stood up as Kate entered, a dark shadow flicking past her through the open door.

'What was that?' Kate demanded. 'You know no creatures is allowed in here.'

''Tis only a cat,' pleaded the child. 'It run out of the brewery just after Big Daniel, all afrighted it was and did run in here —'

'Not — not another toad...' Kate's voice shook, but the child seemed not to notice.

'A cat, I tell ee, a black 'un, a great black 'un with yellow eyes, I seen it afore, come to think, the day our Angel run off —'

'He were never *our* Angel!' snapped Kate. 'No child of my blood but a witchboy born and bred — the son of a witch condemned! I kept it close to shelter him and now I'm well repaid! I dunna want nobody to call him mine, not never again, you hear?'

Prue stared at her round-eyed. 'Why, what's he done?'

'He's killed my Clem, that's what he's done, my Clem as fathered him knowing he was none of his own.'

'He never! What for?' Prue goggled, unable to imagine Angel killing anything.

Kate misunderstood her. "Cause he thought he was mine, that's what for. He took him for my sake, good kind soul that he was, took a viper into his bosom!' Kate sat down on an upturned bucket and began to howl afresh. 'I hope they catch the varmint, before God I hope they do!'

Prue continued to stare for a moment. Then, recognising that no further information was likely to be forthcoming, she scampered off to find the other children, her eyes shining with excitement. Matthew from the forge would be interested, she knew — imagine, Angel a witch!

'And where are you tearing off to?'

It was Nan, Matthew's mother, into whose skirts she had blundered in her headlong rush, and who now held her firmly by the arm.

'Where's Matt, I got to tell him about Angel — Kate says he's a witch and she hopes they catch him — do that mean he'll be hanged?' As Nan did not answer she went on. 'I dunna want him to die, do you? Nan, do you?' She wriggled and twisted, trying to free herself. Nan only tightened her grip, giving her what Kate would call an old-fashioned look.

'Prue — you sure about this?'

'Course I'm sure — let go, you're hurting! I want to go and tell Matt —' Suddenly released, she raced away, scarce able to contain herself.

'Yes, you go and tell him.' Nan spoke absently. And I'll be telling Jody, she added to herself, standing pensive in the bustle of the yard. He'll have something to say about hanging Angel. Oh, I'd stake my life on that!

Eustace stirred and mumbled as the brilliant light found a crack between the bed hangings and came probing into his eyes. He turned away to escape it and met with displeasure the form of the woman still sleeping beside him. He brought a knee up sharply against her soft rump. 'Out!' he growled. 'You should be gone before now.'

She yawned and shuffled obediently out of his reach, pushing her way out through the curtains to search for her clothes. 'You've no need to kick me,' she complained mildly, tugging at the end of a garment protruding from underneath a sleeping deerhound. 'Get up, you!' As Eustace sat up angrily glaring she added hastily, 'Not you, my lord, the dog.'

'Hound, woman, your ignorance appals me! Close the curtain and get back to the forge, I would sleep.'

'Aye, now that you're sated,' she retorted, nettled. 'Kick me out of bed's good enough for me now — 'tis not what you said last night, it was Pretty Nan then as borne your son as'll one day be lord of Buxford —'

'I said *perhaps*!' rasped Eustace. 'I may well change my plans. And whether or no, I'll stomach no impertinence.' He reached out and grasped her by the arm, bringing her face within inches of his. 'Neither will I stand for gossiping. You are privy to my intent only that you may know it is my heir you nurture. Betray me and you'll rue it.' As a whimper escaped her he tightened his grasp. 'Mark me, woman. He is old enough now to dispense with your care and a rattling tongue could undo you! I know what you and your man get up to, don't think I can be deceived. One word out of place...and I will be rid of you both.' For a long moment his eyes burned into hers as she cowered in his grip. Then he flung her from him to cringe in a resentful heap upon the wolfskins.

She scrambled to her feet, snatched up her clothing and, naked as she was, fled from his presence.

When she had gone, Eustace lay frowning, drawing strands of his beard between his teeth to chew on. Last night in his cups he had been unwise, told the simpering fool too much. Now he might have to deal with her before intimations reached Edith. She would never bring the Cornish brat out of hiding if she guessed the truth and all his machinations would have been in vain. Damn Joanna! Joanna, Joanna always the accursed Joanna...who would have thought that after fifteen years with her father dead and discredited she would still be a stumbling-block! And yet she was; even now, when he had given up hope of a legal heir by Edith and fathered at last a lusty son who gave every promise of survival, the shadow of Joanna

81

stood between the boy and his inheritance...He hurled himself out of bed in a sudden access of energy, threw on his velvet night robe and strode out and along the gallery to his wife's apartments.

'Madam!' he thundered, bursting in upon her sleep. 'I must have words with you.'

'God's life, my lord!' Edith groped for her wits, sitting up with an effort, her coif slipping sideways over her thinning hair. 'What's the matter, are we afire?'

'Afire, no — send these cackling geese away.' He gestured impatiently towards the women who had come running at the noise. 'Out, out!' He shoved them through the door and slammed it, roughly dragged the bed hangings aside and thrust his red face within.

Edith shrank, drawing the fur covers higher under her chin. 'The time is not right...'

'Right? When was it ever right?' He barked a laugh. 'No, I'm not here for country matters but to remind you of your vows. Obedience, madam.' He smiled dangerously into her uncomprehending face. 'Produce your daughter; I have been patient long enough. You are not too sick, I presume, to write a letter?'

Edith's mouth dried. This was the moment she had dreaded — and how like Eustace to spring it on her so early, before she had even taken a grip on her senses. She swallowed, her eyes trapped by a throbbing vein at her husband's temple. She heard herself speaking, words that seemed to come from her mouth without ever having crossed her mind. 'No, my lord. Nor yet too sick to care for my daughter's safety — and for yours.' She held her breath, watching his face as it suffused and then turned dangerously livid.

'Be plain, it is too early in the day for riddles.'

Edith prayed and blundered on, snatching words from the air in her desperation. 'I mean, sir...' Suddenly, she had it. 'I mean...that there is another abroad with a claim to Buxford — one who spells danger to all of us while he lives. No — no, hear me out. You will recall some fifteen years ago when Joanna —' she had been about to say 'disappeared' but caught herself — 'went into retreat, that two women were executed for witchcraft?'

He scowled, shaking his head. 'Come to the point.'

'I do, I do. You must recall, it was the last year of King Henry's reign, before poor misguided young Edward stopped the executions. These two were the last to die, an old crone and a young girl, a servant from this very house. I petitioned you to let me question her —'

'Yes, yes, yes, but —'

'But I did not tell you the reason. That girl had consorted with John Pengerran.'

Now she had his full attention. 'So! Go on, go on — speak, what did you learn?'

'Nothing, alas. By then she had lost her wits. But it comes to my mind that she came to us as a wetnurse, with a babe...'

Eustace stared. 'God's wounds...' he breathed. 'It was disposed of, surely?'

Edith swallowed again. This was the moment of danger. 'I...was unwell, unable...the servants succoured it, I hear, in secret. In innocence, they could not know its lineage and supposedly saw no harm. But there's peril in it, to you as to Joanna. The child was male, a son of John Pengerran with a claim more strong than that of the distaff. And he has grown up dangerous.'

'He is not still here!'

'If only he were, it would be simple. He it is who made off with my mare after murdering the ploughman. No servant here would harbour him now, they go in fear of him — the dairymaid swears he consorted with toads, has the Evil Eye —'

'Piss-prophecy!'

'*I* say he lurks in hiding, awaiting his chance. He imperils the life of my daughter, I cannot bring her to Buxford while he lives.'

'I say you will, if you value your life!'

'No, my lord, not in sanity!' Edith summoned all the dignity at her command, looked straight into the gun-metal eyes and lied with valour. 'Kill me and you'll never find

her, since only I know where she is. Think on it, my lord.'
She closed her eyes and sank back against the cushions.

Eustace glowered down at her a moment longer. Then
he rose and stumped off, muttering under his breath,
'We chase the girl, we chase the mare — now we
chase the boy, a pretty game of Barley Broke about the
countryside!'

Edith listened to his retreating steps and drew a long
sigh of relief. If nothing else, she had won a little time. She
was sorry about the boy who might well be the harmless
victim of hysteria. But her loyalty was to her own flesh
and blood: the family of which she was a part, the
daughter who must carry on the trust after her death.
Buxford and its revenues had come with Edith herself to
the Pengerrans. If Joanna had survived she must live
to inherit, or it would pass from the Buxford bloodline
altogether.

Her stomach tightened again as a new thought struck
her. Her union with Eustace had proved barren, unless a
row of tiny coffins in the vault could be counted as heirs.
She had long been aware that he imported women from
the village for dalliance and it was never difficult to identify the current favourite; was it his intention to settle
the estates on one of his bastards? Was she to come to her
death-bed knowing that Buxford would pass not even to
the grasping Pengerrans but worse, to the misbegotten
son of a blacksmith's wife?

It was not to be endured! Joanna must be traced — and
not by him. She, Edith, must find some means to ensure
that she remained in hiding until his death. If that
entailed lying and treachery so be it. Since her girlhood
she had encountered little else.

6

Master Nicholas Bodkyn, upright man, prigger of prancers and sometime counterfeit crank, stepped out boldly in the warm sunshine of May Day. He was well pleased with his world; his recent spell as a whipjack had paid handsomely. The money he had wheedled from the kindly disposed to ease him in the loss of his non-existent ship had fitted him out in fine style from his high felt hat to the expensive leather 'stampers' on his unwashed feet. It was time to change his way of life, he reflected, take things easy for a while: too long as a whipjack and folk might become suspicious. But he did not fancy laying aside his new clothes to return to the life of the counterfeit crank; it was not a comfortable way of getting rich, daubing your face with pig's blood and mire, filling your mouth with soap to make you froth. And there was always the danger of running into some surgeon who could recognise the true falling sickness and catch you out. Nicholas had no desire to be whipped through the streets at the cart's end, he was too fond of his creature comforts. He might be lousy under his shirt but it was of good Flanders linen and he meant to keep it.

He would enjoy a respectable inn tonight, he thought with satisfaction, not the sleazy hospitality of an alehouse. There would be warm welcome, roasted meats…he smiled. There might even be a coney worth the catching. If he played his cards right he could afford to lie low for a while, one good cozenage would set him up as a pedlar, keep him out of sight and out of mind of the justices.

He reached a likely inn in the late afternoon as the sun was beginning its long leisurely descent, and sat down outside with a goblet of malmsey to watch the guests arrive. Only the innkeeper and his staff were within, but it was early yet. He smiled. He could afford to wait.

He was relaxing on the stone bench, legs extended, feet crossed, when a sorrel mare came slowly along the road. Nicholas opened an eye; he took in the sweat-flecked coat of the palfrey. He looked over her rider, a fair-haired countryman with a rawhide patch obscuring one eye and a ripening bruise bidding fair to close the other. His smile deepened.

'My dear young man!' He leaped to his feet with feigned concern. 'I see you have been set upon and robbed — pray allow me to help you as a fellow Christian.'

The gull, who had been drowsing off in the saddle, looked first startled, then suspicious. 'No — due thanks, I can shift for meself.'

Nicholas noted the speech, the lack of shirt, the furtive manner. Better and better, he thought: here was no young richman with a legal claim to such a mount but some thieving stable lad in no position to call on the constables. He put on his most avuncular manner.

'My dear boy…you are upset, confused — small wonder, truly the highway is safe for no honest wayfarer these days!'

'That's right.' Horse and rider edged away. 'I'll give you good day, I'd as lief be home by nightfall.'

'Of course, of course,' soothed Nicholas, his hand already on the bridle, coaxing the mare into the yard. 'But you are in no state to travel on as you are. Come in and recover a little, take some refreshment while I walk your mare. I see she has been galloped, spare her at least if you will not consider yourself.'

His victim hesitated. 'I anna got no money...' he said doubtfully.

Nicholas smiled his warmest. 'Leave it to the Good Samaritan. Some day you may do as much for me.' The rider stumbled as he reached the ground and clung to the saddle for support. He looks dazed, thought Nicholas, and knew a moment of compunction. But it was only a moment: after all, it was the way of the world, the luck of the road. He nudged him towards the bench where he had left the goblet. 'Drink up.'

It was drained at a gulp, producing a splutter and a look of surprise. 'That's never ale!'

'Who said it was?' He chuckled. 'That's malmsey, lad, and the best this side of London.' He noted the calloused hand still stubbornly entwined in the mare's reins. 'Sit you there and rest, I go to fetch more — and a squab pie to tide us over until dinner.' He swept off his new hat, laid it down on the bench like a pledge. 'Then I'll walk your horse while you take your ease —'

'I'll walk her myself.' He staggered to his feet only to fall back again, his head in his hands.

Smiling into his whiskers, Nicholas went inside.

Angel had neither eaten nor slept for three days and nights. Now he sat helpless in the warmth of the sun while the golden glow of the wine soaked into his bones and robbed him of his will. He must get to his feet, walk Bess...give her some wine...she was smiling into her whiskers — no! He jerked his eyelids up with an effort that was almost painful...and again — merciful Heaven, he must not fall asleep! He tightened the reins about his hand, made a final, futile effort to stand up...

He dragged his eyes open once more. He looked about him bemused, alone in the dusk of the courtyard. The reins in his hand ended in two cut ends. As if in derisory payment, pie and a goblet of wine lay beside him on the bench where the hat had been. And when he looked about him for its owner he saw that both he and Young Bess were gone.

His weariness fell away from him. He ran to the

roadway and looked both ways along it although he knew in his heart it would be fruitless. In the past hour many horses must have passed this way and the earth of the road was churned up by their hooves; there was not even a trail that he could follow. He slammed frustrated fists against a tree trunk and drove his head down upon his forearms, flooded by desolation, by grief for Bess, by fury against the rogue who had tricked him — not least by exasperation with himself for having slept...

He gained control of himself at last and walked slowly back to the bench. Until now he had been running without an objective, but now he had one: he was going after Bess. He would know that man's face if ever he caught up with him. Oh yes, he promised him silently: Some day I'll do the same for you, be sure of that!

Midnight found him threading his way through the mean back streets of a village, picking a path between snarling curs, heaps of ordure, drunks and beggars, at one point the rotting carcass of a donkey, searching for somewhere to lay his head.

Asked for permission to sleep in his barn, the inn-keeper had eyed him with disfavour. 'No palliards here. Plenty of alehouses for the likes of you, push on.' The label 'palliard' had made him smart; but he knew he must seem like a beggar, lacking even a shirt and with only a few pence to his name. He had swallowed the slight and trudged on, reminding himself that it could well prove unwise to hang about the inn; it was spacious and looked the kind of place that travellers to or from Buxford might patronise. The last thing he desired was to be recognised.

Rounding a corner he stopped short. In the doorway of one of the houses two women sprawled, one of them very young and very drunk. Both were barebreasted, and the elder of the two was trickling something from a tankard into the mouth of a small child who lay grizzling in her lap. From behind them a din of raucous laughter, drunken quarrelling, oaths and an occasional girlish squeal surged out into the night on a waft of ale, fat bacon and sweating

88

flesh. As he hesitated, the younger girl
invitingly.

'Come in, darling. Good libbege here a...
withal.'

Angel frowned in perplexity. Trugging was the ...
thing on his mind at the moment. And what in the world
was libbege? 'I'm just looking to sleep,' he said.

The women exchanged glances and laughed. 'A pretty
cove from the dewse-a-ville!' The elder added teasingly,
'And where did you lib last darkmans, in the ruffmans?'

He stared at her numbly, unable to decide if she were
speaking some language foreign to him or if it was Eng-
lish, and his brain too dulled to grasp it. 'I dunna understand. I'll try somewheres else...'

'I says you slept in the woods last night — no, don't go.'
She said aside to the girl, 'Watch what you say, he's not
proper stalled to the rogue.' She stood up, tipping the
child uncaringly off her lap, and swaggered over to where
Angel stood irresolute. Her breasts were gross and
flabby and he saw that the nipples were crudely painted.
'So, you just look to sleep, do you? And who sent you to
me?'

'Not you specially, there's an inn a few leagues back
along the road. They wouldna take me in.'

'And they thought I would. Got any money?'

He fished for his few coins, displayed them on his palm.
She folded his fingers quickly over them. 'Keep close,' she
warned, 'or you'll not have them long.' She stood back,
walked slowly around him, eyeing him shrewdly in the
light from the door. 'You ain't from these parts, are you?
And you don't look like no clapperdudgeon to me — that's
to say, you ain't no proper beggar. What you doing so far
from home? No duds, not so much as a shirt, nowhere to
sleep. And where's your licence from your master?'

The girl on the doorstep smothered a loud guffaw.
Angel's heart dropped at the reminder that he needed a
licence to be out of his home manor; caught without it he
stood to be whipped for vagrancy and — which was much
worse — sent back to his parish! He did not trust this

...an; her face was raddled, her expression hard ...neath the professional smile. But he had no choice. 'I ...nna got one, I'm a fugitive.' He held his breath. Watching her, he added, 'I had a bad master, he was about to lop my hands. Dunna turn me away, I'll be gone soon as it's light.'

The bawd stared at him a moment longer. Then she burst into noisy laughter and slapped him on the back like a man. 'Why then, you're one of us! You don't lose a hand without you're caught thieving and that's good enough for me. Come in, lad, warm you by the glimmer and quaff you some booze, then you can couch a hogshead in the strummel.' As he frowned again in puzzlement she linked her arm in his and laughed again. 'You niggle with Marian here, she'll teach you the cant. Pedlar's French they call it, and a fine and secret tongue it is too if you want to talk privily with no fear of eavesdroppers.' She drew him towards the lighted doorway as the girl called Marian lurched to her feet. 'Snoutfair, you are, I'll give you that. And strong.' She pinched the thick muscle of his arm. 'Make you an Upright Man if you've wit to learn...'

Angel, his head reeling with fatigue, was long past the point for arguing or the asking of questions. With a painted doxy on each arm and his eyes already closing, he staggered into the alehouse and collapsed in a heap on its evil-smelling floor.

7

From time to time during the night and the following day
he stirred and mumbled or roused just sufficiently to
shift from his neck the threadbare cat who had huddled
there for warmth while he slept. Her whiskers in his ear
did not disturb him but crunching mouse bones was
another matter: he grunted, rolled her off and turned his
back to plunge again into heavy sleep. In its depths
lurked a dream in which Clem had stolen Young Bess
and Kate lay battered on the brewery floor. Her lips
moved ceaselessly, moaning words that he could not
make out. He knelt over her. 'What ails, Ma?' She looked
distressed, her eyes still closed. 'Toad...in the great
vat...drowning...stalled...' Her voice was fading, changing, blending with that of the alewife...

'Stalled to the rogue, think you? By the Solomon, he's
libbed a long time!'

A man's voice, growling in answer. 'How long?'

'Why, all through the darkmans — and bids fair to
sleep away the lightmans too.'

'Boozed to the eyeballs. Wake him, mistress — we'll
rid you of him.'

'No. He ain't maunding nothing, let him bide. He's
tired, I'll lay he's come a long way from home. Best shift
him, though. Help me...'

He felt himself lifted, carried, set down again, still

unable to wake. As the little cat settled once more on his shoulder, her eyes watchful, her bony elbows peaking through her fur, he was drifting off again.

'Leave him there, he can sleep his fill...' The speaker was Kate once more, settling him to rest in the long-ago days.

He was roused at last by the tramping of feet and a shaft of light that stabbed his eyelids at intervals. He opened his eyes reluctantly, squinting into the setting sun. beaming in through a mean window set low under the eaves; motes of dust danced in it as it flickered on and off between the legs that passed back and forth across his vision, the feet barely missing his face. He sat up incautiously and his forehead struck something hard. Timber. The underside of a table. A delighted cackle broke out from above and he looked up to see a man with a bunch of ribbons tied to his sleeve sitting down to drink, his pedlar's pack safely clamped between his feet. Yawning, he crawled out to look around.

Tables and benches lined the small room, each with its burden of carousing travellers; he made out among them a minstrel with a hurdy-gurdy, a small-time tinker with his back pack and bellows and two men of decrepit appearance applying something from a bottle to the open sores on their legs. His empty stomach churned and he looked away.

From the herbs and the hams hung to smoke in the broad chimney, the greasy pots scattered haphazard and a stack of dubious-looking pies warming on the hearth he took the crowded room to be a kitchen — or rather to have started life as a kitchen, for clearly its function had changed. He guessed the woman who had brought him in last night to be the alewife, now decently covered and stirring something in a cauldron over the fire, fending off a small bare-buttocked child from the stack of pies, taking money, serving ale, using her long spoon to chastise misbehavers and keeping up a stream of good-natured banter at the same time. 'So, you're alive,' she greeted him. 'Marian, here!'

Angel peered through the gathering dusk in which dancing shadows partnered the flames on the hearth. At the back of the room a girl of about fourteen detached herself from a man in a long and filthy patched cloak and came forward into the firelight. A pretty girl with a tangle of red-gold curls and eyes moist as pansies above the dark bruised crescents of a hangover, barely recognisable as the drunken trull of last night.

'Wotchyer, cove. Hungry? Have some ruff-peck.' She held out to him a chunk of bacon. He took it, sorting out a half-penny from his hoard to offer her. She shook her head. 'Paid for. Pannam?' She tore off a piece of black bread for him and sat down companionably by him to eat her own. She reached a sly hand towards the pies but was rewarded by a smart rap on the knuckles from the spoon.

'Fambles off! Them's for customers, not for you. Not till you tip me more cross!'

'Cross?' queried Angel, puzzled.

'Money, she means. Stingy old bawd,' she muttered under her breath, adding aloud, 'Bless the Lord!' in answer to the alewife's prompt challenge. ''Struth, cove, don't tip it to the cat!'

'Why not, she's hungry — dunna chase her off —'

But Marian was on her feet shooing at the cat who fled for cover. 'Bing a waste, you old fleabag! Go on, scat! Back to the ruffmans!'

Her rival banished she returned to Angel and smiled. 'Well, what we going to do with you, eh? What can you do? Hook, curb, nip a bung?'

He sighed. 'I know what I canna do, that's understand a word of your talk.'

'Better start learning then, hadn't you? Now,' she shuffled round to face him, 'nipping a bung, that's cutting a purse. And hooking and curbing, that's ways of filching cheats —'

'Wait, whoa — what's cheats, for a start?'

'Fings! Anything, like — your nab-cheat, that's your hat. And crashing-cheats, them's your teeth — you'd be

93

hard put to it to steal them, mind!' She laughed, showing her own teeth still firmly in place. 'Then there's cozening. That's playing the cards so you always win, primero and the like. But I can't tell you about that, I don't know the tricks.' She slid a mischievous hand across his bare stomach. 'And that's your quarroms — your body. Nice if it wasn't for that scar. Fall in the fire, did you?' She leaned close, whispered in his ear. 'Want to niggle with me? You could have it for nothing.'

Angel drew back. He had fumbled his way to knowledge in the haylofts of Buxford with girls as ignorant and as curious as himself. But the thought of trying conclusions with an experienced whore unnerved him. Blushing, he attempted to turn the conversation. 'You anna told me what you are — I mean — what do you do, what's it called...' he floundered and stopped.

'Me?' She looked at him quizzically before breaking into laughter. 'What I'm called's a bawdy-basket. I sell ribbons and laces and...other favours. You ought to know that!' She tugged at her bodice strings to release her breasts; they were rounded and pert and he felt an unwelcome surge of excitement.

'No!' He had said it too quickly. 'I mean — I thought you'd be a wife.'

'So I am!' she declared proudly. 'Walking-mort to an Upright Man. Not autem-mort, not proper wed by a priest, well, I ain't never seed the inside of a church. But wed by a Patrico, a hedge-priest as is one of us. So I'm his mort all right, and he's my cove.'

'You never seen the inside of a church?' he repeated, remembering Sundays at Buxford with every servant marshalled under the echoing vaulted roof, the ringing of bells and the candles that had gone, then returned only to go again, on and off like summer lightning. 'Why not?'

'Allus been on the road, see. Churches isn't for the likes of us.'

'But this man...dunna he mind about the other men?'

'Lord bless you, course he don't. He never lacks when

I've got it, no more'n me when he has — well, mostly. Mind, I had a better afore him, never beat me nor filched from me — well, hardly ever. Will Kethro. Wonderful he was, real Rome, turn his hand to anything, hooking, curbing — pick a lock with anyone. We used to work the crossbite together.' Her eyes softened. 'Lived like gentry we did, best victuals and Rome-booze — none of your duckspiddle ale. But he was took up last summer. Went to the chats.' The brightness had dimmed from her voice and he thought he saw tears. He waited. She dashed the back of a hand across her eyes. 'Hung him, they did. They all comes to it in the end. Still, my Nick's no fool, he'll last a bit. He'll be back for me soon, you'll see.'

'Course he will,' Angel spoke gently. 'Here, I reckon he's a Rome cove too. Have I got it right?'

'Certain you have!' Her laugh was a brittle defiance of fate. 'You're learning real quick, once you get a jark you'll be set up for anything.'

'A jark?' He felt he was learning a whole new language.

'A jark, a licence — a passport for the road.'

'Oh...that. Like I said, my master'd never give me one.'

'Not a proper one, a counterfeit! There's a pedlar goes round the fairs can do one, seals and all, for a groat. Not the best, mind, a cove caught with one of his last Michaelmas got carted for his pains. Better to wait for Jarkman Joe. He's a pretty-boy, mind.' She winked broadly. 'You keep your back to the wall. But he'll do you the best jark in the business.'

'Hm-mm.' He grinned. 'What do I have to do for it?'

'You have to pay, stupid, tip him what he asks. How else do you think he lives?'

He shook his head. 'Anna got but a few pence. It'll have to be the pedlar.'

She tossed her curls. 'No, you'll have to make more. What can you do?'

He shrugged. 'I worked in a brewery. And I can plough —'

'Gawd love us, I don't mean work, who gets fat on that? No, it's nip and foist as makes your fortune, a good hour's work can feed you for a month. You just have to be —' she trilled her pretty fingers —'a bit nifty with your fambles.' Smiling, she handed him back his own coins.

'You mean picking pockets!'

'I could learn you,' she said, unabashed.

'No doubt,' he said warmly. 'And what if I'm caught?'

Marian shrugged, spread her hands in a comic gesture. 'What if you go home? If that ain't the kiss of the rope on your windpipe I ain't never seed one.'

Angel considered. She was right, of course; at best his hands, at worst his neck would pay, for they had only to find Clem's body to know at once who had killed him. He had no work, no passport and no friends. He had given no thought to the future beyond the forlorn hope of finding Bess, and even to do that he must somehow scrape a living...

Marian had already turned her attention to the advance of another woman, bony and toothless but sporting a velvet gown. 'There's work for you tonight,' the hag was saying. 'A gentrycove insisting on a virgin, won't settle for no other. What about it?'

Marian's laughter was scornful. 'Come on, Meg, you know me, I was broke years agone, even afore my Will. Go find you another.'

'No, no, it's you he wants. Seen you he has, and fancies you still a young dell. Try the surfling water trick, he'll not know the difference.'

'Not me! Molly Wopping shrunk her goods to please a customer and went too far — the poor cove knocked and knocked all night and never gained admittance! Anyways, it ain't honest.' She turned to catch Angel shaking his head. 'Well, make up your mind — here, you laughing at me?'

In the days that followed he became versed in new skills. He learnt to extract coins from a pocket hung with hawks' bells without their making a telltale tinkle, and to sever cleanly the thongs of a purse with a cuttlebung, a sharpened sliver of horn attached to his thumb: that, he reflected grimly, was no doubt the instrument used to cut Bess's reins. He learnt too that the man in the street was all too aware of being among thieves and kept a sharp look-out, but that if a straw applied to the back of the neck was not enough to coax his protective hand out of his pocket, a jostle from behind would do it in order to save himself from falling.

Daily he practised under the watchful eye of Marian, in the intervals of cutting wood and fetching water for the alewife in return for scraps. Evening found him listening to the talk around the tables, chuckling over their travellers' tales, amused as any by the fate of a curber who, fishing with his hook for booty through a window, had upended the contents of a chamberpot over his head. Then, with the ale flowing and the laughter uproarious, their way of life seemed at least better than starvation, its successes worthwhile, its failures merely comic. But at night on the flattened straw of the barn he often lay cold and wakeful, remembering Will Kethro who had died 'on the chats'; Marian saying sadly, 'They all comes to it in the end...'

He turned restlessly on the straw and tried to sleep. Only one thing seemed certain: somehow he had to find Bess. Always in the back of his mind he was aware of her misery, lost and dispirited, exhausted by harsh treatment, and the knowledge ached in him that he was to blame.

By day he took refuge in trying to perfect his craft. But he felt far from competent when without warning Marian said, 'Time to test your skill. There's a puppet show setting up as'll draw a fine crowd. Now's your chance, can't ask for a better.'

His stomach plunged. 'I'm not ready. What if I fail?'

The pansy eyes hardened with a knowledge older than time. 'Don't fail,' she said flatly. 'Come back a rogue so we can get you stalled to it proper. Then you're set up.'

'Stalled to the rogue...that's what the alewife said. What's it mean?'

'It means, what's the word now...'nitiated. That's it.

'Nitiated to the Company of Beggars. Makes you one of us.'

He thought of the distasteful rituals of the Horseman's Word. 'What do you have to do?'

'Don't ask me, never done it, being a wild dell born to the road. You'll find out, I daresay.' She picked up her basket of ribbons and tapes. 'My Nick'll be back tonight, he's the one to do it, him being a Upright Man an' all.'

He called after her, 'Wait! What's an Upright Man when he's at home?'

She laughed, calling back across her shoulder, 'You'll find that out too, first time you meet one on the road! Mind now, don't you come back emptyhanded.' With a toss of her bright mane she was gone.

Angel stood irresolute for a moment, wrestling with mounting qualms. Had he come so far and risked so much to escape a trumped-up charge of theft, only to lay himself open to a genuine one? It was madness, and he knew it! But he was past the point of no return. He reminded himself of Black John who had sired him, and stepped out tight-lipped towards an unknown fate.

The alewife had lent him a shirt of her dead husband's; with a leather strap to kilt it at the hips and a discreet slit in its voluminous folds it gave him a promising poacher's pocket. He had practised his art to a fair degree of success on Marian's dummies, safe in the knowledge that a fumble would not bring disaster on his head. This was different, and already he felt his fingers turning to jelly with apprehension. His mouth dried as he mingled with the people moving towards the market square.

The puppeteers were setting up their booth as he arrived, the man draping a box frame with cloth while two women unpacked the battered puppets and carefully laid them in order. He saw a dragon, a knight in armour, a lady with a steepled headdress, a juggler...he wished he could have been coming just to watch the show.

The crowd was not yet thick enough to cloak his activities, being divided between the puppeteers and a tumbler competing for attention at the far end of the market place. He moved away to make a slow tour of the square, where bustle of a different kind was breaking out. The place was not large enough to support a daily market, and those who lived on the borders of the square never missed an opportunity such as this for extra trade. In minutes stalls and trestles had appeared, those who lacked them standing in their doorways, their produce displayed on the threshold. He strolled among shouting vendors and haggling shoppers, glancing without interest at baskets, rushes in bundles, spindles, stools and spinning wheels, leathern buckets and lengths of homespun; behind one window an old woman was dipping candles, while through an open doorway he could see a potter at his wheel. On a doorstep an old man gnarled as a tree root sat cross-legged, cobbling shoes. Angel picked one up to look at it and it was instantly snatched back.

'Keep your thieving hands to yourself!' The ancient eyes flashed a warning and he backed off guiltily. But the old man's attention had returned at once to his last.

Savoury scents of roasting meat and hot bread wafted towards him from the bakery but for once his stomach did not respond. It was tied in a taut knot of apprehension. Nervously he fingered the cuttlebung, scanning the growing crowd for a likely victim. He noticed a short well-larded man with flour on his hair, his purse hanging unguarded at his belt. He looked like a miller; judging by his build he would not starve for the loss of it nor was it likely he could run very fast. As the beating of a tabor punctuated the noise of the market, the audience began to assemble about the booth. The miller moved forward with the others. Angel moved in behind him, his palms sweating.

Should he cut the purse now, under cover of the move-ment around them...or would the man reach at any moment for his money to pay the puppeteers? Maybe he should wait until everybody was engrossed. But then he might be trapped by latecomers from behind; he had no wish to be caught standing beside his victim when the theft was discovered. Perhaps after all the best time was at the end of the show, when everyone began to move and he could escape unnoticed. He passed his tongue over dry lips, rubbed his damp hands against his breechings.

The showman was bawling, trying to make himself heard above the hubbub. 'The marvellous mystery of Saint George and the Dragon...'

The curtains of the booth were agitated, then opened in a series of jerks to a chorus of 'ooh's and 'aah's from the onlookers. Angel hardly saw what lay behind them. He was preoccupied with searching out a quick way of escape from the square when the time came. Suddenly he froze.

On the fringes of the audience a pedlar was moving, his pack unopened on his back, not crying his wares but with unwonted stealth. This was not the pedlar he had seen at the alehouse, yet there was something oddly familiar about him. Surely...yes, surely he recognised that high felt hat...the man turned his head, and their eyes met for an instant.

The next moment Nicholas Bodkyn, abandoning his intention of cutting a third purse in the space of two minutes, was legging it for his life up the road with an avenging Angel fiery at his heels.

8

Nicholas glanced over his shoulder as he ran. By the Solomon! The fellow was gaining on him, scarlet in the face, his one eye blazing, his legs pounding tirelessly in pursuit. Hampered as he was he could hardly hope to outstrip him and a brawl in the hearing of the townsfolk was likely to end with them both in the stocks. He struggled out of the pedlar's pack harness and flung it back towards him. 'Here, take it in payment for the prancer and have done!' But to his chagrin the other did not pause.

'I dunna want your toys, I want my mare!' And he redoubled his speed.

Nicholas swore. Already he could see two or three figures behind them on the road, and one of them had the too familiar look of a constable. He glanced about him for cover and found it in the shape of a sprawl of farm buildings running down among trees to the roadside. He slackened his pace, leaving the earth track to weave in and out among bushes and brambles, and at his chosen moment dropped among them out of sight.

Angel came up panting and glared about him in frustration. He could have sworn...

Suddenly he was hurtling off balance; a hand clamped over his mouth from behind and his arm wrenched

painfully upward to a point between his shoulder-
blades, he found himself dragged away backwards
through the undergrowth and in through some dark
doorway to be pinned to the ground by the weight of a
man he could not see.

'You young idiot!' A voice whispered savagely in his
ear. 'That prancer was none of yours either — now stow
you, or we'll both be in the pigeonholes!'

For a long time neither of them moved. Angel lay listening for sounds of pursuit on the road outside, until
very slowly his captor straightened up to peer through a
cobwebbed chink, let go his breath in a long sibilance,
and released him. 'They've given up. As for you, you
great lump, you should have taken the pack and been
thankful — now neither of us has it.'

Angel sat up, brushing earth and straw from his
knees. ''Tis likely still on the road. I'll get it after dark —'

'After dark? Some licorish rogue will have it long
before then. I'm going back.'

'Oh no, you dunna!' Angel was on his feet. ''Tis mine,
from your own mouth. Payment for my mare.' With such
a pack he could eat, move about freely, go in search of
Bess…His assailant set off at a run but he was quicker,
his need more urgent, and he reached it first. ''Tis mine!'
he challenged, stooped over it like a hawk.

The older man laughed. 'No more yours than the
horse was! Come, confess to it, you're no innocent
abroad.' He waved a hand towards the thumb with its
cuttlebung still in place. 'Think you I never saw one of
those before? I'm an Upright Man, count yourself lucky
not to be beaten and left for dead.'

Angel lowered his head and set his jaw. 'She was
mine,' he said stubbornly. 'You took her. Now I'm
having the pack.'

The professional smile turned a little sour. 'You'll
have nothing I don't choose to allow you.' From a corner
of his eye Angel saw that he was drawing a club. 'By the
Solomon! A kinchin cove with one glazier gone —'

'I'm no kinchin, I'm eighteen!' Well, near enough…and

102

things were beginning to look ugly. On an impulse he whipped off the eye patch. 'Maybe you seen the Evil Eye before as well?'

He had played his one card in desperation. The result astonished him.

'Jesu, Maria!' The man backed off, looking away. 'Cover it — cover it...' he muttered uneasily.

Angel pressed home his advantage. 'I got the Horseman's Word an' all,' he lied. 'That's why the mare's mine. Buy her, steal her, she's still mine, take her to the ends of the earth, she'll hear my voice and never obey no other. So you best tell me where you got her hid.'

The Upright Man sank down on the bank and wiped his face with his sleeve. 'I sold her,' he said shakily.

'You never...' Angel was aghast, unable to hide his dismay.

The man shrugged. 'What did you expect? I'm a professional, I don't prig prancers to ride myself, I unload 'em and that fast. She went to a gentry cove in London if I recall — mind, I've had a few others since then. Still...' He eyed Angel thoughtfully. 'You said you've got the Horseman's Word. Is that a fact?'

Best brazen it out, he was committed now. 'Here's the frogbone.' He produced it, still miraculously intact, from his pouch. 'Now d'you believe?'

'So you have...so you have, indeed.' The man walked around him, looking him up and down. 'A prigger of prancers and a Whisperer, eh? Now there's a winning combination if ever I saw one.' He stood still, head cocked to one side, stroking his beard. 'That speaks to me that you and I should be in business together. How say you?'

Angel had not the slightest desire to team up with the man who had already robbed him of Bess. 'I'm no horse thief. I just want back what's mine.'

The Upright Man stood up, his composure recovered. 'And so you well may if you come with me.' He swept off his hat with a flourish. 'Nicholas Bodkyn, prigger of prancers, at your service. Together we'll visit the fairs and the markets, you'll see more horses with me in an hour than you'd meet in a day's march. Marry, what better way of seeking out your lost mare?'

That was true enough. But still he held back; the advantage to himself was too fortuitous, that to the other man less easily seen and therefore suspect; and judging by past experience he was likely to come off worst. On the other hand, what other course lay open...

As he hesitated, Bodkyn's hand fell companionably on his shoulder. 'Come, pick up the pack, we'll not fall out over trifles. We'll use it for cover on the road. How say you, will you come?'

Angel stood up and shouldered the pack, reflecting that at least he would have that. 'I'll take my chance,' he said guardedly, earning himself a comic grimace. 'Right, where's the next fair?'

'All in good time, cove, all in good time.' Nicholas's eyes were merry above the golden beard. 'First to Romeville to try our luck.' He slapped Angel again on the back and laughed. 'Romeville, my kinchin, the city of spires. London, "flower of cities all"!'

9

Angel woke, stretched and smothered a yawn as the stench from the street outside seized him by the throat. He looked at his companion. Nicholas was still asleep on his back, snoring a little with his head propped askew upon the pack, his eyes obscured by the felt hat tilted over his face, his mouth open a little and a fine trickle of saliva drawing a snail's trail into his beard. As Angel watched he started up in alarm. 'What — who...oh, it's you.' He subsided again into his heavy sleep.

Angel grinned. How anyone could sleep longer was beyond his understanding. Country habit had roused him before dawn but even without it he would now be wide awake, for here in Southwark, across the river from London, the air was already strident with the voices of girls crying, 'Flowers, fresh and fair!' or 'Hot peascods!' in shrill competition with men shouting, 'Sea-coal, small coal!' and 'Old chairs to mend!' Drawn by the hook of curiosity he stepped over the drowsing bodies of those with whom they had shared the cellar and made his way to where the light of day was prising its way like a knife blade between the bars of a grating level with his face. Peering out he traced the source of the smell to a heap of rotting entrails swept out from some butcher's shop into the gutter. Beyond it he could see only legs: legs of men, women, children, dogs, horses, donkeys and once those of a team of oxen drawing a great wain. Of that he glimpsed only its iron-shod wheels topped by straw and dangling feet, some bare, some buskined and jingling with bells, floating by him dreamlike on a scarf of mist from the river. Players, he thought, wanting more than ever to be out and about; but his companion was still asleep, the pack firmly trapped beneath him.

Frustrated, he drummed his fingers on the ledge of the grating. It was many hours since they had eaten and he was hungry. Across the road, next to a knife-grinder plying his trade in a shower of sparks, he could see a woman selling hot sheeps' feet, but he had no money. Last night's mean lodging shared with rats and vagrants in the cellar of the cordwainer's shop above had cost him his last farthing, for since Nicholas had relieved him of the heavy pack yesterday he had had no chance of opening it up for trade, and belatedly he saw it as a pretext for repossession. There was, it seemed, always some excuse: prices would be better further on, in Southwark perhaps — but no, in London itself...Fool! he thought, mentally kicking himself. Now he would have to await another opportunity. But at least they had dined at Nick's expense last night, and afterwards wandered the lively streets in the shadow of the great spire of St Olafe's, rubbing shoulders with richly dressed young men and painted women, brassily strolling with cool inviting eyes.

'Winchester geese,' chuckled Nicholas. 'Playground of London, this is, outside the City's jurisdiction. Young bloods can do as they please, bullring, beargarden, it's all here for the seeking.'

'I took 'em for whores?' He had found himself walking backwards to stare after the women.

'That they are! All the world knows His Holiness of Winchester owns every pickhatch in Southwark, that's why we call 'em Winchester geese, to vex him. Plump and ripe they are too, but be warned — you must needs rise early in the morning if you'd liefer be plucker than plucked.'

'You need money for trugging,' said Angel pointedly. 'When are we going to open that pack?'

Nick clapped him on the shoulder with a loud guffaw. 'Not here, unless you're minded to give all away! You never moved in such a company of thieves.' He lowered his voice. 'We could try our luck with nip and foist at the bullring among the crowd...but better we stick to the prancers. Tomorrow we'll cross the river to London where the real pickings are.'

He had had to be content with that; and in truth he had been ready enough to avoid the bullring. He had seen a tethered bull tormented by terriers on the green at Buxford, seen a dog trying to drag its useless hind legs after a toss had broken its back, heard its screams drowned by the laughter of the spectators; and his one distant memory of a travelling bearward burning his wretched charge's paws to force it to 'dance' still had power to set his teeth grinding.

Now he moved restlessly behind the cellar grating, impatient to escape the foetid breath of the place, to be out and get on with his life. 'Nick — '

He was cut short by a clumping of feet outside the door behind him. It was flung open and there stood the cordwainer, sour-faced in his leather apron. 'Come on up, you scum! Up and out, the lot of you, on your way!'

A chorus of grunts and growls from the huddled forms on the earth floor answered him as he came down among them, encouraging the more obstinate sleepers with an unloving foot. 'Rouse up now, get on your feet. God rot, you reek like a laystall — you'll have my patrons complaining their boots do stink!'

They stumbled up into the light like sheep, blinking and jostling one another on the narrow steps, herded by their host with a continuous stream of complaints. 'I vow 'tis not worth it for a miserable two pence, I'm like to lose my best trade for the goodness of my heart...' They shuffled out through the workroom where the men and boys who had slept there were yawning as they sorted skins, snapping or grizzling according to age and pecking order. Once in the street Nick nudged him towards the crown of the road. 'Walk in the gutter and you're like to cop a potful first thing in the morning.'

Angel smiled, remembering the curber. 'Where are we bound?'

'London Bridge, for a start. As fine a sight as you've ever seen, I'll be bound — there, look at that.'

He looked, taking in the broad street bordered by houses, taverns, shops crowded cheek by jowl; a few women with stalls set up in the roadway selling pies, codlings, rabbits...a man with a handcart loaded with cheeses. A drover with a pair of oxen. Two girls in heated argument over a basket of eggs. 'No, no, no!' said Nick with impatience. 'Look up there.'

Looking again, he saw that seemingly among the rooftops stood the masts of ships, tall and slim as reeds, the tracery of their rigging dark and delicate as lace against a morning haze suffused with rosy light. Puzzled, he said, 'What're they doing in the town, ships and that? Is it the coast?'

'Coast, no! That's the river — the Thames, the great thoroughfare of London. Wait, I'll show you. There's the bridge, a moment and we'll be on it, but first come and look across. There, see that where the mist's thinning? The oldest pile in London, they do say the Romans built it.'

Angel strained his eyesight to make out a distant shape of turrets and walls crowned by what looked like four large onions looming above the mist. 'What is it?'

'The Tower.' Nick's tone was grim for once. 'Where the saucy lads go who offend the Queen.' Then the blue eyes twinkled with mischief. 'Never fear, you'll not catch the royal eye, it's Bridewell or Newgate for the likes of us. The Tower's for the high and mighty — like the great houses along the Strand, Somerset, Arundel and the like. You can see their gardens from the river, run right down to the water's edge. A fine sight on a fair day, I can tell you.'

Angel was not impressed. An evil odour rose from

below them, compounded of river mud, rotting vegetation, tar...and something else. A breeze was getting up, lifting the river mist to mingle with a pall of smoke from a thousand coal fires, exposing mud flats where he could make out the shapes of children and old women scavenging in the scum of refuse left behind by the tide. He knew now that the other smell was from the dark tinge of the mud in which they floundered ankle deep. Good for crops, he thought, and knew a twist of nostalgia for Buxford. He said in mild surprise, 'You talk about this place as if you loved it.'

Nicholas drew himself up, took a deep breath and savoured it. 'Better than anywhere, cove. Better than life. Born here, hope to die here. Probably will — Tyburn, most like.' He chuckled at his own grisly joke.

Something rounded fell past them to disintegrate on the bank, where a raven took shape out of nowhere to alight upon the remains. Angel stared, aghast. 'Holy Virgin! Was that...?'

'One of them.' Nick was no longer laughing. 'Traitors, so they say.' He gestured upwards to where a forest of pikes bristled the gatehouse, each crowned with a skull, the teeth bared in a ghastly grin of decay. About them wheeled the macabre shapes of kites, fighting over the shredding flesh of the newest, its humanity sadly discernible in the travesty of the face. Angel shuddered. 'Let's get away from this bridge.' He plunged through the gateway into a busy street thronged with people and lined with buildings on either side.

'Away from it?' scoffed Nicholas. 'You only just stepped on it. Look, there's Tom-a-Beckett's Chapel, that's but halfway across.'

'But it's all houses!' His experience of bridges was limited to a couple of beams across a stream. 'You mean there's folk living here, with all water underneath?'

'You don't know much, and that's a fact.' Nick's tone was one of superiority. 'This is London, cove, and don't you forget it. There's things here you've never seen before nor are like to see again. Come here and look down.'

He piloted Angel to a gap between two buildings where they leant over a parapet. Below them water was running with the speed of a millrace, churning and eddying in its desperate haste to get between the close-set piers of the bridge and out to sea. 'See there.' Nick pointed across to the far bank where a barge had pulled in to a landing-stage to discharge its passengers, two finely dressed gentlemen in ruffs and rapiers who were gingerly making their way up a stone stairway shining with slime to the roadway above. 'Too risky for them to go under the bridge, they'll walk along Thames Street and wait for the waterman to pick them up the other side. Don't care to wet their fine feathers with a ducking in the Thames.'

Angel looked with distaste at the polluted water with its flotsam of dead dogs. 'I'm surprised they want to go by river at all.'

'You won't say that when you've seen the streets! Come on, we've dallied here long enough.'

'Where are we bound?'

'First to East Cheap. The market of the world,' he tossed over a retreating shoulder, and dived ahead into the press of people surging across the bridge, elbowed and collided with by those coming from the opposite direction. He moved so fast and so deftly that Angel, unaccustomed to navigating in crowds, had his work cut out to keep him in sight. He was hampered too by the weight of the pack, which he had managed to pick up this morning before Nick had collected his wits; he had thought briefly of slipping away among the crowds and branching out on his own, but second thoughts had seemed best: Nick was undoubtedly his quickest path to Bess, and although he could look after himself in the country he felt less than confident in this teeming city. Later on, when he had learnt his way about, it would be a different story, but for now he hurried to catch up with the tall hat bobbing among the heads of the crowd, pushing and dodging between carts and litters in urgent pursuit of its wearer. As they left the bridge he skidded on a pile of fish heads swept out from a doorway and ran, gagging at the ancient fume steaming up from the gutter.

Nicholas grinned as he caught him up. 'Fish Street, or had you guessed? Leads straight into the market. You can feast your glaziers there for a while, I've got business to attend to.'

'Horses?'

'Horses...oh, like enough...whatever you lack you'll find it in the Cheap. There now, did you ever see the like?'

Fish Street had ended abruptly, spewing them out into a broad highway crowded with people. Over their heads he could see that on the cobbles were set out trestles and stalls piled high with eggs and eel pies, cabbages and candles, live goats and goslings, chickens and cheeses; thyme and turnips, parsley and pomanders competed for attention with shining basketfuls of rainbow mackerel, oranges and oysters vied with pots, pans and pudding-pies in a riot of colour and noise as the hucksters and their apprentices did their utmost to shout each other down. Cutpurses were at work among the shoppers, while a fresh-faced girl with a bucket and ladle led a cow with swinging udders, calling shrilly, 'Milk below, maids!' under the jutting windows of houses four storeys tall. She was jostled by a grimy man with a bundle of sooty brushes shouting: 'Sweep chimney, swee-eep, with a hey derry sweep!' and turned on him with a lively stream of abuse of which Angel was sorry to have missed the words. He turned in amusement to Nicholas, to find that he was no longer beside him. He had said he had business to attend to; doubtless he would be back when it was done.

His attention was caught by a flash of iridescent blue on the breast of a peacock held aloft above the crowd, its high sharp monotone piercing the clamour as it surveyed its surroundings with delicate disdain. Fascinated, he wandered from stall to stall; never had he seen such abundance, such profusion and variety of beautiful things. Everywhere he looked there was something going on: an acrobat performing for pennies, an Egyptian girl gaudy with gold telling fortunes, a beggar fighting off rats with

111

his staff for possession of a sheep's head thrown out by a butcher.

He looked again for Nicholas. He was nowhere to be seen; he knew a moment of annoyance, suspecting that he had been dumped in this teeming maze to fend for himself. So much for promises of helping him to find Bess! He shrugged. He still had the pack; filled tightly with ribbons, laces, coifs, gloves, knives, it would stand him in good stead until he found his feet, and he was glad now that they had sold none of the contents. He hitched up its weight and smiled.

Laughter came wafting towards him, wave upon wave from the far end of the market. Drawn by the enticing sound he moved to join a knot of people gathered around its source, a swarthy man with a flashing gold ear-ring who was playing with some small animal on the end of a chain. As he drew near he saw that it was only the man who was playing. The animal, a small and frightened monkey tethered by a chain to a leather strap about its hips, was being goaded into antics to amuse the crowd by the sly application of a sharpened stick; its wizened face and sad brown eyes reminded him of an old fleabitten monkey once kept at Buxford. Arthritic and querulous, it had moped about the halls until having bitten one person too many it was despatched, unmourned by any but the child he had been; he had stolen its body from the midden to bury it under a tree near the stables, and watered it with surreptitious tears.

Now he felt his hackles rise. The torturer, it seemed, was offering his victim for sale. The price he asked was drowned in the derisive laughter that followed it. 'What did he say?' he asked an old man standing beside him.

'Hundred crowns for that!' muttered the old one. 'He belongs in the Bedlam, he must be out of his wits.'

Angel shook his head. It was too far beyond his means; saddened he turned away. He could only hope for someone kind to buy it. But who was kind to animals? They were workers or they were toys. And this one was a toy.

112

He looked round angrily as he was roughly thrust to one side by two men carrying a litter. A small gloved hand heavy with rings emerged from under its canopy and a woman's voice demanded imperiously, 'Bring the creature to me.'

The swarthy man, his smile ingratiating, jerked the animal towards him by its chain and attempted to thrust it in between the curtains. Frightened, the monkey twisted from his grasp and ran up its chain to his shoulder where it perched, uttering shrill cries of alarm and clutching him tightly about the head until with a muffled curse he contrived to free himself. Seizing the base of its tail with one hand he grasped the animal from behind in a crushing grip and held it up before him. 'There, lady.'

'What does it do? Make it do something.'

Angel was held against his will, unable to drag himself away. He could see that the man was losing his temper, could see the hard fingers boring into the monkey's tender flank, hear the note of distress in its hooting, sense the panic behind the nervous baring of its teeth.

'Do, mistress? Why, what you will, dance, sing, play on the virginals...' The rest was lost in a roar of laughter from all round as it was plunged for the second time into the darkness of the litter. It was hard to be sure of what followed. There was a feminine shriek from the occupant and then the man, his smile congealed to a vicious snarl, was bringing down his stick again and again on a screaming, terrified huddle of dark fur crouched upon the cobbles, its thin arms vainly trying to protect its head.

The next moment he was sprawling under the weight of the pedlar's pack; Angel, the quivering monkey in his arms, was listening to his own voice shouting, 'Take that! 'Twas payment for a horse, I'll lay it'll pay for a monkey, fair and square.'

Scowling, the swarthy man picked himself up. He looked suspiciously at Angel and then back at the pack.

'Go on, 'tis full of trinkets and the like. Open it and see for yourself.'

As the man drew it towards him and began to unfasten the buckles a familiar voice rang out. 'Bing a waste, you fool — it's full of strummel!'

Straw! And stones for weight, no doubt — he would break that Bodkyn! But now was no time to look for him. Thrusting the animal into his shirt he ran, heedless of the panicked raking of its nails, twisting, dodging, doubling in and out among the crowd, not daring to look over his shoulder as the hue and cry broke out behind him. God damn that Nicholas and his trickery! But what had he said about Southwark? Outside the City's jurisdiction? If he could reach there he might be safe. He found the entrance to Fish Street by his nose and bolted down it…but he knew it was too late. It would be a matter of moments before they caught him up, he could not hope to escape across the bridge.

He reached the end of Fish Street just as his pursuers entered the top, and he cut off to the right with a prayer that they had not seen him. The landing-stage he had seen from the bridge must be somewhere close at hand — if he could scramble down the steps out of sight of the road — if only he could find it before they came boiling out of the street and saw him — and suddenly the steps were there — were just ahead — were under his feet…and he was slipping, sliding down the wet stones, barely avoiding collision with a man coming up towards him…and he was safe. He flattened his back against the dank masonry and tried to silence his hectic breathing, not risking a glance above him to the roadway; high overhead he heard the sounds of the hunt break up into confusion and finally dwindle away. He stood still, listening to the lisping of the river lapping the stones, the cry of a waterman inviting, 'Eastward, ho?' as he drew abreast. He shook his head vehemently. The man grinned as he passed on.

At last his heart finished thudding; he drew a deep tranquil breath and sank down on to a step. He peered inside his shirt. The monkey, quiet now, blinked solemnly back. He smiled wryly. He had two mouths to feed now

114

and not even the pack to do it on. If ever he caught up with that turd...

He started at a quiet voice in his ear. 'How now, my son, and what are you running away from?'

10

Angel felt his sinews stiffen in alarm, but his first glance at the stranger reassured him.

A thin man in a soiled white coif and the rusty black gown of a cleric stood on the step above him, slightly stooped with age, one hand extended in a tentative gesture. His clothing hung on him as from a peg and his heavily-lidded eyes looked out uneasily from a narrow ascetic face; a man so tall that he stood awkwardly like an ungainly wading bird, as if he were not quite sure what his knees were up to.

'Forgive me,' he went on. 'I gained the impression that you were in trouble...perhaps in need of counsel?'

Wearily, Angel shook his head. 'In need of more than counsel, father, and that's a fact. There's me and the monkey here and not a crust to share between us, on account of a stranger offering help as only helped himself — if you get my meaning.'

'Ah, my dear son.' The old man lowered himself stiffly to sit beside him. 'The old, old story, I fear. You are young, and a stranger from the country by your looks. And alas, you have "gull" written upon you in letters of fire.' He took a fold of his gown and wiped his face with it.

'I'm not that young. And I know what "gull" means, I anna stupid neither.'

'Indeed?' The faded eyes twinkled. 'Then how, may I ask, do you come to such a pass?'

'Misfortune.' He smiled in response. 'Dunna look like the weight of your purse is like to break your arm, neither.'

'I am a priest, my son. Or rather, I was. When great men die as martyrs to their faith, the humble merely take cover. Now I'm a hedge-priest; a Patrico, as they say. I do what I can for the poor and the sick, and beg my bread like a Christian.'

Angel snorted. 'Christians! You'll not find many of them among the beggars — thieves and rogues and liars to a man.'

'Judge not, that ye be not judged.' The old man got carefully to his feet. 'Come with me now, a full belly looks upon the world with more charity than an empty one. I know a goodwife keeps a pie shop and saves the broken pieces for the poor. There's little enough in my scrip but we need not go begging to Whitehall.'

'Why, what's at Whitehall?'

'The royal palace and its profligate queen. Much waste and rich leavings for him who can fight his way through the rabble about the gates.'

He would have liked to see the palace but clearly this was not the time; he followed the elderly priest to the pie shop where they shared their handful of cold fragments in the busy street, jostled by passers-by and scrounging dogs. When the monkey was offered a morsel he only blinked mournfully, and crumbled the pastry between his little black-nailed fingers.

''Tis maybe not the right thing for him,' Angel said doubtfully. 'I canna rightly remember what they eat, 'tis too long since I saw one fed.'

The Patrico shook his head. 'Looks a little fevered to me. How long have you had it?'

Angel glanced at him sharply, but the question appeared to be innocent. 'Not long,' he said guardedly. 'You know anyone as might know what to do for him?'

He thought he caught a shrewd gleam in the gentle

eyes. 'You could ask the man you got him from.'

He looked away. 'That'd mean going back to the Cheap. I'd as lief not do that.'

'And why might that be?'

'Rogues and cut-throats,' he said lightly. 'Like I said before.'

'And that is all?'

He hesitated, torn between dread of exposure and an urge to confide in this holy father, a gnawing need to confess about Clem and be told that it was not his fault...'Aye,' he said unhappily. 'Aye, that's all.'

The old man shook his head in sad reproach. 'My son, my son...I saw you steal that monkey. Can you not honour a man of God with the truth?'

'You saw? Then you know it was honest trading, I never knew it was straw in the pack, I swear it — '

'Peace, hold your tongue, do you want the world to hear? It seems I must believe you since it pours so from the heart. But tell me, how could you fail to know, did you not buy and stock the pack yourself?'

Angel saw that he was getting out of his depth. 'I — I traded it.' He hesitated, aware that to say for a horse would take him into still more dangerous waters. 'For other goods. With the man I told you of — he tricked me with a pack full of straw.' He smiled wanly. 'You're right, I am stupid. Never take nothing on trust from an Upright Man.'

'An Upright Man, you say? And you, of course, are a licensed pedlar. Of which parish?'

'I did have a licence. I lost it...' He looked to see the world-weary eyes gently teasing him. 'No, forgive me, Father, I tell a lie. I'm a runaway, I never had no passport. I was looking for Jarkman Joe to do me one.'

'Jarkman Joe, eh? No better work to be found — but at a price.'

'Aye, so they say. Only now I lost the pack and canna pay. I don't know what to do and that's a fact.'

'Go home, my son.' The old man's hand was gentle on his shoulder.

118

'I canna.'

'Why not? No good awaits you in this place.'

'I just canna.' It was base to deceive this kind old innocent. Why not give in, confide as he wanted to, share his troubles...At length he said, "Tis Bess, see, her that I run off with. We got parted — well, she went off with another, I dunna trust him, I got to find her somehow and win her back.'

'Forget her, lad. Waste no more tears, the game's not worth the candle, go home and seek a better.'

'No, 'tis not in me.' He was glad to be able to answer without being forced to lie. 'I dunna reckon you ever ploughed a furrow, 'tis not to be expected of you. But if you had you'd know, once you've started you dunna look back. That's me, that's how I am. No turning back till I get where I'm bound and no good for to ask it.'

The Patrico leant back and regarded him with an expression faintly quizzical. 'Welladay, let it not fall to me to discourage such fidelity. Since Heaven has seen fit to guide your steps to me, I suppose I must direct you to Jarkman Joe. He is sometimes to be found at the sign of the Cock in Alsatia, and a passport you will certainly need if you will not be advised. But, look you, no mention of jarks until you have the wherewithal. Meanwhile,' he sucked the last flavour from his fingers and brushed crumbs from his dusty gown, 'to St Paul's and the si-quis door. If honest work's to your taste you may find it there.'

'Wait — what door?' Tucking the ailing monkey back inside his shirt he started up after the old man who was already on the move. 'Where are we bound?' he called after him, dodging and bobbing among the crowd to keep his long-legged quarry in sight.

The Patrico's answer was lost in the hubbub about them, the haggling of women with market baskets and the shrill chatter of the prentices who stood outside every cookshop with laden trays touting the wares of their masters. The slow thud of hooves from behind made him turn to see that, into the narrow street already thronged with people, a man carrying a leather scoop was leading a lacklustre pony with dripping saddlebags, crying, 'Fresh water, fresh from the Fleet!' In his wake swaggered a white-capped youth with a heaped-up tray on his head, shouting, 'New loaves, hot pippin pies!'

Instantly one of the prentices gave an indignant yell. 'A scurvy baker! After him, lads!' The others threw down their trays with cries of 'Clubs! Clubs!' and suddenly the street was in turmoil. In seconds it had emptied, men and women running in all directions, screaming children snatched to safety, dogs barking, rats scurrying for cover, geese and hens awaiting their turn for the pot flapping and squawking in their crates. The intruder turned to flee and the cookshop boys thundered after him, knocking over merchandise and shoppers alike and alarming the pony who whinnied and reared, tearing down a line of washing strung between the oversail of two houses, which two women on opposite sides of the street were struggling to rescue from their upper windows. Terrified by the flapping linen it bolted, dragging its owner until, the rein ripped from his grasp, he was flung off among the ruined pies abandoned by the boys.

'Stop him!' he yelled as he saw his livelihood disappearing up the road. Angel, the monkey tightly clutched under his shirt, was already gaining on the frightened beast, hampered as it was by dangling shop signs and the heavy water bags that thumped against its sides.

'Whoa now, whoa!' He reached for the flying rein just as a slightly-built figure in black stepped out from a doorway directly in their path. There was no time to arrest the pony's progress. All he could do to avert disaster was a sidelong blow to send the victim sprawling to safety in the rank ooze of the gutter.

He brought the trembling animal under control and stood quietly gentling it for a moment before turning to lead it back to its owner. As he did so he was confronted by an amazing apparition.

Staggering to its feet was a figure swamped from head to foot in filth; the plumed bonnet was further embellished with cabbage leaves, the other clothing indistinguishable under a thick plaster of ordure that sent fumes to heaven and an evil smelling drool into the boots. Two eyes opened in the greenish slime of the face and blazed at him, black and furious. '*You!*' The voice, though light and boyish as the build, was nonetheless distorted with rage, almost — was it possible? — with hatred. 'Touch me again and I kill you!'

Astounded, he felt his jaw dropping, his mind an incredulous blank as with a bloodthirsty lisp of steel a sword appeared in the other's hand. 'I dunna believe this!' he spluttered as indignation came to his rescue. 'Look, you! I just saved your life — fine thanks and no mistake!' He turned to the onlookers who were gathering. 'Didn't I save him? He'd be dead else — you saw the runaway.'

His appeal fell on disinterested ears, they were only concerned with the entertainment afforded by the incident and were already sniggering as the unfortunate glared warningly at two boys who had come forward as though to restrain him and retired with loud guffaws and exaggerated gaggings at the smell. His look at Angel still spelt murder, although now it was apparent that an element of doubt was creeping in. 'You flung me in the mire, you knave, you — you codshead!' Although he was reduced to blustering, he clearly had no intention of climbing down. 'Don't think you can fool me, I know you of old, you baseborn jackanapes!'

'You never seen me in your life before!' By now he was struggling to control his own laughter. 'Oh come, you anna serious. You'da been run down without I gave you a shove, what's your fine clothes along o' that?'

He had half expected the youth to see the funny side himself: he could hardly have been more mistaken. Ridicule seemed to have inflamed him beyond the limit of endurance and he hurled himself forward sword in hand with a warning, 'Have at you!'

Angel let go the pony, snatched the stave from his belt and whacked upwards at the sword arm almost before he had taken in that his assailant was in earnest. The hand flew open and the sword went sailing aloft to strike against a chimney, slide down a roof and clatter back to earth to a chorus of jeering approval. Before anyone else could move he planted a foot on it. 'Right, you,' he said angrily. 'Dunna you never come at me with no sword again, you hear! Now run home to your dam and bid her wash your face.'

Begrimed as he was, the other still commanded a degree of caution; bent over his injured arm he resembled a small dark serpent poised to strike. 'Give it back!' His look was a dart of pure venom. 'Before I have you taken up for theft!'

Angel was now incensed beyond discretion. 'Go to the Devil,' he retorted. He gave the weapon a kick that sent it spinning away up the street and walked away, shouting over his shoulder, 'Best douse your head and cool your temper first. He's maybe not as peaceable as me!'

He found the water-seller wringing muck out of his clothing with wry good humour. He handed over the pony and was rewarded with a free scoop of water for his trouble. 'Thanks.' He jerked his thumb in the direction of his fuming adversary. 'Bit different from him over there.'

The water-seller pulled a face. 'Silly young cockbrain. End up in the river with his throat cut if he goes on like that. Now what's he up to, looking for another go?'

Angel wiped his mouth with the back of his hand and looked. The youth had retrieved his sword from the far end of the street and had cleaned some of the grime from his face; but he did not seem ready to move off. Instead he was standing quite still, heedless of the clamour and bustle of returning shopkeepers rushing past him to set their stalls to rights, staring at Angel with a curious, confused expression. Then as if feeling his gaze challenged he turned abruptly and was soon lost to sight.

'Good riddance,' muttered the man.

'Who is he? Seemed to reckon he knew me.'

'Don't know, don't want to. Mind me own business, I do, best you do the same if you want to make old bones. If a stranger bites his thumb at you just look the other way.'

Angel's attention had shifted to his ailing charge, trying to coax it to take a little water from his hand; it looked at him miserably, and shuddered. He must somehow get help for it soon. 'Did you see where the old man went?'

'What old man?'

'The priest, him that was with me when the fighting started.'

'No priest here now. What do you want him for?' he cackled, 'Confession?'

'We were going to find a door. A secret door, I think he said.'

'A secret door?' Suddenly the eyes in the dirty weatherbeaten face were bright with interest. 'Here — you set up to rob some house?'

He shook his head in irritation. 'I'm no thief.' Only by the grace of God, he thought.

'All right, all right! But you won't last long in London if you ain't and that's a fact.' His laughter crackled hoarsely. 'Tell you where it was did he, this door of yours?'

'Couldn't rightly hear for all the racket going on — no more'n I can properly hear you now.' He thought he would never get used to the noise of this place. He cupped a hand to his ear and shouted, 'Paul's, would it be?'

'Don't ask me, mate. Could be St Paul's, all the world meets there in the churchyard. The door'd be the si-quis — '

'The what?'

'The si-quis. Where the servants go for work.'

'Sounds like it might be. Where'll I find it?'

The man shrugged. 'I'm going that way, you can follow if you've a mind. But once there, shove off, don't take kindly to hangers on, I don't. Understand?' He slapped the pony's rump and raised his gritty voice again. 'Water! Sweet water, fresh from the Fleet!'

After a slow trudge made tedious by repeated stops to sell water they came to a halt by a small turreted building hard by a church, surrounded by gossiping women with buckets and pitchers, the roadway obstructed by tall wooden scuttles hooped with osier. Angel indicated the church. 'Is that St Paul's?'

'All in good time, all in good time. This is the Conditte, where we takes on water.' The man was elbowing a path between the women to push to the front of the crowd. 'Well, don't just stand there, give a hand, I got a living to make!'

'You cry it river water,' commented Angel. 'It anna, not if it comes from here.'

'Shut your mouth, can't you!' growled his guide as he struggled with a brimming scuttle. 'Course it's river water, how d'you think it gets in the pipe — think we strikes the rock like Moses and prays for a miracle?'

''Tis roguery.' Angel took the scuttle from him and lifted another in the other hand. 'Folk could fetch it themselves, and that cheaper.'

The good humour vanished. 'They don't have to buy it, no more than I has to put up with you, so stow it if you wants to walk along of me to St Paul's.'

As Angel filled a near-empty pannier from the scuttle he felt a hand clapped on his shoulder, heard again the wheezing laugh. 'Lor' bless ya, you can't make a honest living out of being too honest — if you see what I mean.'

There seemed no answer to that and they finished their journey in silence broken only by the water-seller's cry. It was easier anyway not to make the effort of bellowing above the traffic's din, the ring of hoofbeats and iron-shod wheels upon cobbles, the voices of hucksters raised in barter or in argument. By the time they came within sight of the great steeple he felt numbed and battered by the noise and press of people on all sides.

His companion waved an arm towards a vast building. 'There it is.'

It looked even bigger than Buxford Place with its

multitudes of doors and gateways. 'Which door's the si-
quis, then?'

'How should I know? Go in and ask, there's always
plenty in Paul's Walk.' He whacked at his bored pony and
was swallowed into the crowd.

Angel edged his way slowly through the crush in the
churchyard to where he could see the roof of a great
porch supported by columns. He stepped through the
high arched doorway and stopped dead.

Massive columns marched away into the distance on
either side of him, reaching to a vaulted roof so high that
its swirling shapes seemed to swing about his head as he
looked up. But the interior of this great church, where he
had expected to find cool peace and quietude, was as
noisy and thronged with humanity as anywhere in
London, the folk more mixed even than those without,
the contrast between rich and poor, honest and rogue
more blatant. As he moved among them he was bewildered by their numbers and variety, young bloods in
satins and jewels rubbing elbows with beggars and foot-
pads. They jostled past him in all directions, each intent
on his own business as though none other existed. He had
not thought there were so many people in the world, let
alone in one vast, seething city. He wondered what Kate
would have made of the sight — Kate who vowed that the
number of sheep in High Pasture made her dizzy...He
wished he had not thought of Kate.

He turned his mind back to the business in hand. Doors
there were in abundance, but nothing he could see to
mark out one from all the rest. Perhaps he had missed
something. He made his way past them all again as well as
he could for the crowds, wishing he were taller and could
see over all their heads. It had long been his secret disappointment to have grown to only middle height: Black
John had been a man of stature, so they said, and the discovery of his parenthood had briefly given him hope. But
he knew in his heart that it was vain. After seventeen
summers he was done with growing and would have to
make do with what he was.

Between two heads he caught a glimpse of parchment tacked to a door that he had failed to notice before. Drawing near he saw that from time to time a man in russet or servants' blue would detach himself from the group about it, peer intently and go away frowning. When he had shouldered his way close enough to see, his heart sank. It was writing that they peered at: they frowned because like himself they were unable to read. It had been a waste of time to come here without the Patrico.

He wondered if anyone here was familiar with the sign of the Cock. He was pretty sure that was what the Patrico had said. He caught at the sleeve of a passer-by. 'Pray you —'

To his astonishment the man whirled to face him, a hand already on his sword hilt. 'Unhand me, scoundrel!'

He jumped back, blundered into the body of someone behind him and before he had time to think found himself pinioned.

'A pickpocket!'

'Thieves, thieves!'

'Call a constable!'

'I anna done nothing —' His protests were drowned in the general uproar and he was bundled roughly from hand to eager hand to be flung out the way he had come, the monkey clinging frantically inside his shirt and chittering with fright. Over and over he rolled, trying to protect it with his arms, until they came to rest in the yard outside. With that their persecutors seemed to be satisfied and they abandoned him to pick himself up from the dust.

He sat down on a stone and bowed his head on his arms as depression settled on him. So this was Romeville, the sparkling city that Bodkyn loved so well. He was welcome to it, St Paul's and all. He, Angel, wanted no part of it. Now, with his most urgent peril behind him and the way ahead cold and unwelcoming, his stomach ached with hunger and his spirit ached for home. He thought longingly of the familiar brewery, of Big Daniel, bluff and good-natured...even of Kate and her cross-grained warmth; all haloed now that he could never go back to them. And Bess. What had become of her, what had he brought her to...?

A faint stirring against his skin brought his mind back to the immediate. He peeped inside his shirt. The monkey was regarding him with wistful brown eyes as if aware of his mood. More likely, he told himself sternly, it was looking to him for help. Gently he ruffled the bedraggled fur. 'Dunna give up,' he encouraged it. 'At least we can try for you.'

He got to his feet. There must be someone somewhere who could direct him to Alsatia. But he had learned a sharp lesson about asking the way of strangers. He looked about him vaguely in search of inspiration.

Suddenly his attention was caught and held. Above the intervening heads he could see a familiar tall felt hat, the eyes below it wary as a rat's as they met his.

'Nicholas!' He sprang forward, his former ill-will forgotten. 'Thanks be to God — can you read?'

Nicholas looked slightly affronted. 'That's a gentry cove's frill, I know tricks worth ten of that.'

And I've seen a few of them, thought Angel. 'You mean you canna.' 'Well, no matter. You know your way about this godforsaken place, you can take me to the sign of the Cock.' It would have to be the Patrico after all.

11

Walking alongside Bodkyn, Angel found his thoughts turning back over the incident of the young swordsman and his odd behaviour. 'I know you of old,' he had said; yet surely he, Angel, would remember? He was willing to swear that he had not seen him at the alehouse, his clothes and bearing if nothing else marked him out as one unlikely to frequent such a place. And 'of old' suggested something further back, perhaps as far as Buxford. Had the stranger come there as a guest on some distant occasion? He would hardly have noticed Angel among the outside staff, let alone remembered him...unless by chance he had ridden Bess? It seemed improbable. And yet in some dim recess of his mind there lay something that teased him, something so nebulous he could not lay hands on it...

'You see I got the pack back.' Nick's voice broke in on his reverie. 'They were all so concerned with catching you I was able to nip in and hoist it before they noticed me. You nearly lost it for the second time, you chub!'

He felt his ears burning. It was surely enough to have been made a fool of without being twitted about it by the culprit. 'Suppose you wanted it back so you can cheat some other poor fool,' he said stiffly.

Nick chuckled. 'In a manner of speaking. But it's not what you take it for, there's more than meets the eye

128

among that strummel. Something worth more to me than a mountain of fairings — here, I'll show you.' He drew Angel into a narrow space under the jutting upper storeys of two buildings and swung the pack from his back on to his knee. 'There, did you ever see the like of this?' He drew from the pack what appeared to be a bundle of stiff cloth, awkwardly folded and bound about with webbing. As he opened it out a light stirrup dropped free, then another on its length of webbing, and the thing was revealed: a saddle complete with girths and buckles and with no scrap of leather anywhere about it.

'What's it made of?' It was hard to believe that it had folded so small as to be stowed away inside the pack.

Bodkyn produced a bridle and bit from the same source and grinned proudly. 'Buckram. Weighs nothing — here, feel it. A prigger's saddle, that is, throw it over a likely prancer and away you go, saddled and bridled in no time.'

'Well...'tis clever enough. But who needs a saddle — I'd as lief ride bareback.'

Nick laughed, glancing up from packing his stock-in-trade back among the straw. 'That's how I knew you rode a stolen horse, you poor innocent! You have to be sharper than that to live by your wits. By the Solomon, lad, you'll not last long in London!'

'You talk like everyone's vagabonds like you and nobody decent at all. 'Tain't so, there's this old fellow I'm looking for, only met this morning and he's offering to help me find work — honest work too, not your sort.'

'I know Romeville better than you do, take my word. No one looks after any but himself, life on the high-pad's too chancy and too hard, you must learn to shift for yourself.' He laughed again but with more good humour, and slapped Angel's shoulder. 'Come, be friends. I forgive you, even though you tried to trade our livelihood for a moth-eaten monkey. What did you do with it, by the way, sell it?'

'Got him here in my shirt. He's sick, or maybe mortal hurt inside. Look.'

Nicholas peered and grimaced. 'Don't look up to much. I'd get rid of it.'

He shook his head. 'Once I'm in work I can maybe buy him a physic. That's why I want to find the old man.'

'Your honest fellow, eh, at the sign of the Cock?' His laughter was scathing. 'Yon host hardly knows what an honest man looks like!'

'We was only going there,' Angel pointed out with the overemphasis of mounting irritation, 'to look for Jarkman Joe. And that's because I asked him.'

'Jarkman Joe, eh?' Nick regarded him with a teasing glint of amusement. 'Well now, I wouldn't have thought it, a pretty-boy like him. I'd have thought wenching was more in your line.'

Angel turned his head away in a gesture of impatience. 'I know, I know, Marian made the same jest. All I want him for's to do me a jark.'

'Marian?'

'Wench at the alehouse, back there where the puppets were. She taught me to use the cuttlebung and quite a lot beside. Good to me, she was. Pretty girl...' he added reflectively. It was sad that she was wasted on such a life.

'Pretty, say you?' Fleetingly, Nicholas looked pleased, almost as though the compliment had been to himself. But when he spoke again his voice had a different edge. 'Niggled with her, did you?'

Something fell into place in Angel's brain. By Heaven, he must be *that* Nick — Marian's Upright Man! He was thankful now for the reluctance that had saved him the necessity of lying. 'Too short in the purse,' he joked. Then with a show of surprise, 'Here, you're not Marian's Nick! Well, 'tis a small world and no mistake. She talked about you all the time, said you was a real Rome cove...'

Watching the slow winding down of tension in Nicholas's expression he knew that Marian was deceiving herself: her man might be tolerant of her profession, but only if he did not have to watch.

The Cock fell somewhere between tavern and alehouse in that it offered comfort and good fare but its clientele was dubious. Angel was learning to recognise rogues not by

130

their dress or appearances, which could be deceptive, but by something in their manner that was always alert, their eyes that seemed to take in everything and everyone at once. He and Nick were certainly not the only ones here. He was relieved to pick out the incongruous figure of the Patrico among the revellers, no doubt only here in search of him since they had missed each other earlier in the day. The old man rose to greet him. 'Ah, my dear boy, how glad I am that you have found the place. And our good Nicholas is with you, I see.'

'You know each other?' The revelation was vaguely disquieting.

The Patrico chuckled. 'My son, I must know every rogue in London. Never fear, we are among friends here. Come to the fire and rest you, I am sorry I cannot offer to buy victuals.'

'I owe him a meal,' said Nick, with an odd glance at the Patrico. 'A cut from the spit-roast, Joshua, for my friends.'

As they ate, the rich juices running between their fingers, Angel looked around the crowded room at the assortment of faces picked out by firelight or lantern under the smoke-blackened beams. Hens pecked and crooned among the rushes and a dog drank noisily from a tankard carelessly set down on the floor. This, he recalled, was where the notorious Jarkman Joe was said to be found. He could see no one among the beer-swilling, tankard-banging company who might earn the epithet of 'pretty-boy'. He said casually, 'Where's the Jarkman then, is he here?'

'All in good time, my son, and first the wherewithal. Did you find the si-quis door?'

'Aye, and much good it did me without you there to read the lines.'

'Alas, I was called on to minister to the dying. You understand, my son...'

'Perfectly,' put in Nicholas. 'Business before charity, eh, Father?'

'Not quite how I would express it,' said the old man

131

mildly, laying a gentle hand on the sleeve of Angel who had started up in his defence. 'Ah! I see a soul in need of comfort, I must leave you.' In a moment he was lost to sight.

'So that's your honest friend.' Nicholas's eyes twinkled with malice as he sat mopping grease from his beard with a grimy lace-edged kerchief.

'Aye!' said Angel angrily. 'And I'll thank you to show respect, he's worth two of your sort put together.'

'Undoubtedly, probably more.' He laughed, pounded a playful fist against Angel's shoulder. 'Peace, peace...you'll learn wisdom, given time. You're not offering meat to that monkey, surely to Heaven?'

'I got to do something, dunno what else to try. You reckon anyone here knows what to do?'

Nicholas shrugged, an expression of amused tolerance on his face. 'Who knows? Joshua!' As the taverner looked in his direction, 'Know anything about monkeys?'

The big man shook his head. 'Wait, though.' They followed his glance to where a pair of new arrivals had appeared in the open doorway. 'He might. Used to keep one, so I've heard.' Darkness and rain were falling outside and the two stood within, shaking their cloaks and dousing links in the shelter of the porch, a heavily-built ruffian and a smaller, slighter man.

'Which one? I'll go and ask — '

'Softly,' cautioned Nick. 'You don't go roaring up to him like a bull at a gate, one of the gentry coves is that one.'

'If he's gentry, what's he doing here with this lot?' He had imagined petty crime to be the sole perquisite of the poor.

Nick chuckled. 'In the company of rogues there's questions you don't ask. And the fewer you ask of Jarkman Joe the better, he doesn't take kindly to curiosity. That's him, in the muddied black velvet.'

Angel groaned inwardly as the newcomers moved forward into the light. 'Oh, no...that's never Jarkman Joe!' It seemed to him that all his hopes were dashed in one fell moment. 'If that's him he's not about to give me the time of day.'

'Don't tell me you've got the wrong side of him already?' said Nick amusedly.

Angel could hardly bear to watch as the two seated themselves on a high-backed settle on the far side of the room and were instantly served with a goblet of wine and a tankard. The bigger man was readily classified as a rogue of the rougher sort; matted hair straggled out from under a greasy cap and his ill-assorted garments had clearly been made for several different victims of his trade. His teeth showed black and crumbling when he spoke and a deeply-indented scar on one temple bore testimony to his violent way of life.

In contrast, the youth beside him wore his sombre black with the bearing of nobility. One of the gentry coves, Nick had said; it was easy to see how the description had been earned. It was not so easy to reconcile his appearance with that of the begrimed and infuriated figure of this morning, although the mud still clinging to the velvet doublet was evidence enough that this was he. He made a pool of stillness in the bawdy atmosphere of the tavern, a dark and brooding presence which held its own quality of menace and needed no outward show to reinforce it.

Angel sighed. 'He only come at me with a sword today — took me for another but he wouldna be told. I'd best hold my peace, no good for me to ask him nothing.'

'Faint heart!' jeered Nicholas, tossing off his wine. 'Come, I'll present you to him.'

'No —' But before he could stop him Nick was crossing the floor, insinuating his way between bodies, laughing and beckoning 'Come on!' over his shoulder. He was more than a little drunk, Angel decided, and stayed where he was, turning his back in the hope of going unrecognised.

'You've a face like a thundercloud, my son.' He looked up to see that the Patrico had returned. 'Now what, may I ask, is the trouble this time?'

'Oh, 'tis Nick — well no, not really. I got across the Jarkman today, now Nick in his cups is like to make it worse.'

'How can that be?'

'He knows about monkeys, Joshua says. I'm not sure if Nick's out to help or just to make mischief.'

'About monkeys...hmm. No, not the wisest thing.' The old man looked at him uneasily. 'How did you come to "get across" the Jarkman, as you put it?'

'Knocked him from the path of a runaway horse. He took it amiss, come at me with a sword and all. Water-seller reckoned he'd end up in the river, the way he went on.'

'Except,' said the Patrico drily, 'that if you're the cleverest forger in London there are too many great rogues to be reckoned with for a lesser one to dare put you out of breath.'

'The cleverest in London?' Angel shook his head. 'But he's a mere stripling, his voice anna broke, he canna fool me with that gruffness he puts on.'

'Don't be deceived, my son. There are those who have sorrows the rest of us are spared. The Jarkman is fully grown, and older than you imagine.' He lowered his voice discreetly. 'He is *castrato*.'

'What?' He could not have heard correctly, it was all this noise. What he had thought he heard was inflicted on horses. Pigs, oxen...not on men.

'You are unfamiliar with the term? It is Italian, and means...he was a singer in a great cathedral. A young boy, a fine voice...not to be lost?' He leaned forward confidingly. 'His manhood was sacrificed to Mother Church.'

Angel stared. So he had not misheard. 'You mean...*they cut his ballocks off!*' His involuntary cry of outrage rang through the tavern at full volume, cutting across the hubbub and commanding attention. There was a split second of silence before it broke out again reinforced by a roar of laughter, noise flooding in from all sides to fill the gulf as the company resumed its carousing. All but Jarkman Joe. Silent and white-faced, he sat unmoving, a dark unreadable look fixed on Angel and his companion.

'Have a care,' murmured the Patrico. 'You could make a formidable enemy with that unguarded tongue.'

Angel grimaced. 'Small wonder he bears a grudge

against the world. But 'tis none of my doing and he's fair took against me. There, see how he's looking at me now.'

They had watched Nicholas thread his way between tightly-packed bodies to where the Jarkman sat and engage him in discussion; had seen the Jarkman shake his head with a derisive laugh. Then Nick had pointed towards Angel and the Jarkman's expression had changed dramatically. Now Nick, still flushed with wine, reappeared before them.

'I've got him to look at it! But you've to go yourself, he won't treat with me — wants to see you in person. By the Solomon, must be he fancies you!' He laughed raucously and sprawled upon a bench, waving his empty goblet for a refill.

'Enough,' cautioned the Patrico. 'Already it comes between you and your wits.'

'Stow it, cove, you spoil the fun.' But he allowed him to take the goblet. 'Well, go on, you!'

Angel hesitated. He was anything but eager to go as a supplicant to the Jarkman whose animosity was entirely mutual. But he needed to do something quickly for the patient animal clinging to its slender hold on life. Must he then swallow his pride, bend the knee...It was Nick's taunting 'What's keeping you then, lost the wind from your sails?' that finally sent him shouldering his way between the revellers.

'You're Jarkman Joe?'

The eyes that had been fixed on his face crackled into antagonism at his approach and were swiftly averted. They were darkly beautiful in a disturbing way; too much so, Angel decided. They belonged on a woman.

'Call you me thus.' Whether it was assent or question was uncertain. 'And you, what do you call yourself these days?'

Not ready to give his name, he said, 'I've brought the monkey.'

The Jarkman finished his wine slowly and deliberately, his eyes maintaining their veiled scrutiny of Angel's face. He set down the goblet and the too fine upper lip curled

135

insolently. 'An excellent match, you are most admirably suited.'

A rollick of laughter went around those near enough to have heard and he gritted his teeth; he suspected that this dandyprat had sent for him to pay him out for this morning. 'You said you'd look at it,' he said stubbornly. 'You give your word.' He had not forced himself into this situation to be put off so lightly. 'You better look then, hadn't you?'

The listeners paused in their laughter to look at Jarkman Joe. A flush stained the beardless cheek and the black eyes sparked with malice. 'So? I am looking. And I see no monkey but one.'

Angel felt his hackles rise and suppressed them ruthlessly. 'Patience,' he said evenly. 'Here comes the other one.' He delved into his voluminous shirt and drew the limp form into the light.

For a long disbelieving moment he stood still, staring helplessly at the little wizened body in his hands. It seemed smaller, shrunken from the living creature of this morning, the closed face grey and withdrawn as if life had retreated behind it, locking the door; an empty house with the shutters up. Like Jody's. And it too was gone away...

He heard the forced unnatural voice of the Jarkman. 'Go tell the Patrico I'm not in the market for monkeys, dead or alive.'

Fresh guffaws were breaking out all around him. Anger and humiliation flooded in on his disappointment and he rounded on them, shouting, 'I know what you're thinking, a codshead from the dewse-a-ville trying to raise the dead! Go on, laugh then, very droll — makes a change from the cockpit and the bullring!' They reeled about, slapping their thighs. He turned recklessly on the Jarkman. 'As for you, you puffed up cock-a-dandy —'

Before he could say more he was seized from behind. 'Come away, you lunatic!' Nick must have followed him across the room and was struggling now to drag him away, still raving.

'My son, my son!' remonstrated the Patrico as he

twisted to release himself. 'What did I tell you — it is tempting Providence to entangle yourself with him — Nicholas, hold him fast!'

'I'm trying!' puffed Nick. 'He's a handful, I tell you — be still, you madman!'

Angel, his eyes still locked on the Jarkman, saw him rise, speak to his companion with a jerk of the head in their direction, and to his fury begin sidling towards the door as the other started towards them. 'Oh no, you dunna — let go!' he raged as Nicholas still fought to restrain him.

'Have done, you cockbrain! That ruffian's his hench-man, he'll carve you to cat's-meat before you can cry "A knife!"'

A clout delivered in desperation knocked him off balance. As he staggered backward it was Nick who took full in the face the contents of a tankard aimed at Angel. The Jarkman's man who had thrown it looked momentarily confused as Nick, blinking ale from his eyes, snatched a knife from the nearest belt and, suddenly sober, leaped on to a table with the agility of an acrobat.

Angel, unexpectedly released, made a lunge for the door. 'He anna getting off scot free!' he muttered under his breath. 'He's about to get a flea in his ear — '

'Look out, lad!'

'Take heed!'

A chorus of shouts gave him warning of the ruffian behind him about to bring down a bench upon his head. He turned and dived for the man's ankles as Nick landed pick-a-back on the towering shoulders and brought him crashing down. 'Bing a waste!' yelled Nick. 'It's you he's after — ' The rest was lost to him in the uproar. Now Joshua's voice was added to the hubbub. 'Out, the lot of you! Out, I say!'

The taverner's voice roared in his ears as he was grasped by heavy hands and propelled forward, conscious of a falling back of bodies, cries of alarm and sounds of overturning furniture, seeing nothing through the reddish haze of his fury as he was flung from light into darkness and the slap of rain, to land on the harsh broken

137

cobbles of the yard. For a moment he was jerked to his senses by the jolt of the fall. Then looking up he saw a dark figure slipping furtively through the shadows at the side of the building. 'Come back!' he roared. 'Come back and take your physic!'

The black-clad figure doubled back towards the refuge of the tavern just as Joshua emerged with the second batch of evictions, Nick and the Jarkman's man among them, followed by the rest of the customers pouring out to watch the fun.

'Here!' Nick's voice rang out as a knife came skimming across the cobbles towards Angel. 'Even things up a bit!' He was lost to sight, swallowed up somewhere in the mêlée.

Angel covered ground without waiting to attain the upright, moving swift as a fox to reach the weapon. He missed it by a whisker. It was pinned by the buskined foot of a shirtsleeved youth standing over him, armed and ready.

'Not so fast!' The Jarkman, his escape cut off, was evidently electing to stand his ground with a show of bravado. 'If you're eager to die, do it like a gentleman. Somebody lend him a sword.'

'Aw, dunna talk stupid — ' As he got to his feet a blade was thrust upon him, cold and unfamiliar, its length unwieldly in his unpractised hand. 'I never used a sword in my life!' he protested.

'Then you had best learn fast!' The flat of a blade caught the side of his head and rocked him, drawing blood.

He sprang back. Jesu, Maria — it was coming at him again! He put both hands to the hilt of the sword and used it like a staff, parrying blows, ducking and dodging to the accompaniment of jeering and catcalls on all sides. The occupants of the tavern were now ringed about them holding links and lanterns aloft. Like a bear-baiting, he thought! He did not know who they championed and he did not care, it took all his concentration to keep track of his opponent who moved with a speed and lightness he could hardly credit.

Without warning an expert movement twitched the blade from his hands and a shout of admiration went up from the onlookers. For a brief unguarded moment the Jarkman paused to savour his triumph and in that same moment he was lost. Angel's hard hand closed over the gauntleted wrist and squeezed until he felt the bones begin to give. 'Drop it!'

The swordsman gritted his teeth, but he was almost on his knees. The fingers stretched as if in supplication and the weapon fell to the ground. Angel was taking no chances. He bent and threw it in a whistling arc into the night sky before releasing his hold on a wrist whose thinness had surprised him.

'Right.' He gave a shove and danced back to give himself room to manoeuvre. 'Ballocks or not I've had about enough of you today! Now let's see what you can do without your toys.'

He delivered a cuff that brought a flash of alarm to the face of the Jarkman; he threw an anxious glance over his shoulder and looked for an instant as though he might turn and run. Then seeing that they were still surrounded he turned back to face his attacker, knees bent, hands spread in imitation of Angel's own.

It was apparent that it was now the Jarkman who was at a disadvantage. They circled each other like cats while the exhortations turned to jeers, the onlookers drifted away to watch the other fight which seemed to promise better entertainment. Angel's patience, sorely tried, ran out at last. He closed on the obnoxious Jarkman and fell upon him barehanded, thumping, rolling, pummelling out his fury in an undisciplined orgy and receiving unnoticed kicks, bites and scratches in return for his blows. When all resistance ceased he sat back on his haunches, panting.

'Get up!'

The limply huddled figure shook its head. 'Wait...' The voice was muffled, the face turned away. What trick was he up to, thought Angel.

'Get up!' he repeated, and roughly turned him over. The eyes that met his were stark with terror. His own widened in astonishment as the torn shirt was ripped from the hand that clutched it to reveal skin smooth as marble between the welts, a line of throat and jaw like a cadence of music sweeping down to the curve of a breast.

'You *are* a woman!' he gasped, incredulous. 'You're nobbut a rumpscuttle wench!'

'Silence!'

He sensed a movement too rapid for the eye to follow and felt the sharp kiss of steel at his throat. He found himself squinting down the short thin blade of a poniard held in a strong slender hand.

'One word — ' She spoke between clenched teeth. 'One word of what you know — one false move, and you're dead!'

12

Angel peered through a veil of rain into the finely-boned face that he had surely seen somewhere before. She was drawing together the remnants of her shirt with one hand while the other, gripping the knife as if it were her last slim hold on life, drove its razor edge relentlessly against his skin.

'You shall never have me — *never*, do you hear!'

He held his breath. They were alone now. The spectators had left them, to close in a tight ring about the other pair of fighters. He could hear them chanting 'Kill...kill ...kill!' From somewhere among them a gargling scream spoke of a winning, a losing...Nick was fighting for his life against this woman's henchman. Was the scream his?

He looked at her in disgust. 'I dunna want you.'

For an instant she looked confused, her expression clouded by doubt. He seized his chance to dash away the hand that held the poniard, pinning it to the ground with his knee, peeling back her strong unyielding fingers while she struggled frantically. 'Give up!' he rasped.

Suddenly she was still. Tense. Trembling. 'So be it then.' She drew back her head in an agony of defiance. 'Kill me. Make an end and have done! Why do you wait?'

He should, and he knew it. It was what she expected, what she was prepared for, asking no more quarter than

141

she would give. She had courage, he would grant her that! He released her and sat back on his haunches. 'Get up. You've had the britching you asked for. Now get up and go your ways.'

She stared. 'This is unnatural.' Her eyes narrowed in mistrust and she glanced down at her ruined shirt. 'This is some trick!'

He shook his head. 'No trick. Just lose yourself, dunna cross my path again.'

Slowly they separated, slowly backed away, their eyes still hostile, unregarded now by the watchers who had flocked to the other more exciting scene of carnage, resulting as it had in a bloody slaughter. Angel watched her melt into the shadows, heard the swish of steel over stone as she retrieved her sword, wondered briefly if she meant to return to run him through. But the sound of her feet retreated into silence.

He stood still for a long time in the soft fall of rain, pondering the strangeness of her. Why had she not returned? Why had she not killed him in the first place when she had the chance?

It was not until much later that he asked himself why he had not killed her.

He spent what remained of the night in a lean-to behind the tavern apparently used for storing logs. It was pointless to sue for readmission and in any case he still had no money. And while half of him wanted to know the fate of Nicholas the other half did not want to hear. There could be little doubt of the outcome; the Jarkman's man was half a head the taller and built like a bear — alas for Nicholas, who had also drunk a skinful. He had found the tall hat in a puddle which had felt in the rainwet darkness ominously stickier than water. The knife, too, he had retrieved and stowed in his belt, memento of a rogue who had proved a friend of sorts and for whose death he felt miserably responsible. He thought of Marian, waiting at the alehouse near the Tonne Bridge for her man who would never return. It

142

was, he reflected, only a day's walk away. He might take her the hat, tell her Nick was dead: it seemed the least he could do.

When the sky lightened he eased himself out from among the logs and stretched his cramped limbs. He looked at the hat in the growing light. It had a dried brown stain about the brim; he did not want to show it to Marian like that. He soused it in a rainwater butt and set it on his head to dry.

If he made his way back to the river, London Bridge would take him out through Southwark Gate: from there he had only to set his face south. He tightened the rope about his waist to stay the need to break his fast and started walking. He missed his way several times in the maze of alleys between St Paul's and the Bridge, and the sun was well up and drawing steam from the sodden ground by the time he was clear of Southwark. As he stood at the junction of two roads debating which to take, a hand fell on his shoulder and another snatched the hat from his head. He whirled, knife in hand, expecting an attack.

'Nick, by all that's wonderful!'

'By the Solomon, you're a difficult cove to keep track of! Where are you off to, sick of Romeville already?'

'Ah, Nick!' he laughed delightedly. 'I thought you must be dead of that ruffian what with the booze and all.'

Nick laid a finger alongside his nose. 'Only fox drunk, never fear. As for him — much brawn and little brain, he gave me no trouble.' He dusted his hands together in a comic gesture.

Angel laughed again, shaking his head. 'Well, I dunno. You here, good as new — 'tis the surprise of my life, I must say.'

Nick smiled his most disarmingly and tilted his sodden hat. 'Prepare for a greater. I'm working for the Jarkman.'

Angel's amusement died. 'You're *what?*'

'Why not?' Was it imagination that Nick's tone was slightly defensive? 'His cross is as good as any man's, and twice as plentiful.'

143

'Hmm...I see. Well, it's been good to see you safe but here's where we part company. The less I see of that one the better I'll be pleased.'

'What, feared of him? You pay too much heed to the Patrico —'

'Feared, of that?' Indignation almost loosened his tongue before something prompted him to curb it. Not that he feared her threats, he assured himself, still less that he owed her loyalty. But the underworld would tear her to pieces soon enough without him lending it a hand. He said offhandedly, 'I'll allow he wields a pretty sword, flies like a swallow in his hand. But take that away and he's helpless, canna defend himself no more than a babe newborn. That what he's took you on for, to guard his back?'

Nick did not answer. Instead he gazed into middle distance and said, 'How long have you known him?'

'I dunna. Not before yesterday. Nor wish to.'

'Why do you reckon he wants a watch set on you?'

'On me?' This was going beyond a joke. 'Is that what he said?'

Nick shrugged. 'Among other things. Mainly he's taken on something he can't manage single-handed, some rich gentry mort wanting more than a simple forgery. For the moment I'm come to fetch Marian back to London, you'd best come along where I can keep an eye on you.'

Angel shook his head. 'Sorry. Say Romeville's not to my taste.

'Ah come, what about our pact?'

'I never made no pact, that was your idea, not mine.'

'And what about your mare you were so set on, how will you find her without me?' Nick said artfully. 'Look, cards on the table. My deal with the Jarkman depends on this, it's all or nothing. Say I split the cross with you, fair shares of the snap? I'll help you find your mare and you'll have money to buy her with. Can't say fairer than that. Come, your hand on it!'

Angel hesitated. It was true enough that he had little hope of rescuing Bess without money. And here stood

Nick, hand outstretched, offering a bargain he was no more likely to honour than anything else that he had promised. He smiled wryly, slapped his palm against Nick's.

'Well, let's go and find Marian,' he said. He felt he had aged ten years since the day he left Buxford.

PART THREE
Summer

1

'You're mad!' breathed Nick. He corrected himself hastily, 'I mean she's mad, this gentry mort — does she know what manner of man it is she's pitting her wits against?'

The shrewd eyes of the Jarkman fixed him coldly. 'Spare me your uninformed opinions. You will do it?'

They spoke in subdued voices, their heads bent close across a scarred table in a corner of the Cock tavern, mindful of the fact that they were there on probation since the rumpus of two nights ago.

It was late, a wet and joyless summer evening. The fire burned low in the ingle, spitting defiance at the heavy drops of rain that splashed down the chimney. In another corner four players were engrossed in a game of primero, hugging their cards and eyeing one another like weasels, while in shadowed nooks the short of purse huddled furtively, hoping to steal a night's shelter before Joshua, one-eye sleeping on the bench between his kegs, should notice and evict them on to the drowned inhospitable clay of the road outside. Fowls had settled to roost along the high back of the settle and the tavern mongrel sprawled before the hearth, dozing fitfully between voracious hunts with yellowing teeth along his backbone after fleas.

In the inglenook where the sweet smell of woodsmoke

149

was least tainted by those of rancid food and drenched dog, of stale beer and sour humanity, Angel sat whittling a stick, as far as he could remove himself from the assembled company. He was ill at ease in London with its gloomy overhung streets and its putrid alleys, its evil odours so different from those he was used to, its inhabitants so cocksure and superior; even the dogs looked at him sidelong, suspicious and unfriendly. He had in Kate's parlance 'taken against' the place from his first sight of grinning skulls on London Bridge, and little had happened since to change his opinion. Once let him find Bess, he promised himself, and Nick or no Nick he would forsake this place and every villain in it. Nick, he was confident, would not scruple to do the same to him...He changed his position restlessly. Bess was not young. A few months or even weeks of harsh treatment could send her to the knacker's yard...his mind ran away from the thought.

'Your answer, Bodkyn!' The sharp tone of the Jarkman jerked him back to the present. 'I am committed to this venture, if you are too craven —'

'Not so, hold hard. Just let's have it straight so there's no brabble about it later. I'm to ride to this castle in Northumberland — if I can find it, that is — in a trumped-up livery. I deliver the letter to its lord...and then just disappear? Looks a trifle suspicious, wouldn't you say, not waiting to take the reply?'

'That is for you to do and for me to decide.' From where he sat Angel saw a look of annoyance cross the Jarkman's face to be quickly masked by a smile. 'A challenge for your ingenuity, Bodkyn. Make it appear natural. The Border country's wild enough, take your horse out to walk him and fail to return. Come, why do you suppose I choose you for this errand if not for your reputation?'

Nicholas sat back and folded his arms across his chest, trying to conceal the fact that he felt flattered. 'Yes, well...a detail, cove, a mere detail. And then?'

'And then back here with all speed. For here's the nub:

150

they will be forced to send their own courier with an answer. Look well at that man, know his face like your own and be back here to point him out to Marian as he comes through Islington. You, girl,' her eyes flickered briefly to where Marian's tangled mop sparkled in the firelight, 'will be ready to divert him and bring me his letter while he sleeps. The rest will fall to me.'

Nicholas let go his breath in a long soft whistle. 'So I'm to outride him. You ask a deal for your money, cove. A man must needs go like the wind.'

'You call yourself a horseman, do you not?' Again the challenge, the faintly mocking smile. 'Be wily, gain a start on him. Time your arrival for nightfall. They will need time to consider and compose a reply, they will hardly have it ready before the morning. Seek out the courier, sear his face into your memory and vanish in the night.'

'Straight back without a rest — the horse will be breathing its last, never mind about me!'

'Abandon it, buy another. The patron has gold and she will pay.'

'Hm-mm...Suppose he remembers me?'

'He must not. Shave your beard, dye your hair, do whatever else may be needful, you are recognised at your peril, for if he does not reckon with you be sure that I will!' She leaned forward across the table, seeming to smoulder with some inner fire. 'Look you, Bodkyn, mark me well. This is the weightiest matter you have undertaken or ever will, the fortunes of a mighty family depend on it, the righting of a great wrong. Carry it off and we could all be rich as Croesus — fail, and all our hopes must perish with you.' She sat back, watching him for the effect. 'Now, how say you; are you the man for the task?'

Nicholas looked sceptical. Perhaps, thought Angel, he too saw a show of chivalry in the Jarkman as cause for suspicion.

'It wants thought, cove, it wants thought..."could" you say, we could all be rich, that's not good enough for me. It's payment on the nail for Bodkyn, no "if" and no "could". Nothing for nothing, eh, doxy?' This last was addressed to Marian, who dimpled and demurely lowered her lashes. Angel compressed his lips. Here with Nicholas, straitlaced and modestly covered, she was barely recognisable as the boozy alehouse whore who had brazenly invited him to dalliance. Was no one what he seemed in this godforsaken place? He glanced over to where the Patrico sat quietly nodding off over his beads: there at least was a kind and honest man.

The Jarkman called for a blackjack, and as a heavy-eyed urchin staggered towards them under the weight of tarred leather charged with beer Angel caught the flash of gold and heard the chink of coin upon the table. 'Here's to seal the bargain. When all is accomplished — successfully — there will be more.'

Nick's eyes narrowed. 'How much more? I'll know the final score before I go further. What's more you must pay my mort if she's to play the Traffic, she's losing trade the while she works for you.'

'She may take her price from the courier — but no thieving or he'll become suspicious. My dealings are with you; whom you see fit to employ, you pay yourself.'

Marian's expression congealed to a look that Angel remembered. Nicholas glowered across a pool of spilt beer to where the Jarkman thrust a tankard under the wavering stream from the blackjack. "Tis a two-handed job this, and well you know it — can't hardly lure the cuffin a-bed myself while his letters are filched, can I?' He lowered his voice to a surly mutter. 'Though I daresay there's some might enjoy it.'

'Indeed?' The dark eyes of the Jarkman glittered dangerously in the shadows. Marian could be heard to suck in her breath and the small incompetent potboy retreated in haste. Nick, an indignant red inflaming his cheekbones, went on recklessly. 'Indeed! You'll pay us both or the deal is off. What's more I want to know what this gentry mort's up to before I commit myself. Not being the one, you understand, to walk blindfold into battle.'

152

'Then want must be your master,' came the sharp retort.

Nicholas stood up. 'Then I'll bid you good darkmans, you've seen the last of me — '

'Wait!' The Jarkman's expression was unreadable. 'Sit down and calm yourself, I see Joshua looking this way.' As Nick reluctantly sank down again, 'Now listen to me. You, Bodkyn, are a fool! The lady of whom I speak is heiress to a great estate and will have vast revenues at her disposal — but she can only regain them by trickery. Now, these letters which I shall write and you will carry will be a hazard to her afterwards should their origin come to light. What will she not be willing to pay to keep these forgeries secret? Think on it, man, only think and be patient — '

'Patience don't pay debts, no more do promises, more like she'll have our throats slit to quieten us! Not good enough, cove, not good enough by half. I want — ' he ticked off the items on his fingers — 'the sum fixed, payment in advance, and no more talk of you not paying Marian. I'm not a richman like you, you know — aside of which I've got to pay the Patrico.'

The Jarkman's sardonic laugh cut across his words. 'Ah, yes, we all pay the Patrico, do we not! His path to glory must be well paved with gold by now!'

A chorus of derisive appreciation brought up Angel's head in surprise. Nicholas, plainly furious, glanced in his direction and clutched at a straw. 'Then there's him, the Horse Whisperer — if I don't cough up what he asks he'll put the Evil Eye on the lot of us. I'm not about to wake up blind some morning or have all me toes drop off — '

'Hexes, Horse Whisperers! What next will you think to cozen me with...'

Angel turned his back and feigned sleep. He had no intention of being drawn into a sordid squabble among thieves. He took refuge behind his eyelids as their voices faded...*melting...into darkness...darkness damp and evil smelling...the pain of saddle galls...the ache of constant hunger...exhaustion dragging like a chain as despairingly the weight is shifted from leg to leg on hard*

*uneven cobbles...hay meagre and rotting and alive with
mice, the taste of it tainted with their droppings...the
only water green and foetid as the stagnant air...*

'Bess!'

He woke, his stomach churning, bewildered to find himself back in the tavern. The fire had burned out. The mongrel and the potboy slept curled together on the still warm hearth. Joshua was snoring cosily, his head against a keg, while a heap of tumbled clothing in a corner showed where Nick and Marian slept entangled. At the table where they had sat haggling the Jarkman alone remained, her head bent low over a parchment where her quill moved swiftly, confidently, by the light of two fat candles, the gloves she habitually wore discarded beside her. He shook his head in an attempt to clear it. 'What...what's happened?'

The Jarkman looked up heavy-eyed from her work. 'Happened? What should happen at this hour, the watch has just called three.'

'Three!' He was startled, unable to fathom where the night had gone. The tavern seemed to have emptied in moments while he catnapped. 'I must have slept in earnest.' He stretched himself awake, while as if to give credence to her words a cockerel gave voice somewhere nearby.

She pushed away the parchment and pressed the heels of her hands against her eyes. 'Like one dead, not even the Patrico's blandishments could rouse you. They say the Devil takes care of his own.'

He frowned. 'They say 'tis wrong to speak ill of a priest an' all. That about him taking money. 'Tis true what he says, he does give it to the poor.'

She looked at him enigmatically, then shrugged. 'You'll learn. Tell him nothing you would not have known.'

You'll learn...that was what Nick had said. ''Tis Bodkyn you want to watch,' he said. 'Twist his grandam for a crust of bread — aye, and still cry at her burial.'

'Indeed.' A faint smile. 'Anything to turn a dishonest penny. Such men have their uses.' She was so sure of herself, so arrogant...like a child playing with fire.

154

'Just watch he dunna use you. If he comes out the loser he'll be the one to slit your throat — you seen what he did to your man the other night.'

'The man was a fool. Bodkyn is a man of many parts, well suited to my purpose —'

'Only while it suits him —'

'By God, you try my patience!' The Jarkman's fist slammed down upon the table with a crash that made the dog start up from sleep. 'Pray mind your own concerns, this is none of yours...why do you stare at me so?'

She was right. Why should he concern himself, it was nothing to him. Yet still he peered into the face that was familiar, unfamiliar. ''Tis just...I reckon I seen you somewhere before.'

She treated him to a look of utter scorn. 'Spare me your clumsy dissembling!' She turned away, began collecting up the tools of her trade. Turned back. 'You wish to deny your identity — perhaps, who knows, you have the grace to be ashamed. But don't deceive yourself, Pan, I'd know you in a million!'

'Look, listen...I knew you'd took me for another. Now you call me out of my name. I tell you you never knew me in your life before, now give in and admit it!'

'Do I so?' She faced him, leaning forward, palms flat upon the table top. 'And what of the scar you bear, unto death if I mistake not?'

Disconcerted he drew back, involuntarily folding his arms across his chest. 'What scar?' he said cautiously. Was it possible that she had been there in the forge, and he too young to remember? He searched the blurred ugly memory...but if she had, why did she call him Pan? Intrigued, he said, 'Come on, what scar?'

He saw doubt flit across her face, the shadow of a cloud on a clear day. She stood motionless. 'Show me your back!'

'So you can stick a knife in it?' he chaffed, hauling up his shirt, and was shocked by her response. A look of horror, fear, nausea, dread — he could find no words to describe it but it sobered him. 'There. What do you look to see?'

He turned back to see her standing as he had left her,

lips still parted from speaking, faced drained of colour, the hands braced upon the table top trembling under stress. 'I...see I am disabused...' And then, *'Who are you?'* The words came barely above a whisper. Her eyes glowed wide, scorching in the candlelight. The dog crouched wakeful, a low rumble gathering in his chest, his hackles rising to the tension in the room.

'You see? I told you.' He forced a laugh. 'You look like you seen a ghost.'

The Jarkman's lips moved but no sound came. As she sank down upon a seat he found himself looking at a face suddenly vulnerable. And younger. Much, much younger...'You dunna know me,' he said slowly, probing his memory for an echo of those fine brows arching away like a blackbird's wings...suddenly he had it. 'But I know you!'

'No...no!' She shrank away, staring at him as though she were watching an adder.

'Yes!' Excited, he grasped her cold hands and pulled her to her feet. ''Tis you, this patron of yours as never was — 'tis you, Joanna of Buxford, as vanished from home when I was no bigger than corn. Your picture hangs in Great Hall to this day, the girl with the unicorn.' He chuckled. 'Many's the clipped ear I had for asking who you were but I got it in the end. Mind, I might have known you before but for being more taken with the unicorn!'

With a sudden twist she freed her hands, tossed her head in defiance. 'So, and what do you suppose you are going to do?' Without warning all the old arrogance was back, curdling his sympathy.

'Do?' He laughed unkindly into her face, enjoying her discomfiture. 'Oh, I anna going to do nothing. 'Tis you must do the doing.'

'What mean you by that?'

'What do I mean?' He savoured from the tail of his eye the look of misgiving, of suppressed alarm and laughed again, remembering Bess. 'I mean if you want my silence you must pay for it. Nothing for nothing, eh, doxy?'

'Do not dare to doxy me!'

He had teased her long enough. Catching her off guard he seized her, tossed her up and caught her a couple of inches off the ground. The girls at Buxford had loved it, giggling and melting into his arms. This one hung rigid as a moppet, arching her body away from his and quivering, whether with rage or fear he could not be sure. He gave her a little shake.

"Tis no great price, Lady Rumpscuttle, not to you. Come sun-up, you're going with me to buy a horse!'

2

'You want to crop your hair,' 'tis over long for a man.' Angel threw himself down on the grassy bank of the Fleet, a long stem of timothy grass between his teeth. The day had dawned hot and still after last night's deluge, a day to draw steam from the fields and sweat from the body, damp and enervating. 'Growing it ready for Buxford, are we?'

His companion ignored him. Dazed from a night without sleep she stumbled as she walked, and now sank down wearily by the riverside. Tireless himself, he had pushed her relentlessly in his search for Bess, homing in like a migrant bird on the signals he was receiving. He was aware of being cruel but he did not care: once he had Bess the Jarkman could sleep until Domesday if she wished. 'You hear what I said?'

Not answering, she pulled off the plumed velvet cap and ran her hands through dark tresses that caught purple from the sunlight, leaving damp tendrils on her hot forehead. She scowled. 'Where is this wild goose chase you drag me on?'

Not getting an answer, he too countered with a question. 'What lies to the north of here now we're out of London?'

'Where?'

'That's what I'm asking you. Over there, across the fields.'

158

'Hoxton.' She looked at him suspiciously. 'That's the next village.'

'And the other way?'

'That of Islington, of course.' She raised her head from where she was leaning down the bank to dabble the water. 'Don't you even know where you're taking me?'

'Not till I get there,' he said maddeningly, taking a perverse pleasure in annoying her.

'Small wonder with only one eye to light your way!' she retorted sharply, splashing handfuls of water over her face.

'I got two eyes, sound as yours. Better,' he added, seeing her flinch as she touched a ripening bruise.

'Why wear a patch, then?'

'Ah! You tell your secrets and I might tell mine.'

From the corner of his eye he saw her anger sparkle. 'You'll get no secrets from me, Master Jackanapes. And I have ways of discovering what I want to know.'

'Don't do you much good though, does it? Seeing you got it all wrong about me. I know who you are but you dunna know nothing about me.'

'Do I not? she cocked a quizzical eyebrow. 'I know you hail from Buxford. Have you a passport?'

'You offering to do me one?'

She tossed her head. 'What do you call yourself?'

He hesitated. 'I dunna give my name for fools to mock at. My mother left it me to bless me with, I reckon it was likely all she had. So I dunna tell it no one, not even Nick.'

'As I thought, a runagate. As well you did not lie, it would have availed you nothing. A jarkman makes his living from liars, I can smell one leagues away. So...you are a runagate. Shall we say, a fugitive? The bantering tone was tinged with malice. 'No doubt you would prefer that my lord of Buxford was not informed of your whereabouts?'

The joke was turning a little sour. 'No doubt,' he said slowly. 'And then there's you an' all. Hoyting about in mens' duds, forging jarks when all the good folk at Buxford think you'm dead. What about your loving family, then? Wouldn't they just like to know where their precious Joanna's to be found and what she's up to — and couldn't I just tell them, if so say you was to get me caught?'

They eyed each other with open hostility. Then Joanna smiled wryly. 'Full marks, Master Jackanapes, you are less dull than I hoped. How do I know that when you have your horse you will not sell me to the highest bidder?'

'You dunna,' he said bluntly. 'It seems we got to trust each other.'

'Trust?' An acid laugh. 'A luxury for the dead! I propose to live a little longer, you may do as it pleases you.'

'A bargain, then: I'll not betray you without you've betrayed me first. Your hand on it, Lady Rumpscuttle?'

She said contemptuously, 'Bargains are for fools, those secrets are best kept that do not venture out of sight.' With a dismissive gesture she turned away to douse her head in the water. As an afterthought she tossed over her shoulder, 'And I am Jarkman Joe to you as to the rest.'

'Even when we're alone?'

'Especially then.'

Baffled, he sank back on to his elbow. Any friendly advance on his part was likely to shatter on the same stone wall. Not that he wanted to make friends...but to be fair they had got off to a bad start. He said, 'You talk like I was about to black your other eye. I'd not have done it, not if I'd known. 'Tis not my way with women.'

'It is every man's way with women!' She tossed back her wet hair with an angry flick. 'But I can defend myself.' She fondled the hilt of her sword as she spoke, adding half to herself, 'I shall not go the way of my mother.'

'Your mother...Lady Edith?' In the way of poor men he had imagined the rich to live a life of unsullied joy.

'My mother!' She rounded on him fiercely. 'She is dead, crushed! Have you ever looked into her eyes! Ashes. There is nothing there, no spirit, she's as empty as a suit of armour.'

He said, 'She did lose all her babes one after another. And then you...small wonder if she's unhappy.'

Her laugh was mirthless. 'I doubt she noticed the loss. Her death began the day we came to Buxford. That man!' She stared bleakly before her, a muscle twitching rhythmically at the angle of her jaw. Without warning she turned her angry gaze on him. 'Did God make men or did they all come boiling up from Hell? Answer me that!' She turned again face downwards to stare broodingly into the river.

He was not sure that he could answer it. After a moment's thought he said, 'Seeing you think all men's so vile...why ape them?'

Not looking at him, she said bitingly, 'Because I have no stomach for rape or pillage. No woman is safe in a forest of raging animals.' Again the mirthless laugh. 'Now I do the pillaging.'

Something in her attitude touched him, stirring his compassion. It was fear, he thought; all that bitterness, all that hatred stemmed from fear. He said softly, 'We'm all animals, lovely. You, me, the Lord Eustace an all. Only some is hungrier than others and takes by force. But it dunna fall to all of us to want to.'

She lay very still. Not at ease but like a colt ill broken, quivering for flight at threat of saddle. He studied her, seeing where the throb of light reflected from moving water showed a few fine lines at the corner of her eye; thinking of the breast he had glimpsed so briefly, lovely yet already losing the newborn spring of youth. He said, 'Anna you never loved a man?'

'Never!' The dismissive gesture, the caustic glance.

'Maybe,' he said carefully. 'Maybe 'tis just the right man anna loved you.'

She looked at him sidelong with a curious expression, almost rueful. 'And what manner of man do you expect to love a woman like me?'

It was the first time they had talked without quarrelling. Now he was aware of a strange disturbing beauty, saw her in his mind's eye gowned in russet, skin warmed to peach by an August sun...or stripped of all, her white body gleaming pale in twilight...

He checked his thoughts. She was gentry, he reminded himself: the kind to dress in bombast and farthingale, to frizzle that dark mysterious mane into iron curls forged by a blacksmith. He shrugged, said guardedly, 'There could be some…as might.'

She turned now to look at him; he was caught in the full power of them, those eyes into which a man might fall and never hope for rescue. Then she sat up abruptly, seemed to shake herself. She rose to her feet and her answer came slashing at him like a sword-thrust.

'Don't give yourself airs, Master Jackanapes. I'd as soon be loved by a monkey!'

'I dunna believe it!' He spoke as though stunned, staring before him into the rank-smelling gloom of the deserted stable. 'This is the place, I know it is — I'd stake my life! And there's nothing here.'

All day they had tramped, almost to Hatfield on the Great North Road in pursuit of some illusion in his mind. This was it, he had insisted: here they would find the mare he meant her to buy. Now, hungry and footsore, they stared at each other, he nonplussed and she exasperated.

'Good,' she said cruelly. 'Now perhaps I may be permitted to sleep. So much for your magical powers!' Swaying with fatigue she stopped short of the doorway, glad not to have to enter the foul place, not to be forced to haggle over price in her present state of exhaustion and thankful for the prospect of release from his presence which still filled her with uneasiness. Pan he might not be, but he was far too sharp a reminder of the past. How could they wear the same face, speak with the same voice and not be cast in the same mould? Even to the obsession with animals…She shivered. One could almost think that a race of demons flaxen-haired, blue-eyed and dark-browed had come to inhabit the earth; and this one filled her with a deeper apprehension than the first. Her stomach knotted and she turned to go.

'Wait!' He reappeared in the entrance through which he had gone plunging into the deserted shed as if he hoped to find his quarry somewhere amongst the debris, the heaps of rotting manure, fraying harness, rats. 'Wait, hold hard! We anna found her yet.'

'You find her. My search is for a bed.'

Wearily he passed the back of a hand across his sweating brow. 'If you must, then. Give me the money and go.'

'Oho, no!' She raised a hand in gesture of negation. 'Tired I may be but not so tired as to take leave of my senses. A horse you said and a horse you get, not money. Not from me.' Her brain was too tired to tell her why not and when at a disadvantage she never took chances.

'So much for your promises.' Filthy and dishevelled he emerged from the stinking hovel, his expression so eloquent that she knew a moment of remorse.

Resenting it, she said spitefully, 'Alas, poor Jackanapes! Did I not tell you that promises were for fools?'

Walking away, she glanced over her shoulder. He was standing where she had left him, eyes closed, head bowed against the door jamb in an attitude of despair. 'When you've something to buy,' she tossed back at him, 'you may seek me out again!'

At the time, her wits dulled by lack of sleep, Joanna felt only relief as she walked away. Later, refreshed by a night's rest and restored to mental alertness, she recognised her folly all too clearly. She must have been mad to let him out of her sight! Desperate for money and in possession of her secret, what else would he do but sell to the highest bidder — perhaps even to Eustace in return for a pardon, she thought, turning over in her mind every dread possibility as alarm seeped into her bones. Something must be done and quickly, quickly — but what?

Gaunt with apprehension she scrambled from bed and dragged on her clothes. Someone must go after him, stop him, either herself or another — Bodkyn had not yet left for the North and could not without the letter — or Marian, she was not needed at Islington yet — dear God, where might he not be by now! She stamped herself into

163

her buskins and ran headlong from the place.

The broken-down stable when she reached it was deserted, as in her heart she had known it would be. The Jackanapes was gone, on who could guess what deadly errand. There was nothing to be done but acquire a horse and set her face towards London, stoking her fires to blast Bodkyn for dereliction of his duty.

3

Lady Edith winced as a shaft of light from the setting sun pierced her eyes. 'More firing,' she ordered the maid who sat with her.

'More?' The girl turned towards her a face already flushed by the heat of the room. 'Madam, are you certain?'

'Don't argue, girl.' Edith struggled to control her shivering. 'More logs, build it high. I am chilled to the bone.'

The girl peered anxiously into the white face, the closed eyes. 'Madam?' Timorously she touched a hand to the burning forehead. 'Lady, you are ill! I will send to your lord —'

'No!' Edith jerked herself back to awareness. 'You shall not...' Why did the window rush at her and then retreat? The answer came to her in a throb of alarm. The illness she had so conveniently feigned for her protection and Joanna's had become a fact. She must have eaten something noxious, taken some infection from the air...something destined to undo her if Eustace should catch her weak and off guard...she made an effort as the darkness threatened to close in. 'You are not to disturb him.' She grasped the girl's cool wrist with a parched hand. 'Not my lord, do you hear? Not your master... fetch...' she paused, wrestling with a wave of nausea. 'Fetch an apothecary...' She was losing command of her senses and the thought of her husband's presence filled her with dread. 'An apothecary,' she moaned at intervals as the fever mounted, her conscience racked by the knowledge that her task was unfulfilled...her strength ebbing. She must not die, they must not let her die, not yet...Joanna, oh, Joanna...'Please...please...' She barely heard the sound of her own voice. She felt herself lifted, rolled...A sheep was drinking her blood, clinging open-mouthed to her arm. She tried in vain to brush it away...'No!...no, no...' She was swaying, rolled in blankets, rolled in the sheep — was she dreaming? It was Eustace who drank her blood...he must not find the sheep — no, Joanna must not find it, find Eustace...not in the blankets! She was burning, burning...parched and burning...her bones were on fire. She could see the flames licking past her face, the flames of Hell for her sin of omission, her unfulfilled trust... 'No...no!' Jesu, Maria!...*ave Maria*...find Joanna...'Joanna!'

Her women stood huddled with frightened eyes about the drenched figure of their mistress so swiftly reduced to babbling incoherence in the thrashing dance with death. Their mute faces asked each other the question they hesitated to voice: What were they to do? The apothecary, hastily summoned, had leeched her, wrapped her in the skin of a freshly-flayed sheep, prescribed a posset of yarrow and hyssop and refused to make firm predictions of any kind. It was not, he affirmed, the small pox. If it were, exposure to the fire would have brought out the yaws and saved her life. It was the sweat, he said, backing nervously from the room; they must watch and pray. He would come again in the morning...if he was sent for.

Still she tossed and moaned and the skin of her body stood up in peaks where they pinched it, and still the sweat poured off her as though from a hidden spring. It was all very well, they told each other in worried whispers, for her to say, 'Don't tell Lord Eustace.' Who was to take the blame if she should die? On the other hand, suppose she recovered to find they had disobeyed her...

In desperation they conferred with the chaplain. He pursed his lips, laid out his altar for the administration of extreme unction. And a little before midnight when her delirium was at its highest, took the responsibility upon himself.

It was not the best time to summon Eustace. Not only had he received a disquieting letter from his distant relative Fitznorth, but sultry weather had heightened his appetites and when he had sent to the forge for Nan to assuage them, back had come an answer coolly tinged with insolence: one of her children was sick and could not be left. His wrath rising with his passion, he had been about to order her seizure when the dread thought struck him; suppose it were his own son Matthew who was stricken! In sudden agitation he had risen from his bed and was already pacing the floor when the timid knock came on his door.

'What now!' he barked at the unfortunate acolyte who stood there stammering. 'Why was I not told before?' Shoving him roughly aside, he went striding along the gallery to his wife's chambers. The women fell back as he entered, exchanging furtive glances. 'Well?' he roared.

The chaplain calmly returned his gaze. 'My lord, your wife is unwell. It seems she gave orders that you were not to be disturbed. Doubtless,' he added smoothly, 'she thought to be recovered ere now.'

Eustace grunted. The women, with a rustle of skirts like an escaping sigh, drew nearer. He waved them away. 'What is she muttering about, what does she say?'

He closed on her, bending over the white shining face that twisted and rolled from side to side on the damp velvet of the pillow, a strand of grey hair loosened from her sodden biggin wetly plastered to her sunken cheek. Already she looked alarmingly like a corpse; clearly there was no time to be lost. Her lips moved ceaselessly over chattering teeth, their movements scarcely matching the faint sounds that were jerked from her throat. 'Well, what?' he snapped with impatience.

Her personal maid stepped forward tight-lipped. It was not lost on her that he had not asked how her mistress fared, or even the nature of her illness. She said without expression, 'She speaks her daughter's name, my lord. "Joanna", nothing more.' Thinking with satisfaction, She does not ask for you, cruel man —

'Out!' The word exploded in her face; she found herself with all the others thrust without ceremony out of the room, the door slamming behind them.

'Answer me, *answer!*'

They looked at each other in helpless distress as the sound of his bullying voice, their mistress's piteous whimpering, reached them from within. The youngest burst into tears. 'Oh, my poor lady...'

They looked to the chaplain. With piously closed eyes, his mouth set in a telltale angry line, he was silently telling his beads.

4

In an upper room of Islington's one tavern, Jarkman and Traffic were in conference.

'So,' mused Joanna. 'They seek a one-eyed warlock and a stolen mare. Is that all?'

'Enough, ain't it?' Marian's reply was pert. 'I ain't paid for spying, you know.'

'You're paid to do as you're told,' was the crisp retort. 'What else is afoot?'

'Nought else. Everyone goes in fear of the lord. His lady's took to her bed and don't see nobody. What more's to tell?'

'And that is all he said to you, you're sure?'

'Course I'm sure.' Marian patted her unkempt curls. 'A cove don't bed with a girl to talk, you know. Ask too many questions, he gets suspicious. Still,' she added saucily, 'reckon you wouldn't know about things like that.'

The Jarkman quelled her with a look. Damn the messenger for a tight-lipped Northerner! She needed to know more, much more. Was Edith sick enough to die or merely ailing as she always had? She needed her alive when she returned to Buxford, to vouch for her identity if nothing else. She wished she could have sent the astute Bodkyn there; he would have found out all she wanted to know. But fearing his flamboyant personality might be remembered she had deemed it wiser to send him further afield, to trigger the vital correspondence at its northern end. So far events had proved her right, for Bodkyn had done his job well, returning in good time for Marian to waylay the courier en route for Buxford; by good fortune she had captured the Borderer's fancy and he now lay snoring in another room, keeping a welcome assignation on his way back North.

'A one-eye, you said?' She feigned disinterest as she took the filched letter from Marian.

'That's right, some cove with a fanciful name, Angel or such.' She giggled. 'Don't sound much of an Angel to me, they reckon he killed a man — burned to death they found him, hid in a furnace. Oh, yes, I forgot to tell you that. Important, was it?'

'No...not important. You're sure he still sleeps, the courier?'

Marian laughed. 'Geordie? After what went in his booze? He'd sleep till lightmans even if I hadn't wore him out.'

Joanna suppressed a shudder. How could she joke! 'Wait downstairs, I'll call when you're wanted.' When Marian had gone she sat with compressed lips, trying to subdue a growing knot of tension that twisted her vitals. So he was a murderer, that Jackanapes. Her instinct about him had been right and perhaps it was just as well that he had disappeared. For disappear he had; even Bodkyn's diligence had failed to trace him and the search had had to be abandoned to release the man for his journey north. It was a curious name, 'Angel', disturbing an echo somewhere in her mind. Curious... and memorable. Small wonder that he did not want it known. At least if Marian's facts were right he would not dare go to Eustace...but what if they were not?

It was pointless to ponder what could not be resolved. She carefully unrolled the letter and read:

From the Lord Eustace Pengerran of Buxford

and Pengerran to Sir Reginald Fitznorth:
Greetings.

I see no cause for haste in the matter of consum-
mation of the marriage between your son and my
daughter. Having regard to the state of James's
health and the hazards of the road it would seem
judicious to postpone the occasion for the pre-
sent time. Joanna has been lodged in a house of
religion since her betrothal and shall remain in
the keeping of Mother Church until the celebra-
tion of the nuptials...

Joanna sat back and smiled thoughtfully into the fire.
So, that was his story. She could do worse than use it,
yes, indeed. Bent a little, shaped to her ends. She made
mocking obeisance to a corner of the empty room. 'My
thanks to you, stepfather. You have smoothed for me
the path to your own demise.' For the moment she felt
well pleased; with every move going to plan she could
afford to sit tight here in Islington and wait. Like a
spider, she thought. Weaving a web, lurking in shadow
for the victim to fall in...

  She sighed. It was precisely the waiting that was difficult...and there would be a price to pay. As always, she
turned her mind away from it; she rose and paced the
tiny room which was the best the inn could provide,
returning at last to the table where she pushed aside the
remains of the meal she had eaten, took parchment, quill
and inkhorn from her scrip, and began to write. When
she had finished she removed with infinite care the seal
from the courier's letter, melted its back in the candle
flame and affixed it to the forgery. When after prolonged scrutiny she was satisfied, she held the original
letter in the flame until it was consumed. Only then did
she go to the door, lean over the gallery rail and call
softly to Marian dozing on the hearth below. 'Here, girl!
Put this back in his pouch and be sure you don't rouse
him. Here's for your pains.' She passed down the scroll

171

and the coin, went back into her room and barred the door.

She returned to the table and sat looking at the tools of her trade, debating whether or not to catch up on some of the letters and jarks from which her revenue came. It was late, very late; just the hour at which to confound herself by making some stupid error. She pushed it all back into her scrip and blew out the candle.

Resigning herself to sleep she found it eluded her, she was at once too tired and too taut. She tossed on the narrow bed, trying to compose herself. But her rest was thin and uneasy and ended before dawn with her struggling in the jaws of a nightmare. She sat up gasping, the dreadful scream ringing in her ears, the images still vivid in her mind...a firelit face grinning across a clearing...a knife that struck as a fumbling body jabbed at hers...the blood...the horror of a frightened child...the body rolling away, rolling from above her, the face as it turned grotesquely inflated, the head the size of two...oh God! Oh Jesu, Maria...not that...no, not the Jackanapes —

With a mighty struggle she fought herself free, willing herself back to sanity. Was it she who had cried out or was it part of the dream...? She listened nervously for sounds outside. Nothing. She let go the breath she had been holding. She drew up her knees, dropped her head on her forearms and sat shivering while the room lightened, the everyday world came to her rescue. She remembered now whose the scream was. Not her own but her father's, tortured and dying in the distant long ago; the scream that had haunted her dreams since the day she fled Buxford, the day that had laid waste her life like the sweep of a scythe through standing corn. An evil day for the house of Pengerran, a monstrous wrong that could not go unavenged! And the duty, the right, the privilege were hers and hers alone. Only she could do it...and only she could pay the price. The price, the price...oh, Mother of Heaven, that price! It was bitter indeed that it should fall to her...a sob broke from her before she could stifle it...and another...for the first time in years her iron control had cracked.

She was still huddled there cold and exhausted when the sounds of men and horses milling about in the court-yard below roused her from torpor. She crossed to the window and looked down; Braw Geordie the courier was kicking his mount to a canter, waving an arm to Marian who stood leaning with her back against the gatepost, her tousled curls catching the early light, her bodice unlaced, still drowsy from the night's work. And such work! thought Joanna, torn between disgust and admiration; Give her her due, she puts on a good act, from the way she smiles and waves one could almost believe she enjoyed it. She endures it of course, as any woman must. And if she can...

She shivered, scrubbed at her damp face with the end of her shirt, gathered up her doublet and boots from where she had discarded them last night. She always felt better with them on, as though wearing the padded peascod belly slotted her safely back behind the façade of Jarkman Joe. Lacing up the waistband of her velvet slops, she thought wryly that when she came to the wearing of feminine garments again she might well have forgotten how to put them on. She straightened her back, buckled on the sword-belt and slung the short riding cape across her shoulders; then pulling the plumed hat well down to shade her eyes, she swaggered out on to the gallery in time to meet Bodkyn coming in from without.

'I've found him.' He grinned up at her with a cheeky air. 'He sends you a message.'

'A message? What means this, you should have stayed with him!'

Bodkyn leant back against the door jamb, crossed one foot over the other and set his tall hat at a jauntier angle. 'He said to tell you he's found what he wanted. And that if you don't come, you know what to expect.'

5

In the tumbledown livery stable near Hatfield, Angel
was engaged in a furious set-to with the horseman, a
disinterested slouch in a greasy leather apron.

'You anna fit to have charge of a rabbit!' he stormed.
'Look at these galls, this saddle's never been off for a
sennight!' He hauled it off and flung it to the ground
where it raised a choking cloud of chaff and dung-
flavoured dust. 'Where's she been this past month, I've
searched for her high and low —'

'I don't ask where they're bound, only when they'll be
back,' was the surly reply. 'What's it to you, do you want
a horse or don't you?'

The mare raised her drooping head and blew gustily
in Angel's ear. 'Bess, my poor Bess,' he murmured. ''Tis
all right, I'm here now...' He ran a hand over her coat,
harsh and brittle from the dye with which it had been
darkened. He took her bridle and prepared to lead her
out.

'Here, hold hard, where d'you think you're going?
Can't ride it out without it's saddled —'

'She's not being ridden, not nowhere till she's healed.
Where's your goose grease?'

The man grinned unpleasantly. 'There's geese in the
yard, go and catch one if you're that concerned.'

'That I am, I know this mare — beautiful she was till

174

you laid hands on her and now look at her! Just look, come here and look. You did ought to be ashamed of yourself!'

'Not a lot wrong that I can see. She'll do till summer's end and still fetch a few pence back from the knacker's.'

'Nought wrong! Just look at her knees all broken and bloody — a shoe cast and two loose nails in another — and her back! Look at it, look at them galls, that one'll run to a fistula, see if it don't! To say nothing of her coat all matted with sweat where she's been galloped and never rubbed down nor walked nor nothing — '

'And I says it again, what's it to you?' The man set down his bucket and came over, his attitude mildly threatening. 'Are you come to hire a horse or just looking for trouble?'

'I'm come to buy her!'

'Buy her?' The man walked round him, looking him up and down with jeering amusement. '*Buy*, did you say? Well now, you don't look like no cat's-meat dealer to me. Come to think, you don't look like no buyer neither.' He leaned forward, bathing Angel's face in a beery fume. 'Where's your money?'

Angrily aware that he would be disbelieved, he said, 'I sent for it. To London. It'll be here before nightfall.'

The man gave a loud belch which ended in an ugly laugh. 'Oh, I see. To London, yes, I see. The young gentleman has sent for it to his goldsmith, no doubt? For the purchase of such a valuable animal — '

Before he could say more Angel's knuckles collided with his teeth. He staggered backwards, hit the wall and came fighting back, and the two were still blindly slamming it out when Nick Bodkyn reined in on the road outside.

'How now, young Jackanapes, in trouble again?' He put the horseman out of business with a well-aimed kick to the groin, hoisted Angel to his feet and dusted him down.

'You don't half fight dirty, Nick!' He grinned in grudging appreciation.

'Yes, don't I?' Nick adjusted his hat and smiled disarmingly. 'That's why I win. Is the mare still here?'

'No thanks to this vermin. You took the message, is the Jarkman here?'

'Yes, I did, and no, he isn't — no, wait!' He raised a hand in a gesture of caution. 'There are reasons you should hear, the Jarkman's no fool —'

'Oh, no! A rogue, a cheat and a villain but no fool! You come on a horse?' Already he was out through the door, shouting back over his shoulder.

'The Jarkman's Saracen, you don't think I walked five leagues —'

'Then I'll hear the excuses first hand! You stay with Bess, let no one touch her till I get back!' He swung himself into the saddle and applied his heels.

'I can't do that!' protested Nick in an unwonted burst of selfrighteousness. 'She's not mine!'

'That never bothered you afore as I recall!' He wheeled his mount and headed back towards London, hearing Nick's voice fading, calling after him.

'I've to keep you under my eye, you fool! Come back...'

He was a good ten miles down the road by the time his temper had cooled enough for an honest appraisal of his motives. Nick, he had to acknowledge, could very likely have produced enough money there and then for the hiring of Bess; all that would have been needed was to fail to return her to the stables. It was even possible that he had brought the promised money from the Jarkman; but he, Angel, had not asked. Instead here he was rushing off hot-headed to Islington, leaving Bess to the tender mercies of Nicholas. Why? The truth when he uncovered it shocked him. For the truth was, he was going to see Joanna.

'What manner of man do you suppose could love me?' He had answered the ironic question lightly: 'There could be some as might...'Thinking, only a fool...or a madman. Now he knew.

It came to him that he had known for a long time, that something from the beginning had drawn him to the

176

baffling enigma of the Jarkman, that same something that even in his childhood had drawn him to her portrait in Great Hall. He remembered asking Jody about the picture. About the unicorn. It was a magical beast, said Jody, forgetting to mention that it was not real; it could not be caught by the hunt but if a virgin called to it — ah, now, that was another matter. It would come and kneel to her, lay its head in her lap...Poor beast, he had thought, poor foolish beast. For then the hunt would close in and despatch it while she smiled, or looked away. Would Joanna look away...or would she smile?

He feared he knew the answer. He had seen the monster of hatred she harboured from God knew what grievance past; any man who lingered near her was doomed to feed it with strips of his hide...

The horse had slowed to a walk while he was preoccupied. He slackened rein and allowed him to graze, asking himself if he knew what he was doing. There could be no possible joy for him with Joanna. They were worlds apart; she would never look at him and to pursue her was courting sorrow.

He looked back the way he had come. Why not turn back towards Hatfield, take Bess under cover of darkness and strike north across the mud flats where water stood rankly in yellow floods, and on to the green distance beyond? There they would be safe. No one from Buxford would find them there, he had gone through London like a fox through water, leaving no trail to be followed. He would be free...wouldn't he? He sat gnawing his lip while the bay continued to graze on the sweet herbage lining the road. Already his mind was busy inventing excuses for going on to Islington: Nick and Joanna both owed him money — how would he be able to feed Bess, restore her condition, have her shod unless he claimed it? How could he —

He pulled himself up short, aware of his self-deception. Saracen was standing now at an angle to the road, reaching forward to browse on the bank, as likely to move in one direction as the other. Why not let him decide?

'Come up, boy!' He clucked, gave a touch of his heels...and as the horse started to move found himself turning its head towards Islington.

He smiled as he realised what he had done, remembering the night of the sword fight at the sign of the Cock. Even then, huddled among the logs watching the rain make ducks and drakes on the puddles, he had seemed to hear something whispering that he might never be free again.

He strode into the tavern at Islington as dusk was falling. 'Where's Jarkman Joe?'

'He said to say he's not here.'

Angel looked up at the soft sound of a door closing on the gallery running around three sides of the room, and the next moment was bounding up the stairs. He tried two doors before he could be stopped and burst in through a third. A tangle of elderly shanks and young plump ones thrashing among petticoats told him of his mistake and he withdrew in haste before his intrusion was noted. He stood back on the gallery and called.

'Joe, I know you're here. Come out!'

There was a moment's silence before the occupants of two other rooms looked out to see what was happening. One door remained obstinately closed. He went and pounded on it. 'Come out or let me in so we can talk. Afore I start some talking of my own —'

The bolts slammed back, the door was opened a fraction and a black-gloved hand wipped out and pulled him inside. 'Come in and hold your tongue!' Joanna's voice was hoarse with fury. 'How dare you force your presence upon me! God's teeth, I'll — I'll —'

'Yes, Master Jarkman?' He made an attempt at lightness. 'And what will you do, cry rape, scream for help like a woman...?'

He stopped, shocked by the effect of his ill-judged quip. She was backing away from him, her face ashen. He could see her hand groping behind her, searching for a weapon. Embarrassed, annoyed with himself he looked away.

'Dunna be daft,' he snapped. 'I only come for money. The money for my mare, like you promised.' What a fool he was! Now he had alarmed her, could sense that she was ready to lash out. 'You said I could seek you out when I run her to earth, now I have and I need the cross. Why did you send Nick Bodkyn to tell me nay?'

Already she was regaining her composure. She said frostily, 'I said you could seek me out and so you have. I made no promise about money. You said you wanted a horse: you may have Saracen.'

'I dunna want Saracen! Look, you don't understand, 'tis not just any horse I want, 'tis the one I lost. She's stolen, she's in a bad way — they're sending her to the knacker, did he tell you that?'

'I know very well that she is stolen; from Buxford and you are the thief. That is precisely why you cannot have her. You are the one, are you not?' She spoke quietly, reasonably, regarding him from under those winging brows; again he felt the dark waters rising, pulling him off his feet.

He stammered, 'I...you don't know that, you couldna. You're just guessing.'

Joanna shook her head. 'I have had word from Buxford. They are hunting a one-eyed warlock on a stolen mare. They have only to see you together. Are you trying to run your head into a noose?'

'What's it to you?'

'To me, nothing — except that when you're caught and hanged for murder it is but a step to me.'

'Murder?' he said faintly. So they had found Clem.

'Murder. A small matter of a man roasted to death. Your doing, I believe.'

He breathed again. It could not be Clem, drowned and waterlogged in the brewery. 'No doing of mine,' he said.

'Aye, so say you,' she said drily. 'I'd get rid of the eye patch all the same. And now, I have work to do.'

'You reckon you can dismiss me, just like that? Oh come, 'tis not so easy as all that. Think on, remember what I know about you — '

'Exactly! Which is why I cannot afford to have you caught. One turn of the screw and you would babble all you know.'

'You think I'd betray you, I'd never —' He stopped short. The words had burst out of him before he could stop them, making nonsense of his threat. 'I mean…not like that,' he finished lamely.

Joanna smiled wryly. 'I applaud your sentiments. However, with one foot pulped in the Boot who could blame you for singing to save the other? Be wise, Master Jackanapes, take Saracen and go.'

What she said was good sense, according to her lights. But he was past thinking rationally. All he could see was Bess in her wretched stable, waiting…waiting… 'I canna, you don't understand. I've known this mare since I were a little 'un, she's not just a horse, she's a friend…' He looked in appeal at the Jarkman. The magnificent eyes were faintly amused, a corner of her mouth twitching as though she were trying not to laugh. Enraged, he crashed both fists down on the table. 'Give me the cross afore I come and take it off you!'

'Hah! You'll get nothing of me but what I choose to give.'

'Give it then like you promised!' With a mighty effort he swallowed his anger, resorted to pleading. 'Look… look, only save my mare and I'll do anything — take her away from here, right away, you need never see me again —'

'No!' She thrust forward a face fired with emotion as raw and intense as his own. 'It is you who fail in understanding. Do you think I care if I see you again or not? Your fate is nothing to me, go hang for your folly if the whim takes you. But to fall and bring me down with you, that I cannot allow! I am sworn to avenge my father, not you nor a thousand mares shall stop me.'

Something had turned cold in Angel's inside. 'Avenge …who?'

'My father, Pengerran of Buxford. He who died Black John…'

Her voice seemed to come from a distance, fading as he stood bereft of speech, unable even to listen to what she was saying. He could only stare, watching her lips move while he failed to take in her words. Of late he had been shutting his mind to the rumour that had once seemed so exciting, eager to discount a possibility he could not bring himself to contemplate. Now he could blink it no longer and it hit him like a blow between the eyes. He had told himself the Lady Joanna was beyond his reach, of course he had — but it was only now that he tasted despair. In one bleak hour he had lost her. Lost Bess. Lost everything. Slowly he came back to an awareness of what she was saying. '...you'll not get my gold to undo me with for some broken-winded jade! Be off with you — try a magic spell, you call yourself a Whisperer...' Still he did not move. He had not lost everything, not yet. There was still Bess...and Joanna had what he needed to buy her back. She was mocking him now, her vivid face alight with amused disdain. '...a toad's bone is it not, for beguiling of horses...'

She was laughing at him, openly laughing in the face of his anguish! Something seemed to explode in his brain, flooding his vision with scarlet and blinding him to what he was doing as he hurled himself forward, aware only of the thud of the overturning table, the bite of a poniard, her body wiry and unfamiliar under his as entangled and struggling they crashed to the floor, his frustration and rage against her, against himself, against the underhand blow that fate had dealt him boiling over to engulf him. He hardly heard the voice of the taverner booming up the stairwell.

'Stow it, you up there, I want no bloodshed — '

'Jesu!' gasped Joanna, her face blanching as the knife went spinning from her hand. 'Have done!'

A violent hand seized Angel from behind, tearing him away just as his hand found the purse.

'Can't take my eyes off you for a minute!' said Nicholas pleasantly, slamming him backwards hard against a wall where he stood blinking, dazed by the impact. Nick turned to his employer. 'Is all well?'

Joanna regained her feet and straightened her doublet with an admirable air of command. 'Small thanks to you, Bodkyn! Where have you been? I bade you guard this oaf.'

'He made off with my horse, I had no recourse but to get me another.' He caught Angel's eye, laid a finger alongside his nose and jerked his head in the direction of the yard. 'A poor exchange, but we caught him up in the end.'

Angel did not wait to hear more. He was out and blundering down the stairs, pushing roughly past Marian who was on her way up calling, 'Nick! Nick, you've left your saddle out here for all to see — God's life, where's the fire?' as she was spun around in her tracks.

Ignoring her he ran on down and out into the yard and there, unbelievably, was Bess. Head down, weary, dispirited but safe, standing patiently where Nick had left her, his prigger's saddle light upon her back. Through a blur he saw her take a step towards him as he went to bury his face against her neck.

But as he stood fondling her ruined coat, holding away from her behind his back a hand from which blood poured freely, his thoughts were not solely of her. Instead they clung miserably about Joanna. He should have known, of course he should have known. Rumour had always whispered that Black John was the rightful lord of Buxford, and that being so it must follow that Joanna was his heir. If he had not seen it before it was because he was hiding from the truth. Now he leant against the comforting warmth of Bess while his mind fumbled with the shock of realisation, stunned by the cruel quirk of fate that had led him to love his sister in a way that no man might. He must go away, he told himself; take Bess and go far away where he would never see her again, far enough to escape her, find some other kind of life...soon. When Bess was recovered. Not yet but soon...His thoughts flew back to Joanna, to the look in her eyes when he had taunted her with rape; if some villain she had duped discovered her...

Bess moved restlessly, the scent of his wounded hand making her uneasy. He sucked blood from it, swearing softly under his breath, wrapped it tightly in a fold of his shirt and led her into the welcoming gloom of the stables. There he stood broodingly in shadow, his arms hugging his chest, unable to find words of comfort even for Bess. He had not known he was harbouring hope until he saw it lying dead.

From the upper window three pairs of eyes had witnessed the reunion. 'Ah, ain't it lovely,' sighed Marian in an excess of sentimentality. 'Fair brings tears to your eyes...'

'Very touching,' conceded Nicholas, tongue in cheek.

Only the Jarkman struck a discordant note. 'I find it obscene.' The tone was icy. 'Anyone might think it a lovers' meeting. Since you've foisted that disgusting animal on me, I charge you, Bodkyn — keep it out of sight!'

As they left the room Nick and Marian were laughing behind their hands: evidently the tales they had heard about the Jarkman were true. Anyone might think him a prey to jealousy — indeed they might!

When they had gone Joanna remained where she was, staring down into the empty yard. Now that Geordie was on his way with her letter the euphoria of success was giving way to something less enjoyable. Now began the waiting, the fruitless calculations by guesswork: so many days to reach the Fitznorths, so many to await their decision, so many to ride back. So many to allow for hold-ups. And then the final, the worst suspense of all: watching every hour for his arrival with the letter she both hoped for and dreaded. The letter which would seal her fate.

'There's more to marriage than four bare legs in a bed', so the saying went. As though that were the pleasurable part of marriage and the penalties lay elsewhere! Yet, please God, the boy could hardly have sap in him to do her any hurt; Fitznorth's first letter, which she had destroyed and replaced, had obliquely hinted as much. If Heaven were merciful he might even die on the journey down. It was not easy to imagine him grown into any semblance of a man. If she had ever really believed he would...

She turned abruptly from the window and busied herself with sharpening her quills. In her nervous agitation she broke one and swore roundly. A pox on that Jackanapes, coming back to dog her heels! She had enough on her mind without further complications with him and his wretched horse. Why, oh why, among all the men in London had she had to fall foul of one from Buxford! It was almost unbelievable — perhaps an ill omen, she thought with a superstitious chill. And that strange name, Angel. If he was really from Buxford why did she not remember it? Yet he must be to have known her from her portrait. That being so, she had to concede that his likeness to Pan might be merely unhappy coincidence...or was that an omen too? It was possible that in her judgement of him she was unjust. She shrugged. In suspicion was safety.

It was odd all the same, very odd. From time to time she found her thoughts straying back to the riddle of his name. Not that it was important, not important at all... but it gave her something to think about. Something to take her mind off those bare legs.

6

Sir Reginald Fitznorth read the scroll in his hands for the second time, and the lines of anxiety deepened about his mouth. He glanced up at the courier still standing before him. 'You may go. Go to the kitchens, take your rest till you're wanted.' As Geordie withdrew Sir Reginald turned to where his wife stood threading her needle in the light by the tall window. 'By God, Tilda, he's not to be put off. Sooner the better, that's what he says, get them together and ensure the line.'

Matilda looked over her shoulder with an expression faintly quizzical. A tall woman, not beautiful but blessed with an habitual calm, she had a bony face and large expressive eyes that looked sternly but with humour not far behind. 'What are we to do, then? Yield up the dowry?'

'You know that's impossible!' He left his chair and began restlessly pacing the room. 'It's mortgaged years ago, you know that as well as I do. Nay, we must think of something better than that. Come on, woman, think!'

What he meant was, You must think of something better. Matilda knew it, and smiled inwardly; her husband's bluster did not deceive her. He relied heavily on her judgement and she had the scars to prove it: her fingers were scorched and blackened from pulling his chestnuts out of the fire. She laid down the threadbare garment she had been patching and said mildly, 'You're a fool, Reggie. You know that, don't you? We should have told them the truth when it happened instead of trying to borrow time, now we're in a right kettle of fish. Come now, sit you down, no problems are solved by wearing a groove in the floor.'

'I want ideas, not lectures!' he grumbled, but he came and sat down. 'If I could just gain a little more time I could maybe raise it by selling some land...'

Matilda laughed. 'Who's to buy it? Nay, lad, we're all in the one boat, too close to the Border. If it is nae the Scots it's the mosstroopers, no sooner the stock goes out to graze than it's gone. Only a fool would buy land here who was nae born to it.'

'Yet Eustace would marry his stepdaughter to it.'

'Aye, poor lass! To be rid of her that's none of his own begetting. Nae doubt he hopes for a male heir of his own — which may the good Lord deny him, wicked man, for all the world knows he filched his lands from her father! Besides,' she added in a businesslike tone, 'if she's disinherited so is our son with her.'

'Our son's dead, woman, can you not get that through your head!'

'Aye,' she said calmly. 'Aye...but then, there's more ways of killing a dog than hanging it.' She stood up, a thoughtful expression on her face as her glance took in the fraying tapestries, the sparse furnishings of the room. 'Just think what we could do with the revenues from Buxford...' She walked slowly to the far end of the room where she stood with her back to him, her hands tightly clasped as if in prayer.

Sir Reginald would have given much to overhear her thoughts but he knew better than to interrupt them. To do so might be to lose a brilliant idea in embryo, but it was with difficulty that he bridled his impatience until she spoke. When she did it was to ask a question.

'When the betrothal ceremony took place here she would be what, eight or nine years old?'

'Oh, God's life, what's that to do with it?'

186

'Just answer me, Reggie. Nine years old at most?'

'Aye, thereabouts. Do you not recall how it angered you that she'd been sent so far with only servants?'

'I do, poor mite. But now we may well be glad of it. She was not of an age, you would say, to have noticed my pregnancy?'

Sir Reginald's jaw dropped as he stared at his wife. 'You mean...Young Jamie?' Her only answer was a faint lifting of an eyebrow. Slowly he shook his head...since the baby bridegroom died shortly before the birth of his namesake there had been no contact with Buxford...he swallowed. 'You're no' thinking we could pass him off as his brother?' He got up, took a few agitated steps and sat down again. 'But he's two years younger — and puir Wee Jamie, God rest his soul, was never normal, his recovery would have been a miracle. Nay, lass, Matilda, yon's a dangerous game to play!'

Matilda smiled, fingering her rosary. 'You would not deny the incidence of miracles? Even if sometimes they may need a little help...Remember, only Joanna ever saw him; who would take the word of a child against ours? The chaplain's away with his secret to the grave. No, there's but one snag that I can see: Young Jamie's all too normal and has his eye on the bonny wee Consett girl already. He'll need to be persuaded.'

Admiration, excitement, apprehension all warred in Sir Reginald's brain as he tried to weigh the hazards against the possibilities. At length he drew a long regretful breath between his teeth. 'Nay, hinny, it's that rash...' He shook his head again, still in doubt.

Matilda sat down and placidly picked up her mending. 'Aye, well, it's for you to say,' she said mildly. 'Nae doubt you'll tell me when you've thought of something better.'

Jamie Fitznorth raised his head from the inviting hollow between the new laundry maid's breasts as a shadow filled the doorway.

The steward coughed discreetly. 'Master Jamie — '

'Away, mon, can ye no see I'm occupied!'

187

'Your pardon, Master Jamie. Your father bids you attend him.'

'Bye and bye. Tell him I'm occupied — with affairs of the estate.' He squeezed from his captive a squeal followed by giggles.

The steward looked away. 'Oh, aye. And what will I tell your mother?'

Jamie swore under his breath. He had not had this lass before and it had taken him days to catch her. He could fob off his father with some excuse but his mother was another matter. He got to his feet reluctantly and straightened his clothing. 'What does she want?' he demanded crossly of the steward, brushed past him and was gone without waiting for an answer.

The steward glanced briefly at the flushed and dishevelled girl. 'Be about your business, ye witless whore!' He stumped off angrily, nursing his wrath; if yon wee ram was not tethered they would be lucky to have a maid left on her feet in six months' time.

Jamie too was nursing his wrath. Frustrated and disgruntled, he entered his parents' presence with a belligerent air.

'I'm told you're wanting me, so I'm here. But I've left unfinished business, pray you be brief.'

'So I see,' said his mother drily. 'Possess your soul in patience, we must speak of your marriage.'

'If it's Alison Consett the bairn's no mine, there's more than one slaked his thirst at that bonny bourne!'

His parents exchanged glances. Sir Reginald said, 'It is not Alison Consett. It is Joanna Pengerran.' He seemed to hesitate until a sharp look from Matilda nudged him on. 'Your betrothed.'

'My *what!*' He looked in amazement from one to the other. 'You're havering, Father! I'm no betrothed to any man's daughter to my knowledge.' He recovered himself and smiled jauntily, 'Kisses, no promises, I'm not daft, ye ken!'

'You mean,' said Matilda smoothly, 'you do not remember. Aye well, you were but a weanling at the

188

time.' She smiled with such composure that he could not doubt her word.

'But — but...' Suddenly his indignation found expression. 'Why have ye no told me, you should have told me before! And if I am betrothed, where's the ring, eh? Ye have to have a ring to be betrothed.' He was not certain of that but it was worth a try. He did not want a wife wished on him to curtail his activities, to set walls about his orchard when he was just beginning to taste its fruits. He was fifteen and a bonny young man...he wanted to make sport, not heirs...'Show me the ring!' he said defiantly.

'It is here,' said his mother gently, holding out her palm. 'It was over large on your hand and we feared you might lose it. It will fit you well enough now.'

He stared at it miserably. There was no denying it, no mistaking the thing; it lay in her palm like a shackle, the slim golden half of a gemmel ring. 'Aye, well...I see,' he said unhappily. 'And the other half?'

'Is on Joanna's hand.'

Jamie could think of nothing more to say. An uneasy silence fell on the three of them. At last Sir Reginald cleared his throat and said with an attempt at heartiness, 'Aye, well...you could fare worse, Young Jamie. She was a beautiful child as I remember — not just bonny, mind. Beautiful! Black hair...and the whitest skin I ever saw, aye, that she did. Good family and a handsome dowry — ' He stopped, pulled up short by Jamie's expression.

'So that's it! Aye, now we have it — a dowry! You sold me in my cradle for a dowry — '

'James!' Matilda's voice rang out. 'You'll not address your father so, not in my presence. Marriages, all marriages, are arranged for the good of the family and we each have our duty to the rest. This is yours and you will do it and we shall hear no more complaining.'

Jamie looked at his father. But Sir Reginald refused to meet his eye; instead he rose and stood by the window, his back to the room. 'Your bride is in retreat at

189

St Anselm's Priory north of London. She awaits you there, thence to travel to Buxford for the final ceremony.'

Jamie looked again at his mother. He could find nothing more to say. He bowed to them both and withdrew from the room in silence.

When he had gone, Sir Reginald said heavily, 'By God, Matilda, what have we done?'

His wife squared her shoulders. 'Done, Reggie? The only thing possible. We've done as well for him as we did for his brother, have we not?'

'Aye...aye. But he's not happy, hinny. He'd not do it of his own will.'

Matilda came to stand beside him. 'No, he'd not. And would you have married me or I you if we'd not been forced? I well remember you shouting at your father that he'd picked you a bony brood mare.' She smiled at his shamefaced look.

'Nay, Tilda, I — you were never meant to hear that.'

'Never mind, my dearie, you've made up for it since. And so will he, you mark my words.'

'Nay, lass...we should have told him the truth, given the choice to him.'

'Aye, maybe we should. But he would not have done it. Think on, Reggie — she's ten years older, twenty-five if she's a day. He'll be lucky to get an heir before he's widowed. But when he is, he'll be free to make a choice of his own.'

Sir Reginald brightened. 'Aye, that he will, I hadnae thought of that.' He put an arm about his wife's strong shoulders. 'But he'll never find a brood mare the equal of his dam.'

When Jamie left his parents' presence he went straight to the stables and mounted the first horse he saw. His anger was returning as the numbness of shock wore off, he wanted movement, speed, an illusion of freedom. He kicked his startled steed into action, out through the barbican and over the moors at a gallop, on, on, the wind

190

streaming through his hair and blowing tears of anger from his eyes, on and still on until the horse was panting and flecked with foam...at last he knew he had to stop if it were not to die under him and leave him stranded. He threw himself off and lay pounding furious fists into tear-drenched heather...someone, he promised himself, someone was going to pay dearly for this day's work.

Braw Geordie, on the other hand, was smiling as at first light the next morning he sat his horse while the gates were raised to let him out and on his way. To Buxford in the far-off south of England was a long and tiring ride, but he was not daunted by it; he enjoyed being a courier, spent most of his life in the saddle, had laughingly claimed to have been born in it. Not for him the peat-smoked pleasures of hall and kitchen, give him the broad heath and the sparkling air, the wind that came in singing off the sea. And the freedom to indulge the passing whim, to conquer and pass on...ah, yes! That bonny wee thing at Islington, the one with hair the colour of bracken. Aye, there were not too many like that to be had for the asking. He would be looking out for her on his way to London. And she had said she would wait...he was laughing as the gate was raised, laughing as he kicked his horse to a canter, out through the archway and down the motte to the moorland track that he himself had beaten. It took him in an eastward curve along the coastal edge, skirting the lowland pastures where marauding bands of mosstroopers were a likely addition to the hazards of the journey, the Grahams and others like them, villains without mercy who swept down from the craggy Cheviots to pillage their neighbours' livestock, cutting down anything and anyone who stood in their way. Geordie patted the hilt of his weapon and urged his mount forward; he was glad of his strength that had earned him the name 'Braw Geordie', glad of the tough leather jerkin he was wearing over his doublet. But he would be still more glad to be over the Tyne, past Durham and down into the peaceful vale of

York. 'Aye, we'll take it easy then, lad,' he murmured, leaning forward over the horse's neck. 'Good taverns for me and warm stabling for thysen.'

The light was growing fast now, bounced off the mirror of the sea somewhere away to his left, gulls soaring and screaming overhead in their ceaseless search for food, rising in their hundreds from the grey fastness of the cliffs to wheel and glitter like snowflakes in the first shafts from the sun. Their noise was so strident that he did not once notice the other sounds. The agitated lowing of cattle, the hoofbeats of horses other than his own, the shouts of men...When at last he turned in the saddle and saw them he stifled an oath, kicked frantically at his horse's sides so that the animal shot forward into a gallop, urged on by the alarm in his rider's voice. To turn and fight, Geordie knew, would be to throw his life away...and he very soon knew that he had left it too late to escape.

7

'Must you keep chipping at that stick,' said Joanna distractedly, pausing briefly in her agitated pacing, 'It maddens me.'

'Whittling,' he corrected her mildly, putting away the knife. 'They reckon it calms the blood. Better sharpening wood than sharpening your tongue.'

Joanna stopped pacing and leaned back against the edge of a manger, the heels of her hands pressed to her eyes. 'Perhaps I should try it,' she said wearily. 'Dear God, will he never come.'

She hasn't slept again, thought Angel, wishing there were something he could do. More than a month had passed since their spat over Bess at Islington, and in that time he had scarcely seen her. But from his roost in the hayloft where he slept he had watched through a chink her light burning far into the night, seen her restless shadow pass across and across the window and known her to be in a torment of anxiety.

They had returned to the Cock three weeks ago. The glib tongue of Nicholas had achieved an uneasy truce between them, and it was through his agency that for reasons he could only guess at he had found himself employed to tend the Jarkman's horses: Saracen, Fearless, a strong young gelding recently purchased for Nick to ride — and Young Bess. Whether she had really been

193

smuggled in unrecognised that day, or whether Nick had deliberately lied for the sake of peace he had no way of knowing, and wished fervently that he had found out while he had the chance, for Nick had disappeared without warning before he could be questioned on the subject. There was little he could do now but count himself lucky to be reunited with Bess in a way that also kept him near Joanna.

He had long ceased pretending to himself that he could break away: he knew without a shred of hope that he had left it too late, that if the opportunity came he would not take it. Joanna was on his mind day and night, Joanna good or bad, right or wrong. In vain he reminded himself of their early antagonism, her churlish behaviour and unprovoked attacks; his heart made excuses faster than his mind could frame indictments. It was fear that bred hatred, fear and mistreatment, he had known that since he first had dealings with horses, but even if he hadn't it would have made no difference. It had always been a mystery to him that Kate could accept the harshness of Clem without rancour; now he had stumbled upon the magic that made it so. Try as he would to dwell on Joanna's faults he could no longer see them, dazzled as he was by her unlikely beauty housing so intrepid a spirit. Despairingly he told himself he should be proud to own such a sister: beautiful, courageous, accomplished...Still the sad ache persisted. It was not as his sister that he wanted her.

Now only Bess and Saracen remained in his care, for the courier on whom so much depended had failed to return from the North and Nick had been despatched on Fearless to see what he could discover, while Marian continued her vigil at Islington. Bess had been quick to respond to good food and clean stabling; already she began to shine again and he could well have ridden her away. But still he remained, watchful for Joanna, feeding his guilty passion on occasional glimpses of her taut face as she passed the stables on her way to somewhere else.

Today, he had seen her striding across the yard towards him with a mixture of dread and longing, his heart in his mouth, fearing she had finally woken to the presence of Bess and come to banish them both. But she had walked straight past him, turned and padded back again, pacing the restricted space like a caged animal. And he, after thinking of her so long, so intensely, could find no word to say. Instead he took up a saddle and moved towards Saracen.

'No...no.' She spoke absently, then turned towards Bess. 'I'll try this one.'

For an hour he had waited on thorns. But when she returned she was smiling. 'A nice mare, you have judgement. I shall keep her for my use. Her coat's growing out,' she added. 'You had best renew the dye.' With a glance at his expression she laughed; not in disdain but with a mischievous warmth that enchanted him. 'Did you really take me for such a fool?'

Lost for words he had stammered and blushed, and even as he moved forward into her light it was extinguished. She resumed her restless pacing and he was cast again into outer darkness, kicking himself for a blockhead. Now, seeing her so distraught, he wished he knew how to help her. 'He'll come,' he said at last. 'Or Nick will. One of them, then at least you'll know.'

Since Nick's departure she had prowled about in a nervous frenzy unable to settle anywhere. Now the eyes she turned on him held such anguish that he felt a stab of jealousy. 'And suppose Nick too has gone, deserted me, betrayed me?'

'He wouldna!' he said shortly, praying it was true. 'Nobody's betrayed you, 'tis just something's gone amiss.'

Joanna shook her head. 'I should have stayed at Islington instead of trusting to others. How do I know they have not taken my gold and gone laughing up their sleeves — he and that strumpet, that tuppenny-halfpenny whore!'

'Marian wouldna betray you.' Nick maybe; not Marian

195

of the warm heart and disintegrated morals. 'She's a good enough girl, just never had no luck.'

'Indeed?' She withered him with a look. 'And since you cannot tell a good girl from a whore, who then has played the traitor — is it you?' She was on the move again, pacing, pacing, her hands punishing one another. 'But of course it's you, who else...' Suddenly she stopped, turned to face him. 'The Patrico! You are in league, are you not? You were with him, that night when you came with the monkey. What have you told him, speak!'

This was too much. 'Nothing!' he burst out. 'Why would I tell the Patrico what's no concern of his? I'm not in league, I anna hardly seen him from that day to this. Anyways he'd never believe it, he reckons you're some sort of...of...'

'I am well aware of what he told you, it is what I pay him for!' Joanna's lips compressed to a bitter line.

'You *pay* him?' Despite his new sophistication, he was shocked. 'You pay a priest!'

'He's no priest!' Her laugh was a short sharp bark. 'Scullery boy at Southwark Priory, he picked up the cant from the monks before they fled. Now he poses, abuses the confessional...we all end in paying the Patrico to keep our secrets dark, the follies of others are his merchandise.'

Angel caught his breath, recalling how close he had come to confiding in the plausible old villain. 'I could wish he didna know about you,' he said with feeling.

'Doubtless!' She laughed again and tossed her head. 'Then you could sell me to him for a handsome price. Alas, Master Luckless, you have missed the market!'

Angel felt the hot blood surge up his neck. 'You dunna trust me no more'n you do him!'

'And why should I, tell me that!'

'Because I'm the only friend you got.' He did not know what had prompted him to say that. The words seemed to have crystallised from the air instead of coming from his mind. And yet hearing them, he recognised the truth.

'A pox on all friends!' Her voice was jagged with

nerves, as if tears were not far away. 'There's more peril in them than in enemies!' She turned her back on him and stood, arms folded, hugging her elbows.

'Joanna...' He was filled with compassion. He knew what it was to feel every man's hand against you. And somewhere within that thorny shell lived a different Joanna, he knew it, one who crouched and trembled behind her defences...'Jo, listen — you have to trust somebody some time or there's no happiness in life.' She was silent. Only her head moved a little higher. He tried again. 'There's good as well as bad in folk. You got to give them a chance.'

'A chance to undo me!'

'No! A chance to love you — ' For a moment he thought he had reached her. Then she turned on him, her face a mask.

'I have told you before, I want no love. As for happiness it's a myth, a rainbow, there is no such thing — '

'I believe there is.'

'Then you're naïve enough for anything! Doubtless you believe in fairies, too — Horse Whispering, hah! You'll be telling me next you've seen the unicorn!'

'No!' Smarting he retaliated, lashing out at the spitting hell-cat appearing without warning in his darling's boots. 'No, I anna! But I'll know what to say to him if ever I do — I'll say, "Go kneel to Joanna, she'll be a virgin all her life!"'

For a time without dimensions they glared at each other, their eyes locked. Then the haughty face seemed to crumple. With a strangled sound suspiciously like a sob, she turned and ran from the place.

When she had gone he remained where he was while his anger drained as suddenly as it had risen. He could not believe that he had said what he had, had not known himself capable of spite. And so stupid, so pointless! Having won himself a glimpse inside the shell how had he used it — to reach in and savage her. Unable to be still, he left the stable and went out to walk off his agitation. But the crowded smelly streets lacked the soothing balm of

Buxford; before long he was back more hot and troubled than before. Armed with a tankard of ale he climbed the ladder to his loft to sort out his thoughts in peace.

As his face came level with the hay he saw her: lying crouched with her head on her arms against a pillow of hay, her dark hair tumbled softly about her face, so still that she could have been asleep. As he hesitated she stirred, raised her head a fraction.

'I brought ale,' he said humbly and went to kneel beside her, offering the tankard.

She sat up slowly, not meeting his eyes, and her first words surprised him. 'I am sorry. I abuse you without cause. You are right, I will be a virgin all my life.'

Shamefaced, he said, 'I shouldna have said that, I don't know what come over me.'

She shrugged. 'It's true enough. God knows I'd sell my soul to be sure of it.'

As she took the tankard he saw how her hands shook. 'I reckon some man must have treated you ill,' he said, surprised at his own audacity. He felt a dark rage building in him against the unknown who had left her with such a scar.

'I thought it was you,' she said. 'You look so like him...I could not be sure I was wrong till I heard your name.'

'But you dunna know my name, I never tell it.'

'At Buxford they know it. Angel, is it not?' She took a draft from the tankard and offered it to him. 'Even then I was doubtful. But then at last I remembered your mother.'

'My mother!' His heart gave a painful lurch. 'You knew my mother, what was she like —' Almost at once he wished he had not asked. Who could guess what horrors might be uncovered?

'A serving girl. She went to be hanged on the day I ran away. That's all I recall.' As if she had sensed his disappointment she added, 'She was much attached to you, I remember that.'

'Much attached', he thought; she could not even bring herself to speak the word 'love'...He masked his sadness with a smile. 'I know you dunna really remember. But 'tis nice you said it.'

'Oh yes, I do!' She spoke vehemently, then checked herself. 'I envied you.' She smiled wryly at his amazement and lay back on the hay, picking straws from a strand of her hair. 'The sole luxury of the poor,' she said musingly, 'the cherishing of their children. I suppose I was jealous even then.'

'Jealous?' He furrowed his brow, thinking of Buxford Place with its sumptuously appointed rooms, its long gallery for exercise in wet weather, its fine silks and tapestries, the banquets of rich foods and foreign wines, its prosperous acres...

Joanna turned to look at him, her expression faintly amused. 'You did not imagine that the children of great families are cherished? They are used like pawns in the great game of power, bought and sold to consolidate estates. Be thankful you're a nobody; Master Jackanapes may marry for love-liking if he please.'

He looked away. If only he could...'What about you?' He dreaded the answer, did not know why he had asked.

'I?' She tossed off a short hardbitten laugh. 'I escaped too late, my fate was already sealed.'

'You're...not married?' The thought of her bedded with another turned him sick.

'Contracted. Half married in my ninth year, and to a cradled babe. Cradled...and monstrous!' Her hand moved to cover her mouth, as though by stopping the words she could stop the memory.

It was a moment before he could speak. 'Monstrous... how, monstrous?

Dumbly, face averted, she shook her head.

'Tell me,' he pulled at her wrists, trying to make her face him. 'Joanna, *tell!*'

The eyes she turned on him brimmed with anguish, wrenching his heart. Her voice came barely above a whisper. 'Its head...a great pumpkin lolling on a broken stem...the eyes vacant, unlit...' And she retreated again into her private hell.

He drew a breath of relief. He had seen animals born like that; they never lived. 'If that's why you run away —'

'No!' Joanna straightened herself, lifted her chin. 'No. That's why I am going back.' She spoke now with the calmness of courage, and of resignation. 'It is the only way I can avenge Black John.'

Angel frowned. 'Look...I dunna understand. Are you telling me you want this marriage, that all these letters going back and forth are to bring it about?'

'I need it for safe conduct back to Buxford.'

'But why! Why go back when you've been hid away so long?'

Her eyes were hard as jet. 'To kill the usurper. For justice. For vengeance!'

'Mother of Heaven!' he breathed. This was madness. One slight girl against an army...he trembled for her. 'You'd never get past the guards, they'd cut you to cat's-meat! Send someone else — send Nick, he'll do anything for cross.'

'No! I am sworn, I will do it myself. And besides,' she added on a more practical note, 'I must be there at his death to claim my inheritance.'

So that was it, after all. He felt a plunge of disillusionment at the taint in her motive, as if an oily streak had blackened the bright flame of her valour: it was not for honour alone that she was ready to kill. But then, the avarice and pride of the Pengerrans were legendary; he should have been prepared for it. He shook his head.

'You do not understand, how should you? Lord Eustace is an evil man, more wicked than you know. He betrayed my father and seized his lands, reduced my mother to the lifeless thing you see.'

'And you?'

'He thought to be rid of me by sending me into the northern wilds to make a ludicrous match. I was only a child and did not comprehend, it was all an excitement to me. But if you could have seen his vicious face when I returned unharmed...In less than a year he had disposed of my father and I knew I was in peril of my life. I took refuge with the rats in the gutter and I have lived there ever since.' She dropped her head moodily on her arms. 'Do not ask what he has done to me.'

I can see, he thought; all too well, maybe better than you. 'How did he get your father's lands? And your mother, how did she come to wed him, she was surely grown by then?'

'Abduction,' she said shortly. 'My father, not knowing that, could not forgive her. He thought she had betrayed him.' She raised her head and looked at him with a gleam of the old suspicion. 'So many questions, you want to know too much. Perhaps you are not naïve but very clever after all, what game do you play with me?'

He knew of no way to answer that. He settled back in the hay beside her. 'Too late to worry now,' he said. 'You might as well tell me all.'

8

'I never knew him, my true father,' said Joanna. 'I saw
him only once, a great black-maned lion of a man bellowing out his rage in the hall below while I listened
concealed behind the gallery screen. I do not know if he
ever saw me. From my earliest days he was absent, my
mother and I alone with my grandam in the castle in
Cornwall. Pengerran it was called, I remember that, and
the pride of bearing its name. In my mind there are only
fragments, like half-forgotten dreams; the gaunt stone
rooms, the narrow windows where the wind moaned
softly in summer and screamed in winter, always carrying the scent of salt water, of storm wrack and thundercloud. One memory is of standing on a battlement in
the buffeting of a gale, excited because I was to see
the sea, and held between two women to keep me from
blowing over the edge. They were discoursing above my
head, of the pity it was I had not been a son; I listening,
straining to understand as they spoke of a death remote
in distant France. "Ah, see! She weeps," they said. But I
did not know it was my father then; it was only the wind
that filled my eyes with tears. The real tears were to
follow soon enough.' She turned her head restlessly.
'What possessed my mother to entertain Eustace at
that time I'll never know. Perhaps she was deceived in
him, knowing him my father's kinsman. God knows

what he offered her — care, help with the estates in the absence of her lord, support in her widowhood, who can tell? But from the moment he crossed the threshold darkness fell.

'He had brought with him a retinue like an army. They filled the place, roistering and drinking, brawling with the menservants and terrorising the women. My grandam, poor creature, took to her bed and died, so they said, of grief. And then my mother...' She turned to Angel the face of a bewildered little girl, the eyes pleading, as if she hoped even now to be offered an explanation. 'She disappeared, vanished from my sight. I could not find her — could not — not anywhere...yet I knew she must be there. In the night I would hear the voices, hers beseeching, his like the roaring of a bull, "He is dead, I tell you! I had it from the messenger, you are free!" But if she was free, why didn't she come to me...Once I heard her cry out in pain. I broke away from the servants and ran searching in the darkness along the corridors, over the cold stones on my naked feet until I found a door high up in the tower where her voice seemed to be. I beat upon it, weeping. "Go away!" she cried, but I could not, I clung there shivering and crying and beating at the wood, listening for the feet of those who would come to take me away.

'Suddenly the door burst open and there stood Eustace, towering over me, livid and terrifying. "You will see your mother again when she is mine!" he bellowed. Then he grasped my arm. "No, better — persuade her to it!" And he thrust me in through the doorway. She was lying on the ground, bruised and cut about the face, her hair dishevelled and her clothing torn. She started up and gathered me to her but he ripped me from her arms with an ugly triumphant laugh. "Here's a key shall unlock you, madam!"

'I remember well those words, not understanding what they meant. From that time on it was I who was beaten and starved, she who watched, bound in her chair. "Be brave...be brave!" she exhorted me while I sobbed and suffered, hating her, fearing him, betrayed and helpless and comprehending nothing.' She fell silent among her darkening thoughts.

Angel waited, his eyes fixed on a spider spinning a cobweb between the rafters. Afraid lest a look from him should break Joanna's thread. At last she went on.

'She married him. That evil man, that monster became her husband. "This is your father," she told me calmly. "Tomorrow we set forth for Buxford." I could not forgive what I saw as her treachery. My punishments ceased but at four years old I failed to see the connection; only later I realised, when riper years brought me to knowledge of such things.' She turned her burning gaze on Angel. 'And the real villainy was, my father was not dead. He escaped his French captors and came home, and Eustace had him hanged as a common criminal! *Now* do you see why I must kill him myself? Such hatred as mine must be purged! I need to drive home the blade, watch him shuddering, feel his blood gush hot over my hands —'

'Oh dunna, dunna!' he cried involuntarily, pulled her unthinkingly into his arms. 'Dunna even think it, such thoughts are not for you!'

For an instant she was still as if frozen. Then she spoke, her voice muffled against his shoulder. 'You forget yourself.'

He released her and drew away. 'Your pardon,' he mumbled. 'I shouldna done that.'

'No, you should not,' she said icily. She drew back to regard him with disfavour and added accusingly, 'I have thought before you looked on me too warmly. I warn you, it is not to be considered.'

'I never!' he lied, in dread of exposure. 'Believe me, trust me, I never as much as thought —'

'Indeed? Yet you do more than I pay you for, do you not? You mend my harness, you polish my boots — oh yes, you do! These things are done without my bidding and no one claims the credit, deny it if you can.' He was silent, the hot blood scalding his cheekbones.

'As I thought, it is clear that you hope for other rewards. "Trust me", say you — hah!'

Confused and shaken, he blundered disastrously. 'You can trust me, I swear it — God's truth, how else could it be when I'm your brother!' No sooner was it out than he wished himself dead. The pain of putting it into words was like the pain of telling the bees of a loved one's death; it put the weight of a gravestone on the faint forlorn hope that somehow the impossible might happen and he would find it was not true. He had not wanted to say it aloud, to give voice to that finality even to himself. Now it had been wrung from him in a moment of weakness and he could not unsay it; his love was lost, and he had told the bees.

'My *brother*?' Joanna was staring at him in a mixture of amusement and disdain. 'You're no brother of mine! I'm no tinker's brat, I merely took refuge with them.'

Tinkers...what was she talking about? Out of his desolation he dragged the words. 'I mean...you said Black John's your father. He sired me too.' He turned away, unable to look at her. The next moment her laughter flayed him.

'Your father — hah! Don't delude yourself, Master Jackanapes, *my* father was John Pengerran. Yours was a common tinker who raped your mother in the woods.'

Stunned, he protested, 'You're making it up!'

'Am I so? You don't really imagine you could be kin to me —'

'Why not!' Wincing from the lash he hit out. 'You say that because you're ashamed to own me, you got a spiteful tongue and like to use it!'

Joanna coloured. 'I told you too roughly,' she said crossly. 'You took me by surprise. It's true, just the same, Black John was not your father. Now I suppose you're going to sulk.'

He pulled himself together, tried to speak reasonably. 'Better to know the truth, if truth it is.' It was all too tempting to snatch at straws, and his emotions were already too ravaged to stand a reversal. ''Tis just...I don't see how you could know.'

'I do know. What is strange is that I did not see it before; I knew your father, I knew your dam, yet it was only of late that I fitted the two together. You still don't believe me? Listen: on the day I escaped from Buxford a tinker was waiting at the gate, asking for a girl who had come to us with a babe in arms. I was a frightened child in a ferment to be gone, I told him the little I knew, that they had taken her to be hanged; together we fled to the greenwood, he and I and his two sons. And there I stayed.'

'Well, but…that dunna mean he was my father.'

'He told me so, though at the time I paid little heed. I was curious to know what he wanted of her and he said he was the father of her child. It was only when I heard your name that the pieces fell together; I remembered that she called her baby Angel.'

They both fell silent, each within his thoughts. Then he said, 'How did you come to take me for another?'

'He must have been your brother, he was as like you as two peas. Though Heaven forfend you should be quite as like…'

He shook his head, trying to come to terms with conflicting emotions. ''Tis all so…so…' Scraps of information chased each other without apparent connection. Would he ever know the rest?

He felt a light touch on his arm and looked up to see her smiling. 'Poor Master Jackanapes, have I shattered your dreams?'

He made an effort to respond. ''Tis not that, just I keep changing sires.' He smiled ruefully. 'And I was proud of Black John, even if mebbe it was wrong.' It had been an unwelcome jolt to find him replaced by a tinker, his birth the product of an ugly assault. And then, he had lost his one link with Joanna. Tenuous as it was, unwelcome as it had seemed, it was nonetheless a link. And now it was gone.

'Not wrong,' she said soberly. 'I too am proud.' Then she laughed. 'Come, don't be downcast. Did you really want such a great villain for your sire, a murderer by all accounts and dispossessed of his lands? There is much to be said for your tinker, he had a good heart beneath him grime.'

'If you know any good of him, tell me. All you've said is he raped my mother, that gives me little joy.' Was that why she feared him, he wondered in a sudden flash of insight?

'So he said.' She shrugged. 'He never once molested me, but he was old when I knew him. The boys said he had a wild temper but I never saw it, he seemed to me a sad little man. I remember one night when the others were asleep and he was huddled over his fire, I woke and saw him crying. No sound, only tears pouring down his face. He saw me looking and turned his back; I never knew why he wept.'

Angel was silent; when he looked she too seemed lost in thought, gazing at a beam of sunlight filtered through a chink where motes of dust danced ceaselessly as if trapped. At last she spoke.

'He gave me his protection, such as it was, although he owed me nothing. He thought I'd been kind to his girl, nothing would shake him from his belief. Perhaps he needed to think it, who knows...' She spread her hands. 'I do not say he looked after me, he would not have known how. He taught me his own rough trade and made me work — you see that? A burn from hot metal — but he kept me alive. Without him I would not have survived.'

In the pause that followed he said, 'I'm glad he was good to you. In his fashion.'

She smiled faintly in the gloom. 'Good...yes. I know now what those sour crusts must have cost him. Then I was resentful of my hunger, sullen and tearful as I trudged behind the cart, I who had been the cosset of Buxford! Not a cherished child, you understand, but livestock to be tended for future use; yet I had not known it was possible to live without servants, warmth, clothing or even shelter. I had much to learn. I only knew how much after he died.' She averted her face. 'His end was easy, compared with some. He just...stopped breathing.'

So, the tinker too was dead. He seemed doomed to

discover his forebears only when it was too late. After
a while he prompted gently, 'What did you do then?'

She swallowed, gave a little flick of her head as though
she were shaking something off. 'I was destitute. I joined
up with a band of Moon Men and travelled with them,
trading their horses and sleeping under the stars. But
they never accepted me, they wouldn't teach me their
language. And the men spurred like fighting cocks, I
scarce could fend them off, with the women so jealous I
sometimes saw murder in their eyes. In the end I had to
run for my life.

'I was older by then; I had seen a jarkman's work at a
fair, I knew how to write and with time and diligence I
came to be Jarkman Joe. I had taken on man's apparel
already, to keep what's mine my own.'

'Oh, Jo...'he sighed. He had been all too right about the
terrified colt. Ill-broken, mistreated...and yet, wonder-
fully, the spirit remained unbroken. More than that, he
knew that here at last he had found the real Joanna. He
said softly, 'Small wonder you're afeared of men.'

'I'm not!' Her response was too swift, too edged with
apprehension.

'You are, lovely.' He reached for her hand and felt it
begin to tremble. 'See, you're even afeared of me.'

'I fear no man.' As if to prove her point she left the hand
where it was. Its trembling increased.

He took it in both of his. She averted her eyes as if
shying away from the sight. 'I have warned you not to
look at me like that.'

She was drawing back from him, trying to pull free; he
knew he should release her but he could not make himself.
"Tis all harmless, I promise you —'

'It is not harmless!' She turned to glare at him like a
hunted vixen. 'I should have let you believe you were my
brother.' She snatched back her hand and hid it behind
her, scuttling away from him across the hay. 'I see I was a
fool to undeceive you!'

Dismayed, he stammered, 'No — no, look — I'll be your
brother if that's what you want —'

'I want nothing of you, do you hear me, nothing! I ask no favours nor grant none —'

'But I'm asking nothing of you! Not even pay — I'll see to the horses for nothing, just my victuals...'

'Just so! And who but a brother would be content with that? A brother, or a charlatan — or an angel indeed, not blessed or cursed with the natural parts of a man!'

'Oh, stop it, stop, you're talking lunacy!' Smarting from injustice, he lost his head. 'You think every man you see's lusting after you, well let me tell you you're wrong! Who do you think wants a shrew in doublet and hose with nought of a woman about her...' he stopped. He was doing it again. Why did he find himself saying these things when his heart spoke so differently! Why could they never talk without quarrelling, must it always be like this? 'Oh, Joanna...Joanna...' Contrition flooded him.

Joanna had collected herself, her fear succeeded by the coldest kind of fury. 'Do not speak to me.'

'I shouldna said that, forgive me. I'll keep out of your sight among the horses, watch over you from here —'

'No, no, *no!*' She had been halfway to the ladder. Now she stopped, turned to face him. She spoke slowly, loudly, clearly, as if he were an idiot child. 'I do not want you to. I do not want you to serve me, watch over me, polish my boots or anything else without my leave. I will not be in your debt, do you understand?'

'But, Joanna —'

'But nothing! Be silent, I will hear no more!' Before he could find words, she was gone.

For a long time after the scrape of her boots on the ladder had faded into silence, Angel remained where he was; brooding in the hay-scented warmth of the loft, hearing and not hearing the whisper of mice, the scufflings of martins under the eaves, the soft sounds of horses in the stable below, the occasional clatter of hooves as one was led out into the yard. It was useless to go after Joanna in the dark mood that had come on her so suddenly. She was one on her own, unpredictable as summer rain; one minute telling him the story of her life, the next...he sighed. If only she were really a colt. It was simple with horses, mingle your breath with theirs and you were friends for life, you needed no Horseman's Word to tell you that. If only it were that easy with Joanna! He smiled at the vision it conjured in his mind. Then caught his breath at the thought of that mouth, those heavy-lashed eyes so close to his...

He dropped his head on his arms in a sudden wave of depression. Joanna might not be his sister but she was as remote from him as ever. He was alone; adrift like a fallen leaf in a forest, forever lost to the unseen tree that had grown him. His kinship with Black John had been a myth; he owed him no loyalty to justify involvement in a plot to avenge his death. It was hard enough to see what Joanna owed him, begotten and forgotten as she was; yet loyal she was, and committed, and he could only follow. The time for turning back was long since past.

As he lay brooding in the poppy-rich hay a new thought floated to the surface of his mind. The barrier he had thought insuperable had vanished like dew in the sun. Whatever happened now was up to him; and in the gloom that had descended on him a spark glowed and prospered like a glow-worm in the dark. He closed his eyes to savour its warmth...the homely sounds of the stable soothed him like a lullaby.

When he woke the light coming through the chink was tinged with the rose of sunset. He stretched luxuriously, then made his way down towards the tavern for his evening meal. Bess blew him a greeting as he passed, and he noticed that Saracen was missing. His stomach gave a warning snatch. He strode on into the tavern. Joanna was not there. He bounded up the stairs to her room. The door was locked and his knocking produced a face unfamiliar and not best pleased to see him.

'Looking for the Jarkman?' boomed Joshua's voice from below.

'Where is he?' He leaned over the gallery rail. 'Have you seen him?'

Joshua smiled unpleasantly, swept two hens off a table

and sat down to devour a squab pie. 'Gone without you, has he? Best get after him then. He's paid up and gone this hour past and took his belongings with him.'

'But his mare's still in the stable...'

'That's right, he took the bay. Paid her livery for another month and said he'd send for her. If he don't I can always sell her, I suppose.'

Angel stood still, feeling that his bones had melted. He clutched at the gallery rail, his brain whirling madly. Bess was in good fettle now, ridable and Joanna's preferred mount. Why then had she taken the bay and left her behind? The answer when it came struck him cold. Joanna had set out alone for Buxford. And with God only knew what madness in her mind.

9

Joanna reined in at the fields about Lincoln's Inn and asked herself where she was going.

The prime object of her flight, to put distance between herself and Angel, had been achieved; she was not sure if it was he whom she feared or herself, only that she had to put herself beyond the reach of something half glimpsed that she sensed she could not control. She knew too, that she had done him an injustice, that in their early encounters she had made a fool of herself; this knowledge alone would have been enough to make his presence unwelcome, but it had to be more than embarrassment or chagrin to disturb her so deeply that she could not remain where he was. Damn him! she thought, damn and confound him for disrupting her plans! Now that she had taken her patronage from the Cock she would have to find new headquarters; and, more urgently, having left her lodgings she must decide where to sleep tonight.

She should have got rid of that mare and him with it, why hadn't she! What was it about him that disconcerted her, this tinker's son with his unsettling knack of getting under her guard. She had thought herself an oyster with shell tightly clenched, safely armoured against the buffeting of the sea. No one had ever been allowed to prise it open. Yet the edge of his blade was already in her shell...

Enough! she thought; she was safely away, and was

never going back. So where now? She squared her shoulders, took a deep draught of the summer evening air. She could ride south along the Strand with its palaces, past the Abbey of Westminster to the horse ferry and be on her way to Buxford; but already the threat of sunset was beginning to burn the edges of clouds piled high on the skyline pierced by the steeple of St Giles. If she pushed on now she would arrive near dawn, with nowhere to hide until dark; better to arrive at nightfall with a plan at her fingertips, primed with whatever tidings Bodkyn might bring, and if she could have stayed on at the Cock —

The sound of a hoofbeat behind her turned her head round in alarm. But no, it was not Angel. He had not followed her nor would he, with any luck. Not for nothing had she left behind his precious mare as decoy. Strange how he had traced it after all, and in the very place he had been convinced of. Perhaps there was something in horse whispering after all...

Nonsense! Far more likely he and Bodkyn and the Patrico had been up to some mischief together, plotting to retrieve the mare and re-sell her, a variant of the monkey trick the Patrico worked so successfully. She had seen that hapless monkey poisoned, sold and recovered countless times. Guido sold it in the market, dosed just enough to make it fall sick; the Patrico marked out the buyer and called 'by chance' at his door begging alms, offered to take the creature to one he knew of who could cure it and returned the next day lamenting its death. He returned any money he had been given for the 'cure' and left the gull singing praises to his honesty, then hot-footed it back to Guido for his share of the sale. And when the monkey recovered they started the whole thing again. Until this time, when they had dosed it once too often and it died.

He must be something of a player, that Jackanapes; had she not seen him with the Patrico she would have sworn that his distress was real...what if it was? What if he had truly blundered into the thing by mischance and had honestly come to her for help? Perversely, she could

213

not bear the thought. 'A shrew,' he had called her, 'with
nought of a woman about her.' Small wonder — yet the
words had cut her so deeply that the pain had stolen her
breath. This, she knew in her heart, was why she was running away. She could not, dared not, expose herself to the
risk of such hurt again.

Why she was vulnerable to him as to no one else was
something she refused to look at. It was because of Tim,
she told herself; or maybe because of Potter. She had lingered with Potter among the murderous Egyptians until
death had mercy on him; but if Angel was innocent she
had left him destitute, at the mercy of such rogues as
Bodkyn and the Patrico. And too late, she knew it must
have been his mother's ring that she had sold at last in the
desperate days of hunger...Tim had succoured her, had
died in her arms; she had never admitted how sorely she
had missed him. Tomorrow she would send his son some
money.

She roused up Saracen, who had lowered his head to
graze, and headed him north. First to Islington to see how
the land lay there, to be finally certain that the courier
had not come through, that Marian still lay in wait for him
at the inn. She could leave her few belongings with the
chamberlain there and set up new headquarters in which
to formulate her plans. She smiled, squared her shoulders and urged the bay to more speed. The world was
before her and was about to open up.

Darkness was falling as she headed her mount once more
into the yard of the Cock tavern. A band of players was
setting up for a show, the whole place alive with noise and
lighted links and excitement. She hailed a hostler without dismounting. 'Ho, there! Come here.' The man, struggling with two horses made fractious by the mêlée,
appeared not to hear her and was swallowed into the
darkness of the stables.

Joanna made a small sound of impatience. It was not
her wish to come face to face with Angel, merely to leave
him provided for. It had not been difficult to persuade

herself that it was better to bring the money herself than to entrust it to some Kit Callot more likely to spend it on himself; one moreover who might prattle of the Jarkman's movements at Pickerings in Kent Street, a regular thieves' kitchen which she was studious to avoid. But now it seemed that in pursuing the hostler further she ran the risk of encountering Angel himself. She dismounted, hitched Saracen to a rail and shouldered her way through the merrymakers into the tavern. She would leave the money with Joshua and be on her way back to Islington. She had found Marian still there, happily plying her trade among the brickmakers and ready with assurances that no courier had escaped her vigilance; a ride across the dewy fields to Hoxton had assured her that Geordie had not come that way, and for the moment there seemed nothing more she could do. On reflection she saw that there might be other roads; early in the morning she would set out on a discreet and thorough checking of every possible route.

Joshua's jaw dropped as she entered. 'What, back already? Your horseman's gone looking for you.'

'Has he, indeed! No doubt to remind me I left without paying for his lodging.' Her heart thumping, she counted out the coins. 'When he comes back tell him he's to stay and look after the mare.'

'But he took her with him, said you needed help —'

'He *what?*'

Joshua looked uncomfortable, aware of having been taken for a fool. He said unwillingly, 'He said you'd run into danger, that he had to get after you quick. Well, he's your man, how was I to know?'

'The fool!' Joanna's gloved fist struck the table. 'The blundering, interfering fool! Which way did he go?'

A sullen red suffused Joshua's cheekbones. 'How should I know?' he repeated. 'All I know is he was asking how to get a horse across the river —'

'Jesu Christus!' Joanna did not wait to hear more. She was out into the courtyard before Joshua could draw breath, fighting her way to where Saracen stood waiting.

She sprang to the saddle and kicked him to a gallop. That fool, that idiotic moonstruck clown had gone careering down to Buxford! If he reached there before she could stop him...

Saracen was a strong young gelding but she could not gallop him all the way. She paced and fretted at the slowness of the ferry, and each time she had to slacken pace for his sake felt a torment of anxiety building up inside her. What on earth had possessed the fellow, he must be out of his mind! So he had thought she needed help; such help as this she would be better off without! Now she would be hard put to it to avert disaster, to lay him by the heels before his misguided chivalry blew her whole plan to the Devil!

When after an eternity she drew near Buxford she glanced repeatedly towards the eastern horizon, watching for the telltale lightening of the skyline that would presage the dawn. A westerly breeze began stirring the leaves and a few drops of rain tingled her face. The moon had set and the stars were veiled by cloud: so much the better if it prolonged the cover of night.

Abruptly she was out of the greenwood and on to the common land. She realised that the landscape had changed hereabouts since her childhood; the greenwood no longer swept up to the gates of the parkland as it used to. The villagers must have cleared more of the brushwood for their fires in the intervening years, for now individual elms and oaks stood singly or in groups where once the cover had been dense enough to hide an army. She dismounted and led Saracen back to where he would not be seen when the sun rose, tethered him to the bole of a silver birch.

What now? Buxford was a vast estate and her quarry could be anywhere. She stood still and tried to think lucidly. If she had come on this fool's errand where would she be, what would she have done on arrival? But no, that was pointless; their minds did not work in the same way. Very well, what would he be likely to do? Assuming that he thought she was within the walls. Even he would hardly be rash enough to go pounding on the doors and demanding admittance. What then would be the next move, the obvious course? Would he make his way along the pale, in search of a way in…?

She patted the horse's neck soothingly and prayed that he would be quiet; then she began moving stealthily along the forest border, her ears and eyes straining to catch the smallest hint. A twig snapped and she started violently. A flurry of raindrops was shaken from overhead and she almost cried out at the unexpected soft slap against her face. Once she thought she heard the sound of a voice…a moan or a whisper…it must be some animal, the forest would be full of them. She shivered and pushed on. Oddly, she felt more at risk here in the uncharted forest than among the familiar hazards of the city — there it was again! Human, and yet…inhuman: a soul in torment, a sound full of agony and strain. She froze, listening intently. It was a sound unnatural, muffled, as though… she turned her head, striving to identify it; poised for flight yet paralysed, horribly afraid yet held against all her will, her inclination. There was something in it, something she recognised…

Suddenly she was running towards the source of the sound, crashing through undergrowth to where in the dusk of dawn her eyes could just make out a writhing figure, hand clamped over mouth, pale hair brushing leaves and twigs from the ground in its futile thrashing…

'Oh, God, no!' she flung herself forward.

'The jaws — the jaws!' His voice was distorted, cracked with pain as he tried to stifle his groaning. Her eye followed a trail of blood in the growing light to where his free hand groped towards his ankle, hideously gripped in the iron teeth of a trap. 'Open the jaws — the shackle —'

'Dear God! Oh, you fool, you fool…' She was sobbing, blinded by her tears as she wrenched at the jaws of the trap. They were locked solid, held immovable by something unseen and she could not disengage them. 'May God strike him blind who set such a thing!' It was

217

Eustace, always Eustace, cursed be his soul...'I can't, I can't see how it works,' she cried despairingly. 'Oh, you fool, you poor fool, why must you —'

'There's a spring,' he gasped. 'You have to push it down, stand on it, use all your weight so the shackle goes down. Oh, try, please try...'

She found the spring, a flattened strip of metal rising in a curve from the ground to end in a ring shackle clamping the jaws together about his mutilated leg. 'Stand on it,' he begged. 'Jump on it, anything!'

She balanced her feet near the highest point and bore down. It moved only a part of the way. The jaws loosened momentarily and then snapped back together, wrenching a cry from between its victim's clenched teeth.

'It's no good, I'm not heavy enough, it needs both of us!'

'I canna stand, I reckon the bone's broke.'

'You must. Here, give me your hands. Now get your good leg under you and lean across my back...try again, you can do it — no, don't fall back...if you can't stand lean upon me, it's your weight that's needed — come, try, we can do it together!' At first it did not yield even under their combined weight. 'Hold fast!' She flexed her knees, drove down her feet with a jerk that forced the shackle down at last. Still the savage jaws did not give up their prey. Sickened, she saw that they were embedded in his flesh.

'You're almost free,' she encouraged him. 'But there's more to be done, you must hold on and keep us balanced while I do it. Come what may don't let us slip off that spring.' Slowly, sweating under his weight, she bent down until she could reach the grotesquely swollen foot and contrived to free it, wincing at what she had to do.

'Now!' She swung them both clear with the last of her strength. As they rolled out of reach the spring flew back up and the barbarous trap clanged shut, gnashing its iron teeth like a beast of prey.

Angel collapsed as it relinquished him and she tried to soften his fall, muffling his face against her doublet to suppress the howl that broke from him as the blood rushed back into the mangled foot. 'Hush...oh, hush...it will be all right,' she whispered, distraught.

It would not be all right, she knew it, and so would he when he saw what was done. Mysterious poisons beset such wounds, evil vapours from the air that caused them to rot like putrid meat. 'Don't look,' she told him. 'Don't move and above all make no sound. I am going to fetch the horse.'

She laid him back carefully, thankful to see that he was in a swoon and for the moments of mercy feeling nothing. When she returned leading Saracen, the sunrise was tearing a bright rent in the dove-grey silk of the sky. Its warmth only served to heighten the deathly pallor of Angel's drawn face.

10

'Come, try, you've got to try,' panted Joanna. 'I can't get us both on to the horse unless you help — damn you, stand still!' she snapped at Saracen, struggling to hold him while he rolled his eyes and tried to sidle away. She turned again to Angel who lay blinking and shaking his head. 'Come on, please...*please!*' She looked about her in the fast-increasing light, conscious that at any moment someone might appear to check his traps.

Angel rolled himself with difficulty on to one knee, his face a distorted mask of pain. 'No good to scold,' he gasped. 'He's frightened, 'tis the smell of blood. Give him here.' He reached up to take the reins from her hand, raised his head towards Saracen's and miraculously the laid back ears came forward, the whites of the eyes disappeared and the soft muzzle was lowered to brush his mouth. For all the world, she thought, as if they were whispering. 'Come,' she urged again. 'Quickly, we must be away from here!' She pulled his free arm about her shoulders and hauled him on to his uninjured foot, the other a mangled obscenity from which blood poured relentlessly. Perhaps it was good that it bled, to wash ill humours from the wound.

'Get up in the saddle,' he was saying. 'He wunna move now. I'll try and jump, you grab hold and help me up.' She did as he asked, glad that Saracen was not a taller

220

horse. It was not easy to reach down so far but she managed to grasp a handful of clothing, an arm, as he sprang. 'Higher, try again,' she exhorted as she felt him slipping back, but he was dead weight suddenly and she knew she must manage alone. Exerting all her strength she hauled him up, slowly, inch by inch until he lay limp as a dead man across her saddlebow, head hanging down on one side, legs on the other.

She took a grip of the back of his belt in one hand and clicked softly to her mount to walk on. Her every nerve was screaming for a gallop but she knew that rapid movement would catch the least observant eye. Moving slowly in the half light they might pass from a distance as deer.

The great thing was to travel as far as possible unobserved, to put the greatest possible distance between themselves and this spot. She flirted with the notion of returning to the road and making a dash for it. But with daylight coming their sorry state would certainly be marked and if Eustace was setting traps no doubt he was also patrolling the roads; she wondered briefly for whom, but the question was not her immediate concern, she must find a resting place for Angel before he bled to death. She headed deeper into the forest, biting her lips; she had known these woods well enough as a child, they could not have changed too much in fifteen years. They had been spattered with charcoal burners' huts, used and abandoned when their occupants moved on; somewhere, she was sure she had seen a woodcutter's cottage with half its roof caved in. Anything would do that would afford them shelter and a place to hide, time for her to think and for him to heal...or to die. She brushed the thought from her mind; she was not riding forth to meet defeat. She touched her heels to Saracen's flanks and moved forward with confidence. Summer lightning flickered its dull rose pink all about them and she felt herself crouching lower in the saddle as thunder cracked and raged overhead, trying not to flinch as a fork struck a tree somewhere not far off

221

with a flash and a report like cannon fire; she had never outgrown her childish fear of thunder and was glad that the boy was not awake to witness her cowardice. She must be thankful for the ensuing downpour to wash out their tracks: they must have left a trail of blood as easy to follow as a dodman's silver line on a wall. She leaned down to look; the flow had diminished to an oozing of heavy blackish gouts. He still hung limply unconscious, drenched to the skin and apparently drained of life, but she saw to her relief that he still breathed. Alas, poor Jackanapes...poor rash wrongheaded fellow, God forbid that she should have his death on her conscience. She sighed, shaking her head. She had done nothing to deserve his loyalty. He was younger than she, too trusting and in need of protection. Instead in her bitterness of spirit she had crucified him...

The sun was well up by the time they reached a clearing she remembered. Yes, there was the cottage, its door standing open, its shutters hanging askew, the remains of a saw-horse rotting on the ground. It looked anything but inviting but it was shelter; and the more uninhabited it looked the less likely they were to be discovered. She dismounted, tethered Saracen with his burden to a beam of the porch and went inside. The place had been pillaged of furnishings and little remained: a broken table, a broom with a few worn twigs, a pot with a hole in the bottom. With an effort she forced open the creaking shutters and the movement dislodged a cascade of shingles from the roof, revealing smoke-blackened rafters where a few bunches of herbs hung withered, brittle and cobwebbed above the long dead hearth. There were traces of occupation by mice, foxes, owls...she shuddered; it would have to serve. With the worn broom she swept clean a corner of the floor by the hearth, and heard as she did so a faint moaning from outside. Angel was stirring, slipping half conscious from the saddle bow. She caught him as he fell. 'Come, lean on me, we've found a resting place.' He seemed not to hear, clutching dazedly at the harness for support. 'Let go — and keep that foot off the ground!' She coaxed him inside and lowered him to the floor, where he lay back with sweating face and closed eyes.

'Hold it up!' she snapped in her anxiety, instinct telling her to keep the raw wound from the dirt. But compunction hit her when she saw that he could not.

She dragged off her leather jerkin and folded it into a prop; it would serve for the moment but what when he slept, turned over, tossed about...it must somehow be secured. She glanced at the beams overhead, so low that caution was needed in walking about. Instantly she was stripping off his shirt, tearing strips from it to make a sling, looping it over the cross beam. With infinite care she slipped the other end under his calf. As she began to raise it he started up with a cry of anguish. 'Ah, dunna!'

'It must be kept off the ground,' she said firmly. But now she could see the problem. The foot had slewed sideways at an angle not designed by nature; somewhere in all that mess was a broken bone, and a bone needed support, she remembered that from her days among the Moon Men. They had seemed to have remedies for everything.

She laid it back on the folded jerkin and cast about for a splint. Roughly shaping a piece from the broken table she bandaged it under the wound and contrived to secure the leg in the sling.

'That feels better,' said Angel weakly. He put up a hand to shade his eyes, still watering from the pain. 'I do thank you. I mean,' he hesitated, ' 'tis good of you to tend me.'

Stricken, she said gruffly, 'The wound is foul and must be cleansed. I go to get wine, do you try to sleep. No one will find you here.'

Briskly she fastened her doublet, crammed her hair back under her hat and went out. Saracen was trying to reach the dregs in a decaying rainwater butt. As she kicked it over she heard a faint call from within. 'What is it?' she thrust her head around the door,

'Get fodder for the horse...he's naught to graze about here...'

223

'Horses!' She turned away, impatient to be gone, but he called to her again.

'Jo?'

'What?'

'I lost my patch...'

'Is that all?' She was already in the saddle. 'Forget it, you're better off without the wretched thing.' She found the stream and let Saracen drink, then set off to find the road and a tavern she recalled from long ago, called the Hop Bine.

When she returned with a well-fed horse and a skinful of the strongest sack the tavern could provide, the sun was high and hot, sending long fingers of light down between the high boles to sketch eerie shapes in the mist that rose writhing from the forest floor. Everything looked different in the changing light and she was glad of Saracen's hoof prints to guide her back to the woodcutter's lodge. It occurred to her that if she could follow his tracks, so could a pursuer; next time she went for provisions it might be well to leave him at livery and walk back, so that the telltale track could green over and disappear.

Angel was lying as she had left him, an arm across his eyes, his young face drawn and old in the subdued light. He turned his head as she entered. 'You're back, then. Safe. I was starting to worry.'

'You worry too much about me. If you hadn't...'

He smiled wanly. 'I know. Dunna rub in the salt.'

Joanna sat near him on the floor, her hands clasped about her knees, and slowly shook her head. 'You're such a fool,' she said gently. 'What on earth did you think you could do?'

'Stop you, maybe...help you. I dunno. You weren't nowhere on the road and I thought...'

'Yes?'

He hesitated, avoiding her eyes. 'I meant to kill him. Before you got there. Then you'd be safe...'

There was silence between them, stretched and taut as the string of a longbow. It was Joanna who broke it. She

224

rose to her feet and went striding outside, her thoughts a rabble army she could not marshal. Activity, that was the thing; there was a task to be done and she must do it if life was to be saved. She found a bunker outside, and in it a few old logs and a rusting axe. She breathed a prayer of thanks for Tim Kettle's training and set to work, but it was long since she had handled such things and it no longer came easily. When she had an armful of dry wood she carried it indoors and started a fire.

Angel looked at her in surprise. Both of them were sweating, she from her exertions and he with the threat of a fever.

'I have to heat the wine,' she explained, looking about for a vessel. But there was only one discarded pot with a hole in it; she hung the wineskin itself from the hook above the fire and waited, hoping it would stand the heat.

'This is going to hurt you but it must be done.' She took his knife and passed the blade through a flame.

Angel caught his breath and turned a shade whiter. 'I can stand it.' He cast about for something on which to bite.

Joanna handed him a chipping of oak. 'Scream if you must, there's no one to hear. We've had enough heroics for one day.'

He did not scream. But his back arched, his teeth drove deep into the wood and his fists beat a frantic tattoo on the floor as the blade bit into the aching mass and the wine poured scalding after it. Seared with pity, Joanna worked fast, probing, cleaning with the hot white wine in the raw red jelly that had lost all semblance of a foot. It was hard to believe that it would bear his weight again; what if it did not? She dismissed the thought.

'It's done,' she told him with relief, 'Only the bandage now.' She tore more strips from the eroded shirt and soaked them in the cool water of the brook to bind up the wound; then, finding there was a little left over she bathed first his face and then her own. 'You did well,' she said. 'Was it very bad?'

'Worse than the trap.' His voice was hoarse with

225

strain, he had to clear his throat. 'Didna feel that straight off, not till I tried to pull away. But it sang to high Heaven when you poured in the wine, I thought I was going to puke.'

Frowning, she said crisply, 'You had best gain control of your stomach, you have it to look forward to again before nightfall.'

Throughout the day he dozed on and off, refusing food, taking only the water she brought in her cupped hands. When she came again with heated wine for the dressing he put up no resistance and showed less sign of distress than before. Perhaps it was improving, she told herself doubtfully, but he looked worse rather than better. An ashen pallor showed through his tan and shadows like bruises stained the skin about his sunken eyes. Concerned, she wrung out a cloth and bathed his face again. 'How goes it with you, is it any better yet?'

'Not better,' he said weakly. 'Only...different.'

'How, different?'

'Funny, sort of. Like all that booze had made it drunk.'

'Drunk...' She frowned, teasing her memory for what it might mean and not liking what she found there. His skin was still hot to the touch yet the toes protruding from the bandage felt cool; she brought a brand from the fire and looked closer. Through the rags was seeping not blood but something of a paler hue. As she stripped away the wrappings she saw pus oozing from the wounds, four of them marching across the taut flesh of the shattered ankle, separate and clearly discernible now that the swelling had begun to subside. The surrounding flesh glowed an angry mottled crimson and she was dismayed to see that further away it showed signs of turning black, 'Dear God...' she breathed.

Angel's voice cut across her thoughts. ' 'Tis poisoned, I reckon.' He struggled up to look and fell back, sweating. 'Like when Clem trod on the sickle...'

Joanna refrained from asking whether Clem still had both feet. Instead she pressed her thumbs on the spongy flesh and was rewarded with a spurt of yellow matter, a smell like that from a rotting tooth. 'That's better,' she muttered, surprised that he did not wince.

'What's better?'

'Can't you feel what I'm doing?'

'I canna feel nothing,' he said. 'Just the bone do ache.'

Joanna's eyes slid over to the ingle where the axe stood ready by the pile of logs. Our Lady in Heaven, she prayed silently…don't let me have to use it.

11

'You heard what I said, they're to be taken up!' Eustace half rose from his chair to loom over the bewildered steward.

He had slept little and was short of temper; he had lain awake listening to the distant rumble of thunder, asking himself why no reply was forthcoming from the Fitznorths when they had seemed so eager to get the matter concluded. It was damnable that just as he had evolved a scheme for the removal of three sitting birds with a single stone, the correspondence on which the whole thing dangled had dried up. Delay was one thing, offering him time in which to lay hands on Joanna; total apparent cessation was quite another. He frowned, drawing strands of his greying beard between his teeth. It was so neat a plan, would leave him so unassailably placed...he could not bear to relinquish it. It had come to him in the small hours, a result of the exasperating Edith's perversity: that boy, his cousin's by-blow whom she so obstinately held to be dangerous, was the answer! Let him return of his own free will to Buxford, voice his lineage abroad and the murder of the bridal pair could be contrived so that he would hang for it. That promised to be the easy part; what exercised him was a problem more immediate, whether to write again to Reggie Fitznorth and risk precipitating a wedding with no bride, or to concentrate on a search for her and hazard the whole arrangement falling through. Around and around his mind it ran in a maddening figure of eight, no wonder it was the symbol for eternity! He was a man of action and frustration was intolerable to him. He had been flirting with a decision when the hapless steward interrupted him.

'My lord...you gave orders for them to be set.'

'And now I want them up!' He waved the rawhide eye patch in the steward's face. 'The fellow has been caught and released himself, he must now be entrapped by some more subtle means. The mare has been found, you say?'

'She has, my lord. Neither saddled nor bridled and her coat has been dyed but there can be little doubt. She was standing quietly among the trees not a hundred yards from the spot. Uncanny it was, almost as though she were waiting for someone.'

As no doubt she was, thought Eustace, no doubt at all. He said slowly, 'It is my considered decision that she was not stolen but strayed. You understand me?' The steward bowed gravely. 'You say her coat has been dyed. Keep her close until it has returned to nature. How long, do you suppose?'

The man spread his hands. 'Hard to say, my lord, depending as it does upon the dye. I could ask the head horseman —'

'You will ask nothing, say nothing. Keep her out of sight and wait. When all evidence of theft has disappeared, put it about that the dairymaid's son is innocent and is free to return to his work. Is that understood?'

'Aye, my lord. But...' the steward's tone was puzzled. 'But what of the ploughman, the body in the brewery? It's common belief that the runagate murdered him.'

'Then common belief is wrong!' roared Eustace. 'And you will say so — God's death, do I have to spell out every word, are you so dull! The fox is cunning and must be outwitted if we're to lay him by the heels. As for this — 'he thrust forward the patch on its thong — 'you have

229

shown it to none but me, no other has seen it?'

A vigorous shaking of the head. 'Only the man in charge of the traps.'

Eustace sat back, reassured. 'Slit his tongue. And then burn this — no, better I will burn it myself. And you have never seen it, will speak of it to none. You know the penalty for disobedience.'

The steward made his obeisance and scuttled away. He knew all too well the penalty for disobedience; he had no desire to add experience to that knowledge.

When he had gone, Eustace sat brooding, gnawing the strands of his beard. There was nothing to be lost by taking up the traps; he had only had them set as a half-hearted gesture to Edith, in the hope of lulling her into telling him where Joanna was to be found. Now that he had wrung from her that she knew no more than he did there was nothing to be gained by appeasing her. The truth had come out on her supposed death-bed...but only part of the truth. One question remained unanswered: Why had she lied in the first place? Could she, pale, pious Edith, have deliberately baulked him for reasons of her own...?

Suddenly he sat forward in his chair, his thoughts running like a mill-race. If that babbling whore at the forge had let slip his plans for Matthew — no wonder she avoided his bed, she did well to fear him! Because of her Edith had made a fool of him, and the longer he pondered it the more fiercely his anger smouldered. Nan would be dealt with easily enough...but a lawfully wedded wife was another matter. Why had she not had the decency to die, instead of lingering on as a thorn in his flesh?

12

All night Angel had tossed and muttered, his skin parched and burning; all night Joanna had lain by his side, dozing fitfully in the intervals between bathing his face and restraining him from tearing his leg from the sling and clawing at the bandages, crying out that it itched — that it was burning — once, that it must be killed.

At first light she rose and went out to douse her head in the stream, and came back feeling refreshed though no less weary. He seemed quieter now, whether sleeping or merely exhausted it was hard to tell; she set about rekindling the fire and put the remains of the wine to heat. She was not sure whether it was good or bad to heat the room: she was no longer sure of anything. But it was something to do, something to keep at bay the sense of helplessness that began to oppress her.

When she judged the wine to be warm enough she took down the skin from its hook, and opened the bandages. She caught her breath. The whole of the lower leg was puffy and discoloured as though it had been bitten by an adder. One look was enough to tell her that it was hopeless. She glanced up to see him watching her, his eyes bright slits of fever by the flickering light of the fire.

'How does it look?' he croaked.

She did not answer. Replacing the bandage she offered him the wineskin. 'Here, drink this.' He hesitated, then took a hearty swig, his eyes on the axe.

'You know, don't you?'

He nodded. 'Do it quick.'

'It's the only thing to do, you must believe me. If there were any other way...'

'I know. Dunna feel badly about it, 'tis no fault of yourn. You'd maybe best sit on me, hold me down. And try and do it first time. Can I have the rest of this?'

She nodded, unable to speak, appalled at what she must do. Such a fine strong body to be mutilated...God forgive me, she prayed silently, it is my fault.

She came back with the axe and set the blade to warm in the fire; she had heard that cold steel made the pain more sharp. To take his mind away she smiled, and said, 'You must have had strange dreams last night. You woke and cried, "Kill it, kill it!" Do you remember?'

He lay with his eyes closed in the glow of the wine. 'I was dreaming about my mother,' he said drowsily. 'My real mother. And Clem, when he poisoned his foot. They was...yes, they was killing a chicken. That's what it was.'

'I thought you didn't remember your mother. How did you know her?'

He looked at her, bemused; perhaps by the wine. 'I dunno. But I knew it was her in my dream. And Clem, with this chicken tied on his foot...' He closed his eyes again.

Joanna's eyes opened wide. 'A chicken! Of course, a chicken — dear God, why did I not remember!' She jumped up and withdrew the axe from the fire. The Moon Men, those Egyptians with their cunning ways, they knew! To be sure, they had used a hedgehog, and there were herbs, incantations...but the principle was the same! It was worth a try! She ran out of the cottage and saddled up the horse, then thrust her head around the door to see that Angel was lying with his eyes tight shut, still waiting for the blow to fall. 'Finish your wine,' she called to him. 'Lie there and sleep it off. We're not beaten yet!'

Two hours later she was back with two freshly-killed capons tied to her saddle bow. They were dead but still warm and having been neckwrung had lost no blood. She took one and laid it open with the axe from crop to vent, removed the stale bandage with the suppurating crusts and laid the spatch-cocked carcass over the wound, binding it tightly with fresh strips of shirting. Her patient did not stir. She left him to sleep and sat down to pluck the other chicken for the spit.

Angel came out of his stupor to the smell of roasting chicken. Nauseated, he turned his head aside to vomit and was overcome with shame; he was lying in a pool of urine which he tried to hide as Joanna's face bent over him.

'Don't be a fool,' she said crisply. 'Do you think I would do any differently?'

He tried to speak but the words were washed away with the water she was pouring over him; he floated away on its tide into the darkness. From time to time he surfaced for a moment only to sink again into the cauldron in which he was stewing with the chicken, around and around he swirled among the herbs and the worts, trying to keep his foot from the burning bottom of the pot while Bess muttered incantations...or was it Kate...Joanna had grown an extra foot and was sewing it onto the chicken...his head was turning faster than the rest of him and he was dizzy...dizzy...

The first time he awoke for more than a few seconds it was dark. Joanna was beside him, he could just make out her face in the firelight. All he could feel of his foot was a screaming agony like toothache from the broken bone. 'Did you do it, Jo?' He brought the words with difficulty from his parched throat.

Joanna got up without answering and came back with a cup of liquid. As he struggled to sit up she slid an arm underneath him, propping him against her shoulder to

233

hold the cup to his mouth. He took a sip but it tasted vile and he turned his face away.

'Drink it,' she ordered sternly. 'I walked miles for that golden-rod. It's the cinquefoil you can taste.'

'Lady Rumpscuttle...' He chuckled feebly.

'Don't try to talk, drink it down. You're heavy.'

He swallowed it obediently, shuddering. 'I stink,' he croaked.

'There's worse to come; in a week you'll reek like a jacques farmer. But you'll still have both feet.'

In alarm, he followed the length of his leg to the sling: to his dismay, the foot was still there. She had been unable to use the axe, and who could blame her? But he knew that he was doomed. And if he died, he thought on a wave of anger and frustration, he would have gone without telling her how deeply she was loved. He wanted her to know it, wanted her to have that balm to her old unhealing hurt. He stirred, took a breath — and let it go again. What use to tell her what she would not hear, to press upon her what she could not take...

He closed his eyes and contented himself with leaning his head against her shoulder. 'Dunna go,' he whispered. 'Dunna leave me, not till after...'

Joanna's arms held him with unexpected fierceness as he succumbed to another fiery onslaught of pain; as the drugged wine drew him again into the shadows he thought he felt her tears.

Tink, tink...tink, tink, tink...someone was tapping on the outside of the cauldron, inviting him to come out. But it was comfortable now, no longer madly scalding but only pleasantly warm, he swam lazily in its tepid depths in no hurry to come to the surface.

Tink...tink, tink, tink...There it was again. He screwed up his eyes against the light as he floated upwards into consciousness.

'Good morning,' said Joanna's voice. 'I thought you'd sleep for ever.'

He prised himself on to an elbow and squinted under

his hand at where she squatted before the fire, barefoot in sunlight with the discarded pot between her knees. 'What are you at?'

'Mending the old pot, we might as well make use of it. You've slept two days and nights, are you ready to eat?'

He shook his head, his stomach churning at the thought of food. 'I could drink though. Just water,' he added quickly.

'All in good time,' she said, and dosed him with more of her herbal concoction first.

'I did ought to be dead,' he said wonderingly. 'Why aren't I?'

'All in good time,' she said again, her dark eyes mischievous. 'You'll need a strong stomach before I tell you that. No, leave it alone!' She arrested the hand that reached out to investigate the mis-shapen poultice with the feathers that protruded from the bandages. He was willing enough to do as he was told, recoiling as the foetid odour hit him; exhausted already, he lay back on the pillow of bracken that seemed to have appeared by magic and was asleep again almost at once.

Day by day he recovered strength as the evil stench increased; Joanna waited with a growing excitement, impatient for the moment when she could view the results of her gamble and know that she had won. But she knew that to take off the poultice too soon would be to undo everything. She worked off her pent-up energy in cleaning the cottage; renewing the spent twigs of the broom she swept the floor, tore down cobwebs, carried water from the brook in the newly tinkered pot to sluice over the sick-room corner and its occupant. She discovered a loft above the chimney breast, but the ladder had rotted with the incoming rain and collapsed under her weight.

'You'm restless as an April wind.' He smiled, watched her from under his hand.

'Why do you shade your eyes, does your head still ache?'

'No, 'tis to shield you from the Evil Eye. Nick turned pale when he saw it!'

She laughed. 'I'm of sterner stuff.' She came to kneel

235

beside him and drew down his hand. 'No, look at me. I see only colours of earth and sky, mixed together like the Turkish stone…or perhaps the sea. Nothing to fear.'

'Aye, but now look, when I turn to the light. There, now do you see?'

She caught her breath. Encircling the pupil, between the black and the mingled hues of the iris shone a ring of light. 'It is beautiful,' she breathed. 'Strange, certainly. But nothing of evil, they are fools who told you so!' Suddenly selfconscious, she rose and moved away.

'Kate took it for a witchmark.' He fingered the livid scar that disfigured the smooth tan of his chest. 'Like this I had from my dam.'

'I had wondered how you came by it, that scar.'

' 'Twas what was underneath.' He grinned, selfconscious in his turn. 'They reckoned it was for suckling imps, they burned it off. Me being a witch's child, see, they was frightened I'd be the same.'

Joanna came back and sat down. 'They burned it off? They did that, to a child!'

He shrugged. 'Kate, I reckon, being easy scared and one to believe anything. Like about my ma, Kate held she was a witch; but I never heard nothing of what she did, only what she was. Same as me, they say my eye's evil, but I never done nothing bad with it so how would they know?'

'They know nothing, these piss-prophets! I'll lay if Our Lord himself walked the earth today they would call him Witchboy.'

'You reckon?' After a moment he said, 'I wish I could have known about my mother, though. If she was innocent, I'd have liked to know. I never hear nothing but bad about her. Don't even know her name.'

'I must have known it once…' She shook her head regretfully. 'I'm sorry. Too much has happened since then. But if she had done something to warrant her death, I'd surely remember it. As to her innocence, who knows? Perhaps she did have "powers"…perhaps she came in your dream to save you, where's the harm in that? I don't see why the Devil should have credit for everything.'

236

'What about the Horseman's Word? A Whisperer can stop a horse in his tracks and keep him there all day if he's a mind to; lead him through fire — anything. Some reckon that comes from the Powers of Darkness but I only want it for good. So why shouldn't I seek it?'

She laughed. The notion was ludicrous, she had never seen anyone with such a way with the beasts. 'You don't really think there's a word you can learn that will teach you more than you know!' She saw from the way he coloured that he had taken it as a jibe. 'Come, you mistake me. Merely, it seems to me that this magic you seek, this talisman, may be a thing to know, to carry in the heart, not a word to repeat like a popinjay. Perhaps you already have it, who can say?'

Mollified, he smiled. 'You make a better man of me than I am.'

'Man?' Her laugh was unsteady. 'Don't vilify yourself.'

Unexpectedly he caught her hand and rubbed the back of it against his cheek where a soft stubble of beard bloomed golden on the bronzed skin. 'I am a man,' he said soberly. 'We'm not all vile, Joanna. If only I could show you that, I could make you whole. There,' he touched her frightened hand to his lips and released it. 'See, I let you go free.'

She jumped up instantly, her hand still tingling where he had touched it, and tried to still her jangled nerves with a flurry of activity.

'So!' Her voice came out high and unnatural. 'Tomorrow being the sixth day, we shall see if I've made you whole. Today we must eat.'

She all but ran from the cottage and began aimlessly collecting firewood that they did not need. After a few seconds she stopped and leaned against a tree, flushed and shaking. In dread, and at the same time strangely elated; feeling older, feeling younger in one and the same moment. When her pulses slowed from their racing she turned and laid her head against her arm, fighting down the tears she could never allow. If only, she thought, her throat aching: If only a man could really have been like that...

13

Joanna lay next to Angel in the darkness before dawn, listening to the whisper of midsummer rain, the clear fluting notes that trickled down through high branches from the throats of blackbirds and finches eager for the day, and wondered what was happening to her.

It seemed more than two weeks since she had cut away the stinking bandage with its rotting carcass and cast it, a seething mass of maggots, into the fire. Even as it burned the smell of putrefaction had leaped down their throats and attacked their stomachs, they had crawled or staggered out into the open to retch in the fresh air. But the wound when washed was clean and healthy, and now it was almost healed. He slept peacefully now, no longer waking and thrashing in need of comfort in the night, and she could if she wished have moved her pallet further away. But she had not.

He had spent the intervening time in making a crutch for himself and was already trying to hobble on the twisted foot, filled with the restlessness of recovery and, she guessed, plagued by anxiety at the loss of the mare and an itch to be freed of the splint and go in search of her. She told herself that she did not trust him not to set forth, depleted as he was, and bring down some fresh disaster on their heads; it was common sense to keep a close eye on him. So she rationalised; but she could not

238

blink the fact that she had grown used to the sense of his presence in the eerie silences of the forest at night, had come to welcome the sheltering arm that sometimes fell across her as she slept, the sight of his accustomed face beside her when she woke. She felt comfortable with him, at ease as she had been with no one else, able to laugh and talk freely without the need to guard her tongue. It was as well, she told herself, that having been forced into the role of a woman she had slipped into it so readily; she could hardly go hoyting about the halls of Buxford in buskins and a sword. She had bought a length of homespun from the taverner's wife at the Hop Bine and botched it into some semblance of a gown, explaining to herself that it was high time she learnt to walk in a skirt; and when she went in search of herbs came back with an armful of honeysuckle to sweeten the room...she was not sure why she had done that. She turned her mind away, aware that a chasm yawned at her feet.

No doubt it was the enforced physical intimacy; that, and his helplessness that had thrown him upon her mercy in a way that she would once have found intolerable. Why didn't she now? She did not know, did not understand herself, knowing only that life had taken on a new dimension. That she, who from her searing childhood had kept the rest of the world at arm's length, touching no other and allowing no one to touch her, was learning for the first time the softness of another's skin, the comfort in a simple clasp of hands. Was this what was meant by friendship? If it was, she wanted to keep it.

It was borne in upon her that she did not know how to keep it. All her arts, her verbal skills, were in repelling, defending, maintaining a safe distance; she had no cunning in the arts of bringing near. Angel or Jackanapes, he would soon be on the mend and ready to move on; and uncharacteristically she had not looked beyond the morrow. She had told him so many times to leave her alone; she did not know how to unsay it now. She could hardly offer him employment, sorely though he might need it; the time of master and servant lay behind them, they could not go back to it now. It belonged to the past, and this brief sequestered time was destined to join it. Never again would she know this happiness, and a deep unreasoning sadness welled up in her at the thought.

As if he had overheard her thinking he stirred and yawned. 'Reckon I'll be walking in another day.'

'Yes.' She waited.

He lay on his back looking up into the rafters, his eyes glistening in the dusk. Presently he said, 'Reckon you'll be glad to see the back of me, being nought but a nuisance to you. You'm better off on your own than with my sort of helping. Me losing Bess for you, an' all.'

'No matter.' It sounded stiff and formal. But she could think of nothing else to say, numbed by the shock of his words; he was going away, taking her at her word. It was no more than she deserved. But so soon, it was so soon...

'Well...you got Saracen. And she's likely found her way home by now. To Buxford.'

His words dropped like stones on to a cairn, building a weight like the *peine forte et dure*. He was waiting for her to say something; but she could not speak.

'Anyways,' he said at last. 'You'll be free of me tomorrow. I'll be back on me feet and no more trouble.'

'Yes,' she managed to say. Thinking, Tomorrow you'll be free of me, you won't need me any more. You'll pick yourself up and go on with your life and be lost to me; you, and the closeness of these days and the warmth I never knew about, the whole world of touching and caring that I didn't know I had missed. I'll be alone for ever, locked up like a prisoner in the bleakness of Jarkman Joe. Now it's I who need you...dear silly, blundering Angel, ready to throw your life away for someone else's dream...Her eyes brimmed and she turned away, anguished by the first painful throbbing of life through her crippled heart. As grief overcame her she pressed her hands over her mouth, feeling shameful sobs tear through her and trying to suppress the sound.

She was aware of his hand on her shoulder, his voice soft with concern. 'What is it, lovely? Dunna cry so...'

Helpless she turned towards him, blinded by her tears. 'Oh, Angel...I don't want to be a virgin all my life...'

If there were words to answer that Angel did not know them. He closed his eyes and let his instincts rule him; his arms enfolding her, his face against hers he rocked her gently, consolingly while her sobs abated, her movements answered his and their rhythm changed so subtly that neither was aware of it. Their hands from soothing one another turned to caressing, their bodies to glow and then to ache with hunger until at last they clung skin to skin in joy and dread and were shaken and reborn with little cries, tumbling locked together and still trembling, over and over in the sweet bruised bracken, laughing softly with delight and the sudden newness of it all. At last they were quiet.

'You'm like a foxes' wedding, all smiles and tears,' he whispered, kissing away her forgotten tears.

She opened her eyes, shining under wet lashes, her lips against his. 'A foxes' wedding?'

'When 'tis rain and sun together, we say the fox is getting wed. Like now,' he gestured towards the doorway. 'See, the sun's got up while we were loving.' Outside the raindrops fell to the ground sparkling like crystal in the sharpness of the early light.

'It's beautiful,' breathed Joanna. 'It is all beautiful, everything, everything...' She turned back towards him, renewing her embrace. 'Oh Angel, I never knew! Did you know it was all so beautiful?'

He thought briefly of the girls at Buxford and shook his head. 'No, I never.' He drew back to look at her. 'You're mine, Jo,' he said with pride. 'I was your first, that makes you mine, whatever.'

'Oh, yes...yes. My first, my last...my always,' she murmured dreamily. 'Lightmans and darkmans, all

241

the days of my life...'

She drew him close and the joy in them rose again, swinging them away once more into their new found land.

14

Lady Matilda stood on the cliff edge in the sunlight,
exhilarated by the wind that came in sharp and brilliant
off the sea. She loved her home and was proud of it; let
her distant Percy cousins dismiss it as 'a mere peel
tower', to her it was castle enough with its surrounding acres glowing with heather and gorse, supporting
enough tough little golden-haired cattle to feed them
and the raiding Grahams as well. Or almost enough. As
long as they did not lose the Pengerran dowry. It was
worrying that there had been no reply to their last
letter, and her sleep was disturbed with misgivings
about the deception they had practised. Could Eustace
by any mischance have discovered it? How could he pos-
sibly, since no one knew of it but themselves — not even
Jamie. And yet...

Two months was two months, she reflected, tight-
ening her lips, her eyes following the restless movement
of the surf breaking on the dark rocks below. One rock
seemed to move in and out with the pull of the water, she
noted without interest. Then her attention was fully
caught as she realised that it was not a rock but a softer,
more fluid shape: that of a human body. She shaded her
eyes and peered hard. It was not unknown for the victims of drowning to be washed ashore in the inlet; the
pull of the tide made unexpected arrivals on their shore

and sometimes they had drifted many miles. But there had been no shipwreck on this stretch of the coast for many months, the weather having continued clement since the spring. The next moment saw her running back towards the house, calling to the men who came forward at the sound.

'Quickly!' she gasped. 'Send a party of strong men down to the shore, there's a man on the rocks there, bring his body up!' To their confused enquiries she answered nothing but hurried on to find her husband. 'Reggie!' She burst in on him at last in the armoury where he was checking their store of arms with the steward. 'Reggie, there's a dead man on the rocks. I think it's Braw Geordie, the courier!'

PART FOUR
The Horseman's Word

1

Autumn was beginning to tint the forest, flicking with a careless brush a gold leaf here, a russet there as the long high days of summer slowly dwindled.

As soon as Joanna was out of sight of the Hop Bine, she whipped off her hat and shook her lengthening hair free in the breeze. She had cajoled the ageing taverner's wife into selling her an almost new shift and was longing for the moment when she could shrug off the trappings of the Jarkman and try it on; her masculine shirt although of better linen looked decidedly odd under the homespun gown. Old Robbie the taverner had chuckled when he heard her haggling for the shift. 'You've a wench hid away then, have you?' he had wheezed. 'I vow you young bloods starts purring before you can walk.'

'Aye, she's hid where you'll never see her,' she had countered with her best swashbuckling air. 'Who cares to walk if he can mount?' And she had ridden away amused by her secret joke.

Only when she must did she go to the tavern for stores; the rest of the time she spent happily about the cottage, cleaning and garnishing, or watching Angel, nimbler than she had thought possible with his crutch, while he mended first the ladder and then the roof.

She no longer fretted about the northern courier or his message; they had their being in a world upon which she had turned her back. She had played her part and done her best; if the Pengerran honour was not to be redeemed she could in no way be blamed. What had happened to her thirst for vengeance, she asked herself wryly, knowing the answer: it had been washed away leaving her clean. She had wasted enough of her life in bitterness and self-pity; now with sobering clarity she saw it for what it was, realising that she had wanted revenge not for an unseen father or a mother unloved and unforgiven, but for herself.

Perhaps she had needed hatred to sustain her through the years; but if so, she needed it no longer. She had found something better, more rewarding, more lasting than a single act of violence to fill her horizon; she was chilled by the thought that beyond the death of Eustace had yawned a desert...

She did not ask herself where she was going; all she was sure of was that her direction lay forward and not back. Buxford with its gracious living now seemed as remote as the moon, as did London with its summer stench, its plagues and its pitch fires, its cut-and-thrust existence where survival fell to him who was the first to draw his knife; she marvelled that she had kept her feet in it so long. But both were behind her now; she had put her hand into the hand of Angel and there it would remain. The life of Jarkman Joe had ended on the day of the foxes' wedding.

Until now, she had never indulged her body, had forced it to the limits of endurance without ever taking pleasure in it. Now she was living without thought, a happy animal purring in the sleekness of the sun, turning her eyes away from anything that menaced the idyll that had so unexpectedly blessed her, savouring each moment as though it were her last. She wanted to hide in his arms and lose her memory; and if her shrewd unclouded brain whispered warnings that it could not be, she closed her eyes the tighter and prayed for miracles.

She found herself smiling as she often did these days,

her face warmed and softened to it by the glow she carried within her. Since they had first come close, she had found herself fascinated by small tactile things: the texture harsh yet soft of a shaven cheek, the down of coarse blond hair that covered his body and limbs, glinting against the sun-tanned skin. He was like a faun, she thought, or a young lion...

Except for that scar! The thought of it stirred her anger, causing her to wonder as she always had that he could sustain that knowledge and yet harbour no grievance. 'Life's too short,' he had said once. 'Folk do what they have to, 'tis not a matter of spite. Best to forget what's done and enjoy what's left.' How true, she had thought: and yet how difficult to do...Now, she was learning.

Ah, but the days of persecution were behind him now, and she laughed aloud as she rode through the dappled light, slapping at Saracen's flank to hurry him on. She could hardly wait to get home to Angel, to tell him the good news!

As she came within sight of the clearing she could hear him singing under his breath, splashing in the brook where it widened to form a small pool. She dismounted, stripped off the now abhorrent male clothing and ran to join him, picking her way on bare feet through cool peat-tinted water, between hard stones and scurrying small fry in its depths, smiling and hugging her secret, savouring its possession and the moment to come when she would yield it up.

'Tell me!' he challenged as they wrestled on the mossy bank, their wet pelts shining like fishes. 'Tell, or I'll torture you!' His fingers teased her rib cage, his laughing face hovered between her and the treetops.

'Never! Not by rack nor Boot nor Iron Maiden, not till you give the password!'

'I dunna know it.'

'Ah, but you do...' She adjusted her body under his and their eyelids drooped, their laughter was stilled; there was no more need for words for a long time.

Afterwards she said softly, 'Guess what I heard today from Robbie at the Hop Bine.'

He had rolled on to his side and lay dreamily playing with the little curled hairs in her armpit. 'What then?'

'You're a free man, safe! They no longer hunt you from Buxford Place, you may hold up your head and walk freely wherever you choose. How like you that?' She waited for the joy to happen.

He drew back, puzzled. 'I dunna understand. They was out to lop my hands before I left. And on top of that there's Bess.'

'The mare went home! They're saying now she strayed and it was all a mistake. Oh, do look happy, I thought you'd be so pleased.'

He patted her perfunctorily. 'Course I am. Only there's still Clem. I mind you saying they found a body, if so be it's him they'll know for sure who killed him.'

'But they do, they do! You haven't heard the best of it. They've arrested the brewer for the murder, no one can accuse you now! You can go forth without fear, become your fabulous Horse Whisperer or whatever fills your dreams...' she tailed off. Where was the rejoicing, the shared bliss, the excited plans for the future she had looked for? A cold shadow of misgiving fell across her and she shivered. 'Angel...'

He had moved away from her, his face dark and troubled. 'It wunna do, Jo. It was me killed Clem, I didna mean to do it but I did. Big Daniel's innocent.' He hesitated. 'I got to go back and tell them afore he hangs.'

'But you can't, you can't!' sobbed Joanna, distraught with grief and frustration. 'They won't believe you, you'll never come back to me!'

'I got to save Daniel,' he said with quiet stubbornness.

'No, no, *no!*' she wailed.

For more than an hour she had argued and pleaded and still he was adamant. They stood in the tiny woodsmoked cot that had become their home, facing each other across the ruins of their life. The sun had gone in

250

and they were clothed again, he in his breechings, his knife and stave already at his belt; she in her homemade gown and the shift she had bought with such pleasure only this morning. Now it felt like a shroud.

She made one last despairing appeal. 'Angel, you must try to understand. I cannot survive this if you leave me now. I can never go back to what I was, you have breached my walls, laid me open like a dodman without its shell. Do you not see, for one such as I to love is like leaping from a precipice — there is no going back, no controlling that plunge, no rein that I can pull and cry Slowly, be more wise...If you abandon me now I am utterly destroyed.'

'And what about Dan?' said Angel. 'What if I abandon him?'

'Dan, Dan, who cares about him!' She scrubbed at her face in an attempt to restrain her tears, but they poured down the more because they seemed to move him so little. 'Oh, would I could bridle my passions as you do! How can you stand there so coldly, weighing one against the other, am I then nothing to you after all?'

'You know you are. You know you'm everything.' But his voice held no warmth, no longing. He spoke as if clinching an argument, and one that wearied him.

'I am not everything!' she burst out. 'I am nothing if this brewer is more to you!' The humiliation of her situation scalded her, resurrecting her pride. 'You shall not go, I forbid it. Do you think I am some village wench to be laid in a ditch and forgotten? I forbid you to go, do you hear me, I forbid it!' Her voice rose high on a note of desperation, of near hysteria. 'I am a Pengerran, I will not be shat upon!'

Angel, locked in his dreadful resolve and aching with his own sense of loss, could not answer her. He looked at her and saw again a heartless adventurer wearing the face of his love. 'Aye,' he said at last. 'You'm a Pengerran, caring for nothing but yourself. Else you'd not see a good man die for another's deed. 'Tis what no honest man should do, nor woman ever ask.'

251

'And you are a peasant!' screamed Joanna. 'Go hang then, among your own kind — seek out Nick Bodkyn, go wenching with him and his bawdy-baskets and crust-'o-bread whores — find Marian, your good girl Marian, she's more to your taste, go scatter the hills with your cherubim, you'll get no more of me!' She turned before he could stop her and fled away weeping among the trees.

Angel waited for a time in the silence of the cottage, hoping that she might return. He longed to hold her, to kiss and be reconciled before he had to go; bad enough to part without parting in anger. Not gifted with words, he had never been able to tell her what he felt; he had hoped to show her by deeds, and now there was no more time.

The sun was past its zenith; in a few hours it would be dark. He looked outside and saw Saracen, still tethered where she had left him. She could not have gone far. Perhaps she was waiting, hiding out there somewhere in the shadows, waiting for him to go before she could bring herself to come back.

He sighed, and picked up his crutch. His shirt lay where she had left it in the midst of stitching up its rents. There was not enough left of it to wear. But he took it up carefully and hung it over his shoulder by a finger; took a long last look around the cottage and set his face towards Buxford Place.

When dusk fell he was walking slowly, still holding back in the faint hope that she might appear for a last brief moment, a smile, a glance...he knew it was a dream. He turned his mind to the problem of saving Daniel without taking his place on the gallows. When he had given up hope of that too he still did not hurry, because the goal to which he travelled was not a happy one and the bones of his ankle, crudely set and ill knit, were unwilling to carry him further with or without the aid of a crutch.

He was so preoccupied that he failed to hear the soft tread behind him until too late. Before he could turn his head a heavy weight thudded against the base of his skull and he went down in a whirl of stars.

He woke in total darkness, lying face down in some airless indoor place. Straw prickled his eyes and nostrils and he tried to sit up, only to discover that his hands and feet were roped behind him, his body curving backwards like a bow. His first guess was that he was imprisoned at Buxford Place. But as his aching head began to clear he realised that that was unlikely. From somewhere below him he caught snatches of muffled speech. Muted odours hung on the air; charcoal fumes mixed with the tang of hot metal, horse sweat and the lingering cloying smell of burning hoof…he must be in or near a forge. But where and why eluded him. He shook his head in an effort to clear it and lay dazed until the throbbing ceased, trying to piece together his impressions. He was in a loft. A captive. And somewhere near a forge. His eyes flew open in the darkness. Someone had done away with Jody…and had now seized him as well! Suddenly it was vital to free himself and find a way of escape. He arched his body, twisting and thrashing in the straw in his efforts to loosen the knots. As he did so he heard a heavy tread on the rungs of a ladder, the floor erupted and a head was thrust up through the gap in the glow of a lantern.

'Well now, so you're awake, are you?' boomed a familiar voice.

'Jody!' The name broke from him in joy and amazement. 'I thought you dead! Here, come and untie me, I got to get to Buxford. 'More's the pity,' he added, mindful of his mission.

Jody did not move. 'Oh no, you don't. You've cost me too much trouble to let you go strolling into the lion's jaws.'

'Oh, it's never you done this? Look, cut me loose, I'm on my way to Buxford Place.'

'You ain't going nowhere, least of all up there. Set a foot in that place, you're as good as dead. Nan told me as much.'

So that was it: good old Jody, trying to save him from himself. 'No, 'tis Nan's got it wrong, I'm pardoned. Only they're like to hang Big Daniel if I dunna get there in time.' He renewed his efforts to free himself. 'Ah, come on, Jode — don't just stand there, see if you can find my crutch or summat...'

Jody smiled, and laid his great forearms along the edge of the hatchway. 'Still got the Bone, have you?'

Angel paused in his struggle with the ropes to frown. 'Aye, I got it. But...'

Jody's face showed satisfaction. 'And the Word, no doubt. You was told to come back to me with it. Why didn't you?' There was a note of menace in his tone that dragged Angel's reluctant attention from his more immediate problem.

'I did come back,' he said slowly. 'I was sore in trouble and needing help and you was nowhere to be found. Not you nor Nan, nor the childer. Not a living soul but the cat, out there on the horseshoes...'

Jody picked his teeth with a straw. 'Full moon then, was it? Well, you should have waited.'

'Waited...when I'd just killed a man...' He fell silent, hit by the implications of what had just been said.

'Not another one!' Jody sounded less shocked than exasperated, as though, thought Angel, murder were just an everyday sort of a nuisance. 'And after we rid you of Clem!'

He stared. 'You never rid me of Clem, it was me. I drowned him in the cooling vat.'

'You mean he was dead already?' spluttered Jody. 'All that effort wasted! No wonder he burned so slow, he must have been sogging wet into the bargain!'

Angel felt sick. 'You're saying you burned his body, there in the furnace where I'd hid it...yet you didn't know he was dead? Oh, come on now, Jode, you're jesting, aren't you?' His forced laugh was unsteady. 'Anyways you couldn't, not without being seen — and I never told no one where he was hid.'

Jody shook his head; his smile was chilling. 'You don't

254

have to be there, no more than you have to use tinder and sticks. The power's in the mind.'

Angel looked into his old friend's face and felt a cold hand squeeze his heart. He swallowed. *'You!'* he said hoarsely. 'You're telling me, you're the kind to do such things?'

'Not on my own,' said Jody modestly. 'It takes a deal of power for work like that.' He reached forward and drew Angel towards the edge. 'Look down there.'

Below them in the darkness a ring of faces glowed in the light of a dip. Among them he recognised Nan and her baby and two of their older children; all were upturned and watching him with a sort of unsmiling hunger.

'All for one, one for all.' Jody smiled unnervingly. 'There's thirteen to a coven, my son.'

2

Joanna paused at the cottage door that still stood open. It was evening and the air was heavy with the scent of honeysuckle, the day-long chatter of birdsong hushed to a distant fluting whisper as the blackbirds settled for the night. She had wept out her rage and disappointment; now she had come back to make her peace.

'Angel?' she called softly, and waited. There was no reply. 'Angel?' This time her voice was sharpened by anxiety. 'Angel! Are you there?'

Still she hesitated, unwilling to confirm what her heart suspected: that he had really gone after all. The sight of Saracen standing patiently outside had given her false hope; when at last she made herself go in, when she stood in the deserted place and knew she was alone she was filled with panic. She burst into fresh tears and ran out of the cottage to search the stream, the wood bunker, the ruined shed, crying and shaking her head, 'Oh, no...oh, no...no, you can't be gone, you can't, you can't!' Finally to return and collapse with helpless sobs against the table, beating with her arms upon the unresponsive wood. 'Oh Angel, how could you?...How could you when I need you so!...Angel, come back, come back...'

At length when she had cried herself to exhaustion and into the calm that sometimes follows, she lay down on her solitary bed of bracken and willed herself to have hope. He would come back. They had quarrelled before, and violently, had come near to killing each other...he had always come back. He had gone on foot; his progress would be slow and limping. Long before reaching Buxford he would see sense, would turn and start back to her and they would laugh at his folly, would forgive and make love and resume their life together, sweeter and more precious than before.

She must wait and have faith. It would be a good lesson to learn, patience never having been her strongest suit...She lay sleepless until her burning eyes closed down the turmoil of her mind, drawing her away into fretful dreams for what remained of the night.

In the morning she woke stunned and hollow-eyed, aware of her feeling of misery before she remembered its cause. It came to her in a rush of pain. She swallowed her grief and threw herself into the anodyne of work, scouring and sweeping everything in reach, telling herself she was garnishing the house for his return, gathering fresh bracken for their bed, plucking woodbine and dog roses, hurrying back in case he should have returned while she was absent.

By nightfall of the second day she knew she was deceiving herself. He had not turned back but had plodded on to Buxford, still imagining he could save the wretched brewer, impelled by that same madness that had driven him into the man-trap; and this time there was nothing she could do to save him. Nothing except pray...and this she did, entreating an almost forgotten God, a half-discounted Blessed Virgin, even, in her extremity, the nebulous ghost of his mother. Not that she had any faith in her either; but at least she had once had evidence of her existence.

At the end of the third day when she could endure the suspense no longer, she dressed once more in the Jarkman's clothes and rode to the Hop Bine in the hope of news.

'You've a face as long as Lent,' Robbie hailed her

cheerfully. 'What ails, lost your sweeting?'

The words knifed her but she contrived a laugh. 'Ah well, easy come, easy go. How turns the world while I've been occupied?'

'You mean while she's been occupied!' Robbie's elbow dug her in the ribs, and the old woman's eyes were teasing. 'You'll find another, never fear.'

'Aye...of a certainty.' She was glad of the brimming tankard to hide her face. 'What tidings, then? Any new excitement?'

'Nothing new. I heard they hanged the brewer at Buxford Place.'

'Hanged him?' She was dropped into a well of ice. 'You are sure?'

'Course I'm sure. You didn't think they'd let him off, not after what he'd done?'

'But...did they never catch the other one, then, the first that they were seeking? He's not come forward?'

'Come forward — why should he? Pardoned he may be, but he'd have to be soft in the head to turn up there until the fuss dies down.'

'Yes...yes, of a certainty...' Locked in her walls of ice she set down the tankard, still half full. 'I must away.' She heard her own voice as though from a distance, Robbie and his wife were in another world as she escaped from the tavern to where their eyes could not follow her, out to cool her burning face in the uncritical night air. She felt too scorched with shame and humiliation ever to shed another tear. Soft in the head...yes. But he was not! He was clever, very clever indeed. He had won her, Joanna Pengerran, had enjoyed her and abandoned her when he had had enough. He had not gone to Buxford, he had never gone anywhere near, had never had any intention but had merely seized on it as an excuse to go. She remembered the lack of warmth in his voice when he argued that she was everything to him. He had made a fool of her! Worse, she had made a fool of herself, had fallen in love like any greensick girl, and with one to whom she meant nothing but a passing adventure...Oh God, oh God, oh God how could she have been so blind! So besotted! She, a grown woman who had seen so much of men! Leaning forward over Saracen's neck, urging him forward, she lashed her anger, her sense of betrayal to a frenzy, desperate for anything to forge into a shield between her and the bitterness of her hurt.

She strode into the cottage and swept up the bed of bracken and the flowers and burned them on the hearth; gathered up the gown and the shift and piled them on the fire. Never again would she be so beguiled! If she had been less happy as Jarkman Joe she had at least been invulnerable. Booted and armed, she sat watching the flames consume the reminders of her lapse, and sank the better part of a skinful of Robbie's wine.

In its glow she began to feel better, warmed and strengthened. The whole interlude, she assured herself, was of no importance; she would put it behind her and quickly live it down, take up the threads of her life again where she had dropped them, find out what had happened to that benighted courier. She was born to greatness, to the righting of a wrong, the saving of a great estate, not to break her heart on the caprices of a common peasant...she swallowed hard to rid herself of the lump that was forming in her throat. She tossed her head in a gesture of defiance. This agony would pass like any other, she had only to sweat it out. When she had drunk herself into a stupor it eased a fraction, its sharpest edges blunted to a bearable numbness, her emotions dulled, her thoughts unable to torment her. She rolled herself in her cloak in a remote corner of the floor and sank at last into a heavy sleep.

She woke late the next morning with a rebellious stomach and a pounding headache and crouched wincing with her head in her hands while the full weight of yesterday came crashing in on her. As soon as she could get her legs under her she staggered out, her vision still reeling, mounted Saracen whom she had neglected to unsaddle the night before, and fled the place.

Once clear of the Buxford area she began to feel more calm, a little stronger. Her courage increased with the miles she put behind her and when at dusk she reached the village of Lambeth, saw across the familiar river the smoke-hazed lights of London away to her right, she was riding proudly erect, her head carried like a banner. But her stony face she turned neither to left nor to right, for although every fair head drew her eyes like a lodestone she would sooner die than have it seem even to herself that she was looking out for Angel. The iron will that had driven her so hard now stood her in good stead: she did not allow herself to speculate on where he might be. Suffice it that he had lied, had not gone to Buxford...she wanted to see no evidence of his perfidy. Leaving the ferry she turned north, riding past the sprawling complex of Whitehall Palace with its many lighted windows winking like those of a village through the sunset. Heading across Leicester Fields, avoiding Alsatia to spare herself the sight of the Cock with its lacerating memories of times past, she excused herself from the charge of cowardice on the grounds that the city gates would be closing at this hour, the bellman already on his round with his familiar cry — 'Look well to your locks, your fire and your light...' She thought of his rasping voice with a nostalgia that surprised her. London it seemed had become home to her, filthy, smelly, pest-ridden though it was; and now that her sortie had ended in disaster there was a part of herself that wanted desperately to creep back into her tatty citadel, lick her wounds and pretend it had never happened. But that was only one part of her. The other part, the part that was all Pengerran, was made of harder metal, would not allow her to back down in the face of adversity, and that part knew where she was going now: no longer fleeing aimlessly from an unendurable scene but with a plan, however nebulous, in mind, she was heading for Islington.

She might or might not be able to take up the threads of her plan where she had dropped them, that depended upon the other factors involved, but of one thing she was certain, she was not going to spend the rest of her life in mourning! One day, perhaps, she might look back without bitterness and be able to laugh; now, she needed her anger to sustain her. Thank God, she thought, nobody knew or could ever guess! She still had money and the means to support herself, even if it meant remaining Jarkman Joe all her days; she had only to live down her lapse in her heart and all would be as if it had never been. 'Soft in the head...soft in the head...' Robbie's words kept repeating themselves in her brain. She used them as a lash to whip up her anger. It had been she, not he, who was soft in the head! Never, never, never would she be so fooled again...

She bought a night's lodging and stabling at an inn near Mary-le-bone village, on the pretext of checking all routes for news of the courier; she could easily enough have ridden on the two more miles to Islington and knew well enough that no messenger from Northumberland was likely to have come this way. But if she was still staving off the moment when she must face prying eyes again she did not admit it to herself. She drank herself dull before lying down to sleep, rose at first light and rode on with set jaw, her pride buckled about her like a cuirass. There must be no more cracked and bloody dodman's shell for her.

As she turned in at the courtyard of the Islington tavern her heart gave a violent lurch and began to soar. She sat transfixed, watching the bright head disappearing into the yawning gloom of the stables between the arched necks of two palfreys.

Her resolutions fell away from her like winter leaves. She dismounted to go striding across the yard, struggling for mastery of the sudden joy that marched exulting through her to destroy the mask she had nailed upon her face. The boy turned as she entered. 'Aye, master?'

She stood still, her emotions so violently checked that they left her numb. 'My...my horse...' She passed her tongue over dry lips, leant for support against the door jamb. 'Out there...'

'Lame, is he?' The boy looked bewildered.

She tried to collect herself. 'Yes — no!' She hardly knew what she was saying. Her mind had not been on Saracen. 'Look to it, feed him. Bed him down.'

'Bed him, master? But 'tis barely morning —'

'Do as you're bid!' She turned away swiftly to hide her confusion and walked off, her movements as mechanical and meaningless as her words, leaving the brown-eyed stranger staring after her. She entered the tavern on legs that seemed to have been borrowed from someone else, demanded her key from the chamberlain in a voice she hardly recognised and started up the stairs towards the room she had rented; she could think only of reaching it and locking its door behind her, of escaping into its merciful privacy to recover herself. At the stairhead a too-familiar figure blocked her way.

'Stand aside, old man,' she snapped, her nerves at screaming point.

'No so fast, my son.' The Patrico's tone was smug. 'Or should I say,' he lowered his voice, 'my lady?'

Joanna's head came around with a jerk. He had long known her for female; he had never before hinted that he knew her identity. 'Be plain, I am in no mood for jests.'

He smiled slyly, drawing from his scrip a scroll with neither seals nor ribbon. 'A copy,' he said unctuously. 'Young Marian could not find you and in your absence consulted me. A fair facsimile, if I say it myself. The original went on to Buxford. Now, shall we talk?' He had unrolled it just far enough for her to read the salutation, copied in a laborious hand but still legible. As she lunged for it he whisked it beyond her grasp, waving it tantalisingly at the extremity of his extraordinary reach. 'Not so fast,' he said again with a maddening smirk. 'Nothing for nothing, as our good Nicholas would say. Everything at a price, eh, doxy?' Noting perhaps her expression he went on, 'But perchance you are no longer in the market? An ill-considered choice, but yours to

262

make if you will. I can always sell my information...shall we say, elsewhere?'

Joanna made the effort of a lifetime. She beckoned him to follow her along the gallery, fitted her key into the lock and bowed. 'Pray come in,' she said with a sardonic flourish. 'I perceive my donation to the poor to be overdue.'

'Slow down, can't you, rein in or something, the pace is too much in this heat!' The Patrico's voice was querulous as he mopped his sweating face.

'The choice was yours, old man. You would follow me to London when you could have waited in comfort at Islington. I offered you a civilised deal over dinner but no, you must needs drag your old bones on the road.' She had indeed offered him dinner, on the pretext that she must draw money to pay him from the goldsmith's house in Cheapside where she lodged her gold; but to her chagrin he had insisted on going with her. Perhaps, she thought wryly, he had read her mind.

She had tried in vain to allay his suspicions: 'Come, you know me! One would think you did not trust me to return.'

She had said it chaffingly, and the withered lips had parted over blackened teeth in what might pass for an answering smile. 'Verily, I do not!'

Damn him! 'Nor I you,' she said lightly, 'And therein lies your surety, think how I chafe to lay my hands on that document.'

He had regarded her with eyes as cool as a snake's. 'Then I shall come with you, that you may have it the sooner.' She had given in. A man might surely choose the manner of his death.

And now he was grumbling. 'It is not meet that you should ride while I trudge in the dust at my age!'

Joanna eyed him with disgust. 'When did you last pause to consider what is meet?' She could feel no compassion for the bedraggled figure panting to keep up with her, no compunction for what she was about to do, only anger with him for driving her to it, contempt for his

263

mean and devious nature. 'Come, stir yourself, I haven't got all day.' She urged Saracen to a trot.

'Wait, wait! I need to rest...' His voice reached her faintly.

She glanced behind her to where he stumbled over the ruts, then forward to the road ahead. Nothing either way. But it was a well-frequented road and she could not afford to waste time. 'We rest a few minutes in the shadow of those trees,' she called back, heading her mount away from the track towards a small copse to her left.

She was stone cool now, calm and under control, almost glad of the distasteful task ahead as a diversion from the wound within that still oozed agony through all her attempts to staunch it. In the shade of the copse she crouched in the saddle, her body a coiled spring, her sword arm a talon with which to lash out against a cruel and uncaring world. As the wilting figure came staggering into the copse, she snarled, 'Villain, say your prayers!' And lunged, running him through.

She was unprepared for what followed. He did not drop dead as she expected, nor fall to his knees and beg for mercy. An ugly light flared in the emaciated face and his long arms reached up to wrest the hilt from her hand, even as the dark flow swamped his rusty gown. She had missed the heart!

His eyes bulging with strain, his lips curled back in a dreadful grin he clung, shuddering, menacing, seemingly indestructible, while she loosened a foot from the stirrup to push against his body in a frantic effort to free herself. Now one of his hands had hers by the wrist — was pulling her downwards, trying to unseat her — in a panic she tried twisting the sword — felt it grate against bone — the man screamed but did not let go...Saracen whinnied and reared. She was dragged from the saddle still clutching the reins as the terrified horse plunged and backed in a futile attempt to free himself from the bloody mêlée entangled in his harness...Joanna fell heavily with the dying man on top of her; the smell of his blood, his

264

foul breath, the odours of his body overwhelmed her, the shock and horror of the moment were blotted from her mind by engulfing darkness.

She was roused by persistent dragging at the rein still looped for safety about her wrist. The body above her was heavy and inert and something wet was seeping through her clothing. Nauseated, she clawed and wriggled her way out from under it, spoke words of reassurance to Saracen who was still trying to back away from her, his ears laid back and eyes rolling with fear. 'He's frighted...'tis the smell of blood...' She locked her mind against the memory. But she would replace these clothes as soon as she could, for although her habitual black would call no attention to the stains the sensation of the dead man's blood congealing on her skin made her own flesh crawl with revulsion.

First she must find the letter and recover her sword. The body was slumped in an uneasy huddle face downwards in a nettle patch, and she knew his scrip must be somewhere underneath it. She did not want to touch him, shrank from covering the few steps between them, using the toe of her boot to roll him on to his back. As she did so, he stirred. His eyes opened, and his long fingers closed like claws about her ankle. Terror wild and unreasoning rushed through her veins in an icy flood. Gasping she sprang back, overbalanced — snatched the poniard from her belt and slashed wildly at the hand — the arm — the expressionless face — what remained of her self-control blown to ribbons, sobbing, cursing, blasphemously praying for help, babbling wordlessly until at last it was borne in on her that she had freed herself, that this time it was finally accomplished: he was dead. She scuttled away like a frightened animal, knowing she was safe and yet held in thrall by a deep primeval fear of the dead. It was several minutes before she could force herself to return to the body, unrecognisable now, and recover her sword; she had to use both hands and brace a foot against the corpse before she could withdraw it, watching him all the time in dread that those fingers would once again come creeping at her ankle. She severed the scrip from his belt with a single stroke and was on Saracen's back and away with all speed they could muster, he no less eager than she to leave the awesome place behind them.

A few minutes later, she reined in and dismounted to think things out before going further; she was almost into Clerkenwell, and had no reason for going on to London. Besides, her knees were trembling still, her belly twisting with nausea. Shamefaced, she tried to pull herself together. What had happened to her back there, she who had thought herself capable of killing Eustace Pengerran? Could she really do the deed when the moment came — or would she weaken, fail and be slaughtered like a fowl for the table? Perhaps after all she would have to wait for natural death to overtake him before she could claim her inheritance...yet it was not the possession of Buxford that was her goal but the death of Eustace, the avenging of John Pengerran. Or so she had told herself. Was it for this she had committed murder — and such murder! Oh, damn the Patrico, damn him, damn him, why could he not have submitted to a meal and a quiet dose of poison? She laughed unsteadily, trying to whip up her bravado, and to her own astonishment burst instead into tears. To her consternation she could not stop, even when she thumped her gloved fist against a tree in exasperation at her weakness, and when she drew out the letter and tried to read it not only was she unable to see but her hands shook so violently that she could not hold it still. 'Oh, Saracen...' she moaned, leaning her head against the animal's warm flank. 'What's wrong with me...'

Saracen turned his head towards her and blew softly, and presently she gained command of herself sufficiently to remount and turn him back towards Islington. There she would rest, peruse the letter and decide what was best to do. Recent days had been too fraught with shocks, with disasters; in a little while she would be herself again. After all, she had managed what she had to do, it was only that for some reason she was over-emotional just now.

266

Probably because her flux was due; she had known it to serve her in that way in the past...she made a quick calculation.

She reined in abruptly, sitting bolt upright in the saddle. Her flux should have started twelve days ago.

3

'Why can't I?' wailed Prue. 'It isna fair, I want to learn to fly like the others!'

'You'll do no such thing!' Dorcas, her mother, was scandalised. 'You'll wash your mouth out, what's more, talking of such wickedness, nor breathe another word to a living soul —'

'It anna wickedness, all the childer does it!'

'*What!*' Dorcas's jaw dropped, her eyes opened wide in disbelief. 'All the childer from where? Not from here, I'll be bound! No Christian child from here would be allowed!'

Prue said nothing, until her mother's hand flew out and started her right ear singing, when she burst into a howl. 'All the childer,' she insisted tearfully. 'All them from the village —'

'From Buxford Hovels? I dunna believe it, you lying little minx! You'll be saying next you seen the faery queen and danced with the Devil —'

'I dunna dance with no one, I want to fly! It isna fair, not letting me, Big Jody does it, and his Nan and all theirs, even the babby — aye, and Matthew, him they says is Master's son —'

'You still that prattling tongue!' Dorcas's hard hand made contact again, but this time to clamp over the small wet mouth. 'Now you listen to me. If Master heard

268

of you talking such mischief he'd have your tongue cut out, no second thoughts about it. Now think, are you sure? Oh, stop your blubbering, child, and answer me! Is it true?'

Prue stared uncomprehending, sniffed noisily. 'I do only know what I heard. She said he was, Nan did.'

'Nan did what?'

'Said, you know…' She bent her head and whispered. 'She says he's Master's son.'

'Not that!' Dorcas was scornful. All the world knew that. 'The other, about the flying. Are you certain?'

Prue felt her sense of identity being restored. 'Course I am,' she said with an air of self importance. 'He told me all about it when he come with his dad to see to the horses.' Reminded of her grievance, she added sulkily, 'That's why I want to go.'

'Well, you'm not, and that's all there is to it! And you can stop looking as if you'd pissed on a nettle and get back to the dairy and work. Here,' she scooped up a handful of raisins from a jar. 'Eat these and wipe that look off your face afore some busybody asks you what's the matter. And just you remember, one word out of place and they'll rise up in your gullet and choke you dead. Now get along to Kate.'

When Prue had gone, hiccuping and swishing her skirts, Dorcas stood alone in the kitchen, deep in her thoughts. Nan's Matthew was not the only child at Buxford who could claim descent from the Master, not by a long chalk. Why, even Prue herself…but then she, Dorcas, had never been one to give herself airs, not like the upstart Nan who had lorded it over her so gallingly the moment she had taken her place. She had been forced to swallow the acid brew of humility at the time…but what a chance was this to dislodge the flaunting little whore! What price Lord Eustace's favour when he learnt she had taken his son to a witches' sabbath! But of course it must not seem to come from her, lest the story be discounted as jealous spite. A word to the steward perhaps; or maybe the chaplain…

*   *   *

'What!' roared Eustace. 'She takes him where?'

'To a sabbath, my lord. A meeting of witches.' The chaplain lowered his voice discreetly. 'It is there that they take their orders from Satan, who comes in the form of a goat to receive their homage. They celebrate the Black Mass and other obscenities too vile to mention.'

'And she takes my son there, *my* son? God's wounds, this time the trull has gone too far! Clear out the lot of them, round them up and send them to the Assizes — they shall give up riding their broomsticks for the horse with three legs! Let the Justices look to it, they must hang.'

The chaplain was taken aback. 'Not the boy, my lord?' He had passed on the kitchen maid's tale as duty demanded, but had not foreseen which way it might rebound. 'The child surely is innocent, may be snatched as it were, from the burning...'

Eustace seemed to consider; but it was only for the sake of appearances. Matthew had enough against him as heir to Buxford with the stigma of bastardy, without the added odour of involvement in witchcraft as well; one count he might have lived down, but hardly two. The boy was useless for his purpose. 'No, he is tainted. Let him go with the rest.'

The chaplain tightened his lips. 'I will send the steward to you, my lord,' he said pointedly, and bowed himself out of the presence.

When he had gone, Eustace sat smouldering. All this was Edith's fault! At every turn she had baulked him — if she had not led him to believe she could produce Joanna he would have had the boy Matthew safely under his own roof by now, out of reach of contamination by Nan and her unsavoury sort. It was because of her that the boy must be abandoned to hang with the rest, the only male heir he had produced in all the years at Buxford. Nan in truth had overreached herself but at least she had given him a son. Why should she go to her death and leave the accursed Edith to flourish!

4

'Think you,' Joanna eyed Nick Bodkyn guardedly, 'I could pass for a woman? Given the ruff, the points, the farthingale...what say you?'

Bodkyn suppressed a smirk. 'As well as any, I'd say. But you'd need to bridle that waspish tongue of yours.'

'A shrew, then. But I'd get away with it?'

'None better. What's in the wind?'

'Nothing...nothing.' Damn his perspicacity! She had hoped to get him to procure the clothes without arousing his curiosity, although on reflection she supposed she should have known better. 'Merely, I fancy a change of art. Too long in the one can be dangerous; you know that yourself, do you not? When did you last prig a prancer?'

'Not for a while, cove, not for a while.' He laughed. 'By the Solomon, I thought you'd taken a whim to join the players.'

The capon leg Joanna was gnawing stopped halfway to her mouth. Players! Of course, why had she not thought of it herself — a band of players could be the answer to all her needs, could provide her with costume and retinue for a convincing arrival at the Priory of St Anselm where the Pengerrans were alleged to have lodged their daughter.

In the days and nights since the death of the Patrico

271

she had been at her wits' end. Her flux had not started and she knew now that it would not for another ten turns of the moon: there was no escaping the fact that she was pregnant. Her days as Jarkman Joe were numbered, and Buxford was now her only recourse. Whether or not she found herself able to do away with Eustace must remain in the lap of the gods; her first primeval instinct demanded shelter for her child. Moreover, it must be soon, soon enough for her to pass off the babe as her husband's. The letter had spoken of the death of Braw Geordie, had urged an end to delay in view of the coming of autumn and the state of the roads, and had ended with the announcement that the Fitznorths and their son would proceed forthwith to the rendezvous at St Anselm's. This letter, the most crucial of all the correspondence, had gone on as it stood to Buxford and the way ahead was fraught with terrifying possibilities. What if Sir Reginald and Lord Eustace met? Originally she had counted on destroying her stepfather before they had an opportunity to compare notes and uncover her hoax...she was unable to force her mind beyond the immediate. The first thing to be done was to ensure that she was at St Anselm's before either party arrived, to convince the Prioress at least of her bona fides. After that...Heaven or Hell would provide the answers and she cared very little which. The heart had gone out of her enterprise, reducing it to mere expediency. Mechanically, she had penned a letter to carry to the Prioress, purporting to come from Edith and requesting a retreat for her daughter, a letter with one significant omission: it bore no date. Mechanically she had laid her plans, and mechanically now she put on a face for Bodkyn.

'And by the Mass, you're right! I am caught redhanded...' She got no further. The room swung about her, heat swelled within her so that she thought her head must burst and she staggered out into the open in a desperate quest for air.

In the rank shadows of the alley outside she bent

groaning and gasping as her stomach voided itself. She looked up from vomiting to see Nick watching her, an elbow propped against the wall, one foot crossed over the other in a nonchalant attitude.

'So,' he remarked drily. 'You are but a mort after all.'

For a moment she tried to stare him out of countenance, the handsome cocksure rogue regarding her mockingly from under his jaunty feathered hat. Then another twist of nausea assailed her, making her vomit anew. It was useless to dissemble. 'So now you know,' she admitted weakly.

He grinned. 'I always had my doubts about you. Now here's the proof.'

She straightened, leaning against the wall for support. 'Well,' she challenged wearily. 'What are you going to do?'

'Do?' He looked puzzled.

'Do!' she snapped. 'Bearing in mind my condition. And the fact that I am armed...' She felt herself swaying and tried to evade the hand that shot out, but it merely grasped her elbow and steered her towards a bench, where it pressed down her head between her knees. 'I'm not...entirely at your mercy...' she gasped, knowing that she was.

'Stow you, what nonsense is this?' Bodkyn sounded affronted. 'You've said nothing of why you sent for me as yet. The message was to meet you at the ordinary in Fleet Street, so here I am. And just in time it seems, to see you fetching up your boots. Suppose you just tell me what you want of me?'

Beginning to recover, she turned to stare at him. 'You mean...you are still prepared to serve me...it makes no difference that I am not a man?'

He shrugged. 'What's it to me? Your cross buys the same as anyone's. Given you good service in the past, haven't I? Like I said, I guessed long ago.'

She said wonderingly, 'I cannot fathom you. To have known so long and yet done nothing, said no word.'

Clearly offended, he drew himself up. 'I'm an honest

273

rogue, not the Patrico to bleat to the highest bidder.'

'No, no!' She spoke too quickly. 'That is not what I meant — ' She broke off, colouring as Nicholas's laugh rang out.

'What, country matters — with you? I'd as soon bed with a viper! Anyway, Marian would have my ears.'

'That punk?' How could such a one command fidelity? The words had broken from her involuntarily, but Bodkyn's laughter ceased abruptly.

'Aye,' he said with heavy sarcasm. ''Tis pity she's a whore. What else can she do, she'll have to keep body and soul together if I'm hauled off to the chats...' A good enough girl, just never had no luck. If only Angel's words would not keep coming back to her when she wanted to escape him: his voice ran on and on in her mind like a song she could not lose. Nick was still talking, warming to his subject. '...you're in no case to turn up your nose, virgins don't grow great bellies and you've got one coming or I've never seen the signs!' Again the voice: We'm all animals, lovely...Animals, born to rut and forget. Why could she not forget...

'Peace,' she said mildly. 'I meant no offence, life's hard enough, God knows. Come, let's mend our quarrel and part friends.'

'Part?' he stared. 'You're not serious about the players?'

'Never more so. The world has seen the last of Jark-man Joe. Find me a band of players and then turn your eyes away.'

Nicholas swept his hat from his head and dashed it to the ground. 'What folly is this? They'll not take you in — '

'I'll buy my welcome, they're always in dire straits.'

Nick shook his head. 'It's madness, they're strangers, they're not going to care. Why can't you hide up till all's resolved? A midwife or a dose of penny royal, my Marian knows the game, she'll look after you — '

'No!' The word was rapped out too smartly and she hastened to modify it. 'No, you do not understand, she is not to be told. I have that to accomplish which can only be done in the dark. I shall disappear and no one, not even you, must see where I go. Mark and be warned, friend Bodkyn: he who attempts to follow me, to trace me for whatever reason, is a dead man, I'll have no choice.' She took a gold coin from her scrip, pressed it into his palm. 'Here's for your Marian, tell her nothing of what you know. Wipe me out of your mind and forget you ever knew me, only find me the players and leave the rest to me.' She stood up, still swaying a little. 'We'll not meet again. Send a message to Jarkman Joe at Islington telling where the players are to be found. No need to come yourself.'

Nicholas sighed. He rose to his feet. 'From the good sense of women may the Lord deliver us!' He smiled ruefully. 'At least let me see you safe to Islington. Since I see you are now alone.' She caught her breath, in dread of what more he might say. But he only went on, 'For the sake of old acquaintance?'

'Very well,' she said at last, reluctantly. But she was thinking of something else that Angel had said: I'm the only friend you got. Perhaps after all, he had been wrong that time... 'Look you, Nick,' she went on. 'You leave me there and you never, never look back, not for your life! I'd be loath to kill the only good man I've known.'

5

Angel had only a sketchy estimate of how long he had been imprisoned in the windowless loft. He had tried to keep track from the sounds that reached him from below, the frequency with which he was given food, but the blow to his head had robbed him of consciousness and he had no idea for how long. His hands remained bound, but although his feet were free his crutch had been taken away: Jody had undoubtedly realised that without it he could not hobble more than a few yards. And no amount of argument, either reasoned or impassioned, would persuade him to set him free. 'Daniel's done for,' was all he would say. 'He's no concern of mine. Now you, that's another matter. You broke your blood oath and took off, you're no use to me like that. 'Tis a wrong can't be righted till next full moon and no use you fretting to get out of it.' He had slammed down the hatch for emphasis, leaving Angel to ponder his words. They had a sinister ring, out of keeping with the jovial blacksmith he had thought he knew...He sighed.

Since his stomach ached with hunger he guessed it must be time for the evening meal, when Nan or one of her children would come with a bowl and spoon the contents into his mouth. That, with a pitcher of water and a bucket for his needs, was the limit of his creature comforts. The darkness of the loft made it impossible to mark the passage of time with any accuracy, but he knew that days must have passed since his arrival, that Daniel must indeed be doomed. He had given up Joanna to no purpose, and could not go back...what a failure he had turned out to be. Young Bess he had lost for the second time out in the forest, with only rumour to suggest that she was safely home. He dropped his head on his arms, depressed beyond words; remembering her as she had been before they left Buxford, sleek and shining in her stall beside the Warrior...*quietly munching the sweet meadow hay...enjoying the grooming...the saddle well kept and soft, padded with wool against the chance of chafing...*

When Nan came with his food, she could not rouse him. She shrugged, left the bowl beside him and went away again.

Eustace had given precise instructions to the steward for the rounding up of Jody and his family and had ordered the questioning of Dorcas and Prudence for the names of other members of the coven. Now he turned his attention to setting his own house in order.

He found Lady Edith in her chamber, wanly supervising the embroidering of new hangings for her withdrawing room. She stiffened visibly as he entered, her pale eyes flicking nervously from side to side.

'I come to take you abroad, madam.' He spoke with laboured affability, gratified by her startled look, the blanching of her skeletal face. There was hardly enough life there to warrant the snuffing, he thought, noting the skin already stretched like kidskin over the flat cheekbones. One good fright and whatever soul there was would leave that unappetising body like a candle flame leaving the wax. 'Come, we go riding.' He snapped his fingers in the direction of her women. 'Your mistress's cloak, and be quick about it.'

The maids looked at each other aghast. Their mistress had barely risen from her sick bed and had not ridden a horse for years.

'M-my lord,' stammered Edith. 'I am not yet fit. The fever…it left me weakly…'

As always, he thought. 'Just so,' he said aloud. 'The evening is fine, your mare is returned, what better to restore you than a gentle tour of the park?' As she rose with some difficulty to her feet he added, 'Fear not, your fond husband will be there to take care of you. A turn about the lake, perhaps?' He permitted himself a sarcastic smile. 'Or some dalliance, some quiet talk in unaccustomed solitude…?' Still smiling, he drew her thin wrist through his arm.

Swathed in her cloak against the rigours of early September she complied, moving with drawn face and the eyes of a martyr led to the *auto da fé*. Her women, silenced and in awe, left behind in the hush of the room, drew together as though for protection, not caring to put into words their sense of foreboding.

Edith followed him numbly from her apartments, walking slowly and with unseeing eyes along the length of the gallery, down the broad stairway, through the Great Hall and out to blink in the sunlight for the first time since that day in May when she had gone to give orders to Daniel in the brewery. Now Daniel was dead, his corpse still dangled in its chains upon the gibbet, his flesh gradually shredded by the kites. Others were being seized she knew, Jody the blacksmith and his wife and even his children, the baker, the miller and his son…the list was endless; the life of the village was being destroyed, laid waste by Eustace in his hunger for revenge. For vengeance it was, she had no doubt of that: baulked of Joanna he would pursue the wanton slaughter like a rogue dog fox until his lust was assuaged. Now it was her turn. This, her first venture out of doors since her illness, was to be her last.

It troubled her little to know that she was about to die. In a strange inverted way she almost welcomed it, as a tidy end to her inadequacies, a consummation of her lifetime of losses, a just desert for her failure to help Joanna when presented with the chance. In reality she had lived so long under dominance that the initiative needed for the venture was lost to her; but because her role in life had been to produce results to orders not her own and to bear the burden of guilt when unsuccessful, this truth escaped her. Conscious only that she uselessly inflamed the tyrant's anger, '*Mea culpa*,' she said in her heart, and meekly bowed her head to accept the axe.

The two horses stood saddled and waiting, the evening light blooming the bright coat of the mare. Eustace swung himself on to the massive Warrior's back and waited with ill-disguised impatience while she was hoisted to the saddle of Young Bess by two burly stable hands too shamefaced to look her in the eye. They know, she thought, humiliated. She raised her head and did her best to sit her horse well, trying not to sway as with hooves ringing on the stones they went out of the yard and across the bridge; at least she could die with dignity, not cadging for pity from underlings at this late stage of her life. She had submitted in silence as on her husband's orders — 'Lest your lady fall and be hurt' — the two men had tied her to the saddle, ignoring their embarrassed looks of apology as much for their sake as for her own, her heart contracted to an icy knot of fear by the implications.

Now, her mount on a leading rein in the hand of Eustace, her own hands bound to the pommel, she rode forth from Luxford Place into a nightmare.

Once clear of the gatehouse he spurred the destrier to a gallop, dragging the mare behind him and lashing them on with blows and curses while Edith, her last shred of composure gone, clung on as best she could, white-faced and speechless, unable even to pray. The monstrous shapes of trees and branches came whirling towards her at breakneck speed, menacing, threatening violent death, tearing past or overhead only to be replaced by others while the movement of her steed over the uneven ground came perilously close to unseating her. She had no idea of how far they travelled, time had no meaning for her as the little mare, as

279

terrified as she, flattened her ears and raced madly out of control. At one point she was aware of the gleam of water — the lake, he had said — was she to be driven into the lake? Oh, Holy Mother have pity! The mare was panting now, her sides heaving and her heart thudding, little flecks of foam blowing back from her open mouth towards her rider. 'Mercy! Oh, mercy...' sobbed Edith, her pride deserting her in the face of frightful injury, uncertain death. And now they were pounding along the margin of the lake, the horses' feet churning the mud, bruising the aromatic weed and sending up fans of spray to sparkle in the evening light...

Without warning a shadowy figure seemed to materialise in their path, shimmered for an instant like a mirage against the mist of shining droplets and was gone. Both horses plunged and whinnied in alarm and the mare, her headlong flight abruptly checked, slewed to a standstill and stood coughing and shuddering as her drooping rider lost consciousness and slumped forward over her neck.

Enraged, Eustace started to dismount, intent on catching the interloper. He was partway to the ground with one foot still in the stirrup when Warrior reared alarmingly, cavorted as if stung and with what sounded to the man's startled ears like a shriek of fear bolted in earnest. Dragging his rider by one leg he thundered back the way he had come. With rolling eyes and flaring nostrils he pounded on oblivious of Eustace's cries which gradually gave way to screams as he hurtled back through the woodland, back over the deer park, scattering the grazing does, back at an insane gallop over the cantilever bridge where Eustace, howling and gesticulating in wild panic now, was caught by the arm on one of the side chains and ripped free at last. For a frozen second he hung balanced on the edge of the bridge. Then, before anyone could stop him, he plunged head first into the blackened slime of the moat.

As usual in late summer, the water was low. When more than an hour later the mare came into sight, walking slowly with Lady Edith half fainting upon her back, the men were still trying, albeit with little enthusiasm, to recover the body of their master from the mud. When they saw Lady Edith approaching they ran to help her, letting him disappear irretrievably at last, his eyes open and staring, his mouth and nostrils choked with sewage. And there he stayed.

Angel was released from the horror by his own gasping cry; he lay sweating in the darkness of the loft, uncertain whether what he had just escaped was a shared experience with Bess or fearful nightmare. Had he slept...he did not know. And then, there had been Warrior as well... He shook his head, trying to clear his mind. But already the dream was slipping away, beyond the reach of his thoughts.

Inevitably, after a while they returned to Joanna. He thought of her constantly, alone and deserted for a lost cause. If only he could find a way to tell her what had happened! What was she going to think when she heard as she must that Daniel had been hanged? He shook his head. He knew what she would think, and the knowledge made him ache. He, who had so wanted to heal her wound, had ensured that it would never heal...

A sound below caught his attention. Nan with his food, he thought; then he saw the untouched bowl beside him. Listening, he frowned. There were footsteps, yes...but not those of woman or child...yet they did not sound like Jody's. Somewhere he could hear crying, and a sharp yowl of protest from the cat. Then Jody's voice protesting, 'I tell you he ain't here, he don't live with us no more!' Who was not here? Surely no one had come to look for him...He crawled to the hatch, eased it up a crack and peered down.

The forge was milling with people; men in the livery of Buxford and the local constable with them, Nan and her children crying, Jody blustering and struggling with the men who were trying to arrest him. One of the men looked up in time to see him squinting through his crack. 'There he is, have him down!'

Angel dropped the trap and retreated, but before he could scuffle his way under the straw the hatch erupted and a ruddy face appeared in the opening.

'Oh, no.' The voice betrayed disappointment. 'This ain't him, this is never young Matthew.' There was hesitation. 'Still, orders is to flush 'em all out. Whoever he is he'd better go with the rest.'

6

Resplendent in amber velvet, her dark hair brushed to
the sheen of a blackbird's wing, her throat adorned by
the simple gold chain with its pectoral of pearls in the
form of the initial 'P' which she had kept in secret since
the day she fled Buxford, Joanna sat brooding.

Nicholas Bodkyn, as good as his word, had found her
the band of players she required and disappeared from
her life. Her last connection with her former life was
severed. The players had borne their parts adequately
and having brought her safely here to St Anselm's
Priory, had accepted their pay with alacrity and gone on
their way without asking too many questions. And if the
Prioress thought it strange that her charge should
arrive with so small a retinue and immediately dismiss
them to go home without her, the size of the dowry she
brought for so short a visit recommended the desir-
ability of silence.

In fact, Joanna had laid out her last farthing on this,
her last desperate throw of the dice: if this failed all was
lost, and her chances of survival with it. It was all or
nothing now. She had nothing left of the gold she had
slowly earned and carefully husbanded over the years.
But if she lost this throw, having let Eustace know
where to find her, no amount of money was going to
safeguard her life.

It took all her strength to maintain the outward appearance of calm that was essential, frayed as she was by anxiety, by the questions that only time would answer but which her restless mind never ceased to ask. Who would arrive first, Eustace or Reginald Fitznorth? Would Eustace come at all, or had he already written back with yet another excuse to stave off the wedding, perhaps in time to stop the northern party from starting out? What if they met — or if neither of them came, leaving her here with a growing belly and no more money? She dared not contemplate. She could not see the plump Prioress's bounty stretching further than the purse she had received, neither would she be fooled when the state of Joanna's linen revealed the absence of a monthly flux. She had seen the fate of fallen women and did not envy it. Nor had she any confidence in her future at the hands of Lady Edith, even if she were able to travel so far without funds; she could not imagine those pale cold eyes warming to the news that her long lost daughter was about to make her a grandam by a stable boy. Even the recognition on which she relied might conceivably be withheld under such a shadow.

She had one chance of salvation, and it was slim and precarious: she must meet and marry her bridegroom here at the Priory before the two families met. With that much accomplished she could bend her wits to the prevention of that disastrous meeting for the present time at least. Once the deed was done, they could scratch their heads all they would, they could not then undo it. And as the Queen herself was known to have said, 'Much suspected, nothing proved can be.' Everything therefore hung on the arrival of the Fitznorths before anyone else, and whether or not that was to be was all too much a matter of luck.

The Priory of St Anselm was a small and inconspicuous building and not easy for the traveller to find; and while Eustace undoubtedly knew where it was, whether the Fitznorths did was entirely another question and one that kept her pacing her cell night after night to the accompaniment of the sisters' soft voices in the chantry. The other snag in the skein was the Prioress; she knew well enough that Joanna had not spent the past sixteen years in her care, and she alone of all the nuns was permitted to converse with guests. One careless word from her to the Fitznorths and she, Joanna, was doomed.

Silencing her would not be simple. The Prioress was a practical woman, one of resource and intelligence who had kept her small community together throughout all the troubles of recent years. When as a novice she had trembled with the rest of their handful of nuns at the disendowment of the convents, the preceding Prioress, a lady of noble birth trained to the holding together of crumbling estates, had sidestepped the King's order by declaring St Anselm's a chantry house, and as the foundation was largely supported by private endowments from local gentry for masses for their dead and the respectable settlement of their unmarriageable women, it had survived. When in Edward's reign the chantries had gone the way of the monasteries, the old lady had gone to her long home, leaving the present Prioress to found with the nine sisters a small hospital for the destitute which was little more than a pretext for their continued existence. Mary's Catholic reign had been brief and uncertain and with her Protestant sister Elizabeth now on the throne it was unwise for any to predict which way the cat might jump. The Prioress had brought them safely through so far by lying low and by circumspect behaviour; she was far too astute to risk the disfavour of her patrons by complicity in the plotting of Joanna or anyone else. And yet silenced she must be, by whatever means.

She rose from her chair to pace the room, her hands tormenting each other in reflection of her thoughts. How to deal with this lady, given the circumstances? There must be a way, there must! If only she could think of it. It was out of the question to kill her as she had the despicable Patrico. A wave of revulsion shook her, less

285

for the murder, dreadful as it was, than for the man himself, the baseness of a nature that stooped to trading in the sacred confidences of the confessional...Suddenly she stood still. There was, she was sure, no resident priest at St Anselm's: so far, she had seen the Prioress perform the offices herself. She composed herself, left her room and made her way out through the immaculate gardens to where she could see the Prioress supervising the harvesting of beans by two elderly nuns.

'Mother,' she said demurely, 'will you hear my confession?'

When they emerged from the confessional they walked in opposite directions, the Prioress's eyes sparking with suppressed anger while Joanna's demeanour was of barely concealed satisfaction. In vain had the Prioress protested that she was not authorised to give absolution; she had been subjected to such a show of remorse, so tearful a plea for the unburdening of guilt, such unspoken reproach from the eyes of the two old sisters that she had had no choice but to listen tight-lipped to a fabrication of peccadillos to cover the missing years. Now, although undoubtedly aware of having been duped, she would be obliged to guard her tongue on the subject of her guest's length of stay, for the seal of the confessional was absolute. Only Eustace was likely to be able to bully the truth from her; if he could be fended off until the marriage had been solemnised...

Perhaps, thought Joanna as she watched the retreating figure of the affronted Prioress, there was yet something she could do to make that state of affairs more likely. If her luck held, if the Fitznorths were first upon the scene, might she not persuade them that the Buxford party was unable to come, inveigle them into a celebration of the marriage and turn their noses towards home before they came face to face with Eustace. It would require only one more of her letters purporting to come from Buxford...dared she risk it? If Eustace intended coming here it was by now too late to stop him, and he had only to arrive for her deception to blow up in her face; and yet...and yet once married into the Fitznorth clan she would be under their protection. With or without their presence she could safely proceed to Buxford, and present there any tale she chose to invent. With so much at stake it was surely worth a try...

She withdrew to her cell and there, under pretence of doing penance, forged the last letter. It was addressed to Sir Reginald Fitznorth, to be handed to him on his arrival at St Anselm's Priory by Joanna Pengerran, and purported to come from Lord Eustace Pengerran of Buxford informing Sir Reginald that in view of the protracted ill health of his wife Lady Edith it was his wish that the nuptials be solemnised forthwith at the Priory, whence the Fitznorths should return to their homes without venturing through London, '...for that the small pox doth rage still through the city, her Majesty herself having lately been sick of it nigh unto her death, for which deliverance may God be praised. We would not wish the same foul infection to come upon you or upon ourselves.' That, she thought with a smile, should be enough to dissuade them from lingering. She rolled and sealed the letter and concealed it in the deep pocket under her gown. If Eustace did appear to blast her hopes she must at least be able to minimise her peril by destroying it unseen. Then she resumed her vigil from the window, from which she could survey the approaches to the Priory.

St Anselm's lay on a narrow and little-frequented lane which cut off at right angles from the rutted track known as the Great North Road; it was impossible to guess from the direction of its approach whether the party she could see moving between the distant trees had come up from Buxford or down from Northumberland. Someone, accompanied by a retinue, was heading towards St Anselm's.

Straining her eyes she tried to make out the livery. It was impossible. Only snatches appeared between the greenery, and that so plastered with dust and mire from

287

many days on the road that the colours were totally obscured. Was there a litter among them? There should be, whichever party it was would include a litter, either for Lady Edith or for the sickly bridegroom. She could make out at intervals the plumed heads of two palfreys, those of the unadorned mounts of servants and the humbler ears of a packmule; but no litter. Perhaps, after all, it was some other guest who was expected...but, now that they were visible, those were the colours of Fitznorth, she was sure she remembered them! Elated, yet puzzled, she craned her neck as they came crowding in, filling the tiny courtyard, dismounting with sounds of relief and weariness, two grooms handing down a tall muffled figure who stepped down stiffly from her side saddle to be affably greeted by the Prioress, 'Come in, come in and rest you!' while a second rider flung himself down scowling as though this were the last place on earth he wished to be. He was young and richly dressed, short and sturdy with a ruddy face and keen eyes that seemed to be everywhere, and he marched past the reception committee with no response to their gentle gestures of welcome.

Joanna heard his boots ringing over the stone flags of the hall and then his voice, rasped with displeasure and shaped by a strong Northern accent, came booming up the stairs to freeze her where she stood. 'Well, where's this wife I'm to be cursed with, this famous beauty I've been promised? Bring her forth!'

This could not be happening, she told herself, leaning against the closed door of her cell for support, trying to summon the strength to go out, the wit to find something to say. She had been prepared for a union with a helpless invalid, she had steeled herself for that. But this bullying bridegroom, strong, lusty and bursting with vigour, was something she had not bargained for. How could he have recovered thus, from a pitiable infant with a lolling head the size of two? How could fate have dealt her such a bitterly underhand blow! She could not believe it.

Someone was tapping on her door, softly, discreetly in

the way of nuns. She could of course pretend not to have heard. For a moment she thought wildly of escape, of abandoning her project and running to the stables, fleeing on Saracen to whatever might befall her — surely nothing and no fate could be worse than this — what was she doing here, how had she brought herself to this plight, she must have been mad! Angel had been right, such thoughts were not for her and she should have known it...

The knocking was repeated. Slowly she took her hands from her head, slowly turned and opened the door. 'Yes?' she said dully. The nun outside beckoned her to follow. 'I come,' she said, and closed the door again. She bathed her face with water from the ewer, smoothed her hair and her gown, and slowly went downstairs.

A tall stately woman, divested now of her riding cloak and cradling a goblet between her long hands, turned from the fire to face her as she entered. She looked travel weary and a little tense, but her smile was warm and her grey eyes friendly. 'Joanna, my bonny lass! I'd have known you anywhere, though you'll likely not remember me, Matilda Fitznorth. Your husband's mother.' Did the grey eyes flicker? 'And this is Jamie, you'll not recognise him for a certainty after so long.'

Joanna curtsied deeply, bent her brow over the outstretched hand. 'No, madam, I do not.' She could not discipline her attention, it flitted wantonly from the mud-caked hem of her mother-in-law's gown to the worn rings on her hand and thence to the unstable state of her own stomach. She could not bring herself to look at her bridegroom. Confused, she stammered, 'I bear you this letter, from...my stepfather.' She had never acknowledged Eustace as her father and would make no such concession now.

Lady Matilda took the scroll and looked at her curiously. 'You said, you brought it? From Lord Eustace?'

Joanna felt herself blanch. In her haste she had overlooked the necessity for an explanation of how the letter had come into her hands. There was no time now, she would have to brazen it out. 'Pray read it, madam.'

Matilda opened the scroll and read it to the end. 'I am sorry to hear of your mother's sickness. However, we can await her recovery.'

'Oh no, she would not wish it — '

'I wish it,' said Matilda firmly. 'When did you say this letter came?'

Joanna's heart sank. 'I...' she stammered and was lost. She was saved from answering by the appearance of the Prioress, but her relief was short lived. That lady was carrying a second scroll, also bearing the Buxford seals, which she presented to Lady Matilda before she could intercept it. Dear God, what now!

'It is addressed to Sir Reginald, my lady, but I thought in his absence...It has been awaiting him for a full week.' She withdrew with a glance in Joanna's direction, an unmistakable glint of triumph in her eye. She knows she has undone me, thought Joanna. She cannot know how, but she senses it...In a ferment she waited, her every nerve screaming in the effort to maintain her outward composure, while Lady Matilda broke the seals, opened the scroll and read it. When Matilda had finished she handed her the letter. 'Read it,' was all she said.

Joanna unrolled the letter as though it were the book of doom. She recognised Edith's handwriting immediately. It greeted the Fitznorths and prayed their forgiveness for a wasted journey. While her husband had lived, she explained, she had remained his loyal servant in all things, but since his death had released her from that duty she must now confess that to her great sorrow, her daughter Joanna had disappeared soon after the betrothal and was now believed to have been murdered. Although their most diligent searchings had failed to find her remains, she must be presumed dead and the marriage was consequently null and void.

Joanna knew that she was going to faint but there was nothing she could do to stop it. She clutched at the back of a chair just in time to save herself from falling towards the fire.

*   *   *

She came to on the hard couch in her cell with Lady Matilda bending over her and waving burnt feathers under her nose. Her gown had been opened to the waist to give her air. She started up, snatching it together to hide the network of blue veins, the carmine nipples that betrayed her condition, thankful that there was no one else in the room.

Lady Matilda eyed her speculatively. 'Aye, bonny lass! That's no grandchild of mine you're carrying.'

Joanna thought again of the lusty young bridegroom, the puling baby in its cradle, and pulled herself together. 'No, madam!' she said firmly. 'And that's no husband of mine that you have brought to warm my bed. Now, shall we talk?'

7

Angel woke and stretched on the flattened heap of straw that served him as a bed. He had lain in prison since late last summer and had lost all account of time. From where he was confined he could see nothing of the outside world; stone walls rose around him on all sides unbroken by windows, the only light crept reluctantly in between the bars of a ventilation shaft high above his head, shuddered under the vaulted roof for a few hours each day and slunk out again the way it had come in. The mouldering walls sweated damp on to a chill earth floor, and from the odour of the air that crawled sluggishly through the shaft he judged that it must give on to the moat. His cell allowed him to move six paces in one direction, four and a half in the other; he knew because every day, morning and evening, he paced it out, exercising his legs as best he could in the confined space. By its size, this cell must have been intended for many and he did not know how he came to have it to himself. Unless he was the only prisoner. He was lucky not to be in the *oubliette*: those who went in there were rarely known to come out alive. He knew only two things with any degree of certainty: he was imprisoned at Buxford Place, and he had no expectation of release.

He could only guess at what had become of Jody and the others taken with him. On the day of their seizure they had been herded into the lock-up of some distant town to await a sitting of the magistrates; from there Jody and Nan had been taken, he supposed to a hearing, and had not returned. The gaolers were brutish and uncommunicative and he had been unable to discover their fate; everything including information had its price, and without money for the 'garnish' constantly demanded by the gaolers a prisoner was lucky to retain the clothes he stood up in, let alone be able to eat. With diminishing optimism he had waited for his own trial or release, until after half a year that had felt more like half a lifetime he had been transferred by night to his present quarters, trudging through rain and darkness, stumbling over ruts and through mire on his twisted foot, led by a Buxford man not known to him who had come to collect him mounted on a donkey. From this man at last he had been able to obtain some answers. No, he had not been charged with the same offences as the blacksmith. No, he had not been charged with anything else. No, he was not to be released, because no one had given the authorisation. The town gaol was sending him back to Buxford, but no, they didn't know why he had been arrested. Yes, Lord Eustace had given the order — or so it was supposed. Could he not then be appealed to for clemency? The question brought a gust of laughter and an invitation to try fishing him out of the moat.

Not until that moment had he known that Eustace was dead. He stood still in the downpour, thinking of the implications. Had Joanna...? The donkey went on walking and he was jerked unceremoniously after it. Who, then — he could hardly bring himself to frame the question — who now ruled Buxford, was it Lady Edith? The man shook his head. Not long for this world, she wasn't, not after the trouncing she took the day the old devil went to his Maker. But then, of course, he wouldn't have heard? The Lady Joanna had come back from the dead —

His heart had leapt painfully — Joanna! She had sent

293

to rescue him! But why, then, was he not to be released... touched by a chill finger he listened again as his captor prattled on. In fine fettle she was now, wedded, bedded and full podded, that she was! Been hidden away in the North with her husband — out of the old lord's reach they all reckoned, not stupid, she wasn't — and brought that Lady Fitznorth down with her to see her safely home. Ah, things was a sight different at Buxford now, he could tell him, wouldn't credit the changes made, and mostly to the good, he'd say...

Joanna — his Joanna. Even now if he closed his eyes, he could sense in the darkness the bracken scent of her hair, hear her wondering whisper, 'My first, my last. My always...' She, who had come at last to love him after such hard struggle...or so she said. Now it seemed that in his heart he had always known she was not for him. Full podded, the man had said. He licked his dry lips. 'What...what like is he, her husband?'

The man shrugged. 'Young and bouncy, cut a mite too close to the Scot. But snout-fair enough to please the wenches. "Bonny" — aye, that's the word they Northerners use.'

Not then the monster of her nightmare memory, but a hunting and hawking young gallant worthy of her rank. She was safe now from Eustace, happily wed, her old wound healed by some marvel leaving her able to love like any other...wasn't that what he had wanted for her? It was what he had told himself. By what right, then, did he feel betrayed...? He had trudged the rest of the way in silence, and when his limp began to hinder their progress and his escort offered to let him ride had declined, spending what remained of the night in nursing his aching bone, glad of its nagging to take his mind off the other, deeper pain.

That had been many weeks ago; he did not know how many, but even here in the gloom he had sensed the pulse of spring, felt the disturbance of the earth as it trembled with renewing life. He had tried then, half-heartedly, to make contact with Bess; but he had failed.

Either she was here no longer or he had lost his powers. Or perhaps it was just that he was underground.

Now he stood up and flexed his limbs, stiff after a night of damp and discomfort, and turned to watch the grille through which his daily ration of bread would come. It would not be yet; but since it was the only event of the day, and since there was nothing else to do to pass the time, he set himself to wait for it.

He clung to the hope that some day Joanna would relent and set him free; it was a tenuous hope, but it was all he had. They had parted in anger and pain, and at first he had supposed he was being chastened for his desertion, his imprisonment a salve to her wounded pride. One day when she had punished him enough she would let him go...if she remembered. But after long and sober reflection he saw that he was wrong. Joanna in her anger was swift and bloody; she would kill outright, not inflict a living death. There must be another reason why he was left down here to rot. It was a question he asked himself day after day, night after sleepless night, discarding every answer that offered itself — except one. 'Those secrets are best kept that do not venture out of sight...'

She was mistress of Buxford now, and could deal with him as she pleased. Surely to God she would not leave him to fester in this place! Suddenly he was struck by a new thought, one so obvious he wondered that he had been blind to it so long: in a place as vast as Buxford, was it not possible that she did not know he was here...

When the turnkey came at last to thrust bread and a tankard of water through the grille he caught his wrist before he could withdraw it. 'I want you to take a message. To the Lady Joanna.'

'Oh aye?' The man sniggered. 'They all say that, I shouldn't wonder. Wrote her a love letter, have you? Ribbons and a seal and all?'

He hesitated. He had learnt so much from Joanna, why had he not asked her to teach him to write his name! Even if he knew what to say it could not be confided in this fellow — if in fact he could be trusted to pass it on. He fumbled in his pouch. 'Just give her this. And tell her, him that sends it craves his freedom.'

'Humbly craves,' prompted the turnkey.

'Not humbly, no. Just what I said, no more. I'm sorry I canna pay you for the favour —'

'This is Buxford!' snapped the other, cutting him short. 'None of your scurvy town ways here. Shall I tell her your name?'

He considered. Then shook his head. 'I did her some small service once...Just give her that, she'll know.' Releasing the man, he said unhappily, 'You will do it? I reckon they've all forgot I'm here, I could die before they think to let me out.'

The turnkey chuckled. 'That you could, and wouldn't be the first. The Lady Joanna, you said?'

'No other. My thanks, I'll not forget you when I'm free.'

'If you're free, don't go counting no chickens yet. I'll do what I can. Save pounding me flat feet down here every day if they let you go.'

Angel listened until the last echo of his footsteps died away. Then he sank down in a corner and nibbled listlessly at his chunk of black bread.

'He asks *what*!' Joanna stared in disbelief at the frogbone lying in the palm of her hand. 'Where is he, what does he mean?'

The steward was a methodical man, and dealt with the first question first. 'For his freedom, my lady, as I understand it.' Having brought the message at second hand through the turnkey, a menial he considered too rough to be admitted to the presence, he was uncertain of his ground.

'But where is he — how is his freedom in my gift?'

The steward shifted his feet. 'He is here at Buxford, lady. In the keep.'

'Here...at Buxford...' Joanna felt the room recede, and gripped the arms of her chair. 'Why, man? Why imprisoned here, in God's name what has he done?' The questions were rapped out in quick succession and the man backed away discomfited. 'I do not know why, I swear it! It was something left from Lord Eustace's time, some muddle — I was told that he was pardoned, nobody knows why he was seized again. It seems he was in the blacksmith's house when the family were taken up for practising witchcraft, by some mischance he was caught in the net and never brought to trial. They kept him in the gaol awaiting orders and then sent him back to us.'

Aware of the eyes of others upon her, Joanna took a grip on herself. 'And how long has this...fellow been imprisoned?' She contrived to say it calmly, willing herself to await the answer.

The steward, conscious of his shortcomings in the matter, tried to hedge. 'Here? A week, or two...perhaps longer —'

'No!' She could not keep the urgency from her voice. 'When was he arrested?'

'It must have been,' the truth came grudgingly, 'when the blacksmith was arrested. The day Lord Eustace died. Last summer,' he finished lamely.

'You villain, you villain! He has been here all the time!' Distraught, she tried to cover her outburst with a show of righteous anger. 'This is foul injustice, I will not allow it to smear the honour of Buxford!' That was palpably absurd, considering the abuses of Eustace's time. The curious stares of her women told her that still she was over-reacting; she snatched at the shreds of her dignity and tried to recover the situation. 'An innocent man has been imprisoned without cause and such things are no longer tolerated here. The honour of Buxford is to be redeemed, not further smirched by disgrace — yes, disgrace!' She scalded with a look the unfortunate steward who had opened his mouth to protest. 'Most of all upon you, sirrah, who should know whatever goes on within these walls! Amends must be made, and at once. Release him, send him on his way. With a piece of gold for each month he has been held.' It was so much less than she wanted to give...but more would put him in peril. 'And a horse,' she went on recklessly, 'he must have a horse, the pick of the stables — let him choose. Now take yourself out of my sight!' He would take Bess. She prayed he would take Bess. She wanted that for him at least...She turned her back on the man and stood biting her lips, in dread of breaking down. At the door he paused, diffidently.

'My lady...is it your wish to see the man?'

'No! No!' She almost screamed it at the wretch. It was too late, impossible now...it was all too late! If she saw him, heard him speak...'Go! Go, get out of my sight!' She turned and hurled after the steward the cushions from her chair, breaking into sobs of rage and frustration that brought her women twittering around her.

'Madam —'

'My lady —'

'She must not be upset so near to her time —'

'Restrain her!'

With little birdlike sounds they coaxed her bulk back on to the chair, fussing and fluttering in a way that drove her to distraction. She had lived too long in the free haphazard world of men...or not long enough. She clenched her fists and cried out between gritted teeth, 'Jesu Christus! Let me be!'

At last and with troubled looks they left her in peace. Their mistress had her unpredictable moods over which the elders of the household were wont to wag their heads: they remembered her as a child, and a right little vixen she had been! But they were wise enough to refrain from giving tongue. Outside her apartments, the women conferred. Should they fetch her mother? The idea was dismissed as soon as mooted. Lady Edith was interested in nothing these days, not even her coming grandchild, the scullery-maids were more excited than she. She had been seen to weep for the first time when her daughter arrived home and that had seemed to spell the end of her interest in life; since then she had sunk into a morass of self-abnegation from which nothing could drag her out. No, Lady Matilda was the one. She alone could deal with Joanna; a close friendship had grown between her and their difficult mistress and it was to her that they went scurrying now.

Matilda entered calmly and closed the heavy door behind her. 'Nay, hinny, what's amiss?' She all but ran to where Joanna crouched on her knees, her knuckles showing white where they gripped the carved arm of the chair.

'Help me!' she groaned, gasping as another tongue of fire licked through her body. 'Ah God, I never knew it would be like this!'

8

In the great testered bed of the Pengerrans, propped
like a broken poppet in a cradle of cushions, Joanna lay
motionless. Only her eyes moved restlessly in the deep
bruised shadows of their sockets, making again and
again their ceaseless journey around the carving of the
mullions: down the stem, around the scroll and back
again, up the stem, in and out of the rose...there was no
escape. She wished she could turn away from the light
but her head was too heavy to move. Her hands felt
strangely remote, her legs had been lost to her long ago.
Was this death? If it was it brought no fear but only
peace, a blessed release from the agony that had torn
her day after day, night after night while the furnace
raged and died, raged and died in her tortured body;
days when she had thrashed, sweated, screamed, trapped in that terrifying state and unable to free herself.
She remembered like a bad dream the chaplain — or was
it the Patrico — leaning over her with the sacraments:
'Take it, you must take it. Do you want to burn in Hell?'
And herself dashing the cup from his hand: 'Fool, can't
you see I burn in Hell already!' The old wives who had
whispered in corners that she was too old for the bearing of a firstborn had been right, she would not laugh at
them again... .

Strained and anxious faces hovered in the mists about

her bed; her women, the midwife, the chaplain, his professional detachment unimpaired, Matilda. Lady Edith, her wan cheekbones blotched with weeping. She had seen Edith cry only once in her life before, on the day of her arrival at Buxford. Weary and travelsore she had stood in the alien hall, her knees aching with tension, and been met with the cold, accusatory, 'Where have you been?' 'Do not ask!' she had snapped, and then, her own voice cracking, 'Mother...for your sanity, do not ask!' And in Edith it had seemed that the tears of a lifetime had been dammed up like water in a bag, needing only a touch to bring them flooding through. They had both wept then, not clinging in the consoling way of women, but turned away from each other, isolated by griefs too shameful to be shared...they had always been strangers; they were strangers still. Her restless gaze moved on. The steward, the baby's nurse. The one face she wanted to see was not there. She turned her eyes again to the window. The glass between the mullions was jewelled with raindrops, suddenly illumined as the sun broke through the clouds. The fox was getting wed...

She heard a whisper. 'See, she weeps. The babe, she wants her babe.'

She was being raised, floating as it seemed, her arm lifted with infinite gentleness to curve about the living warmth of the child. She peered with difficulty at the tiny face, the down of red-gold hair, the eyes blue as speedwell wandering aimlessly, unfocused. Would they change colour as she grew...or would only one of them? She would not be there to see...it did not matter, she would be safe...no harm could come to her here. She mustered her ebbing strength to make the words. 'Serafina...she is to be...Serafina...'

Her mother barely paused in mumbling her rosary. Only Matilda bent towards her soothingly. 'Serafina, aye, lass.'

She looked again at the baby, feeling the cramped limbs kick against the swaddlings under the heavy velvet robe; watched the delicate underlip draw down, the pink eyelids squeeze together, a frail protesting cry ringing to the high stone ceiling above. Oh, don't, don't ...she could not bear to see her daughter weep. Dunna cry, lovely...her eyes brimmed at the memory.

'It tires her, bear it away.' Serafina was taken from her helpless arms and given to the nurse, a girl warm with health and country bloom who bared a ripe breast as she cradled the squealing babe. Joanna saw the tiny mouth clamp over the sweet flow like a small limpet with little sounds of satisfaction; tried to smile at the girl who leant close to whisper shyly, 'See, my lady, how well she does.'

Yes, she thought; for she's country bred too, and knows her own kind. They must be good to this girl; she remembered her early life here, visiting her own hurts on those who served her...but I was a child, she pleaded with the memory, only a child, I did not understand...I understood nothing until Angel. He might live to see his daughter ruling Buxford...yet he would never know. She wished she could have told him; would have sold her hope of redemption to see him just once, to be reconciled and know herself forgiven...she closed her eyes and lost herself in the drowning of her tears.

They must be crowding about her now for they were blotting out the light, the chaplain intoning incessantly, holding a crucifix before her eyes...somewhere far away the muffled clanging of a bell...her death knell. It did not disturb her as she drew the darkness abut her like a shroud...it was better this way...now no lusty Young Jamie could defile her, no terrible birth could tear her apart again...and there was nothing in life she could not bear to leave. She had loved Angel, and knew that she would never love again. Even Serafina meant little to her, bringing only pain and fear; only Angel had brought her peace, had blessed her with a summer as magical, as fleeting as the unicorn...From her high window she had seen him go, his bright head drooping in the cold spring light, leading away his beloved Bess through the postern gate. He had turned and looked up, as if some instinct had told him she was there; she had drawn back quickly to avoid being seen. Better for him to go on alone into the world, to put her behind him and become the Horse Whisperer of his dreams, make a life without her and be happy with what he had.

She had kept his frogbone, her one relic. Matilda had it now, to be kept for Serafina until she was grown. Angel would not need it. He had always known the Horseman's Word...it was love...

On Edith's broken spirit her daughter's death fell as just another blow and was dimly felt. It was Matilda who stumbled from the room. In Joanna she had recognised a spirit to match her own; she had admired the wayward child and had come to love the woman — perversely more than her own Young Jamie, who was to her a wastrel and a disappointment. What a wife Joanna would have made for a Borderer! Jamie, she supposed, would have to be recalled to Buxford now; his exile until after the birth had been Joanna's condition for her silence and Matilda had been willing enough to comply. Tomorrow she would write to Reggie telling him that she and Jamie must remain at Buxford as guardians to his daughter. Not that she was, of course...but that was the one secret she had never been able to win from Joanna, not even in response to cajolery. 'Where *were* you all those years?' she had asked her once in an exchange of confidences. And Joanna's eyes had danced with mischief. 'Why, lady, with you of course! In your castle, helping you to perform that miracle upon your son.' They had laughed together, rejoicing in their ability to gull the world. Now she would never hear that laugh again. She knelt beside wilting Edith in the chapel and prayed for the soul of Joanna. But if Edith's prayers were submissive, hers were not. Serafina, whoever her father might be, would never lack a friend.

While the two ladies were secluded with their bereavement in the chapel, and the chaplain was occupied in bringing fresh candles for the corners of the catafalque, the midwife and the youngest waiting-woman were left to prepare the last of the Pengerrans for interment in the vault.

'Stop sniffling, do!' snapped the midwife. 'Never knowed anyone brought back by it yet.'

'Can't help myself. Poor lady, so young and only just come home. Just look at the blood she lost.'

''Tis the curse of the Pengerrans,' muttered the midwife. 'Never a birth but a death in this family, you mark my words.' She collected her basket with its herbs and binders and turned to go. 'Mind you get rid of that foul linen, everything with blood. Bad luck to leave it in the house, see you take it outside — and the afterbirth — and burn it. I'd best be off.'

Still the girl stood looking sadly at the marble profile. 'So beautiful she was...' She turned to her companion with a perplexed expression. 'What was that she said, you know, just before the end...did you understand it?'

The midwife shook her head, impatient to be on her way and get on with her life. 'I couldn't rightly make it out either, didn't seem to make sense.' She paused a moment, looking thoughtful. 'Sounded like "lightmans and darkmans",' she said.